WHERE YESTERDAY LIVES

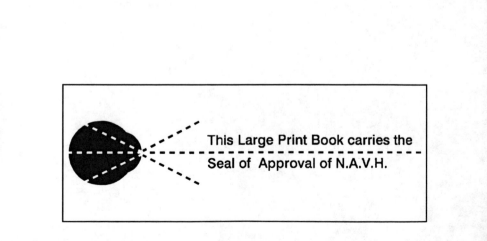

This Large Print Book carries the
Seal of Approval of N.A.V.H.

WHERE YESTERDAY LIVES

SOMETIMES TODAY'S ANSWERS
ARE HIDDEN . . .

KAREN KINGSBURY

CHRISTIAN LARGE PRINT
A part of Gale, Cengage Learning

GALE
CENGAGE Learning

Detroit • New York • San Francisco • New Haven, Conn • Waterville, Maine • London

GALE
CENGAGE Learning™

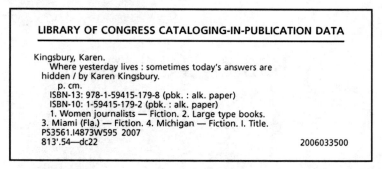

LIBRARY OF CONGRESS CATALOGING-IN-PUBLICATION DATA

Kingsbury, Karen.
    Where yesterday lives : sometimes today's answers are hidden / by Karen Kingsbury.
        p. cm.
    ISBN-13: 978-1-59415-179-8 (pbk. : alk. paper)
    ISBN-10: 1-59415-179-2 (pbk. : alk. paper)
    1. Women journalists — Fiction. 2. Large type books.
3. Miami (Fla.) — Fiction. 4. Michigan — Fiction. I. Title.
PS3561.I4873W595 2007
813'.54—dc22   2006033500

Published in 2007 by arrangement with Multnomah, an imprint of WaterBrook Press, a division of Random House, Inc.

Printed in the United States of America
2 3 4 5 6   20 19 18 17 16

Dedicated to Dad, that in seeing today what could be tomorrow, you would never wonder how very much you are loved.

Mom, for being forever dependable. Your love has no limits.

My husband, my best friend, whose Bible is anything but dusty. Walking through life by your side is the greatest thing this side of heaven. Thank you for loving me enough to tell me the Truth. I love you always.

Kelsey, my sweet daughter. Your love for Jesus is as beautiful as the light in your eyes, the warmth in your smile.

Ty, my tenderhearted boy. I treasure watching you walk and grow in the image of your daddy, as he continues to walk and grow in the image of our heavenly Father.

Austin, our little Isaac. God blessed us with you not once, but twice. You will always be a living reminder that God still works miracles among us. I can't wait to see the great things

He has planned for you!

And to God Almighty, who has for now blessed me with these.

ACKNOWLEDGEMENTS

Like any writer, I draw from my experience and the experiences of others when I bare my heart in a work like *Where Yesterday Lives.* And so I thank these who make up my own yesterdays . . . Donald, of course, and Dad, Mom, Sue, Chris, David, Tricia, Lynne, and Todd. Reporter friends I have known and worked with, and my longtime friend, Lisa. Also thanks to those others who played an integral part in building my scrapbook of rainy-day memories. I remember you fondly.

This book could not have come together without the talented efforts of one very special editor and friend, Karen Ball. Thanks for believing in me and *Where Yesterday Lives.* And thanks for making me a better writer in the process. I'm excited about what God has planned in all this.

Thanks to Dad, Tricia, Gina, Sherri, Michelle, Natalie, Rene, Wendy, and Betty for your feedback and encouragement in the initial process of writing this book. And finally, a special thanks to Rene, Dawn, and Amber for watching my little ones while I snuck an hour or two to write. May God bless your servant hearts.

PROLOGUE

Petoskey, Michigan – July 10, 1998

The first wave of pain seized his chest like a vice grip so that his hand flew to his heart and he gasped for breath. The second wave sent him to his knees. He felt his face contort from the pain, and he forced himself to concentrate on surviving.

Help! The word formed on his lips and died there.

Air refused to move in and out of his body, and his lungs screamed for relief. The pain intensified; the grip tightened. There was tremendous pressure now, as if a cement truck had stalled directly over his heart.

He clutched harder at his chest, ripping a button from his shirt. In the recesses of his mind, in the only place that was not consumed with pain, he knew what was happening.

His body crumpled slowly onto the matted brown carpet that lined the hallway. *Get up!* his mind screamed. But he remained motionless, every muscle convulsing in pain. Sweat beaded up on his forehead and his face seemed surrounded by flames. Frantically he gazed upward until he found the photographs that lined the walls.

His eyes darted across the familiar faces.

Another wave hit, and he squinted in agony, staring at the people in the photos, seeing them when they were young.

When they still liked each other.

He wondered if they knew how much he loved them and suddenly a million memories fought for his attention. Once more he tried to speak, to summon help, but no sound escaped and his eyelids grew heavier.

The strongest pain of all hit then, and in the haze of agony he calculated how much time had passed. How much remained.

He could no longer keep his eyes open — a fact that brought overwhelming sadness. He wanted to see them once more, the photographs . . . the people who lived in them. He struggled with every bit of his waning energy, but his eyes remained closed.

There was a ringing sound in his ears now and he became light-headed. He was fainting, losing consciousness. He told himself that perhaps he was no longer having a heart attack but rather giving in to an overwhelming urge to sleep. He relaxed and let himself be sucked into the feeling.

Then one last time searing pain coursed through his body, and he remembered what was happening. Someone seemed to be shouting at him now.

Wake up! Wake up! Wake up!

He tried to move, to open his eyes. But he was slipping further away and it was too hard to come back. For the briefest moment, he thought again of the people in the photographs . . . and he prayed they would forgive him.

As he did so, the pain eased dramatically.

Then there was only darkness.

ONE

A dense blanket of heat and humidity covered the Florida peninsula the afternoon of July 10, but at the climate-controlled offices of the *Miami Times* the unending process of news-gathering continued at a frenetic pace.

That Friday afternoon, while the city sweltered under record-breaking temperatures, the editors sat quietly at their desks in the center of the newsroom and Ellen Barrett, back from a morning of interviews, worked intently at her computer several feet away.

"Jim, tell me there's not something more to this murder." She held up a news clipping and strained to see Jim Western. Jim sat in the cubicle immediately in front of her and worked the environmental beat, dealing with illegal chemical dumping and polluted harbors. He was not interested in homicides.

"Sounds fishy." His eyes remained focused on his own computer screen and the story he was writing. Ellen watched for a moment, fascinated with his neatly arranged notes, his clean desk, and the way he typed using only his index fingers.

"More than fishy." She reached for her coffee and took a sip, wiping the moist condensation off the notepad where the cup had been sitting. Her eyes traveled across her desk, searching for a clear spot. She alone could make sense of the disaster that was her work area. Somewhere, buried under layers of rumpled notes, was a picture of her and Mike on their wedding day and a Bible he had given her three years ago. It was dusty now, though its pages were stiff and clean — much as they had been when she received it.

Ellen studied the heap of papers and, as she had once a month for the past year, made a mental note to get organized. For now she pushed her keyboard back and set the hot drink in the space it created.

She looked at Jim again. "Guy lives his whole life in his father's shadow, tells his friend he hates the old man, and next thing we know Dad opens the door and gets blown away by an AK-47 on the Fourth of July."

"Some holiday."

"Neighbors think it's fireworks and no one sees a gunman. What does the grieving son do? Hops in Dad's shiny, new Corvette and shows it off to half the people in town."

"Fishy."

"Not to mention the tidy insurance settlement sonny boy figures to get now that Dad's gone."

"Very fishy."

"Know what I think?"

Jim sighed. "What?"

"Prison time for sonny boy."

"Hmm, yes." Jim continued to type, his index fingers moving deftly across the keyboard.

"And won't that be something after everyone's been busy doling out sympathy cards to the guy like he's some kind of forlorn victim? Truthfully, I can't understand why he hasn't been arrested. I mean, it's amazing, how obvious it is."

Jim sighed once more, and this time his fingers froze in place as he looked up from his work. "That all you and Mike talk about at home? Homicide investigations? Must make great dinner conversation."

Ellen ignored him, but she was quiet for a moment. She didn't want to think about Mike and the dinner conversations that

15

were not taking place. She glanced once more at her notes.

"Well, I think the kid's dead in the water. No doubt in my mind. He'd better enjoy the Corvette while he still has his hands free."

Jim continued typing and the conversation stalled. Ellen settled back into her chair and glanced around the office. The newsroom was a microcosm of the outside world and it pulsed with a heartbeat all its own. If a story was breaking anywhere — from Pensacola to Pennsylvania, Pasadena to Pakistan — it was breaking at the office of the *Miami Times.*

The room held twenty-four centers, each with eight computer stations manned by hungry reporters. By late afternoon, most of the reporters were seated at their desks, tapping out whatever information they had collected earlier in the day.

Like the product it produced, the newsroom was broken into sections. News, sports, entertainment, religion, arts, and editorial. Each department had its physical place in the office and operated independently of the others but for the constant relaying of information to and from the city desk located at the center of the room.

Despite the hum of activity from the other

sections, Ellen knew it was the editors at the city desk who ultimately made up the life force behind the paper. They had the power to destroy a local politician by placing his questionable use of campaign funds under a banner headline on the front page instead of burying it ten pages into the paper. A plan to expand the city's baseball stadium could be accepted or rejected based on the way the editors chose to play it in print.

Stories from around the world poured into the office through computerized wire services while editors sorted through reams of information and argued about whether children starving in Uganda was a better lead story for the World News section than Saddam Hussein's latest threat against American armed forces. Whatever was deemed worthy of writing was passed on to the other reporters.

It was a powerful job — one where perspective was difficult to maintain. At the *Miami Times,* editors did not walk in the same hurried fashion as reporters. They sauntered, carrying with them an unmistakable aura of importance and often causing reporters to shrink in their presence.

Except for the editors, Ellen's peers at the *Times* generally enjoyed their jobs, thriving on the kind of pressure that causes stress disabilities in other people. Angry sources, missing information, daily deadlines, mistakes in print . . . the reporters would have taken it all in stride if not for the wrath of the *Times*'s editors. Among media circles, the *Miami Times*'s editorial staff had a reputation for being demanding and difficult to work for.

Reporters at the *Times* credited one man with earning that reputation for the paper: managing editor Ron Barkley.

For three years Barkley had been in charge of the *Times*'s news desk. Every section of the paper had at some time come under his scrutiny, but he paid particularly close attention to the front section. Stories that made the front section were produced by Barkley's general assignment reporters, a handful of the paper's best writers who gathered and crafted stories that did more than entertain readers. Front-page news changed lives. The *real* news, Barkley called it.

If anyone knew Barkley's wrath, or the impossibility of his demands, it was the general assignment reporters. His presence among them had caused more than a little grumbling in the newsroom. Ellen had even heard talk of a union forming to combat

18

what some reporters considered inhumane treatment.

Ellen had once interviewed J. Grantham Howard, the paper's owner, for a piece about the *Times's* evolution over the years. Howard had acknowledged the friction between Barkley and his staff and told Ellen he kept himself apprised of the situation. Certainly the owner understood that Barkley did not make conditions pleasant for his reporters. But Howard was a multimillionaire with a keen business sense and he readily admitted he was not about to disturb the very successful chemistry in the newsroom.

Howard told Ellen he'd kept a close eye on Barkley and found him to be as brilliant as he was demanding. In the years since Howard had hired the managing editor, circulation numbers had reached more than a million on Sundays and advertisement rates had nearly doubled. The same thing had happened at the paper Barkley had run in New York, and Howard believed the editor was the common denominator. Still, whenever Howard would visit the newsroom, Ellen had seen him cringe at the way Barkley treated the staff. Especially her.

"Barrett!" Barkley would boom across the newsroom on occasion, shoving his chair away from his desk and rising to his full height of six feet, four inches. His eyes would blaze as he pointed toward his computer screen. "Get over here! We can't run that story unless you verify those things Jenkins told you. You wanna spend the rest of the year in court?"

His voice would echo off the fiberboard walls of the newsroom as other reporters busied themselves in their notes. Ellen knew they were empathizing with her and envying her at the same time. For all the grief she took from Barkley, Ellen knew the position she held at the paper. She'd heard it too often to doubt it: she was unquestionably the *Miami Times*'s best reporter.

Ellen smiled, and glanced toward Ron Barkley's office. He thought Ellen feared him much the way her peers did. Her smiled broadened. Poor Ron would have been shocked had he known that his prize reporter really thought he was an emotional kitten of a man, a fifty-six-year-old gentle giant, whose rough exterior was only a cover-up for who he really was inside.

Ellen had been at the paper before Barkley's arrival. She had moved to Miami four years after earning her journalism degree from the University of Michigan and had been a sports writer for a year before being promoted to the front page. When the *Times* hired Barkley, she heard rumors that he was hard to work for. She researched his background and found the names of several reporters who had worked for him in New York.

"Tough as nails," a senior reporter told her. "He'll yell and scream and throw a fit until you get the story perfect. But don't let him fool you."

And then the man told Ellen a story she had never forgotten. Ten years earlier Barkley's son had been a bright investigative reporter with a brilliant future in the business. The young man was driving home from the office one night when he was hit head-on by a drunk driver and decapitated. After that, there had been something different about Barkley's presence in the New York newsroom. He still sounded loud and acted angry, but there were times when he would be reading a story about somebody else's tragedy and suddenly start coughing.

"I'd catch him swiping at a tear or two when he thought no one was looking," the reporter said. "Eventually the memories were too much and he needed out of New York."

"You liked him?"

"I understood him. The man knows the

stuff we write about is more than a way to fill a newspaper. Another thing. He's the best editor you'll ever work for. Ignore the rough package and listen to him. He'll make you a better writer than you ever dreamed."

That had been three years earlier, and Ellen had taken the reporter's advice to heart. When other writers fought with Barkley, Ellen Barrett gave in. When he demanded, she produced. When he screamed, she produced faster, nodding in agreement and accomplishing all he asked of her. She learned to rely on the man, ignoring his outbursts and allowing him to fine-tune her journalistic talent with each story. As a result, if Barkley got wind of a sensational tip or a front-page lead, he would always pass it to Ellen.

For her part, the effort paid off immensely. She was the highest paid reporter on staff and her name was known throughout Miami. Twice she had worked on Pulitzer-prize-winning articles and she was only thirty-one years old. She had no problem with the fact that the crusty veteran editor credited his editing practices as the cause of her success. Whatever the appearance of their working relationship, Ellen was not looking for sympathy. The situation suited her perfectly.

She flipped through her notepad and

considered the homicide story on the screen before her. She wanted to scrap the whole thing and write a story blasting the dead man's son, painting him as the primary suspect. But that was impossible unless the police were at least headed in that direction. If only they'd arrest him and make it official.

She tapped her pencil on her notepad and wondered whether she should call Ronald Lewis, the sheriff's homicide investigator. Earlier that morning she'd visited his office and he'd told her there were at least a dozen leads on the case.

"What exactly are you looking for, Lewis?" Ellen had asked impatiently. "The guy's son did it, and you know it."

Lewis had studied her thoughtfully for a moment. He trusted her. She was thorough and truthful and careful not to burn her sources, and he knew that. She'd made sure that when someone talked off the record with Ellen Barrett, the information never appeared in print. It had been a long road, but she had earned the department's respect — and Lewis was no exception. There were things he would tell her that he wouldn't consider sharing with another reporter.

"Listen, you're probably right," he had admitted finally. "But let me make the arrest first, will you?"

That was six hours ago, and now Ellen stared at her story knowing it was noticeably vague and really only half written. She reached for the telephone just as it rang. "It's about time, Lewis," she muttered, picking up the receiver. "*Miami Times,* Ellen Barrett."

"Ellen, it's me."

It was Mike. She relaxed and glanced at her watch. Five-fifteen. He would be home wondering when she was leaving work. Lately their schedules had been hectic; sometimes weeks passed without a single dinner shared together. But that was the price of being successful reporters, she supposed. The success they both had achieved before they married had continued and grown after the marriage. Mike knew the business well, and so had understood the long hours. He'd even been the one to encourage Ellen to keep her maiden name since that was the name people in the industry knew.

"Hey." She softened her tone. "How was your day?"

"Ellen . . ." There was a long pause. "Ellen, I have bad news. Your dad's had a heart attack, honey. Your mom wants you to call right away. She's at the hospital in Petoskey."

Ellen felt the blood drain from her face and she hunched over in her chair, elbows on her knees, feeling like she'd been punched. A heavy pit formed in her stomach, and she pressed her fists into her midsection in an effort to make it go away. She felt nauseous. *Dear God, help me. Deep breaths, Ellen. Take deep breaths and stay calm.*

She had expected this phone call for as long as she could remember.

"He's alive, right?" Her voice betrayed none of what she was feeling.

"Sweetheart, I don't know anything. Your mom said for you to call her. I think you should come home."

She was silent a moment and Mike exhaled softly. "I should have waited until you were off work —" He broke off, then, "Are you okay?"

Ellen squeezed her eyes shut. "Yeah. I'll be home in a few minutes."

Friday was the day Sunday's front-page stories were filed and approved by the city desk. None of the general assignment reporters dared ask Barkley if they could leave before he cleared their Sunday stories. Even so, Ellen stood up, gathered her purse and her notes, and moved mechanically toward Barkley's desk.

He looked up as she approached. "What is it, Barrett?" he barked.

"Something's come up and I need to leave. My story's finished; it's in your file. I'll be at home."

Ellen studied Barkley, waiting, and she thought she saw a flicker of compassion. Maybe losing his son had enabled Barkley to tell when something equally devastating had happened in another's life. His response surprised her.

"Fine." Barkley's tone was almost gentle. He returned his eyes to the computer screen and stretched his long legs beneath his desk. "I'll call you."

Ellen turned, barely aware of her surroundings. She made her way to the elevator, and then to the parking garage outside where she climbed into her dirty, black convertible BMW. Vanity plates on the front and back read, *RTNBYEB:* "Written By Ellen Barrett." She switched off the car radio and screeched out of the parking lot, intent only on getting home.

"Please let him live," she whispered. "Please, God."

When Ellen pulled into the driveway of the

two-story house she and Mike owned near the beach, he was waiting on the porch.

Even masked with deep concern, her husband's face was strikingly handsome. Marked by masculine angles and high cheekbones, punctuated with piercing pale blue eyes, Mike Miller's face looked like it belonged in a high-fashion advertisement or a cologne commercial. For some reason it seemed unfair that he should look virile and healthy when her father was fighting for his life eighteen hundred miles away.

"I'm sorry." He met her halfway down the sidewalk and nervously pulled her close, stroking her hair. "I've been praying."

Ellen remained stiff, unwilling to be comforted. Mike had never known how to deal with the emotional moments in their marriage, and she didn't want him practicing at a time like this. She refused to allow herself to break down. Her father was sick, but he was alive.

There would be time for tears later.

She pulled away. "I need to get inside and call."

Mike followed lamely behind her, and as they entered the house he sat on the couch and buried himself in a magazine. As usual, he would let her take care of making the call. Ellen clenched her teeth, but she couldn't exactly blame Mike. Her father, John Edward Barrett, was fifty-four that year and had undergone triple-bypass surgery the previous summer. Since then he had ignored doctors' warnings and continued to smoke three packs of unfiltered Camels a day. He ate eggs and buttered toast for breakfast, juicy beef hot dogs for lunch, and pizza for dinner. It was fairly certain the news would not be good.

Ellen kicked off her heels and picked up the cordless phone, collapsing in a cross-legged heap on the floor as she studied the message Mike had taken. As quickly as her fingers could move she punched in the numbers for Northern Michigan Hospital in Petoskey.

"John Barrett's room, please." She dug her elbows into her knees and rested her forehead in her free hand.

"Nurse's station," a woman announced.

"Yes, John Barrett's room."

"Who's calling?"

"This is his daughter, Ellen. May I speak with him please?"

"Just a minute, ma'am. Let me get your mother."

Ellen waited, praying against all odds that she was wrong, that the news would be good. Her father's health was poor but he had never suffered a heart attack. There was a chance he might recover completely if he had made it to the hospital in time.

"Ellen?" Her mother's voice was raspy and tired, and Ellen could tell she'd been crying.

"Mother, is he okay?"

"No." A single sob escaped from her mother and for a moment she was unable to continue. Ellen waited breathlessly.

"He didn't make it, honey. I'm so sorry."

Ellen could feel the floor drop away from beneath her. She refused to believe it. "No, Mom, that can't be true. People live through heart attacks all the time. He was —"

"Not this time," her mother cut in. "He died four hours ago. Ellen, he's gone."

"No! Mom, please! He . . . he can't be gone."

"I'm sorry, honey. He loved you so much. You know that."

Ellen was silent as the truth coursed through her veins, searing her, weighing her down. Her father was dead.

"Ellen?"

"Mom —" her voice was barely a whisper — "what are we going to do?"

"We're going to survive and we're still going to be a family."

Ellen nodded and fought a wave of anxi-

29

ety. "Are you by yourself?"

"No, Megan and Aaron are here with me, and Amy's on the way. I've called Jane. She's coming out Sunday afternoon."

"How are they handling it?"

"Not well. Especially Aaron. He hasn't said a word since it happened."

A thousand memories crowded out Ellen's ability to speak, and she realized there was a lump in her throat. Her father was gone, and she hadn't gotten to say good-bye. Certainly Aaron, her only brother, would be devastated. The others, too. *He's in heaven. He's still alive, just happier now.*

Ellen thought about the last time she'd talked with her father, only a few days earlier. He had sounded fine. There had been no warning that it was the last time she'd ever talk to him. She called him often, keeping him up-to-date on her latest assignments. He had always been interested in the little-known details and behind-the-scenes anecdotes that went into her reporting. Now he was gone, and Ellen wondered if she would suffocate from the shock.

"Are you okay, honey?"

Her mother's strained question pulled her back. "Mom, what happened?"

"Well," her mother drew a ragged breath. "He wasn't feeling well when he woke up this morning, and he took a long nap in his chair until about one o'clock. Then he got up and had something to eat. He was walking back to take a shower when he collapsed in the hallway."

Ellen closed her eyes, picturing the familiar house, its aging dark brown carpet and narrow hallways.

"He didn't have a chance. We lost him before the paramedics arrived."

Ellen was quiet for a moment. "When do you want me home, Mom? When's the funeral?"

"Oh, honey, I don't know. I guess we'll have the funeral next Saturday. That's when your father's sister can get here from California. I don't know, it's all happening so fast." Her mom's voice cracked and she began to cry. "I guess none of us should be surprised, but it doesn't make it any easier."

Hearing her mother cry triggered something in Ellen and she felt her eyes well up with tears. Her parents had been married thirty-two years. How did one let go of something like that?

"Mom, you sure you're all right? You shouldn't be alone."

"I'm okay and I'm not alone. Listen, why don't you try to get here Sunday. Jane's plane is coming in around noon at Detroit

Metro. If you and Mike could get here about the same time you could all ride up to the house together. Then we'd have a week to take care of everything."

"Okay. I'll make the plans and call you back. Where will you be?"

"At the house. I've already signed the death certificate so there isn't much else I can do here." Her mother sobbed softly and struggled to speak. "Dear God, Ellen. How on earth am I going to get through life without him?"

Ellen had no answers. She was too busy asking herself the same question.

She finished talking with her mother and then moved into the next room. A shaky sigh escaped her and she stared at Mike. His long body was stretched out on the couch, his feet dangling over onto the floor. He had fallen asleep, still dressed in his designer shirt and tie, the magazine clutched in one hand. She wiped her tears and wondered why she was angry with him.

"Mike." The word came out flat, cool.

He stirred and instantly sat up, wiping a trace of saliva from the corner of his mouth and trying to look awake. "Sorry, honey. What happened? How is he?"

Ellen sat down in a chair across from him and leaned back, staring at the plant shelves that lined the high walls of their living room.

"He's dead. Died before the paramedics arrived."

Mike leaned back and sighed. "Ellen, I'm sorry." He loosened his tie. "Come here."

She paused a moment. Mike had never made an effort to be close to her father, and now that he was gone, she was angry with Mike for not trying harder. He didn't understand what she had just lost — and with all her being she wanted to refuse his comfort.

Instead, she fell slowly to her knees and crawled the few steps that separated them. Then she dropped her head in his lap and gave way to the despair that gripped her.

"Why didn't he take better care of himself?" Her anger brought fresh tears, and they spilled from her eyes. "It makes me so *mad* at him."

Mike stroked her hair and said nothing. Finally, Ellen wiped her eyes and looked wearily up at him. He was her husband, and she believed God had brought him into her life. She loved Mike whatever his shortcomings, but she did not always feel loved by him. He rarely made an effort on her behalf — especially where her family was concerned. Now his attempts to ease her grief seemed too little, too late.

"My mom wants us to be there Sunday afternoon." She leaned up and away from him. "That's when Jane's coming in. The funeral will be later that week, Saturday morning."

"A week from now?" He sounded incredulous.

Ellen blinked twice. "Yes. That's the soonest Aunt Betsy can get there. Is that a problem?"

She saw Mike's hesitation, watched his eyes look away from her, as though he were trying to think of the right way to say something he knew she wasn't going to like.

"Honey," he started, shaking his head, "I've got a baseball game to cover that Saturday. I don't know how I can find a replacement on such short notice."

There was more to it than that, Ellen was sure. She knew Mike wasn't comfortable at funerals, knew he wouldn't be looking forward to spending a week at her parents' house in Petoskey. She loved her family, but she was aware that they had their problems . . . that there would be bickering even as everyone pretended to get along. . . .

Still, the least he could do was be there for her. "A baseball game?"

"Honey, maybe it'd be better if you went by yourself." He searched her face for a reaction. "I could always join you later when I can get away."

She burned with anger and she didn't even try to hide it. Drawing herself up onto her knees, she stared at him. "No, that *wouldn't* be better, Mike." Her voice was even and measured, a study in controlled fury.

"I have a game Saturday. Come on, Ellen, you know how the producers are about last-minute changes."

"Wait a minute. I don't believe what I'm hearing." Ellen's temper blazed. "This isn't some friend's wedding or a class reunion where you can back out and blame it on your work. My father is *dead.* My mother wants us both to come out for the week. Can't you understand that?"

"I'm not married to your mother." Mike looked like he regretted the words as soon as he said them, but it was too late.

Ellen's mouth dropped open. "Fine. *I* want us both there. Okay?"

"Ellen, you know I can't take a week off without any notice. Work is a fact of life." He paused. "Besides, I don't like funerals. I never know how to act."

Ellen's eyes grew wide, full of disbelief and accusation.

He cleared his throat before she could

speak. "You'll have your family there," he insisted. "It's not like you'll be all by yourself." Mike shook his head. "Oh, forget it! You don't understand."

"You don't like funerals!" Ellen stood up and paced the floor. "No kidding, Mike —" She stopped and stared at him. "Me, neither. I don't like *death,* for that matter. But my dad is dead, and I need you there. So don't tell me I don't understand!"

"Don't yell at me. I don't deserve that."

"*What?* I deserve a husband who has complained about attending social events with me since we got married? A husband who doesn't want to go with me to my own father's funeral?"

"It's not that I don't want to go, Ellen. I told you I can't get away. Not on such short notice."

"What if it was *you* who died, Mike? I bet the station could get by somehow without folding."

She went to slam the cordless phone back onto the receiver. She was so furious she was shaking. She turned to face him, and when she spoke, even she heard the hatred in her voice. "What is it, Mike? Some ditzy little news anchor have your attention?"

He stood up, recoiling as if he'd been slapped.

36

"That's unfair."

"Is it?" Her voice was still angry, but softer now. "Is it really, Mike? My dad dies and you won't take one lousy week off work for me? What am I supposed to think?"

Mike looked past her then and reached toward the fireplace mantel for his car keys.

"I don't know what you're supposed to think," he said, pausing by the front door.

Ellen was speechless.

"Listen," Mike's voice was calmer as he continued. "I'm sorry about your dad. I loved him, too."

"Oh, don't give me that! Not now. You never even knew him, Mike. You never *tried* to know him. And you certainly didn't love him. Not enough to take me to his funeral, anyway." She snorted sarcastically. "I get the worst news of my entire life, and *you* can't think of anyone but yourself. What's happened to you, Mike? You're supposed to be a *Christian,* remember? The spiritual leader of the household?"

Mike shook his head. "Oh, don't throw that in my face. Not this time. Besides, I don't exactly see you rushing to the Bible for comfort."

"I'm not talking about comparing my walk with yours. I'm talking about you and me. You're supposed to love me like Christ loved the church, give up everything for me. But not you, no sir. You won't even take a week off work for me. What kind of Christian love is that?"

Mike's shoulders sagged and he sighed loudly, dramatically. "Ellen, I won't let you guilt me into going with you to Petoskey when I have work here in Miami. I could meet you down there the day before the funeral, but I can't possibly get a whole week off with no notice."

"Forget it, Mike." She turned her back to him.

"Look at me, Ellen," he demanded.

She whirled around and put a hand on her hip. "What?"

"You obviously need time to accept the facts." Mike's voice was measured and forced. "Your dad's dead. Nothing I can do can bring him back. You have family and friends in Petoskey, and you don't need me tagging along for a week of funeral preparations. I can probably get out there for the funeral. But that's all. Otherwise the topic's closed."

"Fly out for one day? I need you all week." Her icy anger melted and she began sobbing softly as she turned away from him again. "Forget it. I don't want you there."

Mike was silent, then his voice came from

behind her, cold and hurt. "Fine. I won't go at all." He strode across the room, and flung open the door.

"Jerk!" she shouted, glancing at him over her shoulder so that their eyes met for an angry moment. Then he stepped outside and slammed the door.

She stood frozen in place, studying the door and relishing the distraction of her renewed anger. At that moment it seemed Mike had always been like this, and she cursed herself for marrying him.

"Jerk!" She said it louder this time, even though no one was there to hear her.

She marched across the living room, picked up the telephone, and sat down at the kitchen table. She dialed the *Miami Times,* and in a voice that was almost unrecognizable, she told Ron Barkley that her father had died.

"I'll need a week, Ron."

"Listen, I'm sorry, Barrett." Barkley's voice was soft. "Call us if you need more time."

She hung up and dialed the airline, scribbling flight numbers on a pad of paper and making reservations to fly to Detroit without Mike. When she was finished, she folded her arms on the kitchen table, laid her head down, and sobbed until she thought her heart would break.

Of course she had seen it coming. Her father had heart disease and diabetes, and if high blood pressure and excess weight were any indication, he should have died more than a decade ago. But that didn't make his death any less painful.

"So, this is it, huh, Dad?" she whispered, her eyes closed. "Time to say good-bye."

She silently summoned a strength she had not known she possessed, one she would certainly have to draw on in the days to come. She would go home and face her four younger siblings, all of whom had been unable to get along for years. She would help her mother pick out a casket and plan a service. Then she would see that her father was buried. She would remember the past, walk through it, relive it, and try her best to put it behind her.

"God, help me get through it." But the whispered words felt foreign, as if praying was something she had forgotten how to do.

She sighed and wiped her eyes. How could he be gone, the father who had shared so much of her life? How could she bury the one person who had always believed in her? He was the man who had attended football games with her, teaching her the rules of play even after she'd been hired as a sports writer for the *Detroit Gazette.* There was nothing he would not have done for her, and now she would have to learn to live without him.

Never mind about Mike. She would be on a plane soon enough and then she would have one week before she would see him again. Meanwhile, she had a lot more to think about than what was wrong between the two of them.

Ellen lowered her head back down onto her arms. There had been a time when she thought the world revolved around Mike Miller, a time when she couldn't have imagined a scene like the one that had just taken place. Back when they spent Saturday mornings laughing at *I Love Lucy* reruns and Sunday mornings at church. But somewhere along the path of deadlines and breaking stories and babies that would never be, something had changed.

She tried to think back to the beginning, to the days when she and Mike couldn't stand to be away from each other. Images drifted through her mind. . . . Mike bringing her breakfast in bed on their first anniversary and the two of them giggling for hours because the eggs were rubbery and the toast like cardboard. . . . The birthday when she left work to find her BMW plastered with flowers and balloons, a task that had cost Mike a double lunch break. . . .

It felt good to remember those things — and it forced her to think of something other than her father. The memories raced through her mind like a highlight film and, despite herself, the corners of her mouth lifted as she remembered.

Mike Miller was handsome and intelligent, a Christian man with morals and a sense of humor. He had completely swept her off her feet. But too many times since then he had left her alone when she needed him. If he could let her face the week ahead by herself, then what strength did their marriage have?

Ellen dried her cheeks with the backs of her hands. She would go back to beautiful Petoskey, to the shores of Little Traverse Bay along Lake Michigan, to her childhood home. She would say good-bye to her father, then she would come back to Miami and see if there was still a heartbeat in her marriage . . . or if that, too, had grown ill and died.

Ellen sighed. Every muscle in her body ached. She barely had the energy even to stand. Rising from the chair, she stretched and headed toward her bedroom. She peeled off her clothes, leaving them scattered about the floor, and slipped into a long T-shirt. Then she pulled back the covers and slid between the cool sheets.

She did not often dream and that night was no exception. But in the hours before she finally drifted to sleep, she found herself remembering a time when her father was still very much alive. A time when she and Mike were just starting out . . . when Mike had loved her completely and had done something no one else had been able to do.

He made her forget about Jake Sadler.

As she closed her eyes, she found herself there, immersed in the vivid memories of a time that would never be again.

Two

For as long as she could remember, Ellen Barrett had known what she wanted to be when she grew up. She was not like other little girls who talked of being princesses or famous ice-skaters. Ellen was a writer. It was something that grew from her heart and worked its way through her very being.

As a child Ellen spent hours writing short stories and poetry. Her mother took her for a silly dreamer, but Ellen was nothing of the sort. She was merely a single-minded young girl honing a skill she was certain to draw from in years to come.

When she was ten years old, Ellen first understood her need to place on paper all that already existed in her heart. It was then that she made her decision. One day she would write for the *Detroit Gazette*.

The *Gazette* was the biggest newspaper in Michigan, and after high school, when Ellen began plotting her way toward a journalism degree, it was with the sole purpose of one day being employed by the *Gazette.* A position on staff would mean living in a small apartment by herself, four hours away from her family and the small town she loved. But Ellen wanted a staff position desperately. She would have lived on the moon if it meant working at the *Gazette.*

In 1990, she was in her final semester at the University of Michigan when she was selected to do an internship for the *Gazette.* She was a Christian by then, and many of her childhood plans had undergone significant changes — but not the dream of working for the *Gazette.* From the beginning she saw the internship as an answer to prayer.

"Ms. Barrett," the sports editor said when he called her at her dormitory that January. "We've reviewed your application and selected you as one of our sports interns for the coming semester."

"Sports," she repeated blankly. She had requested an internship in the news department, but her hesitation lasted only a moment. "Fantastic. That'll be perfect. What will I be doing?"

"You'll be taking scores over the phone several nights a week. Of course, you'll need a complete understanding of most of the major spring sports. Baseball, track, softball, volleyball, wrestling, tennis, swimming. And the city league sports, bowling and high-pitch softball. That kind of thing."

He droned on about the details. The job involved taking hundreds of scores and statistics from local sporting events and turning them into brief copy for the score-card in the back of the sports section.

"Sound okay to you?"

Ellen thought quickly. She didn't know the first thing about the rules of sports. She wasn't even sure she knew how to keep score. "Definitely," she said before she could stop herself. "No problem. When do I start?"

"Next week. Stop by the office and pick up your schedule. You can fill out the paperwork then."

When Ellen hung up the phone, she let out a shriek so loud it brought students from several rooms away rushing to see what the problem was.

"I got the internship! I can't believe it! I'm on staff at the *Gazette*!"

The other students rolled their eyes and returned to their business, unaware of the significance of the moment. Within two minutes Ellen was on the phone with her father.

"Way to go, Ellen! That's my girl! I knew

you could do it, honey." Ellen could see his smile as clearly as if he were standing in front of her. "This is only the beginning."

"There's one small problem, Daddy. I've been assigned to the sports department."

"Sports?" John Barrett laughed out loud. "Honey you wouldn't recognize the difference between a ball and a strike. Why would they put you in sports?"

"My clip file included a few sports features I did. Remember?"

"You don't need to know sports to write about the Michigan quarterback's asthma condition. Didn't they ask you if you'd ever covered a game?"

"They asked me if I understood the games."

"What did you say?"

"I said yes."

"Oh, honey," John muttered. "When do you start?"

"Next week. But I don't have classes until then. I could get time off from the restaurant and I was thinking, maybe . . ."

"Get in your car and get here as soon as you can. We haven't had snow in a while so at least the roads are clear."

Her father's voice was kind and understanding. He was a professor at North Central Community College in Petoskey

47

and spring classes didn't start for another two weeks. "I'll give you a crash course on everything you'll need to know. Maybe between the two of us we can fool 'em."

Ellen broke into a smile. "Thanks, Daddy. I'll be there in time for dinner. One thing though." She paused. "If Jake calls, don't tell him I'm coming up. I don't want to talk to him."

"I won't say a word, but he's got it bad for you, Ellen. I'll never understand you two."

"I don't want to talk about it."

She and Jake had dated for six years. But they had been broken up for ten months and the subject was closed.

"Okay, but you're breaking his heart." Her father sighed dramatically. "I'm sure you have your reasons."

I do, Ellen had thought. *Jake Sadler broke my heart first.*

"It's nothing I want to get into. Just don't tell him, okay?"

"Okay, okay. Get your things together and get down here. I'll have Mom fix something special for dinner."

The week flew by in a blur of guidelines and rules and scoring methods. She memorized player positions, team violations, and rules of play. She learned the difference between the high-arc and windmill softball pitches and that a slider was a type of baseball pitch, not to be confused with sliding into base. There were the spikes and sets and digs in volleyball, and whereas baseball gave its batters three strikes to get a hit, volleyball allowed three hits to form a play. She learned about the pin in wrestling, the splits in swimming, and the triple jump in track until finally the rules and terminology didn't seem quite so foreign.

Once in a while they'd be working and the phone would ring. Her mother would answer it.

"Just a minute, Jake," she'd say. Then in a whispered voice, "Ellen, it's Jake. He talked to your roommate and he knows you're here."

Ellen would look up from her pages of sports notes and shake her head. "Tell him I'm out."

Then she and her father would exchange a glance and Ellen would direct their conversation back to sports. She hated to lie, but where Jake Sadler was concerned, the greater evil would have been giving in to her feelings and seeing him. Jake was the only boy she had ever loved and now she could never, ever see him again. There was too much at stake. *My life depends on it. My spiritual life.*

"I'm sorry, Jake," her mother would say. "Yes, we're all doing fine. Yes. Well, I'll certainly tell her you called."

At week's end Ellen was certain she knew at least enough about sports to take phone scores at the *Detroit Gazette.* Her father had been so thorough that she even had time to spend with her sisters and brother.

There were long talks with nineteen-year-old Megan about her troublesome boy-friend, and time spent helping Amy with her homework. Amy was seventeen that year, the quietest of the Barrett siblings, and Ellen enjoyed her company.

On the last day of her visit, Ellen, Amy, and sixteen-year-old Aaron, the only boy among them, played Password until they were laughing so hard they had to quit. Later Jane stopped by and the seven Barretts gathered round the worn oak dinner table as they had done every night before Ellen moved away.

Jane was twenty-one then, two years younger than Ellen. Growing up, the two had been inseparable, but in recent years they had grown strangely distant. Ellen searched for something that would explain the change in their relationship, but there seemed to be no answer. *When I finish school,* she told herself that night after Jane left, *everything will be like it was before.*

The next morning she leaned up and kissed her father on the cheek. It was time to get back to the city. "Thanks, Daddy." Their eyes met and held for a moment.

"Ah, honey." He pulled her into a hug. "You're so grown up now. I can't believe this is your last semester."

"Yeah, I might even pass thanks to you." Her eyes twinkled as she pulled away and grinned at him.

"It'll be our little secret. Deal?"

"Deal!" Ellen's eyes grew watery. "I love you, Daddy."

"I love you too, honey. Let me know how it goes."

"Ellen?" her mother had called from the other side of the house. She'd been packing Ellen a sack lunch for her trip back to Ann Arbor and was a blur of motion, moving across the kitchen, reaching into the refrigerator, then up into the cupboards and back to the refrigerator again.

"Yes, Mother?"

"Now, Ellen, remember to eat these sandwiches in the car while you're driving," she said in a pleasant, breathless voice loud enough to reach across the house. "You don't want to pull off I-75 and risk getting abducted by some stranger at a backwoods gas station."

"Yes, Mother," Ellen said obediently, raising her voice so her mother could hear her.

"And whatever you do, be sure to fill that car of yours with gasoline before you leave Petoskey. You should probably stop at Mr. Gardner's station, right on the way out of town. You remember Mr. Gardner's station, don't you, dear?"

"Yes, Mother."

"He's been asking about you because he wants to send his son, Travis, to U of M next year. He'd love to see you, maybe hear a little bit about campus life and all. Could you do that for me, dear?"

"Yes, Mother."

"You know, that Travis of his is certainly a smart one. He won't have any trouble getting into U of M if you ask me. Of course Travis always did have a secret crush on you, Ellen. He was always . . ."

She continued on. Ellen and her father exchanged a conspiratorial grin and he hugged her once more.

"Go get 'em, honey. You want to know something?"

"What?"

"You're going to be a great writer one day."

Ellen nodded, too choked up to speak.

Her mother rounded the corner with the lunch sack and presented it to Ellen as she caught her breath.

"Don't forget what I said, dear." She leaned over and pecked Ellen quickly on the cheek. "Drive safely and don't take any chances in those small towns along the way. And that sports department is bound to be full of men. I guess there's nothing we can do about that. But don't you let them corrupt you. You're a good girl, Ellen. I understand that this is an important break for you but, I'm concerned all the same. I don't care what the modern school thinks of such things. A sports department is no place for a young lady, so watch yourself and be careful."

"Okay, Diane, okay," Ellen's father said gently. He placed his arm around his wife and pulled her toward him. "Let the poor girl get on the road or she'll never make it back before dark."

Five minutes later Ellen was on her way. Her first night shift at the *Gazette* was two days later and suddenly she was busier than she'd ever been in her life. Her hours were filled with senior level courses, labs and lectures and on-campus reporting. She would finish her course work, grab an apple and a bagel, and fly out the door for the *Gazette.* The days became weeks, and before Ellen realized it the semester was half over.

Once in a while she was allowed to forgo phone duty and cover a high school game in person. But most games were played on the weekend and Ellen's Friday and Saturday nights were spent at the *Gazette,* manning the phones in the sports department. The paper had a system whereby coaches would call in their scores when the games were finished. Ellen took scores from dozens of coaches of sports ranging from track to T-ball, bowling to baseball.

The paper received hundreds of calls each weekend and interns worked the phones until midnight. No exceptions. Ellen was thankful for the work because it left her little time to think of Jake.

"*Gazette* Sports, what team are you reporting?" Ellen would say as she answered the phone and prepared her fingers for action. Then she would cradle the receiver against her shoulder while her fingers flew across the keyboard, transferring the details as accurately as possible into the computer. When the call was finished she would organize the information and file it to the sports desk.

"*Gazette* Sports, what team are you reporting?" The calls continued through the night.

The questions became part of a formula. Who was the winner, what was the score, where was the contest played, why was the game important, when would the teams play again, and how did the winning team manage to win. Space was tight, and details beyond that had no chance of making the paper.

A few interns complained about being used by the paper. There was no pay, no bylines, and no promise of promotion. The hours were long, and Ellen's neck grew stiff while she typed in details about park league T-ball games and high school volleyball matches.

She wouldn't have traded a minute of it.

She had waited tables in Petoskey and then in Ann Arbor for five long years while she earned her journalism degree. Now she was working for the *Gazette. Staff member,* her employee badge said. Ellen took the words to heart.

As the semester drew to an end the *Gazette*'s assistant managing editor John Dower spoke to Ellen's advanced news writing class. Dower was in charge of the news desk. He was pompous and condescending and had all the compassion of a frustrated drill sergeant. Ellen watched him size up the class of seniors and was silently thankful she worked in the sports department.

"Right now all of you are sitting there thinking you're hot-shot reporters about to take the world of journalism by storm." The editor sneered, pacing before the class of fifty senior journalism students. "You think you'll breeze out of here with your University of Michigan degree and waltz your way on to the staff of some big paper like the *Gazette.*"

He stopped and stared at them. "You're wrong. Let me tell you how it's going to be." He began pacing again. "When you leave here you'll move off to a small-town paper, which, if you're lucky, might publish three times a week. You'll work every department, every beat, and make half of what it costs to survive." He stopped and smiled sardonically. "You'll do that for five years before anyone at the *Gazette* will even consider bringing you in for an interview. Any questions?"

Only one student in the room dared to raise a hand.

"Does that apply to interns at the *Gazette?*" Ellen asked.

The editor leveled his gaze in her direction and vaguely recognized her from the batch of interns currently doing time at the paper. "It *especially* applies to interns at the *Gazette.*"

Ellen began brainstorming ways to be more valuable to the *Gazette* staff. Instead of asking only the routine questions when scores came in, she asked a few more, searching for news worthy of more than merely a box score. She hit pay dirt a week later, four hours into a Friday night shift.

She was filing the information from the previous call when a score came in from a young boy named Chin Lee wishing to report the results of a junior-high basketball tournament. As Chin Lee rattled off the score, Ellen saw that the boy played for a school located in a neglected part of town. Most of the players had Asian names. *Strange. Usually the coach calls in.*

Ellen took down the usual information and then paused a moment. "Who's your coach, Chin?"

The boy was quiet a moment. "Uh, well, we don't have a coach. Is that okay?"

Bells went off in Ellen's head.

"Sure, but who works with your team, who makes up the plays for you?"

Chin hesitated. "We, uh, we get together a few times a week and watch tapes of the

Los Angeles Lakers. We see their plays and we learn them. Then we use them in games."

Twenty minutes later Ellen had the phone numbers of the other players on Chin's team and enough information to write a magazine article on the boys.

She stood up from her desk and located the sports editor, Steve Simons.

"What is it, Ellen?" He looked up from his computer screen.

Ellen cleared her throat and proceeded to tell him. Three hours later she had written her first feature story for the *Gazette*. Simons told Ellen it would probably run in Sunday's paper.

On Saturday night Ellen could barely sleep. It was like being a little girl, waiting for Santa Claus to come. Only this time he rode a bicycle and his knapsack carried nothing but a stack of newspapers. The moment she heard the paper smack against the sidewalk outside her dormitory, Ellen rushed outside and tore it open. What she saw made her gasp aloud.

The *Gazette* had played her story on the front page.

After that there were other stories. A ninety-year-old runner attempting a final race in memory of her recently deceased husband; a Little League coach who had taken three boys from his son's team into his home when their parents turned out to be drug dealers. The list grew.

Two weeks before graduation Ellen learned of an entry-level opening in the sports department at the *Gazette*.

"They told us we'd need more experience, but I'm going to go for it, Daddy," Ellen told her father that night on the telephone. "Think I have a chance?"

"Are you kidding, honey? They're probably hoping you'll ask for an interview. Otherwise they might lose you to the competition."

"Pray for me, will you?"

She knew the request would make her dad smile. He had raised them in the Catholic church, and at first when Ellen started attending a Protestant church he had been discouraged, disappointed in her decision. But he was used to the idea now and seemed to enjoy her open discussion of prayer.

"I'll pray, honey. Now get back to school and get that job."

The interview came one week before graduation. Ellen bought a new skirt and jacket for the occasion and then worried that she was overdressed. She was the picture of professionalism as she walked up the marble steps and went inside, but she was assailed by doubts. *I'm too young . . . I don't have enough experience . . . They don't want a woman sports writer . . . I should turn around and go home . . . Who am I kidding?*

She made her way through the newsroom and into the sports department just as she remembered the words John Dower had spoken to her senior class: *"When you leave here you'll move off to a small-town paper, which, if you're lucky, might publish three times a week. You'll work every department, every beat, and make half of what it costs to survive. You'll do that for five years before anyone at the* Gazette *will even consider bringing you in for an interview."*

Ellen entered the sports editor's office and the first person she saw was John Dower. He smiled kindly and motioned for Ellen to sit down. There was no mention of her inexperience.

An hour later she left with her first job offer.

She called her parents with the news.

"I don't know, Ellen," her mother said, her voice filled with concern. "I'll worry about you out late at night covering sports games in a city like Detroit. Working with all those men. You'll have to be so careful, dear. Are there any other women in the department?"

"No, but I've made a lot of good friends, Mom. I'll be fine."

"I just wonder if it's smart for a young lady to be involved in a job surrounded by men."

Then her father got on the line. "Honey, I knew you could do it!" He was bursting with pride. "Aaron and the girls will be so happy when they hear about this."

"I'll be covering high school sports for a while, but that's fine with me. Can you believe it, Dad? Me? A full-time staff reporter for the *Gazette*?"

"It's what you've always wanted, honey."

"As far back as I can remember."

"Before you know it you'll be covering U of M games. Then I'll be down every week."

Ellen laughed. The Barretts had lived in Ann Arbor fifteen years earlier and her father was fanatical about Wolverine football. "So that's why you taught me all that stuff about sports."

"You better believe it. I'll expect sideline passes to your first U of M assignment."

Graduation came and went, and Ellen began working sixty-hour weeks. She covered more high school sports than she thought possible. Newspaper copy was measured in column inches, and most of Ellen's assignments carried a maximum length of twelve inches. But there were times when she was given more in-depth projects, feature pieces on high school coaches and star prep players.

Two months passed. Ellen found a simple, one-bedroom apartment five minutes from the office and bought a few meager furnishings. Occasionally she ate a late meal with the sports staff after deadline on Friday nights, staying out until long after midnight swapping anecdotes and unwinding after an evening of tight deadlines.

Now and then she was asked out by one of her coworkers, but Ellen was adamantly opposed to the idea. There were nineteen writers and a dozen part-time reporters working for the *Gazette* Sports section. As the only woman among them, Ellen would not consider being anything less than professional in their midst.

She spent most of her free time on the telephone with her parents and her sisters. They talked about a hundred different things from boyfriends to school work to part-time jobs, but they respected Ellen's wishes and none of them ever mentioned Jake Sadler.

One day Simons asked to see Ellen in his office. He was an intelligent man in his late fifties with two young grandchildren. Ellen thought he was the kindest editor at the paper.

"The Wolverines have their first scrimmage of the season this Saturday," he said. "We want you there."

Ellen was stunned.

"We'll have a senior writer cover the game, but we'd like to try you on a few U of M sports features and see how you do." He grinned. "Congratulations, Ellen."

The day before the game she was given her press credentials. Ellen stared at them and remembered the long hours taking scores over the phone. She was twenty-three and she had arrived.

Her assignment was a simple one. Interview the offensive coordinator and determine the Wolverines' approach for the coming season. They had a freshman quarterback known throughout the country for his passing ability. Would Michigan stick to its ground game with such a talented athlete leading the offense? Ellen's story would answer that question and reveal the personal side of the coach.

Game time was ten o'clock Saturday morning, and Ellen's apartment was thirty miles east of the stadium. She planned to be there at seven, eat breakfast somewhere off campus, and go over her list of questions before arriving at the stadium at nine. That gave her fifteen minutes before her interview with the coach.

Ellen was aware that this would be her first time to work an event alongside male sports writers who were far more accomplished than she. Certainly the broadcast journalists would be there. Joe Stevens from WGRT, a grizzled veteran with years of sports experience, and Mike Miller from WCBS, a handsome newcomer who had played tight end for Michigan before suffering a career-ending knee injury. Mike was also actively involved with a Christian Athletes' Fellowship and helped out at the local Children's Hospital. He had a promising career in broadcasting, and Ellen admired his work.

She prayed she could earn their respect and come across confident and capable. She planned to work among them often.

The morning began badly. She overslept and couldn't decide what to wear. She finally pulled onto Interstate 94 at 6:45, telling herself she would skip the leisurely breakfast and stop for fast food in Ann Arbor. Half an hour later she was minutes from the stadium, driving along State Street looking for a place to stop.

At the intersection of State and Stadium

Way she stopped at a red light and glanced at the seat beside her to check how much cash she had. But her purse wasn't there. *Strange.* She looked nervously up at the light. Still red. She scanned the backseat of her four-door compact and again found nothing.

At that moment the white van in front of her began to move. *Green light.* She pressed her foot onto the accelerator and scanned the floor of her car once more, desperately hoping to find her purse.

The crash came almost immediately. She jolted up against the steering wheel and then back against her car's headrest.

"Green means go, buddy," she mumbled. Then she looked up at the light and felt her heart sink. It was flashing red. The van in front of her had moved forward only one car-length. She had presumed the light was green and that it was moving on through the intersection.

The van turned slowly into a gas station, and Ellen spied the letters on the side of the vehicle. WCBS.

Oh no. Ellen's heart sank. *They're on the way to the game. Please God, don't let Mike Miller be inside.*

She followed the van into the station and killed the engine just as two men stepped out. One of them was Mike Miller.

Ellen forced herself to get out of the car, furious with herself and the way her face was blushing a deep red.

"I'm so sorry! I thought the light was green and then you stopped and I guess I just didn't see it coming. I mean I've been down this street a hundred times and I've never seen that light flashing red before."

Great. I sound like my mother.

While she spoke, the driver of the van checked out his bumper and brushed off a few chips of paint that had come from the front of Ellen's car. Meanwhile Mike moved closer to Ellen. He seemed to be staring at her shirt and she finally grew flustered.

"Do you mind if I ask what you're looking at?"

Mike straightened and Ellen saw that he was easily six-foot-three. He grinned at her — and for the first time in Ellen's life someone other than Jake Sadler made her heart skip a beat.

"Sorry, miss," Mike said. "It's just, well . . ." He pointed toward her blouse and Ellen followed his gaze. The buttons were fitted into the wrong holes all the way down so that the left side of her rayon blouse hung four inches lower than the right.

Ellen quickly shoved the longer piece of

66

rayon into her slacks. As she did, she bared a layer of white lace that ran along the top of her camisole. Mike raised an eyebrow and smothered a smile.

"Oh!" Frustrated at herself, Ellen yanked the blouse back into place and folded her arms over the section that was now, once again, hanging outside of her slacks.

"In a hurry this morning?"

"Yes, in fact, I am." Ellen was totally flustered and she prayed neither of them would figure out who she was. Perhaps Mike wouldn't see her at the game. With any luck he'd be transferred to a different department or hired by another city.

The driver of the van smiled in her direction. "No harm done, ma'am. Looks like you've got a pretty good dent, but nothing you can't drive with."

"I have my insurance information if you'd like it." She did her best to ignore Mike Miller's partially concealed grin.

"Sure," the driver said. "Never a bad idea after a fender-bender."

Ellen opened her car door and searched frantically for her purse. It contained her insurance card, her driver's license, and her press credentials. Suddenly she knew with sinking certainty that it was back at her apartment.

She pulled out of the car slowly and put her hands on her hips, exposing her uneven blouse once more. "I'm sorry. I can't seem to find my purse. It has everything, all my information."

The driver of the van nodded and Mike tried to contain a chuckle.

"No problem. Everything's okay on our end, right, Mike?"

Mike cleared his throat and tried to look serious. "Well, my neck's a little sore . . ." He rubbed his hand along the base of his skull. He wore leather loafers, dark wool slacks, and a starched white button down which contrasted sharply with his paisley silk tie. He was the picture of cool confidence.

Ellen stared at him beseechingly.

He caught her glance and smiled warmly. "No, I'm just kidding. But you better retrace your steps and see if you can find your purse. That could be a real disaster."

Everyone laughed, though Ellen's sounded a bit hollow, and the men bid her farewell as they climbed into their van. Ellen watched them disappear, then quickly got into her car and headed back toward Detroit.

She had ninety minutes until her appointment with the coach.

Two hours later, still breathless from the morning's events, she walked out of the offensive coordinator's office. She did not have a front-page story, but she had enough information to pull a feature together. The stairs to the press box seemed to go on forever and she was weary by the time she located her seat. She filed her notes and began checking her purse for a pencil.

"I see you found it."

Ellen looked up and found herself staring into Mike Miller's teasing blue eyes. Seating assignments for members of the press were made long before game time, and he was seated right next to her.

Ellen sighed and dropped her head in her hands. "Why can't this day end?"

"Hey, why didn't you say you worked for the *Gazette*?"

Ellen peered at him through the spaces between her fingers. "I was hoping once I fixed my buttons you might not recognize me."

Mike laughed. For the rest of the game he teased and talked with her, and the morning flew by. She had expected him to be ruthless — condescending and unforgiving of the mistakes she'd made earlier in the day. Instead he was helpful. He treated her with respect and consideration and was careful to avoid discussing the accident.

When the game was over Ellen gathered her things. "Guess I'll see you next week." She smiled at him.

"Hey, Ellen, you mind if I get your phone number?"

Ellen felt the heat flood her cheeks. "Oh, the accident. Right. I've got my insurance information here somewhere." She began digging through her purse, suddenly nervous. "I have insurance, really, I do. I just didn't have my purse with me. But I guess you know that, don't you?"

Mike placed his hand gently on her arm so that she stopped talking and looked up at him. He had the palest blue eyes she'd ever seen.

"I don't want your insurance information, Ellen. I asked for your phone number." His smile warmed her all the way down to her toes. "I was hoping you might have dinner with me sometime . . ."

The memory of that smile tugged at Ellen's weary heart, and she rolled over in bed, squeezing her eyes tight against the tears that threatened to fall. If only things had stayed that way . . . if only she and Mike had found a way to hold on to the wonder they'd found together . . .

If only life had turned out differently.

THREE

There was no break in the heat that weekend and Ellen stayed inside where it was cool, sorting through scrapbooks and boxes of tattered memories, drifting back in time. She wanted to find her prayer journal, the one she had kept when she first became a Christian. There she would find the words she'd written after she and Mike first met. And maybe then she would remember the reasons they married, the reasons they should fight to keep their marriage from falling apart. Besides, the task kept her from thinking of her father's death. Right now it was easier to believe she was headed back to Petoskey for a reunion with her siblings than to accept the fact that her father was no longer alive.

Ellen rubbed her weary eyes and gazed at the clock. She had the afternoon ahead of her. Mike was covering weekend sports. When he'd been home earlier their conversation had been stilted, forced. She sighed and reached into a torn cardboard box, sifting through the contents of what once had consumed her heart.

The box contained half-filled journals and what seemed like hundreds of letters. Peering inside, Ellen saw a series of inked-in hearts doodled painstakingly across the top of folded, yellowed notebook paper. She lifted the paper from the others and unfolded it gingerly so the creases wouldn't tear.

It was a letter from Jake.

She sighed. The words had nearly faded from view, the way everything else about Jake already had. She ran her fingers over the wrinkles, glanced at the date and quickly figured Jake must have written it in his junior year at Petoskey High.

"Hey Bucko, what's up?" Ellen read the words silently, and for the first time in years she could hear his voice.

You probably already know this but I've got basketball practice after school. That's a big-time bummer. Know why? I'll tell you. Cuz I'd rather clean my garage or straighten my books. (J.K.) Truth is I'd rather spend the afternoon with you. I know that shocks you what with the hordes of girls flocking around my locker. (Right!!!) Serious now. You're the only one I want to see, Ellen. I mean it. Even if you do like raisins on your salad (sick!) and drive that ugly burnt orange tank. (I made a mental note to never let you drive again. My Bug's the only way to go!) Speaking of which, you and Leslie and Rick HAVE to go to the game Friday night. I think I'll score the big 3-0 and then wink at you like they do in the pros. Plus, we could probably sneak a kiss at halftime. I know, I know. If I'm lucky. Let me know if you can come. Catch you after fifth period. Don't think you can avoid me, either. I'll follow you to the ends of the earth if you ever leave me. You're my future, babe. ILYADYFI, Jake.

ILYADYFI. *I love you and don't you forget it.* Her eyes grew dim and she smiled absently at the long-ago phrase. Last she heard, Jake was still living in Petoskey. For a brief moment she allowed herself to wonder whether he had gotten married, whether he still thought of her. . . . Then she folded the brittle paper and reached back into the box, sorting through dozens of similar notes until she found what she was looking for. Her prayer journal, the first one she'd ever kept. It was dated Spring, 1990.

Humidity had warped the pages, but Ellen could read the entries as clearly as the day they were written. She flipped toward the back of the floral cloth-covered book until she found September's passages. She saw it then, the lengthy entry she had written the night she first dated Mike Miller. Even now the words seemed to dance on the page, filled with the excitement she had felt that faraway day.

Well, I did it. I finally went out with Mike Miller. Ever since we met, our schedules have been too busy to get together. Not that I haven't thought of him and watched WCBS sports more than usual. Anyway, tonight he took me out for pizza and afterwards we walked around the Michigan campus and talked.

We want so many of the same things it's almost scary. He's a broadcaster so naturally we have sports in common. But it's so much more than that. He's a Christian. Raised that way. He said he hasn't had a serious girlfriend since high school because it's hard to find someone who loves God and wants the same things he wants. It's like he's perfect for me. Like God himself brought us together. We even talked about marriage, how it should be forever . . . between a man and a woman equally yoked, people who want to love the Lord, build a family and a home where Christ will be honored. I've only been out with Mike once and somehow I can't imagine marrying anyone else. Of course, I didn't tell him that. I'll wait till the second date at least. Maybe I should pray about it.

Dear Lord, I don't know why you've brought me and Mike together, but I need your help on this one. Is he the man for me, the man I might marry? I need to know. There's something very special about him, something I can see in his eyes. Oh, Lord, help me to be careful around him and take things slowly. And thank you for his faith, his love for you. I pray that you will bless our relationship, whatever it may become. I love you, Lord. Amen.

Ellen remembered how it felt to write those words. She had fallen hard for Mike. *Give me a sign, Lord,* she remembered praying before each date. *Show me if there's some reason I shouldn't give him my heart.* And each time they went out, Mike exceeded both her expectations and her dreams.

"There's just one thing," Mike had told her tenderly when their dating became more serious. "I don't want to sleep with you, Ellen. Not until we're married. I really believe God won't honor our relationship unless we honor him."

Ellen had been stunned. She understood perfectly well that sex before marriage was wrong in God's eyes, but that hadn't stopped her where Jake was concerned. Indeed, she had always felt somewhat self-righteous for waiting three years after she and Jake began dating before giving in to her desires.

When she and Jake broke up and she became a Christian, she understood far better why God asks people to wait. There was a bond between her and Jake that should never have been there, a part of her that she could never get back.

Mike had been honest. He told her he had dated several girls through college and had been sexually intimate with three of them. "It was wrong, and the relationships were empty. A few years ago I made a promise to the Lord. Next time I'd do things his way."

Ellen could still remember how difficult it had been to stay within the physical limits of the dating relationship with Mike. He set a curfew for himself and was out the door of Ellen's apartment no later than ten o'clock each evening. Finally, a year later, they were married. The wedding was beautiful and their honeymoon on a beach near Manzanillo, Mexico, was truly blessed by God, beautiful beyond anything either of them had ever imagined.

Ellen smiled at the memory. There were no words to describe the depth of love they had shared physically and emotionally. They believed God was rewarding them for their obedience, and in those early years it seemed the honeymoon would never end.

Ellen ran her fingers over the words she had written and flipped through the pages of the journal. Mike had been so strong in his faith back then, so sure. Now it had been years since he had talked to her about his love for God . . . months since they had even discussed going to church.

Mike wasn't the only one to blame. She remembered a line from Psalm 51: *Restore to me the joy of your salvation.* Where was that joy now? She closed her eyes and felt the sting of tears. She and Mike were a mess, her father was gone forever, and everything that was ever good about life had changed. The Lord seemed a million miles away.

The phone rang, interrupting her

thoughts. Ellen stretched her legs and reached across the bed for the receiver.

"Hello."

"Hi, it's me."

Jane sounded annoyed, and Ellen braced herself. Her sister had called twice already that weekend to make sure of Ellen's arrival time in Detroit and to report that the other family members were not doing well.

"I think we should have gone today instead of Sunday. You know, I wanted to switch to Saturday, but you and Mom said to wait until Sunday. I think it's a waste of time."

"It's the best we can do, I guess." Ellen stared out her bedroom window at the deep blue-green of the Atlantic Ocean. They were two blocks away from the beach and she never got tired of the view.

Jane was silent for a moment. "What's that supposed to mean?"

Ellen rolled her eyes. Jane had become so testy lately almost anything set her off.

"Nothing, Jane. I'm just saying we'll be there soon enough. I'm not exactly looking forward to this week."

"All you ever think about is yourself, Ellen. I mean it. That's the trouble with you. The world doesn't revolve around what you want. Mom needs us there."

"I know." Ellen tried to keep the fatigue

79

out of her voice, and failed. "Forget it, Jane. Forget I said anything. You're right. We should have gone today instead of tomorrow. Will you forgive me?"

Jane released a short burst of air. "Whatever."

In the uneasy silence that followed, Ellen struggled, wondering what she could say to ease the tension between them. The last thing she needed was to spend a week in Petoskey fighting with Jane. She'd rather not go. Her mind grasped for something neutral to say. "Well, I still have a bunch of things to pack."

Silence.

"So, I guess I'll see you tomorrow, okay?"

Silence.

"Have a safe flight."

Jane sighed loudly. "Sure, whatever. See you later."

Ellen hung up the phone and leaned back against her pillows. She remembered how it had been when she and Jane were kids, before they graduated from high school. They had shared a room together, giggling about the boys they knew and telling each other a hundred different secrets. Regardless of their disagreements during the day, each night before falling asleep they would whisper the same words to each other.

"Good night, Jane. Love you. See you in the morning."

"Good night, Ellen. Love you. See you in the morning."

Ellen's eyes burned at the memory. She couldn't remember the last time they'd said those words.

She thought of the others then . . . Megan, Amy, and Aaron. The five of them had been so close as children. Eventually she and Mike had distanced themselves from her family by moving to Miami. Now Jane was angry most of the time; sweet Megan was twenty-seven and had gotten involved with an abusive, controlling drug dealer; twenty-five-year-old Amy was busy with her own life and never called or wrote to the others; and Aaron, at twenty-four, was unemployable because of a temper so fierce most people were afraid of him.

More than a decade had passed since the Barretts had lived under one roof. Gradually the family had stopped attending Mass regularly, and eventually Ellen's faith had led her away from the Catholic church. Now even that seemed like a lifetime ago. Ellen wished she could remember when they had stopped being the family everyone else envied.

Saturday passed slowly so that by early Sunday Ellen was packed and anxious to leave.

"Have a safe flight," Mike said, pecking her on the cheek as he glanced at his watch.

"Right." Ellen's voice was flat and she refused to look at him.

"Ellen." Mike placed his hand gently underneath her chin and tilted her face toward his. "I love you. Don't let yourself get confused about that just because your dad is gone."

"If you loved me you'd make an effort for me." Ellen's eyes were dry. She was emotionally drained and the week hadn't even started. "I told you I wanted you with me this week. It was important to me, Mike."

"We've been through this before. I can't get the time off and you know that. You knew that when you married me."

"If it was important to you, you'd get the time off."

Mike drew a deep breath. "Anyway, have a safe flight. I do love you and I'll call you in a few days to see how it's going."

Ellen waited until his car disappeared down their street. Then she reached for the telephone and called a taxi. Twenty minutes later the cab pulled up out front.

Grabbing her suitcase, she studied the picture of Mike and her over the fireplace, then headed for the door.

The taxi made its way through the city toward the airport, and again Ellen caught herself swimming in a sea of memories. Like scenes from a movie, flashbacks from her childhood filled her mind and it was all she could do to stop them.

She looked at her watch. Her flight was scheduled to leave at 10:30. She would travel three hours nonstop and land in Detroit just before two o'clock. Jane's plane would arrive twenty minutes later. Megan had arranged to pick them both up and drive them back to the house, four hours north of the city.

The taxi swung into the airport and pulled up along the curb in the area designated for passenger unloading. Ellen moved slowly as she paid the driver and checked her bags with the airline. She wore a simple navy rayon dress that fell nearly to her matching pumps. Her hair was pulled back from her face, tied in a navy silk scarf, and she wore round, dark-rimmed sunglasses that covered nearly half her face. With a lifetime of memories threatening to break free at any moment, she had no room for casual conversation on the flight. Regardless of the people around her, she intended to be alone. The glasses would stay.

"When can we board?" she asked a flight attendant at the gate.

"Go ahead and board now if you'd like."

Ellen made her way down one of the narrow aisles of the Boeing 747, relieved to see that she had a window seat. Three hours alone in the sky. Maybe that would help make sense of her feelings. She sat down, slid the window shade up as far as it would go, and stared at the airline personnel working like so many cogs in a machine to prepare the airplane for takeoff. Ellen wondered if any of them had adult siblings who no longer liked them.

She took a deep breath and realized how tired she was. Because of her early flight she had gotten up at five-thirty. She leaned back, and in less than a minute she was asleep.

"Excuse me." The flight attendant's voice woke Ellen instantly. "We're about to serve breakfast. I thought you might like to know."

"Yes. Thank you." Ellen straightened herself and looked out the window, amazed she had slept through takeoff. She studied the ground below and saw they had nearly crossed the Florida peninsula and were headed for the long journey north across the states. Her eyes narrowed thoughtfully as she gazed upward into the endless blue sky. She couldn't have been sleeping long, but she had been having the strangest dream. . . .

Jake Sadler had been beside her on the plane holding her hand, but instead of being in their early thirties they were teenagers as they had been when they were in love so long ago.

She smiled and closed her eyes. Jake Sadler. She could see his dark brown hair, his tan face, and laughing deep, blue eyes. It felt good to remember him. As she had the day before, she wondered what he was doing, what life had dealt him.

Somewhere, deep inside her, she felt a tug. A nudging. She frowned. Almost a warning. A verse drifted into her mind: *Do not let your heart grow hard to the Spirit's voice. . . .*

Ellen shut her eyes and drew a deep breath. Why on earth had she thought of that verse? She was so tired, she was making no sense at all. There was nothing about her actions or thoughts that need concern her in the least. All she was doing was remembering the past . . . wondering what had happened to an old friend. . . .

And what life would have been like if somehow they'd stayed together.

FOUR

Jane Barrett Hudson was at home when she received the news that her father had died from a massive heart attack. As was often the case, her husband, Troy, a marketing executive, was away on business. Jane had been forced to deal with an array of feelings while changing diapers, preparing snacks, and wiping runny noses.

Koley, her six-year-old, was astute enough to understand that his mother was distracted. But three-year-old Kala, and Kyle, who was barely one, remained demanding as ever, unaware of their mother's emotional state.

Because of the children Jane did not immediately have a chance to break down and grieve her father's death. This was not entirely a bad thing because among the emotions that had assaulted Jane since she'd heard the news was one that definitely was not grief.

She was frustrated that her father had not taken better care of himself, angry that he had left their mother alone, and annoyed about having to leave her small, central Arizona town to spend a week in Petoskey pretending to be grief stricken. But the emotion she struggled with most of all, the one she knew she would have to hide if she was to survive the trip to northern Michigan, was her indifference.

Certainly none of the other adult Barrett children would be indifferent in the wake of their father's death and they would not understand Jane's reasons for feeling so. Therefore, Jane knew she would have to work through her feelings by herself. She was well aware that indifference over the death of her own father was not normal.

I'll be guilty the rest of my life for feeling this way. If only Troy were home. He would know what to say to help me through this.

When Saturday night arrived, Jane sat stiffly in a worn-out recliner, rocking out an anxious rhythm as she waited for her husband's arrival. Nearly two days had passed and she still had not shed so much as a tear.

"Get home, Troy," she whispered. "Please, get home."

Gradually her rocking slowed and her mind wandered as she stared into a blur of yesterdays. Her entire life had been wonderful because of Troy.

The rocker came to a stop and suddenly Jane was no longer in the living room of her Arizona home. She was two thousand miles away in Petoskey, Michigan, working at the Pizza Parlor, meeting Troy Hudson for the first time.

The Pizza Parlor was a noisy restaurant filled with miniature carnival rides, flashing lights, and children's music. While customers ate pizza, a gigantic costumed mouse paraded through the dining area delighting children and adults alike. Every weekend the place handled dozens of children's birthday parties, each of which was conducted by a teenage party host or hostess. Parents left generous tips in return for having someone else manage their children's parties.

Jane met Troy one afternoon at the end of her first week of work. Noise was so much a part of the Pizza Parlor that by then Jane no longer heard it. The tips weren't half what she'd expected and she was in the middle of what seemed like a nightmare birthday party. The birthday boy was a six-year-old monster who screamed at his mother and pinched his party guests. He grabbed pizza off other people's plates and threw a tantrum when he didn't get his own way. He was finally opening presents, and Jane couldn't wait for the day to be over.

"Yuck!" the child shouted as he ripped open another carefully wrapped gift. "More books. I *hate* books!"

"Joey! Be nice to your friends." The child's mother was embarrassed but she clearly had no control over the boy. "Say thank you, Joey."

"No!"

And so it went until Jane thought the party would never end. She was about to rip off her badge and leave without looking back when a large, furry hand tapped her on the shoulder.

Jane whipped around and saw a six-foot mouse standing before her.

"Lucky!" She forced herself to sound excited. "Okay, everyone. Look over here. Lucky's come to wish little Joey a happy birthday."

Lucky bent into a sweeping bow and took Jane's hand in his, bringing it to his over-sized head in a mock kiss. The children giggled.

"Come on, Lucky." Jane pulled the crea-ture's synthetic paw toward Joey. "Come meet the birthday boy."

The mouse nodded enthusiastically and

allowed Jane to lead him to the child.

Joey stood up, looked Lucky up and down, and kicked the mouse on his fur-covered shin.

"You're a fake!" The boy turned to his mother. "You said Lucky was a *real* mouse. I want a real mouse, Mommy!"

"Joey! That's not nice!" His mother was mortified.

The child swung his leg and kicked Lucky harder than before. "I don't care! I hate that stupid mouse! He's a fake!"

Jane expected the mouse to walk away before he got kicked again. Instead, the creature patted Joey on the head several times — Jane noticed the pats were a bit more . . . *enthusiastic* than normal.

Joey yelped, but the noise was so great no one heard him.

Lucky pretended to see someone across the dining room and he waved excitedly. Then he headed in that direction, effectively bumping little Joey out of the way.

"Mommmm! That mouse knocked into me!"

Again no one heard the boy's cry.

"Better watch out!" Joey shouted in Lucky's direction. "Or I'll kick you again."

Jane giggled secretly as the mouse turned around and came back toward Joey. As he did, he bumped once more into the child, as he pretended to look for someone. Several seconds passed before he shrugged and headed back across the diner.

Joey ran toward his mother. "Mommmmmm! That mouse pushed me."

Jane had no idea who was playing Lucky that day but she hoped she would have a chance to thank him. She helped the children sit down and ten minutes later she had just served them cake and ice cream when she spotted Lucky making his way back toward their table.

"Look, boys and girls," Jane said, grinning. "It's Lucky come back to have some cake with us!"

Lucky tiptoed up to Joey's birthday cake. Then, raising a single finger to his mouth, he picked up the leftover cake and acted as if he was going to leave with it.

"That mouse stole my cake!" Joey whined. "Mom, stop him! That's my cake!"

"Don't whine, Joey," his mother said meekly.

Jane concealed a smile. "Yes, Joey, Lucky's only teasing you. Right, Lucky?"

Upon hearing his name, Lucky turned and nodded, balancing the leftover cake in one hand and placing the other over his belly as he shook with mock laughter. He was three feet from Joey and he put one foot in that direction. Then suddenly he tripped over something and lost his balance. Teetering back and forth, Lucky struggled to regain his grip on the cake, but he began to fall.

Momentum carried the great mouse the remaining two steps that separated him from the birthday boy. Suddenly what remained of the cake hit Joey square in the back of the head. Chocolate icing covered the child's blond hair and cream-filled cake slid in gooey chunks down his back. Joey burst into tears.

Lucky brought both paws to his mouth and looked from Jane to Joey's mother and back to Jane. She took the cue.

"Oh, dear! Lucky has had a bad fall, boys and girls. I hope he's okay!"

Lucky nodded emphatically and puffed out his chest. Then he waved politely to Joey and shook the stunned mother's hand. Raising a paw in the air he bid the party farewell and strode across the room the same way he'd come.

As Lucky left, Jane glanced at the spot where the mouse had tripped. There was nothing there.

Jane was doing her party paperwork later that afternoon when a boy with dark red hair and bright blue eyes approached her.

"Hope I didn't cost you a tip on that party today." He smiled.

Jane thought a moment and then her eyes flew open. "You were Lucky?"

"Yeah. I'm new. Troy Hudson."

"Hi, Troy," Jane grinned. "I'm Jane, and yes, you cost me the tip."

"You're not mad are you?"

"Are you kidding? It was all I could do to keep from laughing out loud. I'd have paid you myself to get back at the brat. That cake thing was great."

Troy's eyes twinkled. "Yeah, well, it was just a little leftover cake. Besides, accidents happen." He paused. "Hey, if you're not doing anything Friday night, want to go to the show? My dad's letting me borrow his car."

Jane considered him for a moment. "Sure. I guess you kind of owe me after treating my party to the psycho Lucky act."

"Yeah, well look at this." He lifted his pant leg to reveal a colorful bruise where Joey had kicked him. "Even a friendly mouse like Lucky can only take so much."

Troy was the first boy Jane ever kissed. He was seventeen, funny and impetuous, and determined to remain unattached.

"It's stupid for kids our age to get into these serious relationships," he said during one of their walks home from the Pizza Parlor. "Don't you think so?"

Not anymore, Jane thought, but all she said was, "Of course. There's plenty of time for that when we're older."

"Yeah, like thirty years older." Troy laughed and Jane felt her heart lurch. She had never met anyone like Troy. He liked her the way she was, regardless of whether she ever grew up to be like Ellen.

Summer ended a few weeks later and Troy quit his job at the Pizza Parlor so he could concentrate on senior prep classes at the private high school across town. His phone calls came less often and eventually stopped altogether.

"Someday, Jane, I'll grow up and be ready for you," he said during one of his last phone calls. "But I won't ask you to wait for me. Life goes on. I understand that."

Three years passed and circumstances caused both Jane and Troy to grow somewhat wise and worldly. At the end of that time, Troy finally called.

"Told you I'd call."

Jane grinned madly on the other end. Life had not been kind to her since she'd last seen Troy, but in an instant he infused hope into her heart. They were nineteen and twenty now and Jane believed they were plenty old enough. "Are you a grown-up now, Troy Hudson?"

"I was hoping you might want to go to dinner Friday night and see for yourself."

They picked up where they left off and this time Troy had no aversion to being serious. They dated for the next three years and were married at St. Francis Xavier Catholic Church in the spring of 1991.

Troy knew her like no one in her immediate family ever had. Except Ellen. But that had been when they were little girls. Before their father had let Jane down in a way that none of the others knew anything about. As time passed, Jane built her world around Troy. In the process, she willingly became something of a stranger to her family.

"Ellen's only interested in herself and everyone else has changed. None of us get along," she complained to Troy. "I'd rather spend time with you and our friends than sit around a table listening to one of Aaron's temper tantrums or hearing the latest great news about Ellen."

Troy watched her silently for a moment. "You're jealous of her."

Jane looked at him, incredulous. "Of Ellen?"

Troy nodded thoughtfully.

"I'm not jealous, Troy, I'm disgusted.

Everyone thinks she's got her life so together but what they don't see is how selfish she is. All she thinks about is herself."

For the next two years Jane talked constantly about moving away from Michigan, out west.

"Just think, Troy, we could be done with winters and ice storms and snow-covered driveways."

Jane's enthusiasm was contagious and Troy, who was a high-level sales representative, began sending out résumés. Eventually he received a considerable offer to work as a senior sales representative for a stereo distributor based in Cottonwood, Arizona.

The other Barretts cried and hugged them both as they packed up their things and headed west. But Jane remained untouched by the event.

"I'm going to miss your dad's barbecues," Troy said idly as they drove across country.

"Hmm." Jane was staring out her window.

"They sure seemed sad to see you go."

"That's how people are supposed to act when someone moves away."

Troy took his eyes off the road and for an instant turned to face her. "That's not a very nice thing to say, Jane. Your family wasn't putting on an act when we left.

They're really sad. They love you a lot."

She huffed slightly and her eyes met his. "I've known my place in my family for years now, Troy. I appreciate what you're saying, but believe me, they aren't going to miss me when I'm gone. We're doing the best thing by moving away."

His forehead creased, and she saw the concern reflected in his blue eyes. "As long as you're not running away from something."

"I'm not," she lied.

Over the years, Jane and Troy built a home for themselves in central Arizona. They camped among the pine trees on Mingus Mountain and climbed rocks overlooking the Verde Valley. They hiked Sedona's North Fork Trail and picked wild blackberries along the Verde River. They swam in Oak Creek and marveled over the breathtaking red rocks that brought tourists from all over the world.

Over the next few years they raised a family, and when the children were old enough Troy taught them how to avoid rattlesnakes. They found a local Christian church and Jane headed up the women's group. On summer nights, when Troy wasn't traveling, the two of them would sit on their back porch and watch dazzling sunsets as their children played in the yard.

Occasionally Jane and Ellen would call each other and spend half an hour on the telephone making small talk. Jane remembered once, after such a conversation, Troy had walked into the room and found her crying, her face buried in her hands.

"Honey, what is it?" He was at her side, sliding his arm around her shoulders, holding her close.

Jane drew a ragged breath and shook her head. "It's Ellen. She called."

"Did you two get into it again?"

"No." Jane was still crying, but she fought to regain her composure. "It's just that she and my dad are so close and . . . I don't know, maybe I am jealous of that."

She fell silent, but she saw Troy studying her closely, watching her face.

"You sure nothing else is bothering you, honey?"

"No, really. I'm fine." Jane forced a smile and patted Troy's hand. He seemed satisfied that she was telling him the truth and he got up and went back into their home office.

Jane remembered watching him go and feeling a stab of guilt. The rest of that evening she had wondered if she would ever have the strength to tell him the truth about that terrible, painful dark night. The night her life changed forever.

FIVE

The plane rumbled monotonously and Ellen drew a deep breath, fighting to clear her
head. Nine years had passed since she had
seen Jake Sadler. There was no reason why
he should be making appearances in her
current thoughts as if they'd only broken
up yesterday.

The flight attendant arrived and handed
her a tray of food which she ate absentmind-
edly. When she finished she looked out the
window.

Jake had been there for the good years,
the times when her father was strong and
healthy, and she and her sisters and brother
got along with each other. Maybe that's why
he was on her mind now. Jake would understand what the years had stolen from her.
He'd understand more than Mike ever
could.

She leaned her head back wearily. Even
Jake didn't know about the early days, when

the Barrett family was just beginning. Back then her father had worked for IBM, which everyone in the family always took to mean "I've Been Moved." They lived in seven different cities in seven years and never had time to build relationships with anyone except the people who shared their breakfast table.

I wonder if Aaron and Jane and the others remember how good those times were? Ellen squeezed her eyes tightly closed, freeing two errant teardrops. She knew what she needed to do . . . what she needed to allow.

She needed to remember.

The tears flowed freely now, and she was thankful for the dark glasses. Allowing the memories meant going to a place where her father still lived and laughed, where he still shared his contagious enthusiasm for life. She was afraid that once she found that place, she would never want to leave.

Normally, Ellen did not believe anything good could come from wallowing in days gone by the way some people did, spending a decade recounting it and paying a stranger to analyze it. Still, just this once, as she hung thirty thousand feet in the air, suspended between her present and past, she would go back. She would allow herself to find that faraway place where families are born and love begins. Perhaps if she spent some time remembering her past she would find answers for today and tomorrow. She closed her eyes and savored the moment, slipping slowly into a cavern of scenes from a hundred yesterdays, drifting back to a handful of cities across the country.

Fairfax, Detroit, Jamestown, Kansas City, Dallas, Livonia, and finally Ann Arbor. Ellen had been born in Fairfax; Jane and Megan, in Detroit. The three girls were barely school age when the Barrett family moved to Jamestown, a small country town in upper New York where there had been a hundred things for a child to do. Ellen kept her eyes closed until finally she could hear their voices. . . .

"Ellen, look what I found!" A towheaded Jane, barely four years old, came bounding up the hillside, her small hands cupping the body of a bumpy, brown toad.

"Let's find him a box." Ellen motioned for Jane to follow and the two girls ran as fast as they could back to the house. Gasping for breath, Ellen ran inside and came back with a dilapidated cardboard container.

"Should we put grass in it to keep him happy?" Jane's innocent blue eyes gazed admirably at her older sister.

"Okay." Ellen helped Jane lower the toad into the box and grabbed fistfuls of grass. "I know he's your toad, Jane. But let's say we're both his parents."

"All right. That way he'll have two people who love him."

"Hey, what do you girls have there?" The voice was her father's. Clear, strong, vibrantly alive. He walked toward them, his whole face smiling.

"A toad!" they shouted in unison.

Their father, a systems analyst and one of the most brilliant men to enter the booming new frontier of computers, stooped down and patted the homely creature.

"A fine toad, I might add." He glanced around. "What if we find another one? So that this one will have a friend."

Jane wrinkled her small nose. "No, Daddy. I think one's enough."

He sat back on the grass and looked at Jane thoughtfully. "Well, now, you and Ellen are sisters, but you're friends, too, right?"

Jane smiled at her big sister. "Right."

"Think how you'd feel if someone put you in a box and took you away from Ellen."

Jane's face fell and she reached for Ellen's hand. "I would be sad, Daddy."

"That's how your toad feels." He stood up and swung Ellen onto his shoulders, taking Jane's hand in his. "Come on, now. Let's go find ourselves another toad so that the little fellow won't be so lonely."

The voices grew dim and Ellen opened her eyes slowly, staring vacantly into the sky, wishing she could remember whether they had ever found another toad. Instead, a different scene began taking shape.

Kansas City, late-afternoon. Their mother was seven months pregnant with Amy and had taken Ellen, Jane, and Megan outside their rented townhouse to wait for their father's return from work. Dark clouds filled the sky and there was lightening in the distance. It was tornado season, and the weather bureau had warned that conditions were right for a twister.

Blissfully unaware of the weather, the girls giggled and sang silly songs, watching intently until finally they saw the green Ford sedan round the corner.

"Daddy!" Their delighted squeals rang out, and they jumped up and down as their father parked the car and climbed out. Dressed in a suit and tie, he bounded toward them, a blond, six-foot-two, former football player with bulky shoulders and arms of steel. He swept each of the three girls into his arms, one at a time, tossing them into the air and making them laugh so hard they could barely breathe.

"I have an idea!" He grinned at his wife and leaned down to kiss her.

She smiled. "That's what I love about you, John."

"What's that?" He traced a finger along her cheek and stooped to tousle Jane's hair.

"Never a dull moment. I'm married to the chief memory maker in all of Missouri."

"Tell us, Daddy. Please! Tell us." The girls jumped up and down, tugging on their father's coat sleeves and waiting to hear his plan for the afternoon.

"Let's take a drive." He pointed toward the menacing storm clouds. "Maybe we can get a better view of the storm."

Ellen's face grew troubled. "Daddy, is it safe?"

She was always the worried one, doubting whether the car was working properly and making sure the doors were locked. She was especially nervous about storms, even as a six-year-old. Her father looked sympathetically at her and tousled her hair.

"Of course it's safe. I wouldn't do anything that might hurt my girls."

"It hurts to move away from our friends, Daddy," Ellen said then.

Her father frowned and lowered himself to his oldest daughter's level. "I know that,

106

honey. It hurts me, too. But right now we don't have any choice."

"Will we move again?"

"Probably. But wherever we go we'll be together and we'll always have each other."

Her father's words rang in Ellen's mind, and she glanced out the window once more. What he'd said was true. Ellen and her sisters and mother had grown to depend on each other because they were never sure of anything except the family to which they belonged.

Another memory began taking shape, and Ellen could see herself holding a bulky, oversized chalkboard. There was something scribbled on it, and she was shouting at cars that drove by.

"Park here! One dollar. Park here!"

The image was clear now. The town was Ann Arbor, where the Barretts had lived just eight houses away from the University of Michigan football stadium. Each Saturday when there was a home game, fans would cruise up and down the neighboring streets looking for a place to park.

Nearly everyone on Keech Street parked cars in their driveways and even on their front lawns. Ellen was eight and all week she looked forward to the frenzied excitement of football Saturdays. She would wave the chalkboard to gain the attention of passing motorists. Park here, $1, the sign read. Anxious fans would pull into the yard, and her father would collect the money.

At halftime the family would walk toward the bright, yellow gates of the stadium, and her father would wink at the ticket taker.

"Residents get in free at halftime, right?"

The attendant would smile, size up the trail of children that tagged behind the man, and wave the group inside. They would sit as close as they could to the Michigan Wolverine marching band.

By then Amy was nearly two years old and the family finally included a boy, Aaron Randall Barrett. Even when the weather grew cold and snow covered the ground, their father would carry his infant son to the games, snuggling him tightly beneath his heavy brown wool coat. Their mother usually stayed home to work on dinner and get the house ready for weekend company.

"You're the littlest Wolverine of all," their father would say to the infant Aaron once they were settled into stadium seats. Ellen remembered watching with her sisters as their father tickled and cooed at their only brother. "One day you'll be a big Wolverine, Aaron, and Daddy will come watch you play football every Saturday."

"I'm going to be a Wolverine, too, Daddy," Ellen would say and her father would pull her close.

"That's my girl, Ellen. You can be whatever you want."

When Michigan scored a touchdown, as the team often did, the band would erupt into the familiar fight song and everyone in the Barrett family old enough to talk would sing along.

"Hail to the victors valiant, hail to the conquering heroes, hail, hail, to Michigan . . ." Even little Amy knew to raise her right fist whenever the word *hail* was sung.

Ellen sighed as the memories blended in her mind. Dozens of Michigan games. Every Saturday of the football season for two years.

The plane moved along effortlessly as Ellen tried to capture a glimpse of her father and savor it. She could see him sitting in Michigan Stadium, eyes wide with excitement, cheeks red from the chilly air, cheering the Wolverines to victory. How he loved Michigan football.

Twelve years later, when Ellen was accepted into the university's journalism program, no one was more thrilled than her father. Aaron had not pursued football beyond his sophomore year in high school.

But Ellen knew she had been her Dad's kindred spirit, a child who shared the desires of his heart.

The plane rumbled as it passed through turbulent air, and suddenly Ellen remembered the football season just ten months before her father's death. Michigan had played Notre Dame in a spectacular contest. She'd known he would be watching the game and had called him from Miami during the third quarter to see if he'd caught one particularly good play.

But he was asleep. *Daddy, what's happening to you?* Ellen had wondered at the time.

"Your father's been so tired lately, Ellen," her mom explained when she got on the line. "His health really isn't that good. I'm sure he'll call you later."

Ellen shook off the image of her father sleeping through a Michigan football game. She refused to remember him that way and she drifted back once more to her childhood.

She and her siblings had thrived in Ann Arbor. Her dad had accepted a position with Parsons Engineering, and, thankfully, relocating was not part of the job description. Their family finally had a reason to develop roots and they did so in a matter of months.

With so many children under one roof, almost anything they did became an event to remember. In the winter they ice-skated at Almondinger Park and built snowmen families in the front yard. When summer came they picked blueberries at Hanson's Farm and swam at Half Moon Lake. Best of all was autumn and football Saturdays.

Their mother would easily go along with almost anything their dad wanted to do. But inevitably he was the parent who made things happen. He planned picnics at the local lakes, pajama parties at the drive-in theater, and birthday bashes for each of his children every year.

The family was fiercely Catholic, and their father believed his faith had to be alive to be worth anything. Once, when Ellen was in high school, he had stood for seven hours in the pouring rain before election day passing out Right to Life material.

"If we don't stand up for the rights of unborn children, who will?" he said to Ellen when she studied the pamphlets.

His convictions made him a doer among his peers. Ellen and her siblings had attended St. Thomas Catholic School on Elizabeth Street, and when the school board needed a chairman to raise money for extracurricular activities, John Barrett started a bingo program and ran it single-handedly.

The first Christmas Ellen's family was in Ann Arbor, a young couple from the church came caroling to the Barrett house as part of their holiday tradition. When they left, their dad's eyes lit up and he reached for their mother.

"Let's make that our family tradition, too." For the next twenty years the Barrett women designated a full day during Christmas week to bake holiday cookies, and then the entire family would go caroling.

Their father's favorite story of the holiday season was Charles Dickens's *A Christmas Carol,* and that first Christmas in Ann Arbor he found a brown suede English top hat with a high crown like those worn during the Dickens era. He wore it caroling every Christmas after that.

For two years they loved Ann Arbor as if they'd lived there all their lives. Their mother's sister, Mary, and her family lived three hours away in Battle Creek. Many weekends the Barretts would pile into the station wagon and set out for a raucous get-together between the two families.

It was during the Ann Arbor years that Ellen remembered her dad's football physique becoming soft, giving way to a lack of exercise and overindulgence. He had a voracious appetite for everything in life and food was no exception.

"You're the best cook in all of Michigan," he would tell his wife, kissing her on the cheek as she cooked up yet another gooey dessert or hot batch of cookies. "Keep 'em coming."

When the Barretts thought up fun things to do on the weekends, whether a Sunday drive or a trip to the lake, they always stopped for a treat.

"How 'bout a milk shake?" their dad would suggest, pulling the station wagon over in front of the local ice-cream parlor. If they were at the movies it was popcorn and licorice and frozen bonbons. At the lake it was cookies and rootbeer floats. The children were too active to be affected by the heavy foods, but their father spent much of his day sitting in front of a computer, and it wasn't long before his expanding midsection began to jeopardize his health.

Food wasn't his only vice. By then he had been chain-smoking cigarettes since he was fourteen years old. In the 1970s reports were released stating the dangers of smoking. Ellen's dad was one of the doubters, brushing off the reports as political posturing and premature hysteria. He kept his cigarettes in his shirt pocket, close to his heart, and smoked almost constantly. Smoking was a part of his image, his character. He had no desire to give it up.

Then in late February 1977, the Barrett world changed completely. One night Ellen overheard her parents talking to their Aunt Betsy in California.

"No, we haven't told the children yet," her father said quietly.

"It's not going to be easy for them." It was her mother's voice, and Ellen crept out of bed and sat at the top of the staircase where she wouldn't be seen.

"Yes, it's final." Her father's again. "We'll move to Petoskey before the spring semester. Yes. That's when the job wraps up here. Right. I'll be teaching a full load of computer courses at the community college. I know. It's a dream come true."

Tears sprang to Ellen's eyes. They couldn't possibly leave Ann Arbor. She and Katy Bonavan were best friends and they'd promised to stay that way forever. She gulped back tears as she stood up and tiptoed back into her bedroom. Jane was still sleeping.

"Jane," she whispered. "Wake up."

Jane was eight that year and she opened her eyes, looking disoriented and afraid.

"What?"

"Jane, we're moving."

"We are?"

Ellen nodded quickly. "Yes. To somewhere called Petoskey."

Jane's eyes grew wide with concern. "You mean we're moving to another country?"

"Yes. I think so."

"When are we going?"

"In a few months."

Jane raised up onto her knees, still half-asleep, and hugged her older sister tightly. "It's okay, Ellen. We'll still have each other. I'll be your best friend wherever we go."

Ellen smiled through her tears. "I know. Love you, Jane."

"Love you, too." Jane collapsed back into bed. "Good night."

A month later they watched their belongings disappear on a moving van headed for Petoskey. Then they climbed into a station wagon loaded with pillows and suitcases and drove away. The neighbors lined up along the street to say good-bye, many with tears in their eyes.

"Come back and visit!"

"Don't forget to write!"

Ellen was ten and old enough to know that people would forget and visits would be rare, if ever. She began crying as they passed

Almondinger Park and she didn't stop for three hours. Petoskey, with its shoreline community and Victorian houses, was not in another country, but it might as well have been.

Ellen's father was quietly understanding. He had promised his children they would not move again, but this time there had been no choice. The Parsons plant in Ann Arbor had closed down and he had accepted a teaching position at North Central Community College in Petoskey. By June that year they had settled in a neighborhood just west of the college. They bought a four-bedroom, corner house with towering maple trees, a wraparound porch, and a fenced backyard.

While her siblings adjusted quite naturally to the move, Ellen began eating to appease her loneliness. By the time she was in junior high she was a hefty twenty pounds over-weight.

She began spending more time writing. She kept a journal and wrote poems, which she shared with her parents.

"Hmm," her mother would say thoughtfully. "I guess I don't really understand it."

Ellen would take the poem to her father. He would shut out the rest of the world and read it thoughtfully, sometimes with tears in his eyes.

"Sweetheart, it's wonderful," he would tell her. "Someday you're going to be a famous writer."

"Oh, Daddy!" Ellen would blush. "Do you really like it?"

"It's fantastic. Can I keep this copy for myself?"

The first four years in Petoskey were innocent and carefree, despite her struggle with weight. In summer their dad would get off work, squeeze into his swimsuit, and take the family for a late-afternoon swim at Petoskey State Beach. The sand stretched for what seemed like miles, and Ellen and her brother and sisters would play volleyball in the shallow pools near the shore. Despite his own worsening problem with weight, Dad could still palm a volleyball and rise halfway out of the water for a serve. Mom would laugh and wave from a nearby blanket, thoroughly content to watch the others play.

The summer after she turned fourteen, Ellen began noticing boys. She became keenly aware of the way they paid attention to other, thinner girls. One afternoon she went home, rummaged through her parents' bookcase, and found a dusty old paperback called *Dr. Stillman's Quick Weight Loss Diet.*

The front cover promised a fifteen-pound weight loss in one week. Determined to keep her plans private, Ellen whisked the book into her bedroom and studied the doctor's diet plan.

The next morning Ellen ate three eggs for breakfast, cottage cheese for lunch, and only the meat from her dinner plate. No fruit, vegetables, bread, or sweets passed her lips, and in three months she went from size twelve jeans to an eight. The diet was neither balanced nor healthy, and twice she nearly fainted because of low blood sugar. But it worked, and that summer she slimmed down even further when she sprouted three inches, seemingly overnight. By the time she started high school that fall she had been approached more than once by a representative from a local modeling agency.

"Daddy, please, can I get new clothes for school?" she asked her father one night.

He smiled at her. "Of course, honey. I'm so proud of you for losing weight. Pick out whatever you want. By the way, maybe you can share your secret with me sometime." He patted his stomach, which had continued to grow.

"Ah, Dad. That's just you. Don't worry about it."

He didn't.

Ellen had fairly danced through her first year at Petoskey High School, thriving on the attention she received from her class-mates. That year in physical education class Ellen met a girl named Leslie Maple, and the two were instant friends. They both rode skateboards and wanted to try out for Petos-key's cheerleading squad. They had shoulder-length dark hair and light green eyes, and they were both tall and slender. They even lived in the same neighborhood, just around the corner from each other. From the beginning, people mistook Ellen and Leslie for twins, and the girls delighted in letting people believe it was true.

It was a perfect year except for one thing. She and Jane had grown apart. Her father pulled her aside one day to share his obser-vations about the situation. "Honey, I think Jane's feeling left out. Why don't you spend some time with her."

Ellen realized her father was right. She had been so busy making friends and cel-ebrating her new popularity that she hadn't made time for Jane. She felt bad about Jane's hurt feelings and even tried to talk to her once. But Jane would be at Petoskey High in a couple years and then they would have more time together. Sure enough, when Jane entered high school, she spent most of her time with Ellen and Leslie and the problem seemed to dissolve.

Besides, Ellen was too caught up in her own life to worry about Jane. There were football games and cheerleading practices and Friday-night parties to attend. The next year, Ellen discovered the greatest distraction of all, one that would change her life forever. Jake Sadler.

Until that time Ellen's father had been the only man in her life. But Jake was like an unquenchable thirst — he consumed her from the moment they met, leaving little room for father-daughter talks.

At the thought of Jake, Ellen drew a deep breath and stretched her legs. She checked her watch. The plane had been in the air for two hours, which meant they still had an hour to go. With a sigh, her thoughts returned to Jake.

They had dated six years before breaking off their relationship, and even then it was another two years before they learned to live without each other. They dated throughout Ellen's three years at North Central. The same time period when her father lost his job and did something no one ever thought he would do — wrote a note to his family, pulled together a few belongings,

120

and left.

The memory brought Ellen instantly back to reality. She sat up straighter, took a magazine from the back of the chair in front of her, and flipped through the pages.

Some things were better left in the past.

Six

It was nearly midnight when Jane heard the front door open. She was sitting in the recliner, rocking slowly, hypnotically, staring at a blank television screen.

"Sorry I'm late." Jane watched Troy drop his things near the front door. He came to sit on the arm of the chair and put a hand on her shoulder. "I wanted to be here. I can't imagine how you must feel."

Jane looked up at him without expression. "I'm not devastated, if that's what you mean." Her eyes were dry. "I haven't been close to my dad in years. You know that."

Troy raised an eyebrow. "Okay. But he was your dad, after all, and now he's gone. That has to hurt, Jane."

"It's *supposed* to hurt. That doesn't mean it does."

"Jane, don't be strong at a time like this. It's okay to cry."

"Why should I cry, Troy? My dad didn't

122

love me. Why should I act like I'm suffering now that he's gone?"

Troy stood up and collapsed in a heap on the couch a few feet away. "Here we go," he muttered. "What do you mean he didn't love you? Of course he did. I saw how he treated you."

"Did you see how he treated Ellen? I'm not blind. He didn't love any of us the way he loved Ellen."

Troy shook his head and stared at his brown loafers. "Jane, you're wrong. You're forgetting the good times. Your dad loved each of you five kids the same."

Jane resumed her rocking and turned to stare at nothing in particular. Troy did not understand because he did not know everything about her past. He knew neither the facts nor the way they had affected her life. She took a deep breath and stopped rocking.

Perhaps it was time.

"Troy, there's something I want to tell you, something I never wanted you to know. But it's been inside me for so many years that if I don't let it out, especially now with my dad gone, it's going to kill me."

Troy leaned slightly forward. "All right. I'm listening."

"Promise me it won't change anything."

"I love you, Jane. Nothing could change that."

"All right, then. It goes back a long way. I'll try to take it from the beginning."

Jane drew in another deep breath and closed her eyes. "As far back as I can remember I was part of a pair, of Ellen and Jane. We shared a room, played together, fought together, and got in trouble together. At Christmas we received duplicate presents. We wore identical clothing. We were inseparable."

Jane smiled at the memory. Of course, there had inevitably been a leader among the two: Ellen. She decided what games they would play, what songs they would sing, and which programs they would watch on television. Because Jane was always seeking Ellen's approval, she was compliant and went along as she was expected to do. She never considered crossing Ellen or suggesting something that Ellen might not agree with.

Over the years that relationship had produced two very different personalities. Ellen was outgoing, gregarious, and a natural leader. Jane had always been considered the quiet one, shy and unsure of herself in public situations.

Jane shook her head. "Even when Ellen

went through a period of being overweight," she said quietly, "she seemed to have more friends and more self-confidence than I did. So I suppose it only made sense that Ellen gained Dad's attention, his praise and admiration. Whatever I could do, Ellen could do better." She gave a hoarse laugh. "Once, when I was seven, I realized how much approval Ellen received for writing poetry. So I tried to compose a poem of my own. I brought it to Daddy, timidly making my way to where he sat watching a football game in his easy chair."

" 'Daddy, look,' I said, handing over the scribbled prose. 'I wrote this for you.' "

"What did he say?" Troy asked softly, and Jane looked away.

"He read the piece and smiled at me and said it was wonderful." Emotion burned deep inside her at the memory. "I was so thrilled. I really thought he was talking about my poem." Her voice broke, and she had to wait a moment before she could go on. "But before I could thank him he told me it was wonderful I wanted to be a writer like my big sister. 'Have you shown this to Ellen? She could probably help you put it together, honey. Make it into a *real* poem.' I was crushed, but Dad had already gone back to watching television and he didn't even notice. I just walked to the kitchen, opened the cupboard, and pulled out the trash basket. Then I ripped the poem into a hundred pieces." She sighed and studied Troy.

"Go ahead," he said softly. "I'm listening."

She drew a deep breath and continued talking.

There were other times she'd been hurt. While going through puberty she gained eighteen pounds. She'd been chubby, but not nearly as overweight as Ellen had been. When Jane reached her highest weight, Ellen had already lost hers. One Saturday afternoon the summer before Jane started at Petoskey High, she and her mother purchased school clothes and then staged a fashion show for her father. When it was finished, he pulled Jane close beside him and smiled at her.

"You look beautiful, honey. The clothes are really nice."

Jane smiled, allowing the praise to warm her body. Her father was pleased and all was right with the world.

"And don't worry about your weight. Ellen lost hers at about this age. I'm sure you'll slim down, too, and then you'll be just as popular as your big sister."

Jane had felt her face flush with embarrassment. She'd been very sensitive about her excess weight and her cheeks had burned in shame. Again, her father didn't notice.

"You're lucky to have Ellen. When you get to Petoskey she'll help you make a bunch of new friends. You're a lucky girl, Jane."

Jane nodded and stared at her shoes. She suddenly felt uncomfortable in the new clothes and she wanted to get far away from her father and his hurtful comments.

"Hey," he continued, "don't worry about how you look now. When you lose weight, I'm sure you and Ellen can go shopping and get some real nice skinny high school clothes."

Jane nodded again and turned away so her father wouldn't see her tears. Then she ran into the bedroom she shared with Ellen and ripped off the new clothes, stuffing them into her closet. For the next two days she ate nothing. She wanted desperately to be rid of her plump figure before the week was through.

Instead, on the third day she found a freshly baked batch of cookies in the kitchen, grabbed two handfuls, and ate them in her room. She would eat whatever she wanted even if she never looked like Ellen.

High school was more of the same. She'd been cast immediately into the role of Ellen Barrett's little sister. "At first I didn't have or desire a separate identity." She frowned. "But Ellen ignored me when we were at school. She seemed almost embarrassed of me."

"How so?" Troy asked, and she told him of one incident in particular.

Jane had worn a light blue, oversized nylon windbreaker to school nearly every day that year. The jacket gave her a way to hide her less-than-perfect body, especially in light of Ellen's slim figure. The last thing she needed was people comparing her and Ellen at Petoskey High the way they did at home. But one day Ellen pulled Jane aside and fingered the jacket in disgust.

"Jane, you've got to get a new jacket. You wear this thing every day. Everyone's talking about it."

Jane struggled for an answer, her cheeks red hot with shame. "I like it," she said finally.

"Well, I think it makes you look fat. If you want people to like you, you need to wear something else."

A few days later, Jane overheard Ellen

talking to their mother.

"Mom, pleeease!" Jane peeked into the room and saw that Ellen's arms were crossed and one hip jutted out in frustration. "You have to make her wear something else. It's embarrassing."

"Ellen, you should be talking to her about this. It's between you and her."

Jane was furious as she listened, but she was afraid to say anything. She needed Ellen if she wanted to survive at Petoskey. Her eyes stung as she ran out of the house and slammed the door. The noise brought Ellen and Mom into the foyer and Jane heard them calling her. But it was too late. She walked through the quiet, tree-lined streets of Petoskey for an hour. Then she came home and shut herself in her room.

Jane fell silent for a while, then shrugged. "Things were never the same again between me and Ellen."

"I'm sorry."

Troy's quiet sincerity touched her deeply, and Jane bit her lip, then went on. "Mom must have said something to Ellen because she didn't say another word about the jacket. I still hung around with Ellen, but by that time I was making friends of my own. Friends who were outside the circle of popular kids Ellen associated with. By the end of my sophomore year, I'd made friends with a group of quiet, studious types who didn't care about the clothes I wore. I could tell them secrets about Ellen, things I would never have shared with my family."

Jane's comments came back to her as though she'd said them just yesterday. "I told them Ellen was a snob. I told them she was stuck-up and self-centered; and that all she ever thought about was herself. I said I could barely stand living with her."

She swallowed painfully, then looked at Troy and smiled weakly. "It was about that time I met you. I knew I'd never love another boy like I loved you. But then you were gone and I had no idea whether I'd ever see you again. By the beginning of my junior year I had grown taller than Ellen and lost twenty pounds so that I was actually quite thin. I was pretty enough —"

"You were beautiful," Troy broke in. "You still are."

She smiled at him. Her father had said the same thing, but she hadn't believed him, either. Unlike Ellen, Jane had lacked confidence and charisma and therefore still could not compete with her.

Her lips pressed together. Of course, on the heels of telling her she was beautiful, her father had gone on to add something about Ellen giving her makeup tips.

Finally, in her senior year, Jane was free of Ellen's shadow. That was when Jane began doing things she had never done before. She went on dates with older boys and came home well after the family's midnight curfew. She bought a bicycle and rode through the dark streets of Petoskey to Magnus Park on Friday nights. There she would meet her new friends and drink beer. Eventually her parents forbade her from going out. Jane still found a way to do what she wanted, only now she no longer asked her parents' permission.

She stopped studying and her grades plummeted. The conservative outfits she had worn in her first three years of high school were replaced with tight, black outfits borrowed from her new friends. She wore heavy mascara and carried an air of defiance that caused her parents great concern.

At one of the parties Jane attended that year she had met a long-haired man in his midtwenties named Clay. He was the leader of a local rock band, Jungle Fever, and Jane began dating him secretly.

By that time Ellen was involved with Jake Sadler. Popular, handsome, basketball-hero Jake. Everyone liked Jake. But Clay was hard and mean looking, with a viper tattoo that wrapped around his left forearm. He was a rebel, and Jane knew better than to bring him home. Her mother might have made an attempt to be nice to him, but the comparisons between Clay and Jake would have been too tempting for her father to resist.

"I didn't know any of this." There was a kind of shocked sadness in Troy's eyes. "I'm surprised your parents put up with it all."

Jane shrugged. "They didn't. Not for long."

She could still hear the tone of her father's voice when he'd finally confronted her. She had broken the rules and ridden her bike to a party. When she came home, it was two in the morning.

Her father was waiting. He'd stared at her with an expression she'd never seen before.

"Jane, you're being disobedient and rebellious and we cannot tolerate it any longer."

Ellen was gone that night, sleeping over at a girlfriend's house, but that hadn't kept Dad from making a comparison.

"When Ellen was your age, she would never —"

"Stop!" The shout came out before Jane could think, and Dad raised an eyebrow. Well, she'd started it so she might as well finish. She met his surprised gaze. "I don't want to hear about Ellen. All I've heard since I was a little girl is how Ellen does *this* better and Ellen does *that* better. Well, Ellen's no saint, Dad. She's probably spending the night with Jake Sadler instead of staying at Leslie's house. She lies to you all the time, but you don't see it because you think she's so perfect. She's not! She never has been!"

Her father had been stunned. It was completely out of character for her to accuse Ellen of such a thing.

He shook his head. "I don't think Ellen's a saint. I think my children are wonderful people, fully capable of making wrong choices. We've certainly seen that these past few months. Besides, this isn't about Ellen. It's about you. I want you to stop coming home whenever you please and start respecting our curfew. Do you understand?"

"I understand." Sarcasm dripped from her words. "But Daddy, don't tell me that each of us is wonderful. You love Ellen more than you love me. You always have."

Dad's face grew angry at the accusation. "Listen, Jane. I do not love any of my children more than the others. I am proud of Ellen, yes. She was an honor student, a cheerleader, an editor on the school paper. I'm her father and I have a right to be proud of her, don't you think?"

Jane rolled her eyes.

"I'm just as proud of you, young lady. But I won't tolerate excuses for bad behavior. You will obey my rules or you will be punished, do you understand me?"

Jane's eyes grew damp and she ignored his question. She ran to her room and slammed the door.

The next day, before Ellen returned home from her friend's house, Jane packed some belongings into a knapsack, flung them over her shoulder, and set off on her bicycle. She rode four miles to the house where Clay and the other band members lived. They were having a speed party and Jane was invited. The idea was completely new to Jane. She and Ellen sometimes drank at parties, but they had never dabbled in drugs. For that reason alone, Jane decided to attend the party. She would be different from Ellen if it killed her.

But that night she had more in mind than the drugs. Jane had experimented sexually with Clay but had not yet lost her virginity. Now she'd made up her mind. She would stay at Clay's house for a week and spend much of it in bed with him. So what if it went against everything her parents had taught her, everything she had learned at church over the years? So what if Clay didn't love her? Neither did her father.

But that night after taking one hit from a cigarette dipped in liquid speed, Jane grew violently ill and threw up on the living room rug. Looking disgusted with the mess and frustrated by her inexperience, Clay relegated her to a back bedroom.

"Lotta fun you are. Stay there until you can party like the rest of us." He slammed the door.

Her heart raced and she could barely catch her breath. She struggled for an hour to stop vomiting. When she felt better she climbed out the bedroom window, crept around the house to where her bicycle was parked, and sped off. She spent that night and most of the next day at her friend Rochelle's house, sorting through her feelings. Rochelle had seen the changes in Jane and was thankful she had come to her senses before making a grave mistake.

"Clay is worthless, Jane. Let him go."

Jane nodded and suddenly Troy's words had come back to her: *Someday, Jane, I'll grow up and be ready for what we have between us.*

"Thinking of Troy?" Rochelle had asked.

"Yep."

The two girls stayed up into the early

hours of the morning talking. Jane promised Rochelle she was through with Clay and the fast crowd, but she could not bear any more comparisons to Ellen. She was determined to explain this to her father.

When she phoned her parents they were frantic. They had contacted the police and searched for her throughout the night.

"Jane, where have you been? We've been so worried."

"Never mind, Dad. I have something to say."

There was an uncomfortable silence and Jane knew her father was probably at a loss for how to deal with her. Ellen had never challenged him this way, she was sure. But she was equally sure the time had come to make her feelings clear.

"What?" His voice was gruff with disapproval.

"Dad, don't ever compare me with Ellen again. Please."

"Jane, I never meant —"

"Dad, please. Don't talk about it now. I've thought things through and I'm ready to start living the way you want me to live. I'm sorry about the past. Just don't ever compare me to her again."

Dad was silent and Jane wondered if maybe he was crying. "I won't compare you," he said finally. "But I will insist that you come home now and start acting like the responsible young lady we've raised you to be."

Jane was satisfied with that. The trip away from home was worth every minute if it had finally made him aware of her feelings.

After that Jane still felt she didn't quite measure up in her father's eyes. But at least her shortcomings were no longer verbalized.

Jane paused a moment, catching her breath and collecting her thoughts. "Is there more?" Troy asked, taking her hand.

A sadness fell over Jane then, and for the first time there were tears in her eyes. She tightened her grip on his hand.

"You okay?" He moved closer, and she fell into his arms.

"Hold me," was all she could manage between sobs. "There's more."

The worst was yet to come.

SEVEN

Jane sat back against the cushions.

"Are you okay?" Troy asked. "You don't have to do this, hon."

She nodded. "Yes, I do." Reaching out, she took his hand, then closed her eyes, letting her mind drift back. Back to the events that took place after her graduation from high school. She held Troy's fingers tightly, grateful for his love. For his support. She needed both desperately if she was going to finally tell him the truth.

"It was the summer of 1986." She paused. "The summer Daddy lost his job."

Jane remembered the details of that ordeal like it was yesterday. Her father had left the security of his long-time position as professor at North Central Community College for a lucrative offer with a promising new company in Traverse City. It was a forty-five minute drive one way, but the company offered him nearly twice his previous salary and a benefit package that included a pension plan and complete medical coverage. It was an offer too good to pass up, and her father took it willingly.

"Up until that time, things had been modest. Oh, we never had to do without. But my parents did what everyone did those days: they used credit cards and second mortgages to buy material goods. They bought our Petoskey home for only $39,000, and by 1980 it was worth three times that. Each time the value of the house grew by $20,000 or so, Mom and Dad borrowed against it and paid off the cards." She shook her head. "Dad's new position could have offered him a chance to finally pay off their debts and reduce their mortgage payments."

"Could have?"

"Yeah, but Daddy didn't have the job five weeks before he and Mom bought a new van, new clothes for all five of us kids, and a time-share vacation condominium in Lake Geneva. There were dinners on the town, steak barbecues, and personal computer components." She grinned. "It was like Christmas every day.

"One night we were all gathered at the table for dinner and Daddy got this funny-looking grin on his face. He pulled a box

139

from his suit coat and gave Mom the most beautiful string of diamonds you ever saw. No one could believe it."

Troy looked surprised. "I'll bet."

"He told Mom he'd never been able to shower her with gifts. If money weren't a problem, he said, he'd give her gifts like that every day."

"It must have felt good for him to do something like that."

"It didn't feel so good when the debts piled up. I heard Mom ask Dad once if we could afford everything, and he just assured her that his new job would take care of all our financial worries."

"Sounds like an exciting time," Troy remarked, and Jane gave him a grim smile.

"You have no idea. Four weeks later, on a Monday at the end of June, Dad's supervisor approached him with bad news. They had lost one of their most lucrative contracts, an oil deal with Saudi Arabia. The company was downsizing. They had to let Dad go. And there was no severance pay."

Her father had been stunned. He spent the rest of the week waking at his usual time, dressing and pretending to go to work while he looked desperately for a new job.

He approached his previous employer and spoke with the president of the college.

140

"They said they'd love to have him back, but they were filled for the semester. They couldn't get him on staff until January." She paused, closing her eyes. "It was June. When nothing else seemed immediately available Dad began to panic. On Thursday night he wrote a letter to us." She opened her eyes and met Troy's stunned gaze. "I know it by heart. . . . 'Dear Diane, Ellen, Jane, Megan, Amy, and Aaron. I have failed all of you miserably. My company lost a contract and let me go last Monday. I have looked for a job but there is nothing. The college can't take me back for seven months so I have let you down and I am sorry.

" 'You will notice that the computer from the back bedroom is gone. I hope to sell it. I'll send money when I do and there should be more money later; I'm sure you'll know what to do with it. Diane, my life insurance policy is in my top drawer. I love you all. Please forgive me for what I must do. Your loving husband and father.' "

"Did you find the letter?" Troy's question was filled with sympathy.

Jane shook her head. "Mom did. It was in a business envelope propped up on Dad's pillow. She told us about it that afternoon. She said Dad had lost his job and gone away for a while. We were stunned. We just sat

141

there, staring at her." Jane grimaced. "Of course, Ellen was the first to recover. She asked where Dad was. Mom sighed and said she wasn't sure. That he'd send us some money soon."

In her mind's eye, Jane could still see the loss on her mother's face, the confusion in her brother's and sisters' eyes.

"Maybe he's trying to find work," her mother had finished.

"How could he do that?" Ellen asked and she closed her eyes so the others couldn't see her tears.

"Maybe it's just a vacation," Megan had mused. She was fifteen and always the optimist back then. "Maybe he needs a little break so he can work things through."

"Why didn't he take us?" Amy asked. She was thirteen and there was naked fear in her green eyes.

Aaron said nothing. He folded his arms across his chest and stared at the floor.

Jane remembered studying the others and rolling her eyes.

"He didn't take us because Megan's right." Mom had tried so hard to sound re-assuring. "It's something like a vacation, except this time he needs to be alone. Sometimes adults need time to themselves." She looked at the other children and tried to assess their feelings. "Jane, do you understand?"

"Sure." She'd allowed hatred to fill her eyes. "Dad doesn't love us so he left."

"Jane!" Her mother reached gently toward her and touched her cheek. "That's not what's happened at all. Of course your father loves you and all the rest of us. This must be very hard for him."

"Yeah, Jane, why don't you just shut up!" Ellen had shot back, tears spilling onto her checks. "You're always so rude to Dad. Why don't you give him a chance. He'll be back anytime and then he'll explain the whole thing."

"He'll explain it to you, maybe, because he loves you. But he doesn't care if he leaves me, and that's the truth."

Ellen clucked her tongue against the back of her teeth. "Not another poor Jane story. You always think people love you less than everyone else. It's all in your head, Jane. Why don't you grow up?"

"Girls!" Their mother's voice was loud and it stopped the argument. "We all need to stick together. I won't have any more arguing." She paused. "There's something else."

She dismissed the younger children and asked Ellen and Jane to remain. Their dad had never done anything like this before, she said, so there was no telling when he might come back. She told Jane and Ellen that she was planning to find a job and begin working immediately, but several weeks might pass before she received a paycheck.

"We have a house payment coming up. You both have jobs this summer and I may need your help." There was shame in her eyes and the girls had to strain to hear her. "I hate to have to ask, but we don't want to lose the house."

The girls nodded, stunned by their mother's request. They had never considered their parents' finances before. Suddenly their firm foundation was shifting badly.

"What did you say?" Troy asked quietly, breaking Jane's flow of memories.

"We said we'd do whatever we could to help." Jane shifted, restless.

"You don't have to go on, hon. Not if it's too hard."

She reached out to touch his face. "Yes, I do. You need to know this. We heard nothing from Dad that night, and early the next morning Ellen left the house. She said she'd be back later and not to worry about her."

"Did Ellen ever tell you where she went?"

Jane nodded. She had, indeed.

With the sun still making its way into the sky, Ellen had driven to Magnus Park and found it empty. The tourists had recently returned to their homes in Chicago and Detroit and the town was noticeably quieter. She walked through the thick grass toward a shady knoll overlooking the water. No one would bother her there.

She stared at the blue-green bay and thought about the position her father had left them in. His actions tore at her loyalty to him as nothing else had.

After a while, her thoughts drifted and she considered her own life. She had missed so many classes at North Central the year before that she had been placed on academic probation.

"You're a smart girl, Miss Barrett," the dean had told her. "We would welcome you back should you change your study habits. But we will have to limit your course load until you can show an improved attendance record."

The probation was her fault. The reason, of course, was Jake Sadler. When he wanted to see her, she went regardless of her schedule. What was a history class when she could spend an afternoon with Jake?

After being put on probation she figured that perhaps she did not need a college degree, after all. She had not told her parents, but she planned to drop out of school and enroll in a course for legal secretaries. But her father's disappearance had changed everything.

A gentle breeze blew off Lake Michigan that day, and Ellen stared beyond the bay toward the open water. For the first time in her life she realized how utterly dependent the six of them were on their father. She thought about Jake and their plans to marry someday. Certainly she relied on Jake and would do so even more if they married. If he left she would be heartbroken.

But she would not be broke.

She later told Jane that in those solitary moments she decided she would never be financially dependent on Jake or any other man. She would never wonder where the next house payment was going to come from.

Suddenly the idea of quitting college seemed utterly ludicrous. She would reenroll at the community college. She would attend her classes, regardless of Jake's persuasive invitations. She would work harder than ever to earn high grades and then she would transfer to the University of Michigan where she would work until she had her bachelor's degree. Jake had made her forget her dreams, but now they were convincingly clear. She would study journalism and become one of the best reporters ever.

When she married, she would never place her husband under the financial strain her father had been living with. She stood up, brushed the sand off her shorts, and headed for her car.

"It was a turning point for Ellen." Jane turned to meet Troy's eyes. "She told me she knew it with everything in her. Even her walk was different, more confident, the picture of determination." A wry smile tipped her lips. "She said there would be no notes left on bedroom pillows for Ellen Barrett. No matter what happened with Dad, she was sure of that much."

"Sounds like a defining moment for her," Troy said, and Jane nodded.

"It's strange, though, how the same event affected each of us so differently." She sighed and forced herself to continue.

When her father didn't return home by Saturday evening Jane did something she hadn't done in months. She called Clay's friend and found out where the band was playing that night. By then she had saved up enough money to buy a small used car. After dinner she drove ten miles along the shore of Lake Michigan to Charlevoix where the party was already underway.

"I moved through the crowd of drunken, drugged party-goers and wondered what I was doing. I thought about my father and his eternal comparisons and I had the strange sensation that I was someone other than Jane Barrett, almost as if I no longer had any attachment to the Barrett family whatsoever."

She closed her eyes, fighting the tears. Troy squeezed her hand, offering her silent encouragement as she went on.

"This tall, dark-haired stranger with bloodshot eyes came up to me then. He looked me over, and I could tell by his expression that he liked what he saw. I guessed he was about twenty years old, completely stoned. But his approval fed something . . . a hunger, I guess, deep inside me. He was handsome in a dangerous way and he dressed like one of the band members even though I had never seen him before. I — I smiled at him."

How she regretted that smile. Even now, so many years later, she wished desperately that she'd just turned and walked away.

"I'm the new drummer, and you're Jane Barrett, right?" His words had been slightly slurred.

"How do you know?" Jane had batted her

eyes, playing with him.

"Everyone knows about Jane Barrett. Used to be Clay's girl. The only blond who ever dumped Clay on his royal behind."

He laughed at the thought and put his hand on Jane's bare shoulder. She savored the sensation and felt a stirring in the pit of her stomach.

"It's warm in here." His voice was husky. "Let's take a walk."

Jane had looked into the young man's red-rimmed eyes and decided no harm could come from taking a walk with someone who thought she was beautiful. She nodded and allowed him to slip his fingers between hers as they turned and headed for the door.

"Hey, Squid-man, where you headed?" The voice could barely be heard above the din of the party, and Jane turned to see another band member making his way toward them.

"Taking a walk," the dark-haired stranger shouted in reply, squeezing Jane's hand tighter. "Be back before the next set."

The band member smiled and flashed an okay to the couple as they headed out the door. They walked more quickly than Jane would have liked and headed away from the party, down a narrow sidewalk that led to a private beach. In a matter of minutes the roar of the party had disappeared, and Jane felt suddenly awkward in the silence between them. She wondered if she was crazy, walking hand in hand with a perfect stranger, someone so stoned he probably didn't remember his name.

He glanced at Jane, tripping and nearly pulling her down on top of him. As he struggled to regain his balance he laughed. "You sure are pretty, Jane. Clay must have been messed up for weeks when he lost you, huh?"

Jane wrinkled her eyebrows, not sure what he meant. "Clay was a jerk, to be perfectly honest."

"Yeah," the young man laughed as if he'd heard the funniest line ever. "Right. A jerk."

They stepped off the paved sidewalk and began walking on the sand. There were clusters of bushes and trees along the beach and dozens of dark places.

"Let's go back." Jane tried to twist her hand free from the stranger's. "I'm cold."

He stared at her, the laughter gone, and tightened his grip. "We can't go back now, we haven't had any fun yet." He turned toward her and pulled her into his arms, holding her fast, kissing her hard.

Jane pushed him away and wiped her face with the back of her hand. She was suddenly terrified. "We took our walk, now it's time to go back."

Suddenly the stranger shoved her hard with both hands so that she fell backward onto the sand. The spot was pitch dark, surrounded by dense brush. In the distance she could hear water lapping softly against the shore. A faint scent of honeysuckle from a nearby garden mingled with the smells of the bay.

"Hey!" she cried. "What do you think —"

"Shut up! Don't pretend you don't like it. I heard all the stories from Clay. You'd tease him all night and never give in. Well, you're gonna give in tonight, baby. Right now."

In an instant, he ripped at her clothes.

"No! Get away!" Suddenly she thought of the one person who had always saved her from trouble and she screamed his name. "Daaad! Help!"

The stranger laughed at her as he pinned her to the ground. "Your daddy's not going to help you now."

She screamed again and fought to be free of him. But she was no match for his strength and he slammed his hand over her mouth.

"Don't say a word, or you're dead. Got it? Just relax and enjoy it. Let old Squid-man teach you a thing or two about teasing."

For what seemed like an eternity the stranger savagely raped her. When it was finally over, he stood and kicked her in the ribs. "You look like something a cat would bury." He laughed cruelly, then bent down, picked up a fistful of sand, and threw it at Jane's face. "Good for nothing witch," he snarled. "You tell anyone about this and I'll say you begged me for it."

Jane waited until the sounds of the party began to fade before she crawled back into her torn clothing. She wiped the sand from her eyes and mouth and made her way through the shadows back toward her car. When she got home, she slipped into her room, changed her clothes, and ran a finger over the painful bruises on her arms and legs. There was blood on her underwear and she stuffed them in a bag, which she buried quietly in the trash.

Then she stared in the mirror at the woman she had become that night and wondered at the lengths she had gone to convince herself she did not need her father's love.

"Daddy," she whimpered at her reflection. "I only wanted you to love me for who I am. Oh, Daddy, I miss you."

She cried herself to sleep that night and

every night for a month.

Jane fell silent, hanging her head. Twelve years had passed since that horrific night, but she could still feel the pain, still smell the musty wet sand and the sickly sweet honeysuckle.

What must Troy think of her? Fear filled her, but she pushed it aside and turned to look at him. He watched her, his eyes filled with pain and compassion. He opened his arms, and with a sob of relief Jane collapsed in his embrace. She cried deep, gut-wrenching sobs.

"Th-that," Jane said when she could speak again. Tears streamed down her face as she lifted her head and stared into her husband's eyes, "was how I lost my virginity. The same week my dad left."

She sobbed loudly, painfully.

"Shhh, it's okay, honey." Troy stroked her back, speaking words of love, telling her how proud he was of her for finally trusting him with the truth. "I love you, Jane. I'll always love you."

"I loved my dad. I wanted his love," she cried. "I wanted it so badly. Then he left, and I tried to find it somewhere else. Instead I got raped."

With a shuddering sigh, she straightened.

The memories had left her exhausted, almost dizzy. "Dad came home a week later and found another job. Six months after that, he was rehired by the college."

Troy's arms came around her and he held her tightly. Jane would always remember the expression on Troy's face. He obviously understood now. By the time her father had returned home, the damage was already done. How could she grieve his death, when, in her mind, her father hadn't existed for more than a decade. He had died twelve years earlier on a musty, sand-covered beach in Charlevoix, Michigan.

EIGHT

On Sunday morning, two days after her father's death, Megan and her mother attended an early church service. For forty-five minutes the priest droned on about being a servant of the church and how best to imitate the lives of the saints. Not once did he make reference to their father's death.

Afterwards, arms linked, Megan and her mom made their way back to the family van where they were silent for a moment. The service had been a disappointment for her mother, Megan could tell. The poor woman had hoped to receive some comfort from her church family. After all, they had belonged to St. Francis Xavier Catholic Church for twenty years.

"That was terrible," Megan said quietly as they drove out of the church parking lot.

"It was a bit disappointing," her mother conceded, keeping her eyes on the busy tourist traffic that congested State Street.

The church was located in the Gaslight District where dozens of quaint shops added to the annual draw of tourists. July was the busiest month of all.

"It was more than disappointing. It was sinful. That priest knew we were upset and he didn't even acknowledge us." Megan fumed as she tightened her seat belt. Certainly the priest knew who they were and what had happened! Mom had spoken with him the day before to arrange a date for the funeral. "Dad took us caroling to that priest every Christmas for the past twenty years." She turned to stare out the van window. "And not even a smile or a hand on the shoulder, nothing to help us believe we'll get through this."

Megan and Amy had attended the church's grade school, and their mother volunteered her time as a catechism teacher. The Barrett family had sat in the same pew every Sunday for two decades, Megan thought angrily. But still the priest had failed to help them in their time of need.

As they drove, Megan remembered an incident two years earlier when her father was in the hospital with circulation problems. Mom had called St. Francis Xavier and requested that the priest visit John in the hospital.

"I'm sorry," she was told. "That hospital isn't in our area."

"What? It's only three miles from the church," her mother had protested.

"I'm sorry. You'll have to contact the priest of a church closer to the hospital. I believe that would be the Catholic church in Charlevoix. That's the way the system works."

Overall, Megan believed St. Francis Xavier was undeserving of John Barrett. When they moved to Petoskey her father had offered his assistance in fund-raising, but he was told the church had all the help it could use. Her father never forgot that, and in Megan's opinion, he never viewed St. Francis the same way he had once viewed St. Thomas in Ann Arbor.

The women drove home in silence and sat outside for a moment.

"I need you to help me clean the house, Megan." Her mother looked weary, and Megan was worried about her. "We'll have the girls home tonight, and in a few days people will arrive from out of town. I want the house ready."

"Fine."

"And don't worry about what happened at church today. I'll be all right. Grieving is a private matter for me, something between God and me. I don't need a priest hugging me and telling me everything will be okay."

Megan nodded, and the two went inside. The cleaning started in the kitchen.

"I think Ellen's right," Megan said thoughtfully as she worked alongside her mother. Ellen and Jane had both left the Catholic church years earlier and attended small, nondenominational Christian churches in their separate communities. "Ellen says the Catholic church isn't concerned with people's private lives and that —"

"That's her opinion," her mom cut in, making it clear to Megan that she did not want to talk about the ways in which the Catholic church, according to Ellen, might be lacking. Megan knew her mother had participated in very few religious discussions since Ellen and Jane had abandoned their Catholic upbringing. Still, she'd always made it clear she accepted their decisions and believed there were good things about the churches they attended.

Mom also made it clear that she was aware that St. Francis was not a perfect church, but that did not change her opinion of the Catholic church as a whole. Besides, she had been Catholic as long as she could remember and she would be Catholic until the day she died. Regardless of what anyone thought.

"But, Mom, don't you think that was cold? It's like no one even knew Dad existed at that church. Even after twenty years."

"Your father loved being Catholic. He understood that the priest at St. Francis is a busy man. Now I think that should be the end of the conversation."

Megan shrugged. "At least at Ellen's church everyone cares about each other. When someone dies they pull together and —"

"Megan, that's enough. Now check the calendar and tell me what time the girls' flights are coming in."

Megan stared at her mother. All their lives she had refused to talk about controversial matters. Whenever the discussion made her mom uncomfortable she changed the subject, as she had just done. Megan let it go and checked the calendar.

"Ellen's in at 1:30, Jane's in at 1:50. I need to leave here no later than eight-thirty."

"Well," she wiped her hands on a towel and rubbed her eyes. "I hope the girls won't bicker this week. The rest of you either. Your father would have wanted everyone to get along."

Megan rolled her eyes. "Mom, don't even say such a thing. Of *course* everyone will

159

get along. We haven't been together since the reunion two years ago. Everyone will have a lot of catching up to do. Besides, we have Dad's funeral to think about. You don't think planning a funeral is going to cause us all to start fighting with each other, do you?"

"It could."

"Mooooom. Please. We're adults, after all."

"Honey, you don't know your sisters as well as I do. I'm just going to say a special prayer that Ellen and Jane get along. I'm worried about them the most. It's important to me."

"If you think it's necessary."

Her mother sighed. "You know, sweetheart, you missed a lot all those years you dated Mohammed. Sometimes I think they created a vacuum in your life."

"Meaning what?" Megan knew she sounded defensive.

"Meaning you have a tendency to see your brother and sisters the way they were when they were all very young. Things have changed since then, Megan."

Megan watched her mother as she continued scrubbing the kitchen sink. She felt tears forming in her eyes. "We still love each other, Mom."

"I know, dear, I'm sorry. I didn't mean to say you don't love each other." She was quiet a moment. "I hope you have time to really help each other this week, maybe cry together. I think that would be good."

They heard Aaron lumbering down the hallway toward the kitchen. Megan swiped at an errant tear and sniffed loudly, composing herself. "Mom, you think Aaron would want to go to the airport with me?"

Diane picked up a wet pan and began drying it. "Well, dear, probably not. He hasn't said much since Friday and I don't think he'd be very good company."

Aaron walked into the kitchen, opened the refrigerator, and grabbed an apple. He looked tan and freshly showered, and Megan wondered what he was thinking, how he was handling their father's death.

"What'd you say?" he mumbled.

"Hello, dear."

Megan glanced at her mother. She always made an effort to sound cheerful when she talked to Aaron, almost as if she was afraid to make him angry.

"Megan wanted to know if you'd like to go to the airport with her."

Aaron grunted, rubbed his apple on his jeans, and left the room.

"Would that be yes or no, Aaron?" Megan

called after him.

"I said no!" Aaron's voice boomed through the house from his back bedroom.

"He's going to be great company this week," Megan mumbled.

Sometimes she wondered if Aaron was still angry with her for dating Mohammed. But how was she to know he was a drug dealer? It wasn't until they'd been together a while that she found that out. And by then it was too late to leave him. . . .

Once Aaron had pulled her aside and snarled at her, "That idiot is worse than the slime from a septic tank. And you're nothing but a scumbag for dating him, Megan. Don't give out your last name. I wouldn't want anyone to think we're related."

She had long since forgiven him for his harsh words. She realized that essentially her brother had been right. Dating Mohammed had been a crazy thing to do. But she couldn't help but wonder if Aaron still held a low opinion of her for those wasted years.

She looked at her mother. "I'll assume he doesn't want to go."

"Now, Megan," her mom pleaded. "Don't be sarcastic. He's going through a hard time right now, like all of us. Try and understand."

"Oh yes, I know the story. Aaron's had

162

such a hard life and so on and so forth. You'd think he was raised in an orphanage the way people talk about him sometimes. 'Poor Aaron. Raised in the same house as all those girls.' I guess they don't know that he was the only one who had his own room and the only one who went golfing on Saturdays with Dad while the girls stayed home and did the housework."

"Megan, dear. Be nice."

"I will," she said sweetly, brushing a single lock of hair off her damp forehead. "Don't worry. We wouldn't want to make Aaron angry, now would we?"

Aaron always blamed his temper on the fact that he was raised with four sisters, as if that alone was enough to drive someone insane. Megan clenched her teeth, not wanting to let her frustration with Aaron spill over onto her mother. "I'm sorry." She closed the dishwasher and pushed a button to start the cleaning cycle. "I'll try to be nice."

"Thank you, Megan. It means a lot to me. I really don't think I can make it if you children don't get along this week."

Megan took out the broom and tilted her head thoughtfully as she swept the kitchen floor. After all these years their mother still referred to them as children. She glanced at her watch and saw that it was eight o'clock.

The front door opened, and they heard Amy's voice.

"Hi." Amy rounded the corner, her husband, Frank, by her side. Her eyes were bloodshot and she looked like she hadn't slept. "We're here."

Frank sat down immediately and began thumbing through a computer magazine. Amy remained in the kitchen. She leaned against the counter and stared at her mother and sister working together.

"Is there anything I can do?"

Their mother smiled warmly at her youngest daughter. Amy had always been quieter than the other Barretts. Family theory had it that since her older sisters were so busy talking, she never had a chance to say anything. But Megan didn't buy that. She was convinced Amy didn't want to talk about her life. She was a private person. When she finished her child development courses at North Central in 1992, she'd married a computer wizard. They were a reserved couple who preferred to spend their time alone. Megan considered her sister. None of them really knew or understood Amy — and that seemed to be fine with her.

The one member of the Barrett family

who seemed to understand Amy perfectly was their mother. According to Mom, Amy was much like she had been at the same age. Amy was the only Barrett daughter with their mother's jet black hair and green eyes. Megan smiled. The similarities did not stop there.

Mom had always admitted she desired little in life except to be John Barrett's wife and the mother of his children. She did most of the cooking and cleaning, even after taking a full-time job at the telephone company. She never complained. In her opinion a woman should take care of the home, regardless of her busy schedule.

Of all her daughters, only Amy was the kind of wife their mom had been as a young married woman. She met her husband's needs much the way Mom had always met Dad's needs, right up until his death. Amy would never cause a conflict, and for that reason their mother was especially proud of her youngest daughter. Amy had been a simple child and now, though she was married and working at a local day care, Megan saw her as a simple woman.

"There's a load of laundry in the dryer if you wouldn't mind folding it," Mom said, hugging Amy close.

Amy nodded and did as she was told.

"Want to come to the airport?" Megan put the broom away and helped Amy carry the laundry into the living room where they dumped it on an oversized chair.

"No. You guys don't need me."

Megan looked at her younger sister strangely. "What do you mean we don't need you? We're all in this together. He was your dad, too."

"I know. I just mean they'll probably feel more like talking if I'm not around."

Megan's eyebrows came together in a puzzled frown and she glanced at Amy's husband. "I'm glad you understand her, Frank. I sure don't."

For several minutes she helped fold laundry, making small talk with Amy and Frank. Then she picked up her purse and kissed her mother on the cheek.

"Bye." She studied her mother's face, then added softly, "Why don't you get some rest, Mom? We'll probably be up late tonight."

Her mother nodded absently. She folded the kitchen towel, set it on the counter, and looked up. Megan saw the tears in her eyes.

"It's hard to believe he's gone, isn't it?"

"I know." Megan felt tears of her own. "Sometimes I wonder how we can all be a family without him."

Her mother sniffed, wiping at her eyes. "I

166

keep thinking I've got to stop crying. I won't be able to get through the week if I don't get a grip."

"No, that's not true. You go ahead and cry." Megan put an arm around her mother. "You were married to him forever. You can cry for a year if you want."

Her mother uttered a short laugh, and Megan hugged her tight.

"It's so good to have you back, Megan," Mom whispered into Megan's hair. "My sweet, sweet girl. There were times when you were dating Mohammed . . ." Her voice trailed off, choked by deep gratefulness. "Thank God he brought you back."

"I know." Megan sobbed softly and allowed herself to be hugged like a little girl. "I'm glad Daddy lived long enough to see me come to my senses."

"He prayed for you every day." Her mother pulled back and studied Megan's eyes. "We got through that time, and if we all pull together we'll get through this, too."

Megan nodded, tears still streaming down her face. Wracked by the ache in her heart, she prayed her mother was right.

NINE

Traffic at Detroit Metropolitan Airport did not hold to a specific rush hour. Regardless of the time of day, bumper-to-bumper cars snarled and knotted around the airport's massive loop causing delays for weekend and midweek travelers alike. Megan Barrett fought for position amidst hundreds of motorists and parked her compact car not far from the terminal where her sisters would be arriving.

It was ninety-two degrees and the humidity hovered at just above 80 percent, trapping the city's pollution so that the skyscrapers pushed their way through a murky brown layer of smog. Megan glanced at her watch and picked up her step. It was nearly one-thirty; Ellen's plane would be landing any time now.

The jet was gradually descending, and Ellen peered out the window, scanning the aerial view of the city. The air around the plane had become thick and dirty, and she wondered how she had ever enjoyed living in Detroit. At least in Miami breezes off the ocean kept the city air relatively clean.

She lifted her gaze through the hazy sky toward upper Michigan. Interstate 75 made an almost direct route from Detroit to Petoskey, north up the center of the state. It took between four and five hours to reach Petoskey from Detroit, but as long as it wasn't snowing, the Barretts had never minded the drive. The countryside was quietly rugged with deep green pastures, towering Ponderosa pines, and shimmering picturesque lakes.

Years earlier when her family had made the drive, her father would comment on the lush groves of pine trees or the endless sea of wild grass or the glassy lakes along the way. His favorite part of the drive was just before they reached home, as Highway 31 curved along Lake Michigan and dipped down along the water for a breathtaking view of Little Traverse Bay and the Petoskey shoreline.

"Behold," he would say, sweeping his arm grandly across his body. "The beautiful bay."

The pilot lowered the landing gear and Ellen put her seat in an upright position.

She had flown into this airport a dozen times, and each time her father had been waiting when she got off the plane. Even once when she flew for business and had access to a rental car, her father insisted on meeting her.

"If a father can't meet his daughter at the airport, then things have gotten pretty sad," he'd say with a smile.

"I don't know, Dad, it's a long drive."

"Don't worry about it, Ellen. It's not a problem. I enjoy it."

She closed her eyes and sighed, wishing with all her heart that he could be there now, at the end of the ramp, peering over the heads of strangers as he searched for her face. Just one more time.

The three-hour flight from Phoenix to Detroit was relatively easy for Jane, despite the fact that she had the children with her. Troy had a sales convention in Los Angeles and would join her Friday morning, the day before the funeral. Jane was used to Troy's traveling and she never even considered asking him to cancel the convention and spend the week with her in Petoskey. She and her siblings would have to choose a casket, plan the service, and help their mother survive until the funeral. Troy would have only been in the way.

Jane glanced at her pretty, blond children sleeping in the row beside her. She could picture having more babies. She was patient and fair and had long since learned the art of listening to her little ones.

"Mommy, know what?" one of the children would ask.

Jane would stoop down and look the child in the eyes as if there was nothing in the world more important than the words he was about to say. "What is it, honey?"

The child would smile and proceed with a story while Jane remained captivated until he was done. Her response was something she had learned in her weekly care group at Verde Valley Christian Church. Growing Kids God's Way, the program was called. Through it she and Troy had learned dozens of parenting skills. Listening to a child, they had agreed, was often the most effective way a parent could communicate love. More than anything, Jane and Troy wanted their children to feel loved.

She smiled at them now, absently running her hand across each of their three foreheads. They would miss Papa, as they called him. He had been a hands-on grandfather. He bounced them on his knee, read them bedtime stories, and played silly games with them. It had been during their recent visits, when her father would spend time loving her children, that Jane had actually felt close to him. There were no Ellens in John Barrett's life once he became a grandfather.

As the plane landed, Jane wondered how Ellen was handling their father's death. She was probably devastated. For a moment, Jane felt guilty for being gruff with her on the telephone. There seemed no way to bridge the gap that lay between them.

She ran a hand through her short-cropped blond hair and silently asked God to help her get through the coming week. She was not looking forward to seeing Ellen so upset. It would only make Jane more aware of the relationship she had never shared with their father.

The plane landed gracefully, gliding down the runway and turning toward the proper terminal. Jane glanced at her watch. Ellen's plane would have already landed, and she and Megan were probably comforting each other.

Jane stared out the window of the plane, her teeth clenched. *Just as well that I'm arriving a few minutes later.*

Still wearing her round-rimmed sunglasses, Ellen exited the plane, her leather bag slung over one shoulder. She searched the crowd for Megan and finally spotted her waving, working her way through the crowd.

"Ellen!" Megan's arms were around Ellen's neck and her eyes stung with tears. Ellen hugged her sister tightly They stayed that way for a while, unaware of the people streaming past them.

"He usually meets me at the airport and —" Ellen's voice broke. "He should be here, Megan. I can't believe he's gone."

"He had a good life, Ellen, we have to remember that." Megan was crying, too, and she kept her hands on Ellen's shoulders as she pulled away and looked intently at her. "He loved us with all his heart."

Ellen nodded. "I know," she sniffed. "But I miss him so bad it hurts."

"Me, too." Megan handed her a tissue and picked up her bag. "Come on. We have to meet Jane in a few minutes."

Jane had taken the same airline and would arrive just two gates away.

"You look good, Megan," Ellen glanced at her sister and thought how much more attractive she was than . . . before. Megan was thin and curvy, with long legs that had finally stopped growing when she reached five-foot-ten. She wore her dark blond hair much like Ellen's: cropped to her shoulders and fashionably styled. Ellen smiled as she noted the masculine glances being directed at the two of them. Despite their tear-stained faces, they made a striking pair.

"How's Mom doing?" Ellen asked as they found seats near the gate where Jane would be arriving. "I've talked to her ten times since Friday but I can't really tell without seeing her."

Megan nodded. "She's handling it. Aunt Mary's been over a lot cooking and spending time with her. Mom's been expecting this for a long time, you know."

"We all have. I used to think of Dad as being terminally ill so that it would be easier when he died."

"Did it help?"

"Not at all. There's no way to be ready for news like this."

"I knew his health wasn't good, but I thought he'd live another twenty years. Wishful thinking I guess."

"Remember when he lost his job and left for that week?" Ellen adjusted her sunglasses.

"Yeah. Vaguely." Megan leaned back in her chair and crossed her arms over her stomach. "That was a bad time."

"After that he was never the same."

"Healthwise, you mean?"

"Everything. But especially his health. Even after he got another job there was one problem after another."

"The blood clots."

"Blood clots in the lungs, blood clots in the heart, blood clots in the legs. Phlebitis put him in the hospital every ten months until he had his veins stripped. Then there was the high blood pressure, and by then he was probably a hundred pounds over-weight."

Megan nodded. "At least." She paused a moment. "He was a tall man, but that's too much for anyone."

"I remember taking a health class in college and the professor told us the warning signs for a heart attack. Male, over forty, obese, smoker, high blood pressure, stress, diabetes. When Dad was diagnosed with diabetes four years ago, he was like a loaded gun ready to go off. It was just a matter of time."

Megan sighed. "I know. But he defied the odds for so long I kept thinking he'd get one more chance. Even when I got the call at work that he'd had the heart attack I thought he'd be okay."

Ellen swallowed the lump in her throat and nodded. "Me, too. Just like last year when he had the bypass surgery. Remember when he had the angiogram to see how badly blocked his arteries were?"

Megan nodded. "I was there. They had him laid out on this cold, steel table with technicians and doctors buzzing around doing the test and putting nitroglycerin under his tongue. 'His heart's not gonna make it if we don't do surgery right away.' That's what the doctor said."

Megan shook her head, and Ellen reached out to take her sister's hand.

Drawing a steadying breath, Megan went on. "I remember looking at this huge screen where Dad's heart was on display for everyone to analyze. You know what I thought? With all their technology those people didn't know a thing about Dad's heart. He was more than another heart patient and I wanted to tell them so. For some reason that scene always stays with me."

"I didn't think he'd live through the surgery." Ellen recalled her fear that day. "But when he did I guess I thought he was finished with heart trouble."

"I know. I was sure he'd die on the operating table," Megan admitted. "We all sat there in that waiting room crying and thinking we'd never see him again."

Ellen sniffed and sat straighter in the padded airport chair. "At least we got another year, right?"

"But I wanted *ten* years. Twenty —" Megan's voice broke again. "I wanted him to walk me down the aisle when I get married some day. Like he did with you and Jane and Amy."

"I know." Ellen squeezed her hand. "Me, too."

They were silent then as Jane's plane pulled into position and passengers began streaming off. Ellen and Megan stood up and searched for their sister and the children.

She appeared carrying baby Kyle and holding three-year-old Kala's hand. Koley walked along beside them, handsome in a pair of shorts and an Arizona tank top. Megan waved, and Jane and the children headed toward them.

"How was your flight?" Megan hugged Jane and bent over to tousle the children's hair.

Jane set several bags down and took a deep breath. "Good, actually. The kids slept the whole way."

Ellen moved closer and hugged Jane. "You doing all right?"

Jane returned the hug, but Ellen didn't miss that she seemed slightly stiff. As she pulled away Jane smiled sadly. "Yeah. It's not easy but I'm surviving. You guys okay?"

Ellen nodded, and Megan began crying again. She put an arm around each of her sisters. "We have to be there for each other now that he's gone."

Ellen said nothing but noticed that Jane seemed to ignore Megan's statement as she pulled her children close and struggled to pick up her bags.

"Let's get the luggage and get home," Jane said. Her eyes were cool and dry. "It's a long drive, and I'm sure Mom needs us."

They collected their bags and returned to Megan's car. The children were buckled into the backseat so the adults could share the front and catch up on the latest details.

"So, what happened?" Jane asked when they were all in the car. "Was there any warning?"

Megan shook her head, looking over her shoulder as she backed out of the parking space and merged with the airport traffic. "He seemed perfectly normal the day before. In fact, I got home from work early Thursday and spent an hour telling him about all the personality conflicts at the office. He was a little sleepy, but other than that he was fine."

Ellen, too, wondered what her father's last days were like. Her mother had been too distraught to talk about anything more than the bare details, and Ellen was hungry for more information.

"No chest pain?" she asked.

"Nothing." Megan steered the car out of the airport and west onto Interstate 94. "Then on Friday morning he was supposed to play golf with Aaron but he was too tired. After breakfast he fell asleep in his old easy chair. When he got up and walked down the hallway to take a shower, he collapsed."

"Who was home?" Jane turned around and gave the baby a pacifier. The other children had fallen asleep.

"Just Mom. She heard him fall and knew right away that he'd had a heart attack. She called an ambulance and tried to wake him up, but it was too late."

Ellen felt the tears again as she pictured the scene. She was thankful she hadn't been there.

"How long did it take the paramedics to arrive?"

"Not long." Megan kept her eyes on the road as she talked. "Mom tried to do CPR after she called for help, but on a man Dad's size it's pretty hard. He was already dead when the ambulance got there."

"It wasn't up to Mom to do CPR. That's the paramedics' job. They should have at

179

least tried." Jane crossed her arms and looked suddenly angry. "People can be brought back from that point, you know."

"Jane." Ellen turned so she could see her sister plainly. "His heart quit. There wasn't much they could do about that."

Jane's eyes were hard. "You don't know everything, Ellen. I worked in the medical field and I know for a fact there are things they can do even after a person's heart has stopped."

"You were a dental hygienist, Jane. Most people would not consider that 'working in the medical field.' It's not like you were a nurse."

"I know more about medical issues than you do, okay?" Jane sat stiffly between her two sisters and snorted angrily.

Ellen wanted to argue, to force the issue, but instead she just drew a calming breath. "Well, either way, he's gone." She leaned forward looking past Jane to Megan. "He didn't have any symptoms or anything?"

"His neck had been bothering him, but everyone said that was just muscle tension. Dad thought he'd injured it playing golf."

"Didn't his neck hurt right before the bypass surgery?" Ellen asked.

"That's what I said. But the doctors swore

the neck pain had nothing to do with the heart."

There was silence for a moment.

"Well, like you said, Megan, they didn't know anything about Dad's heart." Ellen's voice was noticeably softer. "Only we know what kind of heart he really had."

"Here we go," Jane muttered.

Ellen turned toward her. "What?"

"Nothing."

"No, tell me. What do you mean, 'Here we go'?"

Jane looked like it was all she could do to tolerate Ellen. "It's just that you're so dramatic, Ellen. The rest of us have been expecting Dad's death for years. You can't tell me it caught you by surprise."

Heat flooded Ellen's face, and she drew back as if she'd been slapped. "No, I'm not surprised. I'm *hurt*. And I want to remember who he was as a person and not just his health problems."

Jane's lips thinned. "You're right. Sorry for bringing it up." She looked straight ahead, and Ellen exchanged a quick look with Megan.

Ellen changed the subject. "Anyway, what are the plans so far for the funeral?"

"Nothing, really. Mom's waiting until

181

we're all together so we can decide what to do."

Ellen leaned back against the headrest and closed her eyes. An hour passed in silence.

"Megan, when was the last time you talked to him?" Ellen finally asked. She remembered her last words with her father. Surely her sisters and brother did as well.

"It was Thursday night. He was watching TV with Mom and me, and I had to be up early in the morning for work. I kissed him good night just like I would any other time, and he smiled at me. You know that smile where you can see that he loves you and he's proud of you?"

Jane looked away.

"Yeah." Ellen smiled and nodded. Her eyes glistened with fresh tears.

Megan's voice was soft. "It was that smile. 'I love you, honey,' he told me. I told him I loved him, too. And then I drove home to my apartment and went to bed. That was the last time I saw him."

Ellen squeezed her eyes shut and hugged herself tightly. She did not regret moving to Miami, but she would have given anything to have been there that night. She could picture her family, watching television and swapping commentaries on the program. What would she have said if she'd been there and known it was his last night?

"How 'bout you? Do you remember the last time you talked to him?" Megan switched lanes and then looked question-ingly at Ellen.

Ellen nodded. She wiped at her tears and struggled to speak. "It was Wednesday. I was working on this murder case and I thought I had it figured out before the police. I called and told him the details. He listened and asked questions, like he always does. Then I asked him how he was feeling and he said he was fine. The doctors had given him a clean bill of health not too long ago and he and Aaron were going to try and get back into golf so he could lose some weight."

"Same old story." Megan smiled.

Ellen tossed a quick glance at Jane. She didn't seem to be listening to their conversa-tion. Instead she stared blankly at the road before them. Ellen shifted restlessly, won-dering if her sister was aware of the uncom-fortable feeling her silence was causing. She turned back to Megan.

"Same old story, all right. He even said he had picked a date toward the end of the year when he was going to stop smoking . . ."

"Again." Megan finished.

"Again." Ellen sniffed, grinning sadly at

the memory. Their father had tried to stop smoking so many times it had become something of a hobby. After his bypass surgery he refrained for several months, but once he started up again his children refused to believe he would ever stop.

"Anyway, he seemed upbeat, and we talked maybe thirty minutes. Then he told me to keep up the good work and send him the article when it ran in the paper. I usually send him copies of my big stories, so I told him I would. He told me he loved me and that he was proud of me for my work on the paper —" Ellen's voice cracked. She cleared her throat, and went on. "I told him I loved him, too, and that was the end of it. I never found out the information I needed and I was going to call him Friday to see if he had any ideas. A lot of times I would call and pick his brain. Sometimes he helped me find a lead when nothing else worked." She shrugged. "You know the rest. By Friday night it was too late."

"At least we both told him we loved him," Megan said. There were more cars on Interstate 75 heading north than usual and Megan remained focused on the road. They had just passed Flint and had two more hours until they reached Petoskey. "I'll bet Aaron hasn't said those words to Dad in years. I wonder how *he's* feeling."

"Has he said anything to you?" Ellen hadn't spoken to him since their father's death. Aaron usually spoke in one-syllable words and seemed to have two basic personalities: bored or on the brink of losing his temper.

"No. He hasn't talked to any of us, really."

Ellen settled back against the headrest and stared out her side window. Another hour passed and she thought about her brother. There was a time when Ellen had made an effort with Aaron. She had sent him encouraging Bible verses and occasional letters. But sometime later she heard through her father that Aaron did not appreciate her efforts at correspondence.

"He thinks you're preaching to him," her dad said gently. "I know you're trying, honey, but maybe you'd be better off to just let him be. You can't change him, you know."

The news hurt, and for months Ellen considered calling Aaron and explaining that she had written the letters only because she cared. But she never called and she stopped writing after that. Although there was no tension between she and Aaron, they hadn't said more than ten words to each other in the past two years.

"What about you, Jane?" Megan broke the silence. "You remember the last time you talked to Dad?"

"I didn't talk to Dad much. Whenever I called I talked to Mom."

"I know, but do you remember the last time you talked to him?" Megan pressed, clearly frustrated and determined to work Jane into the conversation.

"No, I guess not. He probably told me to give the kids a hug and kiss or something. That's usually what he'd say."

Ellen sighed and turned to Jane. "He loved *you,* Jane. Not just your kids. Sometimes you act like he didn't."

"You don't need to tell me that. I know he loved me. But he and I weren't close like you two, or like he was with Megan. And that's something *you* don't understand, Ellen."

"That was your choice." Ellen raised her voice. "You never spent time with him or talked to him or sat down to keep him company. What did you expect, Jane? You have to be around someone if you want to be close to them."

"Well, it didn't seem to matter how far away *you* were. You moved eighteen hundred miles south and you were still closer to him

186

than any of the rest of us."

Megan sighed. "Come on, you guys, don't fight. Dad loved us all. We have to lean on each other now and get through this together. The past is the past."

"I'm not fighting." Ellen returned her gaze to the road. "I just don't want her making Dad out to be some cold-hearted guy. It's time to say good-bye to him and I don't need her cheapening it."

She glanced at Jane again. "Maybe you two weren't close but don't go talking about it. The rest of us want to remember him in our own ways this week. Understand? I mean, you did love him, didn't you?"

Jane held her head a bit higher and clenched her teeth. Ellen was surprised to see tears fill her eyes, but they didn't spill over. It was as though Jane was refusing to cry. Like so many times before. Ellen longed to know what it was that troubled her sister so deeply, why she seemed so set on believing the worst about their father.

"Of course, I loved him," Jane said finally.

"Well, then, let's focus on that. All of us, all right?"

They continued north along Interstate 75 through the Mackinaw State Forest, past Higgins Lake and the Alpine town of Gaylord, on up to Highway 68 past Burt Lake and then to Highway 31. They drove over the slight grade and finally saw water as the road curved left and headed along the shore of Lake Michigan and Little Traverse Bay.

"Behold, the beautiful bay." Ellen could hear her father's proud words.

He had been right. The bay held the deepest, clearest blue water Ellen had ever seen. Even the Atlantic Coast could not compare with the pristine, majestic beauty of upper Lake Michigan.

In a matter of minutes they passed the summer community of Bay View. The social and financial elite from Chicago and Detroit owned the homes in Bay View. They were summer homes, supplied with electricity and water from May through August only.

Megan braked for a light, and Ellen studied the grand houses, their intricate Victorian designs and double-wraparound covered porches. Many of the homes were more than a hundred years old, but most had been completely restored to their original color and design. The neighborhoods swarmed with luxury cars while homeowners sat outside in porch swings, enjoying the dazzling view of the bay.

"Dad loved those summer homes," Ellen whispered.

Traffic was thick, and every other car on

the road seemed to carry tourists. During most of the year, Petoskey had a population of six thousand. In the summer, that number doubled. Ellen remembered how exciting the tourist season was when she was a teenager. She would sit at the beach with her family and watch all the new boys playing touch football and volleyball on the sand.

The town put its best foot forward during the summer months and there was something exciting about the increase of traffic each June. Of course, some residents hated the tourists, cursing them for clogging up the city streets and making downtown Petoskey's Gaslight District nearly impassable.

But tourism was the leading industry in Petoskey, and everyone in town benefited from a strong summer season. Those who grumbled knew enough to keep their feelings to themselves. After all, the inconvenience lasted only three months.

There was something comfortable and reassuring about August, when the summer residents went home and the town returned to its simpler ways.

Megan drove up Spring Street over Bear River and turned left on East Mitchell Road. She continued past Stone Funeral Home into a sprawling subdivision of country homes and restored turn-of-the-century farmhouses. She turned right on Lake Avenue, drove past five houses, and then finally there it was: the yellow-and-brown two-story house where the Barretts had lived for twenty years.

Built in 1954, their house had been restored gradually over the past several decades. The covered porch had been used for everything from first kisses to card games, heart-to-heart conversations and family sing-alongs.

Ellen was glad the house looked the same. The willow trees still anchored it on either side. The interior would be the same as well, just as it had been when she lived there. Vaulted ceilings in the foyer, walnut railing up the stairway to the bedrooms on the second floor, dark brown carpeting throughout, a spacious country kitchen with a faded yellow-tile countertop.

They turned into the gravel driveway and parked behind the other cars. Their parents owned two acres of rolling grassland. After living in a Miami subdivision, she thought her family's backyard seemed to go on forever. They climbed out of the car and helped the children out of their seat belts as Mom walked out to meet them.

Jane was instantly at her side. "Mom, I've

been so worried about you."

Ellen and Megan lagged behind with the children, and for an instant Ellen felt a pang of jealousy as she watched Jane and their mother embrace. Jane had always been a kindred spirit with their mother, while Ellen struggled to gain her approval. Ellen wondered if their mother had seen how much Dad loved her and Megan and had compensated by giving more of herself to Jane and Amy. Or perhaps her mother was still upset that Ellen was the first to leave the Catholic church. Either way, now that her father was gone she felt suddenly alone, without an ally.

Ellen studied her mother. She looked too thin and her face was drawn and pale. There was more gray in her hair than there had been two years earlier when Ellen was last in Petoskey. Her mother's eyes had dark circles beneath them, and every move she made looked painful.

Jane must have noticed the changes, too, for she looked worried. "How are you, really, Mom?"

"I don't know." She started crying softly and she put her arms around Jane's neck. Megan and Ellen quietly rounded up the children and joined Jane and their mother on the sidewalk.

"I'm sorry, Mom." Ellen placed a hand on her mother's back. "I wish he was here so he could say something to make us laugh again."

Her mother nodded and straightened, wiping her tears. She leaned over and hugged Ellen. "We'll be all right. We're together now. Come on, let's go inside. We can talk there."

Inside, Amy and Frank sat on the living room sofa and Aaron filled the matching oversized chair. His legs took up half the floor space in the room. He wore dark sunglasses and his arms were crossed tightly in front of him. Ellen thought he looked like an angry prisoner, daring anyone to get past the walls that surrounded him.

Amy stood up and hugged her sisters, then leaned over to kiss the children.

"Where's Papa?" Kala asked. She was still half asleep, her wispy blond hair pressed against her face from the long car ride.

"Oh, honey," Amy said and her eyes grew damp. "He's in heaven now. But he's very, very happy there and you know he still loves you, right?"

Kala started to cry. "I want my Papa." Jane lifted the child into her arms to console her.

Amy turned to Ellen, and the two hugged

while Aaron remained motionless in the chair.

"Hi, Aaron." Ellen positioned herself so her brother could not help but see her.

Aaron grunted, which told Ellen little had changed. She wondered what kind of war was raging inside his head and heart that he had to work so hard to hide his feelings.

"Did you bring your bags in?" Her mother glanced at Ellen as she shut the door and searched the living room.

"No. I think we're staying at Megan's. Is that right?" Ellen didn't want to assume anything. Not with Jane on edge and their mother an emotional wreck.

"Right." Megan looked at their mother.

"Well, I suppose." Mom shrugged. "I just thought we could all stay here and be a family again. Like old times."

Ellen cringed inwardly as she imagined trying to share a shower schedule with Aaron and Jane.

"Mom, I think we need more space. Especially for the children." For once Ellen agreed wholeheartedly with Jane. "We'll just be at Megan's at night so we have a place to sleep and shower."

"Oh. Well, I guess." Their mother looked slightly put out. "Your Aunt Mary is staying with me so I guess I'll be okay."

"Mom, if you want us to stay here, just say so," Ellen jumped in. She felt pierced by guilt.

"No, no. That's all right. You go on ahead and stay with the girls. Amy and Frank will be at their house so we wouldn't have all been together anyway. It's fine."

Everyone found seats around the living room, and Jane put the children in the den to watch cartoons. When she returned they rehashed the events that led up to their father's heart attack. They talked about his unhealthy eating habits, his lack of exercise, and his habitual smoking. Everyone agreed that certainly his death was not a surprise. They talked about how much better it was that he had died quickly without any pain or suffering and how terrible it would have been if he had died from diabetes complications.

"He could have lost his legs or his kidneys," their mother said. "Or worse, his eyes. That would have been so hard for your father."

Ellen felt sick as she pictured her father blind or without legs. Mom was right. Had he lived much longer the amputation of his lower limbs would have been a very real possibility. He had varicose veins and terrible circulation. Over time the diabetes would only have made the problem worse.

Ellen sat in silence as the others talked about how their father was in a better place now.

"He knew he didn't have long," her mother said quietly.

"What do you mean?" Ellen looked at her mother in surprise.

"When we were in Las Vegas last spring he told me he didn't think he'd live much beyond the end of the year."

"What? Why didn't he tell *me* that?"

Jane rolled her eyes but Ellen ignored her.

"I don't know. I guess he realized he hadn't followed the doctor's advice after his surgery and he figured he was using up his last chance. He told me his quality of life had slipped and he didn't want anymore surgeries or any drastic measures taken. He was at peace with God and himself and he was ready to go."

"Mother, he was only fifty-four!" Megan said angrily. "He should have been thinking about how he could change his life and get himself healthy again."

"Megan," their mother said softly. "It's been a long time since he was healthy. You know that."

There was silence and then the reminiscing started again, as though they had to talk

195

about every memory, every recollection they could think of — as though that somehow kept him alive and in their midst.

When they had exhausted every subject concerning their dad's poor health, they started over and talked about his last day again. Through it all, Aaron sat stone silent, unmoving and apparently detached from the others.

Finally at six that evening, during a lull in the conversation, Megan stood up and massaged her temples.

"I'm going for a walk," she announced. "Anyone want to come?"

Ellen rolled onto her feet and stretched her hands over her head as she yawned. "I'll go. Mom, what are we doing for dinner?"

"Pizza. It'll be here in about thirty minutes."

Ellen looked at Jane, determined to make an effort. "Wanna come?"

Jane shook her head quickly. "No. That's all right. I need to change the kids and get them a snack. The cartoons are over and they need some attention." She hesitated. "Besides, I'm sure you two will have plenty to talk about without me tagging along."

Ellen ignored the comment. "Aaron?"

He uttered an imperceptible sound.

"Aaron, would you like to take a walk?"

Ellen could feel the rising tension but she was determined to get an answer from him.

"I said, no! Are you deaf?"

Ellen turned, ignoring her brother's outburst. "Mom, we'll be back in a while."

She joined Megan outside, leaned against the front door, and sighed. She had never worked so hard to be kind to people in all her life.

"Wonderful, isn't it?" Megan seemed to read her mind and grimaced sadly.

"You feel it, too?"

"The tension? Of course. Aaron and Jane are like time bombs, and who knows what Amy's thinking."

"Tell me something, Megan." Ellen walked down the stone sidewalk toward the road and Megan fell in alongside her. "I know I've been gone four years and things change for everyone . . ."

"That's for sure."

"But what in the world happened? When did we all get to be strangers?"

Megan's eyes narrowed and she stared upward, still walking. When she spoke her voice was a strangled whisper. "I don't know, Ellen. I just don't know. But it's something we've got to figure out, or I'm afraid we'll never get back to being a family again."

TEN

There were no sidewalks so the girls walked on the right side of the worn road. The temperature had dropped considerably and a cool breeze filtered through the ancient maple trees that lined the street. Megan and Ellen rounded the corner.

"Gosh, what's wrong with Jane?"

"Oh, you mean Miss Congeniality?" Ellen uttered a short laugh. "I've been trying to figure that out for years."

"She's not being fair to Dad, do you think?"

"I don't know. She thinks Dad didn't love her like he loved you and me."

"That's crazy." Megan slowed her pace, clearly frustrated.

"I agree." Ellen shrugged. "But those are her feelings. I just wish she could remember the good times."

Megan kicked up a piece of asphalt. "I keep thinking of that Thanksgiving several years ago before she and Troy moved to Arizona. You were in Miami, but everyone else ate dinner at Mom and Dad's. All through the meal Dad kept saying how we should consider all God had given us and be thankful for what we had."

Ellen gazed at the treetops, remembering. "He loved the Lord, that's for sure."

"Always did." Megan paused. "Anyway, that evening when we were done eating he found one of those heavy paper plates Mom keeps around. He piled it high with turkey and potatoes and lime salad and pumpkin pie and then he wrapped it up in clear plastic."

Ellen stopped walking and looked at her sister. "I never heard about this."

Megan sighed. "That's because Jane never talks about the good times. She remembers things the way she wants to remember them."

We all do, Ellen thought. She started walking again. "So, what happened?"

"Well, Dad and Jane left the house and went driving around the Lamplight District looking for one of Petoskey's two wandering alcoholics. It wasn't very long before they found that older guy draped across the sidewalk in front of Michael's Doughnuts."

"What happened?"

199

"Dad and Jane got out of the car and walked up to the guy. Dad handed him the plate, wished him a happy Thanksgiving, and told him to remember how much God loves him."

Ellen smiled warmly, imagining the scene. "How'd you hear about that?"

"I was there when they got back and Jane told me all about it. She said Dad had tears in his eyes when he handed the man the plate. When they got back in the car, he told her he was proud of her for being a wonderful daughter and a terrific mother."

"Maybe we should remind Jane of that when we get back," Ellen offered. They walked past a sprawling farmhouse that had been renovated the year before. "At least she'd have one good memory."

"I don't know. She'd probably get mad at us for talking about her behind her back. That's how she's been lately."

"You think so, too?" Ellen folded her arms and glanced at a barking dog across the street. "I thought it was just me."

"No, I've seen it. I just don't say anything." Megan hesitated. "I want everyone to get along so badly. I missed a lot of years when I — when I was gone. Now I'm back. You and Jane have your husbands and your own lives far away from me. But you two, and Aaron and Amy and Mom are all I have. I think it's about time for us to be a family again."

Ellen sighed. "It's not that easy, Megan. Time passes, things change. I can't explain it but I can feel it. We're all different and we can't go back to being something we were twenty years ago."

Silence settled over them as they walked.

"How's everything with Mike?" Megan said after a while.

Ellen laughed, but she knew it sounded bitter. "I'm not sure I want to talk about it."

Megan studied her older sister carefully. "I thought something might be wrong. Mom said Mike was coming with you. When I found out you were flying by yourself I thought it was strange."

"He has to work. At least that's what he says. He also says he doesn't care for funerals."

Megan cringed.

"Yeah, tell me about it. He actually told me I didn't need him, that I'd have lots of people around for support."

"Let me guess . . . you don't agree?"

The sun was setting, splashing brilliant hues of pink and orange across the northern Michigan sky. Ellen stopped walking and allowed her eyes to drift. When she looked back at Megan she shook her head angrily.

"No, I don't agree! I wanted him to come with me and he refused." She was quiet a moment. "That's how Mike and I are doing."

Megan was pensive as they resumed walking. "Mike's a great guy, Ellen. Don't judge him on this. You know he loves you."

Ellen shrugged. "I used to think so. But it's not just this. Weddings, concerts, social events, lots of times he doesn't want to go with me. What kind of love never makes a sacrifice for the other person?" She studied her feet and kept walking. "I don't know. Sometimes I think we're drifting apart."

"You guys going to church?"

Ellen shook her head. "That's a big part of it. How can God bless our marriage when we've all but forgotten about him?"

"I can't believe you guys aren't going to church. I always thought you were the perfect Christian couple."

"No one's perfect, Megan. Least of all Mike and me."

"Did something happen? At church I mean?"

"No, nothing like that. We just got busy. One thing led to another and now it's something we don't talk about. Like we're too far away from it all to go back." A lump formed in her throat and she had to fight a wave of tears. "I think I'm starting to feel that way about Mike, too."

"He is coming for the funeral, right?"

"We left it up in the air. I told him I didn't care if he stayed home, and he told me that was fine with him. I guess I'll have to talk to him sometime this week so we can decide what to do."

They turned a corner and headed back toward the Barrett home. Megan thought a moment and then glanced at her sister. "Know who I saw the other day?"

"Who?"

"Jake Sadler. Over at the hardware store buying lumber. He's building a fence for his parents or something."

Ellen's stomach flipped. She forced her voice to remain unchanged. "How's he doing?"

"Same as always. Single, tall, beached-out, and gorgeous. Guys like Jake never change."

Ellen's eyes narrowed. "I haven't seen him in so long. Probably ten years, I'll bet. Eight at least."

"He asked about you, wanted to know if you were still happily married, the whole nine yards."

"What'd you tell him?"

"Ellen! What do you think? I told him of *course* you were happily married." She hesitated. "You are, aren't you? I mean there's nothing really wrong with you guys, is there?"

Ellen picked up a loose rock, took aim, and threw it at the trunk of an old maple tree. She stared at her sister. "I guess not. I just wondered what you told him." She fell quiet then, but warning bells sounded deep inside her. . . . *Don't do it. Don't go there!*

She pushed her thoughts aside impatiently. It only made sense that she was thinking about Jake a lot lately. After all, her father's death had made her think about the past, hadn't it? That's all it was. Remembering a time gone by . . . a love that could have been . . .

The bells grew louder — and with them, Ellen's determination to ignore them.

The sisters stopped in front of the aging yellow Victorian, the home they had shared for so many years.

"I look at the old house and I can still see Dad sitting on the porch, smoking, waiting for us to come over for dinner. That year before we moved we probably ate here twice a month." Ellen stared at the house and saw it as it had been a decade earlier.

"Yeah, I know what you mean. I see him sitting beside the front door in that heavy jacket and that old caroling hat, handing out Halloween candy and pretending to be scary. He must have given out more candy than anyone on the block."

"And the kids knew it." Ellen tilted her head, smiling despite the tears that filled her eyes.

Megan laughed softly. "He did that every Halloween for as long as I can remember."

"And then in December he'd be there climbing up that old broken-down stepladder, covering the house in lights. He sure loved Christmas. Remember that time when someone stole the lights from Candy Cane Lane?"

Megan nodded, a sob lodged in her throat, as Ellen reached over and gently squeezed her sister's hand. Candy Cane Lane was an upper-class neighborhood that ran along the lake in Charlevoix. Twenty years earlier residents there agreed to erect stunning Christmas displays, complete with thousands of lights, moveable figurines, piped in music, and special effects. Three streets participated, and each was given a different name for the Christmas season. Carolers' Lane, Bell Lane, and Candy Cane Lane. The Barretts visited the neighborhood every

Christmas as part of their holiday traditions.

Then one year vandals struck and stole the lights from several houses. For the first time ever, the home owners talked about stopping the tradition. Determined to show his appreciation, Ellen's father went to the store and purchased dozens of light strings. He put them in a bag and left them on the porch of a Candy Cane Lane home owner. He taped an anonymous note to the bag: "We enjoy what you do. Please don't let one Scrooge ruin it for the rest of us. God bless you."

The newspaper got wind of his act and ran a story. After that, others followed John Barrett's example until the home owners along the three streets had more than enough lights to make up for what had been stolen. The tradition continued.

"He was something else, wasn't he?" Megan finally said.

Ellen nodded and put an arm around her sister, hugging her close. "Come on. Wipe your tears. Let's go in and see if Aaron's still glued to that chair."

ELEVEN

A feeling of doom hung over the house Sunday night when Mike Miller returned from covering the baseball game. He'd done a particularly professional job of reporting the close contest that night, both throughout play and later during post-game interviews. Before he left the field, one of the producers had approached him.

"Mike, they say you're a natural. You have national sports written all over you, man. You must be living right or something."

Normally the producer's comments would have sent Mike sky high and he would have sped home to share the news with Ellen. But she was in Petoskey, and ever since their disagreement on Friday, nothing felt right to Mike. He was jumpy, nervous, and there was a hard knot in his gut that wouldn't go away. Dread, deep and frightening, burned at him.

He was afraid his marriage wasn't going

to survive.

"How'd everything get so messed up, Lord?" He wandered about his living room. Almost in answer, he paused by the bookcase and found himself staring at the binding of his leather Bible. *Maybe later. After I eat. Maybe it's time to get back into the Word.*

He tossed his jacket on the back of the chair and glanced at the clock in the kitchen. It was just after nine. Ellen and the others would be together now, probably seated around the Barrett dining room table.

Mike sat down at his own empty table and stared at the portrait of Ellen and him that hung over the fireplace. As he had been doing since Friday evening, he second-guessed his decision to let Ellen go by herself to Petoskey. He could have found a replacement to cover the game. So what if he didn't care for funerals? Ellen was right: *no one* enjoyed funerals.

But he still could not stomach the idea of spending a week watching the adult Barrett children tear each other apart. Ellen always talked about how close she and her sisters and brother had been growing up, about the memories they'd made together. But based on what he'd seen of her family, Mike wondered if she wasn't imagining things that had never happened.

He remembered a dozen times when he and Ellen had been at a Barrett family gathering only to leave early because of the tension that all but crackled in the air. In some ways that was why they had moved to Miami. Yet, when Ellen was away from them she called often, wrote once a month, and there seemed to be no conflict at all.

"We get along better when we're two thousand miles apart," Ellen had often told Mike. "I think that's the secret."

Especially when it came to Ellen and Jane.

The strangest thing about Jane, in Mike's opinion, was that away from Ellen she was a wonderful person. Sadly, Ellen knew it, too.

"Have you ever seen how her friends treat her? How she treats them? They love her, Mike. She's bubbly and funny and happy. She's the greatest in their eyes."

Mike listened sympathetically.

"Why can't she be that way with me? I'm her sister, after all. I love her more than any of them, and she treats me like dirt. Sometimes I feel like walking up to her and saying, 'Hi. I'm Ellen. Let's be friends.' Maybe if I pretended to be a stranger, she'd be nice to me."

Mike was puzzled by Jane's attitude. Especially after Jane and Troy were married and began having children. Koley was born in 1992, and Ellen tried to make herself available on the weekends to help Jane when Troy was on business trips.

Mike recalled the time Ellen stayed at Jane's home and watched the newborn baby one Saturday so Jane could sleep. Mike had come to pick Ellen up just as Jane trudged wearily from her bedroom.

"How was he?" she asked.

"Just fine," Ellen cooed at the baby and tickled his cheek. "Get any sleep?"

"Yeah. Thanks."

Ellen studied her sister. "You know, Jane, you look really good. You'd never know you had a baby two weeks ago."

Mike had been surprised at the cool look in Jane's eyes. "What's that supposed to mean?"

Ellen paused, clearly at a loss. "Nothing. Just what I said. You look good."

"Listen, don't make fun of me," Jane barked. "Just because you're Miss Cosmopolitan with the sleek figure doesn't give you the right to comment about me —"

"Whoa, Jane, Ellen was just being nice," Mike broke in.

She ignored him. "Just wait, Ellen. Your turn will come. You'll get stretch marks on your stomach and crease marks on your chest and you'll be struggling to find your old shape. I can't wait for that day. Imagine, Ellen Barrett, chunky and out of shape. That'll be a sight I definitely don't want to miss."

Tears welled up in Ellen's eyes and she stood up, passing the baby to Jane.

"I have things to do, Jane. Call me if you need me."

"Are you trying to say I can't do this on my own?"

Mike wondered if he had missed some segment of their conversation. He could not understand what had triggered Jane's anger.

He took Ellen's arm and led her across the living room to the door, growing angry himself when he felt how Ellen was trembling. Jane followed after them, crying and waking the baby with her shouting.

"Don't worry about me, Ellen! I don't need you. I can handle this mothering thing all by my —"

Mike closed the door on the rest of the sentence. They walked to the car in silence, then drove straight to Ellen's parents' house where they were staying for the weekend.

"It's like she hates me and I don't even know what I've done wrong," Ellen cried when they were in their room.

Mike had his opinions about Jane but he kept them to himself. That afternoon he convinced Ellen that Jane must have been suffering a hormonal imbalance. "You know, that baby blues thing, postportem or something. I heard about it on *Oprah* once."

"Post*partem.*" Ellen sniffed. "Maybe you're right."

"Come on, honey. She'll be fine in a few weeks. Don't take it personally."

But privately he didn't think hormones could excuse Jane's actions toward Ellen. They certainly could not explain her bitter attitude before the baby was born.

Through the years Ellen had found several opportunities to address the issue directly with Jane.

"Why do you hate me, Jane?" Ellen would ask. "What have I done to hurt you? What can I do to change so that you'll be civilized when we're together?"

Whenever Ellen asked such a question Jane would do something that completely baffled Ellen. She would cry and accuse Ellen of saying hurtful things and trying to upset her.

"Do you think *your* words don't hurt *me,* Ellen?" she'd shout, tears coursing down her face. "You have a wicked tongue and you don't care how it hurts people."

Inevitably Ellen would apologize. For six months or a year the sisters would get along, visiting by phone from their separate homes and talking about surface subjects.

Mike shook his head. Problem was, they never discussed the real reason behind Jane's resentment. Mike thought it was almost as if Jane was hiding something from Ellen.

The cycle made Mike tired just thinking about it. He could only imagine how it had taken its toll on Ellen over the years. Poor Ellen. She had been so close to her father and Jane had been so distant. Undoubtedly, now that he was dead, Jane would be upset with Ellen over that fact, too. She would probably accuse her of being their father's favorite. If Jane did that, Mike could only imagine the friction that would develop between the two oldest Barrett daughters that week.

As if the tension between Jane and Ellen wasn't enough, Ellen's other siblings had problems of their own — some considerably more serious than Jane's anger.

There was Megan, who at twenty-seven was finally beginning to live again. For a five-year period, from age twenty to twenty-five, she had spent much of her time dating a drug dealer. The man had convinced her that her family didn't care about her and that Ellen, especially, was trying to change her into something she could never be.

As a child Megan had looked up to Ellen. She imitated her and planned to be just like her when she got older. Megan was a brilliant writer with an art for communication. Like Ellen, she was a natural leader and had dozens of friends. She was also, unquestionably, the best looking of John Barrett's daughters. Whereas Ellen was beautiful and Jane quietly pretty, Megan was gorgeous. She had blue eyes big enough to fall into and cheekbones that seemed carved by an artist. Her skin was the color of pale honey and her dark hair hung halfway down her back. On top of that she was gifted with the voice of an angel. When she entered a room, her presence demanded the attention of every person there.

When Megan was in eighth grade Ellen gave her a handwritten book with personal advice on how to survive high school. Megan read the book hungrily, fascinated at the advice Ellen had written for her. She wanted to be everything Ellen had been and more.

Then, unexplainably, she dropped out of cheerleading in her junior year and began dating loner types. When she was twenty she met Mohammed, a Goliath of a man with Middle Eastern roots and a forest of dark hair that covered his body. The few times Mohammed visited Megan at the Barrett home he never wore shoes or spoke directly to John or Diane. His eyelids remained half closed and there was something condescending in his attitude toward everyone in the Barrett family. Especially Megan.

Mike remembered the first time Mohammed visited the Barrett family. It had been a big family get-together.

"So, what is it you do for a living, Mohammed?" John had asked, spreading a thick layer of butter on his bread and helping himself to an extra serving of gravy.

"Things." It had bothered Mike, the way Mohammed refused to make eye contact with John. Several others at the table had exchanged curious glances.

It made sense now, but at that time none of them — except Megan, of course — knew that Mohammed was a pusher. Everywhere he went he carried a briefcase packed with marijuana, cocaine, and two loaded pistols.

Mike learned later how Mohammed had taught Megan to listen to blank cassette tapes for subliminal messages from "helping-demons," and when Megan didn't cooperate, he'd beat her or put his fist through the windshield of her car.

"If you leave me I'll kill your parents," Mohammed would threaten her. He was five years older than Megan and she believed him completely. The relationship continued.

For years, Mike had watched as Ellen tried unsuccessfully to bring Megan to her senses.

"Don't preach at me, Ellen!" Megan would scream. "Not everyone is perfect like you. Besides, I don't do drugs and I'll date whomever I want, so don't try to run my life. At least Mo isn't some plastic phony like Mike!"

Long after Mike and Ellen moved to Miami, Megan was still caught up in the destructive relationship. By the time she finally broke it off with Mohammed, so many years had passed that the chasm between Megan and her sisters was almost too vast to cross. Mike had seen firsthand at family get-togethers how the tensions remained. This week would be no exception.

Then there was Aaron, the only son. His father's pride and joy. Aaron was strikingly handsome and had always boasted a string of girlfriends. But he was lazy and utterly dependent on his parents for survival. By the time he was twenty-two he had been fired from seven construction jobs. He was six-foot-four, built like a professional line-backer with the strength of five men his size. Once his temper flared in the workplace most employers found it simpler to let him go than to deal with his outbursts.

Mike remembered once when he and Ellen had flown back to Petoskey for a family reunion. A dozen or so family members had gathered at the Barretts' house for a barbecue and spirits were high. They were seated around the dining room table when Aaron waltzed in after work and helped himself to two hamburgers and a full plate of fixings.

"It's a potluck, Aaron. Did you bring anything?" John Barrett had asked when Aaron pulled up a chair and sat down.

Aaron slammed his fork down and threw his plate across the room. Diane gasped as the burgers fell apart and landed on the carpet, splattering ketchup on the dining room wall. Aaron glared at his father, stood up, and went into the kitchen where he slammed the dishwasher shut breaking dozens of dishes.

"Aaron!" Diane had gasped.

Unrepentant, Aaron glared at his father and stormed down the hallway toward his bedroom. Mike remembered John Barrett's expression as he looked at the others, clearly shocked and embarrassed by Aaron's actions. Then he excused himself and went back toward Aaron's room to deal with the situation.

The exchange could easily be heard by everyone at the dinner table.

"We cannot tolerate that behavior, son," John had said, his own voice trembling with controlled rage. Aaron was two inches taller than his father and fifty muscled pounds heavier.

Aaron responded with a string of profanity, telling his father to mind his own business. Then, as was too often the case, he blamed his parents for treating the girls better than him over the years.

"I always got in trouble for things they did!" Aaron's voice echoed through the house. Mike pushed his plate aside. Another meal spoiled by Aaron's tantrums. "Do you know what it was like growing up in this family and being the only son?" Aaron shouted. "I bet you didn't ask *them* to bring anything to the meal. They do whatever they want, and I'm the one who gets the shaft!"

There were more profanities then and finally Mike walked purposefully down the hallway and put himself between John and Aaron.

"Come on, Aaron, let's take a drive and talk this through," Mike said.

Aaron glared at Mike and swore at him, accusing him of being a meddler and reminding him that he was not part of the Barrett family. Then in a sudden burst of intense anger he lifted his fist and held it inches from his father's face. Diane, who had come to see if she could help, screamed. "Someone call the police!"

Aaron swung his fist furiously, but at the last moment he turned his body so that his hand slammed completely through his bedroom door instead of hitting his father. Pulling it free from the splintered wood, he continued to swear at his parents, punching a series of holes in the door.

"Aaron, stop it!" John tried to wrestle him away from the door, but Aaron was out of control. He jerked away from his father's touch.

"John!" It was Diane's voice. "Leave him alone. You'll have a heart attack!"

"That's all right!" Sweat dripped from his face as he struggled to stop Aaron's destructive temper tantrum. "He's my son and he's not going to behave this way in my house."

Mike had watched, ready to step in if necessary, amazed at Aaron's strength as he ripped his bedroom door completely off the hinges.

"I hate all of you!" he screamed.

He pushed his father out of the way, shoved past the others, and stormed out of the house. The Barrett family stood motionless, stunned, as they heard Aaron screech away from the curb in his pickup truck.

It was neither the first nor the last example of Aaron's explosive behavior.

Mike remembered a time when Amy, then eighteen, had told Aaron he was a loser. "When are you going to get a real life?" she had asked.

In response, Aaron had walked out to her brand-new car and kicked his work boot deep into the passenger door. As far as Mike knew, the damage had never been repaired.

Mike had leveled with John Barrett one day. "He's making your life miserable. Maybe it's time he found his own place."

"Well, Mike, I'll tell you. There are times I wonder what I did wrong with Aaron. Sometimes I think he's still a little boy trapped in a man's body. But we have our good days, the times when we go golfing and get along." John took a deep breath and slowly released it. "Besides, we have no throwaway kids. Aaron can stay here as long as he needs to. That's what family is all about."

Mike had his own opinion about what Aaron needed, but since the conversation with John had proven fruitless, he'd decided to keep his thoughts to himself. With John. With Diane. Even, most of the time, with Ellen. Shaking off the sour memories, Mike stood up slowly and headed into the kitchen for something to eat. The more he thought about the Barretts and their assorted conflicts the more he was thankful he hadn't gone to Petoskey.

I love her, Lord. You know I do, with my very soul. He passed a hand wearily over his eyes. *But I can't spend a week with her family. Not even for this.*

He took a hot dog from the refrigerator, heated it in the microwave, and placed it in a cold bun. Then he looked at the telephone. He should call Ellen. He sighed and stuffed one end of the hot dog into his mouth.

No, it would be better to wait a few days — give her time to forgive him for not going with her.

He walked past the phone, past the portrait of him and Ellen, past the bookcase and the unopened Bible, and found a comfortable spot on the sofa. Then he kicked up his feet, grabbed the remote, and ran his finger deftly over the power button. Before flicking on the evening news he wondered once more whether Ellen was still mad at him. He thought again of Jane and Megan,

Amy and Aaron, and he shuddered.

He was glad he had stayed home. Ellen would simply have to understand.

TWELVE

By the time Ellen and Megan came back inside, forty minutes had passed and two half-eaten pizzas were laid out on the dining room table. Their mother was on the telephone, talking in hushed tones, and Jane was in the den reading a book to her children. Amy and Frank had gone home for the night. Only Aaron remained in the living room, positioned in the chair as he had been when they left.

"How's it going?" Ellen sat down near him and leaned over her knees, studying him. Megan took the cue and left the room for a slice of pizza.

Aaron turned and stared at the wall.

"Aaron, you'll feel better if you talk about it. We're all going through the same thing."

Aaron smothered a sob and wiped a tear as it fell from beneath his dark glasses. He stuck his chest out and crossed his arms more tightly around his body. He had always absolutely refused to cry. He wasn't going to give in now, Ellen guessed, especially not in front of her.

"He-*llo?*" She held out the last syllable, aggravated. "Aaron? I'm trying to talk to you."

"Don't want to talk." Aaron rose to his full, towering height and hitched up his jeans. Then in one movement he grabbed his keys from the ledge near the front door and left without saying a word.

"Who's here?" her mother called from the kitchen as the door slammed shut.

"No one. Aaron just left." Ellen wandered into the kitchen and took some pizza. Her mother was still on the phone and she raised her hands, silently asking Ellen where Aaron had gone.

"I don't know. He's not talking to me."

With a sigh, her mother returned to her conversation. Ellen moved in beside her and began helping with the few dishes from dinner.

Aaron climbed into his full-size, silver-and-black pickup truck and headed down Mitchell. In a matter of minutes he reached Spring Street and turned right toward the water. He slipped a Garth Brooks CD into his car stereo and blasted the music — as if that could take away the pain in his heart.

He drove, unsure of where he was headed until he pulled off Highway 31 and turned right on Country Club Road. Suddenly he knew where he had to go. He headed the same way he had a hundred times, making the necessary turns and stops until the street came to a dead end on a hill overlooking the Bay View Country Club. He turned the music off and stared over the golf course, across the eighteenth hole, out toward the bay.

The clubhouse was just to his right and although it was after eight, there were still people leaving, heading for their cars. During July, Petoskey stayed light until nearly ten. He shifted his foot to the gas pedal and drove through the parking lot toward the roadway that divided the course's front and back nine. He passed what was probably the last cart of the day heading back to the clubhouse, then he pulled into a gravel area just off the road so that he faced the golf course. Trees on either side made the spot private, and Aaron killed his engine.

The only sounds were the gentle rustling of trees and the distant traffic on the highway. Over the tops of the trees that lined the ninth fairway, the bay was still visible, and Aaron saw that the sun was moving slowly toward the water. The course would be closed in a few minutes. He could be alone here.

He took a deep breath and then, surrounded by the silence of the empty golf course, he gave himself permission to feel.

Bitterness and anger flooded him. How could his father have done this? How could he have left him?

His anger swelled as he unleashed it and memories ran rampant . . . memories of times he had been mad at his father, times when he had been punished more severely than his sisters, times when he had hated his father for being so hard on him.

"Son, don't tell me they hit you first," he could hear his dad say. *"You're a boy and no matter what happens you don't hit girls."*

As far back as Aaron could recall, his sisters had ganged up against him. They had teased him and threatened him and once they even put eye shadow on twelve-year-old Megan's cheek so that their father would believe Aaron, three years younger, had hit her.

Aaron closed his eyes and remembered the hard spanking he'd gotten for that.

"Dad, I swear I didn't do it," he had yelled throughout the punishment.

But John Barrett was not a man interested

in excuses. He punished Aaron and let him know in specific terms the extent of the punishment he would receive if he ever hurt the girls again.

Even after he had received the unfair punishment, the girls did not let up. He remembered a little miniature wind-up robot he'd bought with his own money when he was seven. The girls found it and placed it in the ice-cube tray so that it froze under water. Aaron searched the entire house before finding it in the freezer. The girls had thought it was the funniest thing ever.

Seventeen years later he could still hear their cruel laughter.

The afternoon breeze had stilled and the trees barely rustled. Aaron kept his eyes on the golf course, his anger building with each memory. There was another incident, when Aaron was eight. He had been given his own pack of gum and did not want to share it. Led by Ellen and Jane, his sisters had taken out each piece, chewed it, and rewrapped it. Then they placed it back in the package with a handwritten label across the front: ABC Gum. Give it a Try.

Aaron's eyes narrowed angrily and his grip grew tighter on the steering wheel. Already Been Chewed. *Ellen probably wrote that.* Ellen, who pretended to care about him these past years, but who had treated him miserably when he was little. Ellen, who had stolen John Barrett's attention away from him.

There had been a time when he didn't care about Ellen and her relationship with their father. No matter how much Ellen did right, she couldn't play football. When Aaron was a young teenager, football had been his surefire way of winning his father's attention.

Aaron played offensive lineman for Petoskey, and John Barrett was at every game. He cheered louder than any parent and was quick to compliment his son's burst of speed off the line of scrimmage. But after two years on the varsity squad Aaron could no longer fool himself. He had the size and speed to be a college player but he had one very big problem. He didn't like the game. He was only playing for his father's approval and after his sophomore year, he could no longer pretend.

"Son, is it true?" Aaron could still hear the disappointment ringing in his father's words. "You quit the team?"

Aaron remembered hanging his head. "Yeah, Dad, it's true. I'm really not into football." He had looked up then, expectantly. "You're not mad, are you?"

"Son, of course I'm not mad. I'm disappointed. Not for what I've lost, but for what you've lost. You were really something out there. You can quit the team and it won't change how I think about you. But maybe you should give it some more thought. You could play college ball with your size, son."

"Dad, I'm done with football. That's the end of it. All right?" Aaron spent the rest of the evening in his room certain that his father would never again view him the same way.

That was 1990, when Aaron was sixteen and Ellen had just graduated from college with her journalism degree. She was hired to work for the *Detroit Gazette* sports section and cover high school football games. That season instead of watching Aaron play, John helped Ellen. He gave her pointers and helped her understand football so that she could write better stories.

With Ellen and their father spending so much time together talking about football, both in person and on the telephone, Aaron felt as if he had ceased to exist in his father's eyes. As long as there wasn't a blizzard, Ellen would come home each Saturday and watch football with their father. They talked about first downs and reception averages and kickoff returns while Ellen hung on every word the great John Barrett said.

The whole thing made Aaron sick. There had been a time when he cherished taking in a football game with his father. After Ellen's indoctrination into sports writing, Aaron no longer wanted anything to do with the game.

"Aaron, come on out here and see this." His dad would wave to him from his easy chair. "It's the big game. Michigan and Ohio State. We're about to score."

"I'm busy," Aaron would shout from the next room. "Maybe later."

Why bother? He'd figured there was no point. Ellen so monopolized their father's attention that Aaron no longer had any interest in watching sports with his father. In fact, he had no interest in doing *anything* with his father, and for years there seemed to be a distance between them no bridge could span.

Then Ellen moved to Miami, and the relationship between Aaron and his father improved dramatically. Overnight the two men discovered they had something in common: golf.

Until his father's triple-bypass surgery the year before, the two of them had spent four or five mornings a week shooting nine holes before work. They would be at the course by six and finish before eight. They golfed in Harbor Springs and Charlevoix, and sometimes even Traverse City. But their favorite course was the grassy, tree-covered spread at Bay View Country Club.

Aaron allowed his eyes to scan the greens. They sloped gently downhill from the road in a velvet carpet that seemed to extend all the way to the bay beyond. How many memories had he and his father made here? It had been on the neatly mowed grass below that he had told his father his girl-friend was pregnant. Aaron would never forget the pain in his father's face that morning.

"I won't tell you I'm not disappointed." He paused. "But son, you need to do the right thing and stand by the girl. She's go-ing to have the baby, right?"

"Right. She doesn't want an abortion."

"Well, let her know that we'll do whatever we can to help."

Three months later they were on that golf course again when John asked about the girl, and Aaron broke down.

"She lost the baby, Dad." Aaron had swiped at his tears, embarrassed at the show of emotion.

"I'm sorry, son." His father had faced him

and put an arm on his shoulder.

"I know it wasn't right what we did." They were far out on the seventh tee where no one could see them at that early hour of the morning. "But I was ready to love that child. I don't know, Dad. It's like I miss him. Even though I never knew him. Do you think I'm crazy to feel that way?"

Aaron would always remember the compassion in his father's eyes at that moment. "Son, an unborn child is a child nevertheless. I understand your pain."

No one but he and his father knew about the lost child. And that morning his dad shared something with Aaron that he said he hadn't shared with his other children.

"Your mother had a miscarriage once, too," he said softly. "It was two years after Megan was born and your mother was already five months pregnant. The baby was a boy."

There were tears in his father's eyes. The two hugged and Aaron felt like a little boy again, safe in his daddy's arms.

When they pulled apart, his father smiled sadly. "Believe me, I understand how you feel. A week doesn't go by when I don't think about your brother, how old he would be, what he'd be doing now."

Aaron thought of a hundred other such

moments he and his dad had shared on the golf course. Even when he began having bouts of rage and punching holes in his bedroom door, his father would forgive him and in a few days the two would be back out playing golf.

On the course, Aaron would apologize and his dad would shrug. "Forget about it, son," he would say. "I love you. I always will."

Then he and Aaron would spend another morning talking and teeing off.

But there was something Aaron never said to his father, and the knowledge of that omission burned at Aaron's soul. He had run out of time. His father was gone, and in all their years together, through all the feelings Aaron had shared with no one else, he never once had the courage to tell his father the most important thing of all.

It was growing dark and the course was becoming more difficult to see. Finally, knowing that he would explode if he didn't give in to his desperate grief, Aaron grabbed the steering wheel and laid his head on his forearm.

There, finally, he cried.

Torrents of angry tears spilled from his heart as he remembered the man he had loved and admired, the man who had known him as no one else had. He would give anything, he thought, to be here in the morning with his father preparing to shoot nine holes of golf. Just once more.

He sobbed violently, remembering the hateful things he had said in anger, wanting desperately to take them back. He remembered the last thing he had said to his father . . .

Thursday night Megan and his parents had been watching television. For once he didn't have a date so he'd gotten dressed in his jeans and boots and made plans to meet his buddies at Denim 'N Duds, a country dance club just out of town. He was running late and as he headed for the door he did not intend to waste time telling his parents good-bye.

But his father heard him leaving.

"Son? You going out?" Dad called from the den, his voice pleasant.

"Yeah. Dancing." Aaron leaned into view and cast an impatient look at his father.

"Okay. Have fun." Just before Aaron turned away he caught his father's smile. That warm, full-faced smile that assured Aaron he was loved beyond anything most sons would ever know.

He could have stopped then and said good-bye or wished his father a good night in return. But instead he turned away and walked out the door. That was it. The last time he saw his father alive. His last chance to say the most important words . . . words he had never shared with his father.

Aaron squeezed his eyes tight, but he could not shut out the truth. His father was gone and there was no more time. No time to say the one thing that should have been said.

"Why?" Aaron shouted, slamming his hands down on his steering wheel. There was a cracking sound and he looked at the wheel. A hairline split ran along the top.

Good. Who cares? Who cares about anything?

He climbed out of his truck then, walked around to the back, and jerked open the tailgate. There inside were his golf clubs, a complete set that his father had given him four years ago for Christmas. Angry, nearly blinded by his tears, Aaron pulled the bag from the truck bed and flung it toward the edge of the hill overlooking the course. He strode angrily toward the fallen clubs and then, one at a time, he hurled them with all his might toward the ninth fairway.

When he was finished, when the bag he had toted alongside his father's was completely empty, he sat down on the grassy hill and sobbed. The rage was gone. Minutes became an hour until finally he gazed out toward the golf course again and pulled himself up. For a moment, in his mind's eye, he thought he could see his father in the shadows. Yes, there he was. Waving to him, calling him to come down and play some golf.

"Dad!" Aaron yelled. "Daaaaad!"

"Son?" The image was fading and his father seemed to be having trouble hearing him. "What are you saying, son?"

"Daaad!" Aaron shouted as the image faded completely. "Dad . . . I love you!"

His words echoed over the empty golf course, ricocheted off the sturdy maple trees, and faded softly into the gentle breeze that drifted off the bay.

THIRTEEN

No one said anything to Aaron when he returned to the Barrett home that evening. Instead, his arrival at just before eleven o'clock gave the others a reason to turn in for the night. At Megan's apartment, Ellen and Jane were politely civil but the strain between them was mounting. When they made it through the night without an argument Ellen sank onto her bed with a relieved sigh.

The next day their mother had plans with Aunt Mary, so the three oldest sisters took the children to the park, talked about their father, and shopped for the week's groceries. Remarkably, there were no blowups between Ellen and Jane. It was late afternoon before they reported back to their parents' home. Amy and Frank arrived moments later.

"I brought dinner," Amy said as she struggled through the doorway. She and

Frank carried sacks of submarine sandwiches and potato chips.

Her mother hugged her gratefully. "Thank you. This is wonderful." She took the bags and moved them toward the dining-room table. "Perfect timing. I had no idea what to fix tonight."

Jane busied herself feeding the children while Ellen, Megan, and Aaron silently helped themselves to a sandwich and found a place in the living room. Amy and Frank passed out drinks and then sat down at the dining room, turning their chairs to face the others.

"Do we know what we're doing for the service?" Amy's tone was soft. "I have a few ideas."

Ellen studied her youngest sister. Amy's comments were always made tentatively. She was extremely sensitive to what others thought of her opinions and she had been known to suddenly leave a gathering if she felt offended. As far back as any of them could remember, Amy rarely interjected her opinion in a conversation, and now that she wanted to talk everyone sat a bit straighter and gave her their attention.

"We have a lot to discuss and I want input from all of you children." Their mom had fixed a plate and joined Amy and Frank at the table. "I thought we could get together tomorrow and spend the day working out the details."

"Fine," Ellen and Megan said in unison, and Aaron grunted his approval.

"Of course . . ." Jane said, "I don't know what I'll do with the kids. They're good, but they can't sit still for most of the day while we talk. I guess I'll —"

"Jane," their mother interrupted. "Relax. Aunt Mary will watch the children. She told me she'd be at Megan's apartment first thing in the morning and stay with them all day if necessary."

Jane's chin lifted defiantly, and Ellen and Megan exchanged a quick glance. "Well, if that's in order," Jane said, "then fine." She placed the rest of her sandwich on the plate and stood to gather her things.

"Where are you going?" Amy looked at her.

"If we're going to be here all day tomorrow I think we should make it an early night. I want to spend some time with the children."

"Yeah, but I wanted to talk about music. I remembered last night that Dad really liked that one song, you know, about the rugged cross, the one where —"

"Amy," Jane looked down at her youngest

sister as if she were a small child in need of a reprimand. "That's why we're getting together tomorrow. To talk about rugged crosses and everything that goes with them."

Amy was quiet for a moment, and from where she sat across the room Ellen knew instinctively that Jane had gone too far. The youngest Barrett daughter turned to her husband and nodded. In an instant they were on their feet, headed for the door.

"Amy, you don't have to go just because Jane's leaving." Their mom stood up too. She put a comforting arm across Amy's shoulders.

Ellen raised her eyebrows and stared at the floor. She hated the way their mother treated her youngest sister like a baby. Amy was twenty-five years old and a married woman, after all. Still, the moment things didn't go Amy's way, Mom was immediately at her side, making her feel better.

"I'm leaving," Amy announced to her mother. "If Jane doesn't want me to talk about the service, I won't talk at all."

"What?" Jane shrieked. "I didn't say any-thing to make you leave. Don't blame *me* for your weird behavior."

"See!" Amy said to her mother. Tears filled her eyes and she looked overwhelmed. "We can only talk about something if it's okay with Jane." She wheeled around and faced Jane, who was standing nearby with her mouth open in mock astonishment. "Jane, nobody made you the boss of this family. Why don't you keep your opinions to yourself?"

"What*ever!* I was only stating a fact. This isn't the time to talk about rugged crosses. That's why we're getting together tomorrow."

"But if I want to talk about rugged crosses today, then I'll talk about rugged crosses today!"

Jane's hands flew to her hips and her face grew red. "That's right, Amy. I forgot you were so sensitive about every little thing. I guess we should all just walk around watching what we say. Wouldn't want to hurt little Amy's feelings, now would we?"

Ellen cringed and glanced into the kitchen, wishing she could escape. Jane had definitely stepped over the line with that last comment. Megan and Aaron had moved to the table and were busy eating their sandwiches, pretending not to hear.

"Jane!" Mom fired a scolding look at her second daughter. She had positioned herself between the two sisters, ever the peacemaker. "That wasn't very nice."

"Come on, Frank." Amy took her husband's hand and turned to her mother. "Forget about tomorrow." She looked angrily at Jane. "I won't be where I'm not wanted."

"Amy, don't say that." Their mother followed Amy and Frank to the front door and out into the warm evening. "I want us all here tomorrow. It would mean so much to your father and —"

Her voice grew faint as she trailed after them, leaving an uncomfortable silence in the Barrett home. Jane remained in the center of the room while the others looked at her expectantly.

"Well, what's everyone looking at?" she demanded. "Come on, Megan, Ellen. Let's get the kids and go. Obviously I am not wanted around here."

Ellen stood up and stretched, hoping some of her anxiety would dissipate when she got back to Megan's apartment. Then she gathered her things and those of the children. Just as they were about to leave, their mom returned. Everyone could see she had been crying.

"Don't worry, Mother, I'm leaving." Jane spat the bitter words as she moved toward the front door, the baby on her hip. "I wouldn't want to upset your precious Amy."

Ellen wanted to kick Jane, to make her

think about what she was saying. She looked at her mother, worried, but Mom just drew closer to Jane and took her daughter's face in her hands. "I love *all* of you girls very much, Jane. But I wish you could make more of an effort to get along. You know how sensitive Amy is."

"I know, but I think we need to stop babying her. It's a bit ridiculous."

"Maybe you're right. But there must be a better time to deal with her than the week of your father's funeral. We have a lot to do tomorrow, and I want all of you here."

"Is she coming?" Jane's disgust was clear in her voice.

"I hope so. But please, girls —" Mom looked at Ellen and Megan — "try to get along tomorrow."

"Don't look at me, Mom, I'm doing everything I can," Ellen said. She was carrying Kala and hoped they could get out the door soon. "Why would I come all the way from Miami just to fight with everyone? I want us all to get along, too."

"Right." Jane muttered under her breath, casting a look at Ellen.

Ellen stared at Jane, wondering yet again what she had done to make her sister so angry, so resentful of her.

She glanced at her mother to see her eyes

had filled with tears once more and she seemed on the verge of losing control.

"See, Jane?" Mom pointed out. "That's what I mean. That wasn't necessary. Comments like that tear us apart at a time when we should be holding each other up."

Jane sighed and looked suddenly sheepish. After several seconds she spoke and this time her voice was humble. "You're right. I'm sorry. I guess I must be tired. Besides, no one ever sees any of this from my point of view. . . ."

Ellen exchanged a knowing glance with Megan. Jane's behavior could not be written off just because she was tired. She had been rude and unkind through much of the evening and there was no excuse for her attitude. Ellen shifted her weight, adjusting the child she still held in her arms. She watched Jane impatiently and waited for her to finish so they could leave.

"I didn't mean to upset Amy," Jane continued. "But it'll be hard enough for everyone to spend an entire day planning Dad's funeral. The last thing I want to do is spend tonight talking about it, too."

Mom nodded and put her arms around Jane. "I understand. It's hard for me, too. He was my husband, remember?" She looked at Ellen and her sisters. "I'm going to ask that you girls do everything you can to get along tomorrow and the rest of the week. Understand?"

Jane nodded and returned her mother's hug.

"Ellen?" Mom asked.

"Sure. I'll try. That's all I can do."

While they were saying good-bye, Aaron stood up and left.

"Honey, are you going somewhere?" Mom asked as he slipped past them and headed for his truck.

"Out."

The Barrett women watched in silence as he drove away.

"He probably just needs time alone, Mom," Jane said. "Don't worry about him."

"I know. Go ahead now, go home and get some rest before tomorrow."

The moon was full and there was a warm glow over the sleepy neighborhood as Megan, Ellen, Jane, and the children left for the night. Diane watched them go and then went back inside. She shut the door and locked it. Her sister, Mary, had a key and would be over later to spend the evening with her.

She closed her eyes and realized how consuming silence could be. That was one

245

sound that had seldom filled her home. There had always been family parties, barbecues, jam-making sessions, and dozens of kids filling the halls with laughter. Life at the Barretts' had been a whirlwind of activity, with John always at the center.

Diane looked at the empty living room and thought how sad and lonely a house full of memories could be. She picked up a photograph of her and John at Amy's wedding and studied it. She could still picture him as he walked Amy down the aisle. And Jane, and Ellen before that.

For just an instant she was angry with John, angry that he hadn't heeded the doctors' warnings and given up smoking, angry that he hadn't changed his eating habits. If he had loved them, why hadn't he taken care of himself? He would be alive today if only he'd had the will to change.

Then, just as quickly the anger disappeared. Diane's tears fell onto the glass frame and she carefully rubbed them off with the edge of her faded cotton blouse.

"John, my love," she whispered. "What am I going to do without you?"

That night in a small house three miles away, Frank was doing all he could to comfort Amy, but he was having little success. She had locked herself in the bathroom and was sobbing so hard Frank thought she might pass out. She had already vomited twice, and Frank wondered if she was having a nervous breakdown.

"Amy, please! Come out here so we can talk." He had been trying to get her out since they got home. His voice was gentle but firm. "We can't talk about it while you're in there."

"No! It's my problem, Frank! My family has always treated me this way. There's nothing to talk about."

"But I love you," he said softly. "I want to help. Come out so I can hold you."

Finally, after fifteen minutes of pleading with her, Amy opened the door and collapsed in Frank's arms.

"I'm sorry," she sobbed. "I didn't mean to shut you out."

He led her to their bed in the middle of the room and with one arm around her waist he sat down beside her. "Tell me about it, Amy. I'm here for you. I'll listen."

Amy struggled to calm herself. "It's been like that for years." Her breathing came in short, fast bursts. "Wh-whenever I say anything or try to make a suggestion, someone cuts me off. It's . . . it's like my opinion isn't worth anything because I'm the youngest."

"Aaron is the youngest," Frank corrected gently.

"Oh, I know that." Amy was frustrated as she reached for a tissue and blew her nose. "But I'm the youngest *girl,* and Aaron doesn't talk to anyone, anyway. So I might as well be the youngest."

Frank was silent, encouraging her to continue.

"All my life they've shut me out of their little threesome. Ellen, Jane, and Megan. I was too young to go to the movies with them, too young to go to parties with them. And to tell you the truth, Frank, after a lifetime of sharing a house with them, I don't even really know them."

A sob caught in her throat. "I love them, Frank. They're the only family I have besides you. But when I'm with them I feel like a stranger. They don't call me or write to me or ask me about my life. It's like I'm some kind of fixture in the room. They expect me to be there but they don't expect me to say anything important or to feel hurt when they leave me out."

"Amy, I'm sure you don't feel that way all the time. This is just a hard week. You're all under a lot of pressure."

Amy shook her head fiercely. "No, it's

more than that. My father treated me the same way. Like a tagalong. You know, I tried to think of one time when Dad and I did something special together by ourselves, without any of the others, and I couldn't remember one. Not one single time. I never said anything, never complained about being left out. So no one thought I had needs and hurts and feelings. Now I'm all grown up and I feel like an outsider in my own family."

"They love you, Amy. Really, honey." Frank stroked her shiny dark hair.

"I don't know, Frank. Look at Jane, the way she treats me. You can't think she really loves me. And Megan, she's too caught up in her own life, just like Ellen. Aaron practically hates me because I stand up to him."

"Your mother loves you. Don't forget how much she cares."

"I know." She seemed calmer as she turned to Frank. "You know something strange? Even though I can't think of any special times alone with my dad, he's at the center of every happy childhood memory I have. I was such a serious kid, I might never have learned to laugh if it wasn't for my dad."

Suddenly she was crying again, and he pulled her close.

"Oh, Frank, I'm going to miss him so much."

"I know, honey, I know."

"Do you think he knew how much I loved him?"

"Of course, sweetheart. Of course he knew."

"But I'm not sure I ever really told him. You know, in those exact words."

"Amy, he knew. Believe me."

She struggled to speak. "I loved him with all my heart. He was bigger than life, my hero, my daddy. Frank, he was my laughter. How am I going to live without him?"

Her sobs grew harder and Frank understood. They were coming from a place Amy did not visit often. And so it continued.

Hours after the others had forgotten about Amy's hurt feelings, Frank held his wife close while she cried for the man who, long ago on a carefree yesterday, had taught her to laugh.

FOURTEEN

Tuesday morning a thick layer of gray clouds came off the bay and covered Petoskey, making it unseasonably cool for July — and appropriately dismal. Just before eight o'clock Aunt Mary arrived in typical timely fashion, chattering about how good it was that everyone could be together to make plans for the funeral and what a wonderful support system they were for each other.

"I just know your mother will be so pleased, what with everyone back together under one roof. I'm sure you'll all work well together, planning the service and making decisions for your mother. You know, this is one of those things where everyone really needs to make their suggestions and see them carried through because, well, after all he was . . ."

Ellen stopped listening and returned to the bathroom to finish her makeup. Aunt Mary meant well. It was just that the woman was hopelessly out of touch with the way they were feeling. Until Aunt Mary arrived, the three sisters had been lost in their private thoughts, savoring the heavy solitude and the relative lack of tension it afforded them.

Running a brush through her hair, Ellen stared at herself in the mirror. For an instant she wondered how much she had changed since she was in high school . . . back when Jake thought she was the prettiest girl in Petoskey. She dismissed the thought as quickly as it had come.

She had long since perfected the art of disregarding thoughts about Jake. In the early days after she embraced Christianity, Ellen learned from Scripture that the best way to steer clear of a weakness was to never entertain thoughts about it. Jake was her strongest weakness back then, so when thoughts of him came she refused to entertain them, recalling instead specific memory verses from the Bible.

Memory verses. Ellen met her reflected gaze thoughtfully. *It's been years since I've even tried to commit a Bible verse to memory.* For an instant she was pierced with guilt, but she shrugged that off as well. *Later. When I'm back home and things are settled. Then I'll get back into the Word.*

She ran a dab of clear gloss over her lips and when she was satisfied with her appearance, she gathered her purse and a pad of paper. They had a long day ahead of them. It was one thing to make suggestions, and quite another to plan a funeral service. Ellen intended to take notes and help them stay on track so they could finish by the end of the day.

Her sisters were ready to go when she walked back into the main room. Jane was rattling off instructions for the children, advising Aunt Mary to call if there were any problems.

"We'll probably come back for lunch, at least I will if I can get a ride." Jane glanced at Megan. "Is that okay?"

"Sure, we can all come back for lunch. We'll probably need a break by then, anyway."

Ellen nodded. "Sounds good."

She was not about to disagree over lunch plans. Not when they had so much to work through that day. The three sisters bid their aunt good-bye and left.

"She's a talker," Megan said as they walked to her parking space outside the building.

"Yes, that must be where Ellen gets it," Jane added.

Normally Ellen would have laughed. There was no secret in the fact that she was a talker or that she had received a fair amount of teasing for it over the years. But in light of Jane's attitude the last few days, Ellen felt attacked. Still, she said nothing. There was more satisfaction in keeping peace.

Ellen looked at her sisters. "Is Amy coming? Did anyone call Mom and find out?"

Megan shook her head, but Jane snorted sarcastically. "She'll be there. That whole little demonstration last night was just a big play for attention. When Amy wants attention, Amy gets it."

Her comments were met with silence. There was no point defending Amy when to do so would just bring further conflict. The ride to the Barrett home was quiet, and Ellen wondered if that was the secret to peace with her sisters. Simply stop talking.

They arrived at quarter past eight, just as Aaron appeared from his bedroom, shaved and showered. For the first time in two days he was not wearing his dark glasses. Five minutes later, Amy and Frank pulled up.

"Oh, thank God," Mom muttered quietly. She settled into one of the dining-room chairs and watched the couple make their way up the walk and into the house.

Ellen studied the room. Mom had arranged a circle of seating for the occasion. Aaron claimed the oversized stuffed chair, the one their father had always used, while Amy and Frank shared the sofa with Megan. Jane sat on a chair in the corner of the room and Ellen completed the circle by taking the chair between Aaron and their mother.

It felt good to gather for a reason, Ellen realized. It almost seemed to give them some sense of purpose. Since Sunday night she and the others had been helpless to do anything but talk about John Barrett's terrible health and how his death could have been prevented and how relatively wonderful it was that he hadn't suffered. Now . . . she studied the faces around her. Now they were ready to take action.

"Well." Her mother's voice was shaky but she managed a weak smile. "I'm glad you're all here. We have a lot to plan and I want us to do it together. Your father would have wanted it that way."

Ellen prepared to write as her mother flipped through several pages of notes and turned to the first page of a small booklet.

"The priest told me we can plan whatever kind of funeral service we want. I had no idea where to start so that's one of the reasons I wanted you all here."

Silence.

"Father Joe gave me this little book." She held it high. "It gives us a guideline we can follow as we make decisions."

"Father Joe?" Ellen asked.

"Yes. He's new at St. Francis."

"He's not officiating at the funeral, is he?"

"I don't know, Ellen. Do you have a problem with Father Joe?"

"Dad didn't even know him," Megan cut in.

"Yeah," Ellen agreed. "Father Jim is the one Dad knew. He's the one we brought cookies to when we went caroling, right?" She looked at Megan for support.

"Right, Father Jim. Mom, the funeral should be led by someone who knew him."

Jane clucked her tongue. "Like it matters. The people at St. Francis don't know each other, anyway."

"It *does* matter," Ellen said softly. "We don't want some guy up there saying how sad it is that John Barrett died, and, gee, it would have been nice if he'd known him. The minister in charge of a funeral should at least know something about the deceased."

"He's not a minister, he's a priest," Mom corrected.

"That's not true, Jane." Amy met her

sister's gaze. "I happen to know many of the people at St. Francis quite well."

"Oh, sure you do." Aaron shifted positions restlessly.

"Who cares who knows each other at St. Francis?" Jane's eyebrows met in the middle of her forehead and she glared at Amy. "I was just saying that it doesn't matter who says the funeral."

"I think it does." Ellen was quiet but firm.

"Well, excuse *me*, Ellen." Jane crossed her arms angrily and sat back hard. "Forget I said anything."

"Come on, Jane." *Control my tongue, Lord,* Ellen prayed. She waited a moment, calming herself. "Don't take it personally. It's just that we should do our best to have Father Jim officiate the funeral because Dad knew him. I think it's only right."

Their mother wrote something on the pad of paper. "What about you Aaron, Amy? Do you think it matters who says the funeral?"

"Dad's dead," Aaron said simply. "He won't know whether it's Father Jim or Father Joe or Sam the Barber."

Amy was silent.

Ellen looked at her brother curiously and was struck again by the emotions that must be warring inside of him.

"At least I'm not the only one," Jane muttered. "I agree with Aaron. Who cares which priest says the funeral?"

Ellen looked around the circle at the faces of her family. "Whatever. If that makes everyone happy." She stared at her blank notepad and tapped her pen nervously. *Well, Lord, I'm obviously not prepared for this . . .* She had expected resistance from Jane, of course, but she had not planned on Aaron siding against her, too. "I just thought it would be nice to have someone who knew Dad say a few words at his funeral."

"There's nothing wrong with having someone who knew your father speak about him at the funeral," Mom said. "In fact, that's something else I want to talk about. I think it would be wonderful if each of you could write something and read it at the funeral. We don't have to discuss it yet but be thinking about the idea."

"I'm not getting up in front of a bunch of people and reading something," Amy announced. "No way."

"Me, neither," Aaron said. "What's the point?"

Their mother sighed. "It's a chance to tell the world about your dad, who he was in your life. Maybe by doing so it'll be easier to let him go."

"I could write a book about him and it

wouldn't be easy to let him go," Ellen said lightly. "But if you want us to do something like that I'm in. I love putting my feelings into words."

Jane sneered. "I think we know that, Ellen." She took on a high-pitched voice. " 'Ellen Barrett, the great writer.' I'm sure you'd love to write something about Dad and I'm sure you'd enjoy making the rest of us look bad while you were at it."

"Jane! Stop that!" Mom ordered.

Ellen stared at Jane, astonished. Only a blind person could miss the hatred in her younger sister's eyes. *Jesus, help us! This is such a disaster.* She drew a deep breath, then put a hand on her mother's arm. "It's okay, Mom. I'm under no delusions here. I know how Jane feels about me."

Jane glared at Ellen but remained silent.

Their mother looked at each of them as they sat there. "What I'm saying is that, rather than having a priest do all the talking, I'd like you five children to help us remember who your father was and why we loved him. Don't make any decisions about my idea one way or the other. Just think about it."

Thankfully, the disagreements seemed to ease after that. They spent two hours discussing which Bible verses best reflected their father, when they should be read during the service, and who should read them. They decided to stay with the twenty-third Psalm, a favorite of their father's since he'd recited it aloud as valedictorian of his graduating class in college. Megan would read that passage.

"What about the Serenity Prayer?" Ellen asked. "Dad always liked that."

"That's not a Bible verse, Ellen. The priest wanted two Bible verses." Jane's tone was condescending, and Ellen had to fight the urge to slap her.

"Mom, did the priest want us to plan the service or not?" Ellen asked.

"Yeah," Amy interjected. "He said we could plan it ourselves, right?"

Ellen realized that Amy was probably taking her side to annoy Jane, and the thought only raised Ellen's anxiety level. Amy didn't hold a grudge so much as she nursed it, breathing life into it as long as possible. After the fiasco the night before, Amy would be upset with Jane for months.

"Yes, Ellen, that's right." Mom's tone was even as she answered. She seemed determined to remain unaffected by the tension in the room. "We can read whatever prayer or poem or Bible verse we'd like. Ellen, why don't you read that prayer to us. Do you have it handy?"

"Yes, I jotted it down over the weekend in case we could use it." She flipped through her notepad. "Here it is. 'God grant me the serenity to accept the things I cannot change, the strength to change the things I can, and the wisdom to know the difference.' "

There was a moment of silence.

"That sounds like Dad," Aaron said finally, and Ellen raised an eyebrow in surprise. She had heard her brother talk more that morning than in the past four years combined.

"Okay, then. Unless someone objects, I think maybe Ellen should read that at the service."

"What if *I* want to read a Bible verse?" Jane's eyes were hard, her tone defensive. "Why should Megan and Ellen be the only ones to read something?"

"Well then, pick something," Mom said pleasantly. "Everyone can read a verse as far as I'm concerned."

"No, that's all right." Jane looked away, the picture of persecuted martyrdom. "It's probably better this way. Ellen and Megan are better in front of people. Dad would have wanted them to read."

"Well," Megan stood up and reached for

her purse. She looked and sounded disgusted with Jane's attitude. "I've had about enough for a while." She turned matter-of-factly toward Jane. "You said you wanted to go back for lunch. It's eleven-thirty. I'm ready if you are."

"Oh." There was obvious hurt in their mother's voice. "I thought you could all have lunch here. We're finally together and getting something done. Why don't you stay and I'll fix something for everyone?"

"We could," Jane said as she collected her purse and headed for the front door. "But I need to get back and see the kids."

Ellen was torn. She didn't want to spend any more time with Jane than was absolutely necessary, but she agreed with Megan that they needed a break from the discussion. She hoped their mother would not be too disappointed.

She shrugged. "I guess I'll go with Megan and Jane. Is that all right, Mom?"

Her mother's crestfallen expression belied her words. "I suppose. I just thought we could spend the entire day together and continue the plans while we ate."

"We'll be back right after lunch. And don't worry —" Jane crossed the room and hugged her mother — "we're working things out, and I think it's going very well so far.

Dad would approve."

Ellen stared in stunned confusion. How could Jane be so thoughtless one minute and so gentle the next?

"Think we'll be done before dinner?" Jane asked as she headed for the front door.

"I hope so. This is exhausting." Mom stood up and stretched. "Maybe I'll take a nap while you're gone."

"Good idea," Jane hugged her again.

"Be nice . . ." Their mother's voice broke. "Please, Jane."

Jane pulled back, studied Mom's face, then nodded slowly. "I will. I'm sorry."

Quick tears stung Ellen's eyes. *Lord, I will never understand Jane. Not for as long as I live.* A sad desperation filled Ellen as she followed her sisters to the door.

After the three sisters were gone, Diane Barrett gave a small sigh. *Oh, John, what's happened to our family?* She wasn't sure how much more of this tension she could take.

Amy and Frank rose from the sofa and moved toward the front door.

"Frank and I are gonna get some hamburgers. You want one, Mom? Aaron?"

Diane smiled at her youngest daughter. "Sure, honey, thanks. Let me give you some money."

"Aaron?" Amy looked at him expectantly.

"A double. No onions." Aaron stood up and lumbered into the den where he flipped on the television. The others could hear what sounded like a golf competition underway. Aaron watched for a moment and then turned the channel.

"Talkative, huh?" Frank broke the silence Aaron had left in his wake. Frank managed a plastic smile from behind his thick, round glasses. There were beads of perspiration forming along his thinning hairline, and he looked especially tense.

"I'm sorry, Frank," Diane patted his shoulder as he and Amy prepared to leave. "Don't take it personally."

Frank shrugged and shook his head quickly. "He's very immature. That's not something I take personally."

Diane bid them good-bye, thankful that Frank was an intelligent man. He was thirty-eight and had come into Amy's life at a time when she was trying to decide what to do with her future. She was a pretty girl with a fuller figure than her sisters. She hated the way men ogled her chest whenever she went out. Before meeting Frank she had confided in Diane that she was seriously thinking about becoming a nun.

In response her father had taught her how

to use his computer to tap into electronic bulletin boards. After that, Amy spent hours chatting with people she could neither see nor hear. Until then, she had never found a social niche that suited her. But when her fingers made contact with the computer keyboard, she entered a world that seemed custom-made for her alone. It was a world in which she had thrived.

A few months later she began having nightly computerized conversations with a man whose screen name was "Franco." She was going by the name "Aimless," something her friends had called her in high school. After exchanging photographs in the mail, they finally agreed to meet one afternoon at a busy restaurant. Six weeks later they were engaged, and Frank quickly found his place in their family. He and John could talk for hours about computers. John had even said that, in Frank, he saw himself as a young man: intelligent, idealistic, and replete with limitless energy.

Frank ran his own business assembling computers and selling them through mail-order advertisements. He easily earned enough money to keep Amy quite comfortable. After they were married Amy continued working at the private day care, but they certainly did not need her income to make ends meet.

Frank was slightly plump and more than a little balding. He had almost white blond hair and was only an inch taller than Amy. From their first meeting, Frank doted on Amy and gave her the security she craved. Diane thought they were a perfect match.

She watched them now as they drove away, and suddenly she felt exhausted. The sadness was so tiring, so gut wrenching. She wondered if she would ever wake up feeling refreshed and free of the burden John's death had placed on her. She closed her eyes and rubbed her neck. Then she padded slowly down the hallway, past the spot where John had died, back to the bedroom they'd shared for twenty-one years. The pillows still smelled like him.

In two minutes she had cried herself to sleep.

FIFTEEN

Back at Megan's apartment, the sisters found Aunt Mary struggling with the children. Kyle had refused his bottle and spit up his applesauce on Megan's living room floor. Kala and Koley had fought all morning over what toy belonged to whom, who had played with it longest, and whose turn it was now.

Aunt Mary looked on the verge of a breakdown.

Jane stepped into the middle of the chaos and calmly directed her children. In minutes there was peace again.

"Kyle, get your pacifier," she told the young boy. She walked to the spot where his playpen was set up. "Now lie down on your blanket and close your eyes." She knelt beside him, stroked his forehead, and hummed softly. The child was asleep almost instantly.

Next she looked at Koley. "Were you

mean to your sister?" she asked softly. Megan disappeared to her room and Ellen found a chair off in the distance where she could watch Jane interact with her children.

"Yes, Mommy." Koley's deep brown eyes were remorseful, full of shame.

"Was that the right thing to do?"

Ellen wondered if Jane caught the irony in her statement. After all, she hadn't exactly been kind to *her* sister that morning.

"No, Mommy."

"Well, I want you to go give Kala a kiss and tell her you're sorry."

The little boy did as he was told, hugging his small sister so tight she could barely breathe.

"That's fine." Jane motioned her children closer and kissed each of them on their foreheads. "I love you both very much and I know you're going to behave better for Aunt Mary this afternoon while we're gone. But right now I want you to find a spot on the floor and lie down. It's nap time."

Ellen watched, amazed. Jane made parenting look easy, and Ellen wondered whether she would be so patient if she had children.

Once the children were settled Jane fixed herself a sandwich. Megan joined Ellen at the small table, and Aunt Mary rested on the couch, exhausted from the morning.

"Are you sure you can stay and watch them this afternoon?" Jane asked. "If it's too much I can probably take them to Mom's."

"No, no —" Aunt Mary straightened herself and tried to smile — "Really, it's all right. I think after they have a good nap everything'll be just fine. In fact, I think I'll go out and pick up something to eat before you leave."

Jane nodded. "Don't rush. And thanks again, Aunt Mary. I'm sorry they were such a handful."

"Oh, it's no problem. You all have a lot to work out and this is the least I can do for your mother."

Aunt Mary and the girls' mother were very close; they had been for as long as anyone could remember. Like Ellen and Jane, they were only two years apart, but somehow through the years they had forged a camaraderie that superseded petty resentments.

When Aunt Mary was gone, Ellen sighed. "She really seems frazzled. Too bad we can't just take the kids back to Mom's with us. I think she could use a break."

Jane lowered her sandwich and stared at Ellen, her eyes glittering.

"If you're trying to say that my children

aren't well behaved, then maybe you'd better keep your comments to yourself."

Ellen threw her hands in the air in mock surrender. She had tried unsuccessfully to ignore Jane's comments all morning, but this was it. She'd reached her limit.

"Jane, no matter what I say you take it wrong."

"Well, then, here's some advice, Ellen. When it comes to other people's kids, keep your mouth shut." She snorted. "Of course, you've never been able to keep your mouth shut about anything."

Ellen stood, her body shaking with anger, and stared down at her sister. "What *is* with you, Jane?" She realized she was shouting, but she didn't care. Across the room one of the sleeping children stirred. She struggled to regain her composure. "Exactly why is it you hate me?"

"Be *quiet,* Ellen," Jane hissed. "You'll wake the kids."

"Oh, now it's the *kids* again. *Listen* to yourself, Jane. Listen to how you talk to me whenever the kids are involved." Ellen lowered her voice, but she couldn't hide her rage. She was losing control. "You treat me like I'm some inept, brainless woman who has no idea what to say or do around someone younger than eighteen. Well, get

270

off your high horse, sister *dear.* You're a wonderful mother, but just because I don't have children doesn't mean I don't know anything about them."

Jane raised her eyebrows sarcastically and picked up her sandwich. "If you knew anything about children, you wouldn't have chosen a career over motherhood. But that's just my opinion."

The words were a slap that took Ellen's breath away. Her eyes filled with tears; her face twisted in pain. "Grow up, Jane! You're so caught up in your own little bitter world that you don't even know what you're saying —" Ellen broke off, and two tears trickled down her face.

Megan dropped her head in her hands and sighed. "You guys, this is so stupid. You know you love each other, so why don't you just apologize and get over it."

Ellen spun to face her. "Megan, this has nothing to do with me. I've done everything humanly possible to get along with Jane, but she's determined to make life miserable for me. Am I the only one who sees it?"

"I don't know." Megan stood up abruptly. "You guys'll have to work it out on your own. I'm not taking sides." With that she headed for her bedroom.

"I'm leaving," Ellen announced.

"We'll leave together. In about thirty minutes."

Ellen looked at Megan. "No. We won't. I'm walking back to Mom and Dad's." Ellen swung her purse over her shoulder and marched toward the front door. The Barrett home was two miles away, but Ellen would have walked ten rather than spend another minute in the same room with Jane. She stared at Megan before she left. "I'm not mad at you. I just can't take her abuse anymore."

Jane shrugged, took a bite of her sandwich, and watched unsympathetically as Ellen walked to the door. "Get over it," she muttered. And then to Megan, "She's always overreacting about something."

It was a thick, humid afternoon and Leslie Maple wandered outside her Pennsylvania house toward her mailbox. She sorted through a stack of items as she made her way back in. Credit-card offers, advertising, an insurance statement. Then she saw it. A hand-addressed, pale blue envelope postmarked Petoskey, Michigan. The town where she'd grown up. She set down the other mail and carefully ripped open the blue paper. Inside was a brief note and a newspaper article.

"Thought you'd like to know about this," the note read. "Take care and drop me a line sometime." It was from Carolann Hanson. Carolann had graduated from Petoskey the same year as Leslie. And Ellen Barrett. Leslie smiled at the thought of her best friend from high school. When Ellen moved to Ann Arbor, Leslie had been devastated, but it had helped that she and Carolann began attending Bible studies together and meeting once a week for prayer. Leslie and Carolann still exchanged Christmas cards and remembered to pray for each other's families.

Leslie opened the clipping and saw that it was an obituary. Her heart sank and tears flooded her eyes. John Barrett, Ellen's father, had suffered a heart attack and died. Leslie remembered Mr. Barrett vividly, his broad smile and the way he made Ellen's friends feel so welcome in his home. She and Ellen's other friends had loved Mr. Barrett and even called him Dad when they stopped by to visit. He was just that kind of parent.

She sighed and thought of Ellen, of how devastated she must be. Then as naturally as she lived and breathed, Leslie bowed her head and began to pray.

■ ■ ■ ■

By the time everyone was back in place at the Barrett home it was one-thirty. Ellen sat in stony silence, not even looking at Jane. The anger between them was palpable, and the room was almost electrically charged with tension.

Their mother studied the faces before her, and sighed. "First, I think we need to take care of whatever happened between Ellen and Jane."

"No problem here," Jane said flatly.

Ellen stared at Jane. *Two could play that game.* She turned and smiled at their mother. "Everything's fine."

Their mother looked skeptically at her daughters. Across the room, Frank yawned and checked his watch.

"Well," she continued, "I know there's a problem between you two, but if you don't want to talk about it then let's get on with it. We still have a lot of planning to do."

"About the music," Amy jumped in. "Like I was trying to say last night —" She cast a disgusted glance toward Jane — "I think it would be nice if someone played that rugged cross song."

" 'The Old Rugged Cross,' " Jane

snapped, providing the title of the song self-righteously.

"The church has offered its organist and soloist for Saturday if we're interested. So maybe we could make that a solo number early in the service," their mother said. She wrote something down.

"You're right, Amy," Megan said. "Dad loved that song. I think we should ask the soloist to sing it."

Mom nodded. "What do you think, Aaron? Girls?"

"Fine." Aaron was wearing his dark glasses again, and Ellen thought his cheeks looked tearstained.

"Fine," Jane added.

"Ellen?"

"Sure."

"Sure? Does that mean you'd rather have a different song?"

"No, Mom." Ellen was drained, and she felt almost sick. The walk had done little to ease her anxiety. She'd been too angry to feel like praying, so she'd spent the time thinking about her father first, and then about her marriage. In her haste she had forgotten her notepad, and she felt help-lessly unorganized and a bit adrift without a distraction should the conversation become too heated. *If Dad were still alive I'd be able*

275

to count on his support. But her father wasn't alive. He was gone. Forever. And Ellen felt his absence more keenly with each passing moment.

"Ellen?" her mother asked again. "Would you rather have a different song?"

Wearily, she tried to explain herself. "I don't want a different song. It's just hard for me to get excited about songs that will be sung at Dad's funeral."

Her mother sighed. Ellen thought her mother had sighed more these past days than in her whole life.

"Ellen, dear, no one's asking you to be excited. It's a fact of life. We have to plan his funeral service or it won't get done. Try to understand."

"I know. I'm sorry."

Mom looked at her notes again. "Now, Megan. Have you considered singing at the service?"

Megan stared at her feet and fumbled her fingers uncomfortably. Ellen wondered at the hesitation. Everyone knew her sister had a beautiful voice, so much so that she was a favorite at local weddings and Christmas pageants. "I've thought about it." She hesitated. "I just don't think I could pull it off, Mom."

"Are you sure, honey? Your father loved to

hear you sing."

Megan nodded. "I'm sorry. It would be too much for me."

"Okay, then, I think other than that we'll just let the organist choose whatever music she wants."

There were nods of approval around the room.

And so it continued.

Their mother led them from one topic of concern to another. They decided to use roses throughout the church since their father loved red, and they agreed on a time for the service. Next they spent an hour discussing whether to use a two-page program with their dad's picture on the front or stick with tiny prayer cards. Once they decided on the two-page program, they worked another two hours on the contents.

They agreed to pick out a coffin on Thursday and to make Friday the private and public viewing day at the mortuary. Ellen and Aaron were opposed to the viewing, but their mother was adamant.

"It's important that we have a chance to say good-bye and see him as he'll be when we bury him. It makes it more real."

Ellen shuddered at the thought. "He's already gone, Mom. I mean, we can look at his dead body but we won't be looking at him. That's just a shell of who he was."

"Mom isn't interested in your theology lesson, Ellen." Jane's tone was typically dry.

"Girls! That's enough. We're having a viewing and that's final."

Their mother sorted through her notes and glanced at her watch. Ellen followed suit. It was five-thirty. There were cold cuts and various breads and salads in the refrigerator and they had planned to eat no later than six. They weren't finished, but Ellen hoped they would take a break soon. They could always finish after dinner if necessary.

"Okay." Mom glanced at her notes once more. "We still have to decide whether we want a full Mass or a shortened service where we do more of the talking."

"A Mass is too impersonal. Especially at St. Francis," Megan said. "Besides, I thought we were each going to write something about Dad and read it at the service."

"We talked about it but we didn't decide anything." Amy glanced around the room. "I couldn't get up in front of that many people if my life depended on it."

"Same here," Aaron grunted.

"I think I've changed my mind on that. I agree with Amy and Aaron." At this pronouncement, everyone in the room turned and stared at Ellen.

"You don't want to write something about Dad?" Megan was clearly shocked.

"Not for his funeral." She had thought about reading a eulogy and decided against it during the walk from Megan's apartment. "I've written him a thousand things in the past. He's gone now. I can't imagine summing up a lifetime of feelings in a two-minute eulogy. It'd be impossible. Let's forget it."

Jane cocked her head to one side and considered Ellen's statement. "I think we should do whatever Mom wants. Regardless of how Aaron and Amy —" she hesitated for effect — "and *Ellen* feel."

"Well, then —" Ellen stood — "maybe it's time to wrap things up for the night and get back to the apartment." It was all Ellen could do to keep her tone civil. It was obvious that Jane had agreed with the idea of individually prepared eulogies to spite her. Ellen was sick to death of her sister's petty behavior. She just wanted to get back to Megan's before she unleashed her rising anger on Jane, despite her mother's request that they get along.

"Sit down, Ellen," Jane ordered. "We're right in the middle of trying to work this out. We all heard what Mom said. She wants us to write a eulogy, however brief, and read

279

it at the funeral. I think we should at least give her idea a chance."

Ellen pinned her with a glare, then smiled sweetly. "And I think Aunt Mary's probably ready for a break after watching your children all day. Why don't we stop for now, pick up the kids, and come back later?"

Jane's face grew red. "I don't need *you* telling me when to give Aunt Mary a break. I can handle my children perfectly fine, thank you. That is one area where you can't possibly know more than I do."

"Here we go," Megan muttered under her breath while the others squirmed uncomfortably.

"Jane, hear me out." Ellen's words were carefully controlled, but they did not hide her frustration. "You know the kids gave Aunt Mary a hard time this morning. Why make her work longer than she has to? Let's take a break, get the kids, and come back."

Ellen clenched her teeth so hard they grated together. Being around Jane was like being subjected to mental torture — and she wasn't finished yet.

"My kids are not the big problem you make them out to be." Jane raised her voice. "What would *you* know about raising kids? Like I said earlier, anyone who would choose a career over motherhood certainly has no room to comment about another person's children!"

Ellen felt her control dissolve. Angry tears filled her eyes and she clenched her fists, driving them into her knees. "Jane, you are the coldest person I know! What happened to you? You and I used to be best friends when we were little and now look at you!"

"We aren't little anymore!" Jane spat.

Aaron got up and headed outside. The others left the room one by one until finally there was only Ellen and Jane, staring angrily at each other.

"No, we're not little anymore," Ellen said. "That's true. But we're still sisters and nothing can change that." Ellen began to sob. The fight was gone from her voice and in its place was a terrible sadness. "I'm sick of you treating me like some kind of cosmopolitan ice queen. I have feelings, too."

Jane remained silent while Ellen's sobs became more convulsive. "Mike and I . . . we've tried to have children —" She broke off.

I can't, God. I can't tell her this.

But she knew she had to. When she tried to speak, the words came out in grief-stricken sobs. "I've . . . I've lost two . . . babies, Jane." She tried to catch her breath but the sobs continued to wrack her body.

"Do you have any idea how that feels? To know there's a life inside you, and then . . . then . . . it's gone?" She drew in several quick, jerky breaths and then exhaled slowly, trying to compose herself. "Right now . . . I'm . . . I'm just not ready to try again."

Jane's lower jaw dropped and her eyebrows raised slightly. She looked instantly remorseful. Ellen wrapped her arms around herself protectively, and suddenly her mother and Megan were there, putting their arms around her.

"Oh, sweetheart, I didn't know," her mother said. "Why didn't you tell me?"

"Dad knew. He told me not to say anything to anyone else if I didn't want to. It was too hard to talk about it."

"Honey, I'm so sorry." Mom hugged her.

"Ellen." Jane's voice was low, full of misery. "I'm sorry, too. I never guessed . . . And I've been such a jerk today. I don't know what's wrong with me." She looked away quickly, but not before Ellen had seen the look in her eyes. Jane was lying. There was a reason why she'd been behaving so terribly but she was refusing to tell them.

Why won't she tell me, Father? Ellen's heart cried. *How long will this go on?*

When Jane turned back to her, there were tears in her eyes, too. "I'm — I'm sorry about your miscarriages. I didn't know."

Ellen's anger rose again. "Of *course* you didn't know. How could you? You hardly talk to me anymore. But does that give you license to be angry with me for being childless? I swear, Jane, you think you're the only one in the world who's hurting."

Ellen pulled away from the group and headed for her parents' bedroom. "I need to be alone for a while."

No one followed her.

Once inside she shut the door and sat down on her father's side of the bed. She stared at the telephone through a blurry veil of tears. Since Sunday she had been so busy defending herself and avoiding Jane's wrath that she hadn't called Mike.

She remembered their argument the night before she left, and she was angry all over again. She wouldn't call him. Not now when she was so upset. He would only think he was right about not coming to Petoskey.

She took a tissue off her father's nightstand and blew her nose.

"Why, Dad?" she whispered brokenly.

She missed her father so badly. And now she was trapped in his house, surrounded by reminders of him, and faced with at least one sister who didn't even like her. She clenched her jaw.

"I want out of here." She glanced around the room, desperately seeking an escape.

She had no car; she would probably be stuck at the house until late that night. Her eyes fell on the Petoskey area White Pages.

Suddenly an idea hit her.

It was crazy . . . or was it?

She picked up the phone book and considered what she was about to do. She thought about the way Jane had made life miserable for the past three days. Then she thought about Mike and how he had refused to make even the smallest sacrifice for her sake.

With angry resolve, she took a deep breath and thumbed through the book to the S section. Scanning the columns of names and numbers she finally found the one she was looking for.

Jake Sadler.

She picked up the telephone and dialed his number. Then she held her breath and waited.

That night, in the brand new wing of the First Baptist church fellowship hall in Pine City, Pennsylvania, Leslie Maple and twenty other women were meeting to discuss the need for a church prayer line. The conversation was heated.

"If someone wants prayer they can call

their closest friends and ask for it," Erma Brockmeir said. She sounded self-righteous and she knit her brows together in distaste.

"That's right," someone else spouted. "Anything more and we'd have ourselves a full-fledged gossip channel."

Leslie Maple stood up and waited until the chatter died down. "If we are to believe in the power of prayer," she began softly, "if we are to take the Lord at his word and lay our requests at his feet, then we have no choice. We must pray when we are alone and when we are together. We must pray constantly and we must pray as a body. A prayer line is the best, most efficient way to let the congregation know when someone is in dire need of prayer."

She stared beseechingly at the women. "If we are not willing to be part of that kind of prayer," she hesitated, "then we are failing to do what Jesus wants. We are failing him."

Several of the faces about the room softened and Imogene Spencer positioned her aluminum cane and slowly struggled to her feet. "As the church secretary at First Baptist, I, for one, think Leslie is right. Sometimes we older women need to listen to the younger set. Their ideas may be different than what we're used to, but it is a disgrace to think we have grown so deaf to the Spirit of God that we cannot hear his wisdom in the their youthful words." She paused. "I say we start the prayer line today. As soon as we can find people who will make it work." She studied the women and cleared her throat. "Now, can I see a show of hands." She raised hers high over her head. "Who else is willing to join the prayer line?"

The ladies looked from one to another, then slowly a teary-eyed Erma Brockmeir rose her hand. Two women in the back row added their hands, and in the front row an entire section lifted theirs. Leslie grinned and pulled Imogene Spencer into a hug as the remaining ladies raised their hands.

"Well, my dear," Erma said. "Let's get busy. How exactly do we start a prayer line, anyway?"

SIXTEEN

Jake Sadler twisted the cap off a cold bottle of Pepsi, sank deep into his leather sofa, and closed his eyes. He had taken orders for more than a hundred windows that day and he was exhausted.

He reached down, picked up a week-old copy of the *Petoskey Times* and flipped to the Lifestyles section. There, sprawled across the top of the page, was an article about his company.

"Sadler's personal touch is the best thing to happen to windows and doors since the discovery of wood," the article stated. That explained the high number of orders he was getting. A person couldn't pay for that kind of advertising. Odds were good he'd reap the rewards for weeks to come. Jake studied the news clipping, remembering how it had been at the beginning. Sadler Custom Windows and Doors had been born in the early 1980s, after construction in Northern

Michigan had slowed and often left Jake unemployed. Quick research told him that thousands of homes were nearly thirty years old and in need of renovation. Especially the custom homes that lined the shores of Harbor Springs, Petoskey, and Charlevoix. He tinkered around with several French and Victorian designs and finally launched his own business. Thereafter, his company supplied custom windows and doors specifically for those homes.

That was six years ago and now his business had grown beyond anything he had imagined. It brought him a hefty six-figure income and required him to employ three additional men.

Jake lived like a man who knew the definition of success. He owned a large split-level home in Harbor Pointe, a premier, gated community situated on the northern peninsula of Little Traverse Bay. Technically the home was in Harbor Springs, but through windows of his own design he could gaze across the bay at the shores of Petoskey. The city limits were barely twenty minutes away.

He had a new boat, a new truck, a self-employed pension plan. Even before the article in the *Times,* his business had been thriving, gaining notice throughout Northern Michigan.

Still, Jake was restless, vaguely dissatisfied with life. He was busy at work and sometimes went out socially, but there was no one special. There hadn't been since Ellen Barrett.

"The business needs me," he told the women who had come and gone over the years. But he knew that wasn't completely true. Every now and then when he'd walk through his neighborhood or relax on his back deck, staring at the bay, he would think about Ellen . . . and wonder.

Tonight was one of those times.

John Barrett had died that past Friday. Jake heard the news hours later from his high school friend, Andy Conover. Andy worked as a technician in the hospital emergency room and was on duty the day John Barrett had suffered his heart attack. When a nurse mentioned the patient's last name, Andy became curious. He called Jake as soon as he got home.

"What was Ellen's dad's name?"

"Ellen Barrett?"

"Yes, what was her dad's name?"

"John. John Barrett." Jake was struck by the urgency in Andy's voice. "Why?"

"Oh, man, I thought so. We had him in ER today." Andy paused. "Jake, he's dead. Massive heart attack. Guy didn't have a chance."

The news hit Jake hard, and he hadn't stopped thinking of Ellen since. Certainly she would come out for her dad's funeral. She was probably already in town. She and Jane and the other Barretts.

Jake took a swig of his drink and wondered if there were still problems between Ellen and Jane. Back when he and Ellen were together it seemed he was constantly acting as referee for the sisters. In the end they had always worked things out, but Jake's last year with Ellen had been one of the worst.

That year Jane and Ellen had shared an apartment a few miles from their parents' house. It was 1988 and Troy was not yet back in Jane's life. Somehow, Ellen managed to look back on that year as a happy one. Jake remembered differently.

Jane was forever upset with Ellen for leaving dirty dishes in the sink or piling the trash so it overflowed. Ellen often forgot to tidy the living area and was, in general, a poor housekeeper. She planned too many activities for too short a time and inevitably her house was the first thing to suffer.

Ellen's messy habits had not been a problem outside of home. But as a roommate, Ellen's messiness was wearisome and Jake thought Jane had every right to express her concern. What bothered Jake back then was Jane's tone of voice when she spoke to Ellen. Jake would listen between the lines and what he heard was a lifetime of hate and resentment there.

The strangest part of all was that somewhere behind intricate layers of unexplained bitterness, the sisters really did love each other. Jake was sure of it.

He drew a deep breath and set down his drink on the varnished maple coffee table. Ellen. It had been years since he'd seen her but he had never stopped thinking of her. Her memory was so real he could almost touch her.

You blew it, he told himself. *You let her go and now you'll spend a lifetime regretting it.* He sighed and reached for the remote control just as the telephone rang.

He reached out to lift the receiver. "Hello?"

Silence.

"Hello?" Still nothing.

He was about to hang up when a familiar voice said, "Jake? It's me. Ellen."

Jake sat up straight, his eyes wide, his heart suddenly beating faster. "Ellen . . . how are you?"

"Well, not too good, really." He thought

he heard tears in her voice. "My dad died . . . last Friday."

"I know. Andy was at the hospital. Andy Conover. He called me that night." She didn't say anything, but he heard her sniffing. "Ellen, hey, are you crying?"

She still didn't answer. Memories of her flooded over him, of her tender heart, her love for her father. This had to be killing her.

He tried again. "Where's your husband? Isn't he there?"

She released a single sob. "No. He didn't come."

"You're not doing well. I can tell."

There was no response. Only the muffled sound of Ellen's cries. Jake stabbed his fingers absently through his hair. Her crying made him ache, made him willing to do anything to take the hurt away. "What can I do, Ellen? Tell me."

She sniffed loudly and regained control of her voice. "I . . . I don't know. I mean, that's why I called. Everything's kind of crazy around here and . . . well, I guess . . . Could you come over and pick me up? Take me somewhere so we could talk?"

"Sure." He looked at his watch: eight-thirty. "Let me change clothes and I'll be there at nine. Okay?"

"Okay. I'll be out front."

He hung up slowly, then sat there, staring at the phone, dazed. Had that just happened? Had Ellen just called him?

He exhaled a long, slow breath. Yes, it had happened. And he knew, as clearly as he knew anything in his life, that Ellen needed him. And he would be there for her.

Ellen hung up the phone and stared at her wedding ring. What in the world was she doing making plans to spend an evening with Jake Sadler? She didn't know . . . and right now she didn't care. She needed someone . . . someone to listen, to care. She left her parents' bedroom and headed for the front door.

"Where are you going?" Her mother looked at her, surprised.

"Out."

"You didn't eat and you don't have a car. There's nowhere you can go on foot at this hour of the night, Ellen. It wouldn't be safe."

Ellen released a short laugh. "At this point anything would be safer than here."

"Ellen, please —" Mom began, but Ellen stopped her.

"No. I called an old girlfriend." *Why am I lying? Why not just tell the truth? I'm not going to do anything wrong, for heaven's sake!*

But she couldn't tell them. She didn't want to deal with their reaction if she did. "She's picking me up and we're going for a drive. I'll have her drop me off at Megan's apartment later on. Don't worry about me."

"What about the funeral service? We didn't figure out about the eulogy. Whether you five kids will each read something." Clearly Mom was tired and frustrated. She wanted them to stay together until the plans were finished.

"Whatever you decide is fine with me." Ellen walked outside and shut the door behind her.

She was dressed in denim shorts and a white T-shirt, and suddenly she felt six years younger than her age. She found a place on the cool grass and sat down to wait for Jake. Then she tried not to think about how she'd done that very thing at least a hundred times before, long ago, when life had seemed so much simpler.

So much happier.

Inside the Barrett home, Jane heard the front door close and looked up from her dinner.

"Who was that?"

"Ellen. She's going out with a friend. She'll meet you and Megan back at the apartment later."

"That's nice." Jane had really tried to be more civil since Ellen had told them about the miscarriages, but she couldn't keep the tinge of sarcasm from her voice. "Shouldn't she be here? We haven't finished working out the funeral plans."

Their mother shrugged. "She said she'd go along with whatever we decided. I think she needs time away."

"Well, then, let's decide whether or not we're going to write separate eulogies and read them at the funeral. I think we should do it because it's something Mom wants."

Jane looked around the table, waiting for a response.

"Well?" she said when they were silent.

"I don't like it, but I'll do it," Amy said finally. "Mom, it doesn't matter if it's short, does it?"

"No. Make it as long or short as you like."

Aaron shook his head. "I can't write something like that, Mom. You know how I am."

"I'm not asking you to write an essay, Aaron. Just a few words about your father and what you'll miss the most."

Aaron was quiet a moment and Jane wondered if he might actually cry. He nodded abruptly, then rose from the table.

"Fine. I'll try."

Megan wiped her mouth with a napkin. "I already said I liked the idea."

"And Ellen said she'd do whatever we wanted, so I guess that settles it. Right, Mom?" Jane looked at her mother expectantly.

"Seems like it. You'll have to let Ellen know tonight. Other than that, I think we're about done."

"I'm going to bed," Aaron announced.

"So early?" The disappointment was evident in Mom's creased forehead, in her pained expression.

"Yes." Aaron's voice was defensive. "I need to work on what I'm going to say. Is that all right with you?"

True to form, Mom backed down. "Sure, honey. I'm sorry. We'll see you tomorrow, then."

The others finished their dinner and gathered in the den to watch television. Since that didn't interest her, Jane borrowed Megan's car and set out to relieve Aunt Mary of her children. As she walked across the front yard she passed Ellen. She said nothing to her then or ten minutes later when she returned with the children in tow.

What Ellen had told her had struck deep. Had it been any other person, any friend, who had shared such a struggle, Jane would have known what to say, what to do. But this was Ellen. And with Ellen, Jane simply didn't know any way other than anger.

Silence seemed the greatest kindness she could extend.

Ellen watched Jane as she left the house, then returned later with her children. Twice Jane walked right past where she sat waiting. Both times she hadn't even looked her way, hadn't said a word.

Even strangers say hello.

She stared down the street, disgusted, hurt. Why had she even bothered to tell Jane anything? Why had she thought it would make a difference? They were sisters, but that didn't seem to matter. They couldn't even get along in the wake of their father's death. No, nothing mattered between her and Jane anymore. Nothing but the anger.

Ellen looked at her watch and saw that she had fifteen minutes until Jake would be there. *Forget Jane. Think about something else.*

For a moment, her thoughts drifted to Mike, but she shut that down. The last thing she needed after the unceasing doses of Jane's anger was to think about her fights and struggles with Mike.

She looked up at the sky, closed her eyes wearily, and let her mind wander. . . .

What would Jake look like after so many years? Would he still have that same smile, the one that had always warmed her all the way through? Would his eyes still sparkle? Did he still have that deep and unrestrained laughter?

Stop! Her conscience jabbed at her, and she sighed. It was wrong to think about him that way. She had loved him, truly she had. But that was another time. He was coming to meet her as a friend. Nothing more. And that's all she wanted. A friend. Wasn't it?

She sighed softly. At that moment she was too tired, too weak not to miss Jake and the way life had been when they were together. Back then everything had seemed so . . . right. Her father was well, she and her sisters got along, and she hadn't a care in the world. Everything about those years was peppered with Jake's presence.

Finally, like dear, long-lost friends, the memories came flooding back — and Ellen entertained them willingly. She ignored that still, small voice warning her to take every thought captive for Christ, and she drifted back to a breezy afternoon at Petoskey High School.

The day she first set eyes on Jake Sadler.

SEVENTEEN

It was the fall of Ellen's sophomore year in high school, and cheerleading practice had just started. That afternoon Ellen and her best friend, Leslie Maple, were working out with the squad in the physical education area when Stacy Wheatley appeared fifty yards away with a boy Ellen had never seen before.

"Isn't Stacy supposed to be practicing?" Leslie asked quietly. Their cheerleading coach, Mrs. Black, was a stickler for punctuality; Stacy was already ten minutes late.

Ellen ignored Leslie's comment. She was too busy staring at the boy to answer. "Who's *that?*"

Leslie squinted across the field, shaking her head. "I don't know."

The boy was tall, with dark brown hair cut close to his head. He wore only his athletic shorts, and his tanned and toned stomach was attracting the attention of several cheerleaders. He looked like he belonged on a tropical island as he teased and flirted with Stacy.

"I think that's Jake Sadler," Leslie said after a moment. "He's new."

"Freshman?"

"Yep. Came from the middle school across town."

"Sure beats anything the sophomore class has to offer."

"That's what everyone's saying."

Stacy and Jake walked closer. He lifted her hand, kissed it, and bowed like a Renaissance man before winking at her once and turning to go.

"Oh, *brother,*" Leslie whispered.

"Stacy!" Mrs. Black's voice boomed across the field. "Stop messing around and get over here where you belong. You have two minutes to get that uniform on."

Red-faced and giggling, Stacy ran into the girls' locker room to do as she was told. When Jake turned around to wave one last time he caught Ellen watching him instead.

For a long moment Ellen was caught in Jake's curious stare. He studied her, almost as though trying to remember where he'd seen her before. Then he flashed her a wide grin and winked, the same way he'd winked at Stacy. In an instant he rounded the corner and disappeared from sight.

Ellen felt herself blush and she couldn't hear Mrs. Black's instructions. With all her might she tried to concentrate on the routine but she kept seeing Jake Sadler's blue eyes instead.

"Ellen?" a voice boomed. "I said move to the grassy quad with the other girls and stretch out. Are you awake?" It was an Indian summer afternoon and Mrs. Black was hot and frustrated. "If I could only get you people to listen."

Ellen moved sheepishly toward Leslie.

"You okay?" Leslie nudged her. "You look spaced out or something."

Ellen nodded and Leslie raised a single eyebrow. "It's that Jake guy, isn't it?"

Ellen said nothing and pretended to concentrate on stretching her right hamstring. She lowered her upper body over her leg and avoided Leslie's probing eyes.

"Ellen, that's it, isn't it? Tell me I'm right. You're thinking about Jake Sadler."

"Of course not," Ellen hissed. She would be mortified if Mrs. Black heard them. "He's obviously dating Stacy. Why would I be interested?"

"Right. I'm your best friend and you expect me to believe that. Come on, Ellen. I can see it clear as the nose on your face. He knocked you flat out, didn't he?"

"Stop! We're gonna get in trouble."

"No sir, Ellen," she whispered loudly. "We're not going to get in trouble. *You* are. Especially if you get your heart set on Jake Sadler. He's had a different girl on his arm every day since school started. And school only started two weeks ago. Forget him."

Ellen nodded. "Okay. Fine. Now let's practice."

"So you admit it! You have a thing for the guy, don't you?"

"Shhhh! Get to work."

Long after cheerleading practice was finished and Leslie had dropped Ellen off at home, the image of Jake Sadler consumed her and left her stomach a twisted mess of butterflies. The next morning before class she was talking to a group of friends when she spotted him, sitting by himself at the other end of the covered lunch area. He was watching her, and when she caught his gaze he grinned. Ellen squelched a smile and excused herself from the group. Despite her nervousness, she walked the twenty feet between them in an unhurried manner.

"Hi." His eyes danced with challenge and Ellen's heart skipped a beat.

"Hi." She sat down across from him and stared at him questioningly. "You're new?"

Jake nodded. "Jake Sadler."

"Ellen Barrett."

"I know."

"How'd you know?"

"Who doesn't know Ellen Barrett?"

"Apparently you know quite a few people. Like Stacy Wheatley, for starters."

Jake stretched, and Ellen noticed the muscle definition in his arms. "Stacy's just a friend. We knew each other in junior high."

"You guys looked pretty friendly yesterday."

Jake shrugged. "That's me, I guess. Can't seem to break the flirt image."

"Apparently not."

The bell rang then and Ellen stood to leave. "Well, see you around."

"You'll be over there at lunch, right?" He pointed to the spot where the cheerleaders and football players hung out.

"Right."

"I'll look for you."

That afternoon Jake found her and gave her a note he'd written during class. She read it while he was buying milk and ended up spending the entire lunch hour by his side. They laughed and teased and kicked at each other's feet, so that by the time the bell rang half the school was talking about them.

"Okay, what's the deal?" Leslie asked in their sixth-hour English class. "Everyone saw you with Jake Sadler at lunch. I want every detail."

Ellen smiled. "He's cute, isn't he?"

"He's gorgeous. So what? I'm telling you he makes eyes at a dozen girls every day."

"Oh, Leslie, just because he flirts a little doesn't mean he's a bad guy. Give him a break."

"Okay, but don't say I didn't warn you."

Time and again over the next six years, whenever Jake broke Ellen's heart, Leslie would remind her that she had seen it coming.

"I warned you, Ellen," she would say. "Dump the guy. He's dragging you down."

But Leslie's efforts never changed anything. From that first day she saw him, Ellen was addicted to Jake the way some people are addicted to drugs. Even when she knew he was bad for her, she could not bear to be apart from him.

At first they'd decided to just be friends. They tickled and teased, but they kept their relationship platonic. Jake was just too popular with the girls. They hung on Jake's every word; they followed him to and from classes and giggled when he passed by. Ellen, too, received more than a little attention from the opposite sex. Neither of them was ready to be exclusive.

Still, they walked together between classes, sat together when her cheer squad took breaks at football games, and talked on the phone almost every night.

"Well, have you kissed the guy yet or what?" Leslie would ask and Ellen would shake her head.

"No, I told you. We're just —"

"I know, I know," Leslie interrupted. "You're just friends. But that's not how it looks. That boy's mad about you, Ellen. And I think the feeling's mutual. The whole thing spells trouble."

"I'm telling you, we're friends. Nothing more."

Then, things changed. Ellen had known for months that her feelings for Jake went deeper than friendship. And one evening, he told her what she'd been waiting to hear. They were walking together, and ended up in a small park. They found a bench and sat down. Jake had been unusually quiet, so Ellen turned to him. But before she could say anything he turned to her, his expression serious. "Something's happened."

She stared at him, and fear washed over her. Was his family moving? Was he in love with someone else, someone who didn't want them spending time together anymore? She was silent, willing him to continue.

He took her hands in his, slowly rubbing his thumb along her fingers. "I'm not sure how you're going to react."

Just say it! her mind screamed. For once she didn't have anything to say. She was too frightened at the thought of losing him.

"The thing is . . . I think I'm in love with you."

Ellen stared at him blankly. "What?"

He didn't reply. Instead, he held her gaze for a moment, then reached up to cup her face with his lean fingertips. Slowly he lowered his head and, for the sweetest minute of her life, pressed his lips to hers.

The memory of that kiss still took her breath away, still warmed her heart . . .

They'd both been breathless when they drew apart. They stared at each other, nervous about the line they had crossed, drowning in a sea of first-time emotions.

"I love you, Ellen," he'd finally said, and joy had coursed though her.

After that there was no turning back.

Ellen and Jake were together through the summer and her junior and senior year. She turned eighteen after graduation and he was seventeen with one more year left at Petoskey. That summer she camped with his family and spent half her days swimming with him at Magnus Park. They played Ping-Pong and Frisbee and backgammon and chased each other in the shallow water along the shore of the bay. They kissed and held hands and studied a hundred sunsets. The days wore on and they were inseparable.

When school started that fall everyone they knew felt shut out of their relationship.

"I don't know, Ellen," Leslie said. "I think it's all a little too good to be true. Let's see what this year brings, now that you're not on campus with him."

Ellen scoffed at her friend's warning, but Leslie proved to be right. Jake was a senior that fall and better looking than ever. Ellen, meanwhile, was miles away at North Central Community College.

Every girl at Petoskey knew that Ellen wasn't around to monopolize Jake's attention. As far as they were concerned, Jake didn't have a girlfriend. They chased him for all he was worth. He found notes on his car, notes in his locker, and mysterious phone messages on his answering machine.

One day Leslie called and told Ellen the news she thought she'd never hear.

"Ellen, I don't like to have to tell you this, but, well . . . it's about Jake."

"What about him?" Ellen had just walked

into the house from a day of classes and was fixing herself something to eat.

"You sure you want to know?"

"Don't be so dramatic, Leslie. Whatever it is, just say it."

"Okay. Well, you know how my brother's a senior, right?"

"Right. So?" Ellen opened the refrigerator and pulled out a loaf of bread, stretching the phone cord to its limit.

"Well, I guess Jake's been spending a lot of time with Candice Conner. You know, the J.V. cheerleading captain."

Ellen's heart sank. She set down the bread and pulled out a chair from the kitchen table. Her lunch was forgotten.

"Are you sure?"

"Billy says you'd never know he has a girlfriend by the way he acts at school. It's been that way since September."

Ellen didn't want to believe Jake had betrayed her, but that night Jake told her the truth himself.

They'd decided it was better to see other people. Ellen refused to let Jake see how much the situation had hurt her. But after he left that night, she cried for two days straight. She listened to sad songs on the radio and stayed up late writing poetry about lost love.

Then one night after two weeks of hearing nothing from Jake she was watching television when she heard the sound of his car horn in front of her house. She ran to the front door and peeked through the curtains. It was Jake. He honked again and she went outside, running lightly in her bare feet to the driver's side of his Volkswagen.

He was crying and he reached for her hand.

"Jake, what's wrong?" She was suddenly worried something had happened to him or his parents.

"I'm so sorry, Ellen!" He slammed his right hand against his steering wheel.

Ellen was quiet. She hugged herself tightly to ward off the chill in the air and waited for an explanation.

"Candice chased me, Ellen. I swear. She wanted to go out and finally I thought what the heck. It might be fun." He dried the tears off his cheeks with the back of his hand. "I was wrong, Ellen. I don't want her; I want you. I've never stopped wanting you. The problem is sometimes I want to date other girls. It's like I can't make up my mind."

Ellen's knees were weak and she tried to think of something to say.

"I know you don't want me around, not

now when I'm not ready to be your boyfriend again. But could you at least talk to me, be my friend like we used to be?" He looked up at her. "I need you, Ellen. I miss you so much."

Then he reached around to the backseat and pulled out a dozen red roses. He handed them to her and there were fresh tears in his eyes. "I love you, babe."

Ellen wanted so badly to tell him to leave, to never come back unless he was sure he wouldn't break her heart. But she knew as surely as she had the first time she'd seen him that she could not turn him away. She sighed and took his hand, fitting her fingers between his.

"Okay. But just friends." she said softly. It was a wish, a way of trying to save face. She missed him terribly and wanted to believe she could spend time with him even while he dated other girls. For an instant she thought about Leslie's warnings, but then she put them out of her mind.

She smiled and Jake's eyes lit up. "Park," she said simply.

He did, and they spent two hours on the porch swing in front of her house talking about the time they'd missed and savoring the fact that they were together again. When he stood up to leave, he pulled her into his arms as if nothing had changed between them. But before he could kiss her she leaned out of reach.

"Don't mess with my heart, Jake," she whispered. "If you're dating other people then we can't . . ."

"I know," Jake put a finger to her lips. "I'm sorry. It won't happen again."

But they both knew it would. The more time they spent together, the more difficult it became to remain platonic, and finally one night Jake told her he wanted things to be the way they were.

"What about the girls at school?"

"I want you," he insisted.

She sighed and twirled her finger through a lock of his shiny hair. "Ahh, Jake. How can I say no?"

"I love you, Ellen." He kissed her softly.

"I know. Me, too."

Their relationship deepened as they grew older. Soon the youthful romance became something much more serious. Finally, after being together for three years, though it went against everything she'd been taught, everything she believed in, Ellen gave in to her desires and Jake's and they began sleeping together.

From time to time guilt would stab at her and she'd close her eyes, fighting back tears.

Father, forgive me . . . she'd pray. *But you know we love each other. And we're going to get married. Someday. I just know it. So it's not really wrong, is it?*

Her only answer was silence.

For three years their relationship continued. They slept together, camped together, and made promises to marry each other. But every time Ellen thought things were going great, Jake would break up with her because of another girl.

After six years of the roller-coaster ride with Jake Sadler, Ellen wondered what had happened, how she had fallen so hard and lost control of her life. She wondered if the reason she continued to go back to him was the challenge of changing him. She wondered if she was crazy.

One night she was lying in bed, agonizing over yet another letdown with Jake, when her heart suddenly began racing, thumping wildly about in her chest.

She sat up, struggling to breathe. *I'm dying!* Sweat began to bead along her forehead and she climbed out of bed, moving quickly down the hallway to her parents' room, where she knocked on the door. After a minute, the door opened slightly and her mother's bleary-eyed face appeared.

"Ellen? What's wrong?"

"My heart." She shivered as she put a hand to her chest. "It's racing a mile a minute and I feel like I can't breathe."

Her mother led Ellen out to the living room and sat next to her. "You need to relax, dear. Take a deep breath and hold it."

Ellen did as she was told.

"Now, let it out slowly."

The air seeped out of her mouth, and she felt slightly more relaxed. "Now what?"

"Do it again." Her mom rubbed her back, talking to her in a soothing voice. After five minutes, Ellen's heart stopped racing and she was calm again.

"Go get some sleep now, but I'll make a doctor's appointment for you tomorrow."

The doctor's diagnosis was simple: she had suffered a panic attack.

"Is there anything in your life making you feel out of control?" he asked.

Ellen thought of Jake and uttered a short laugh. "You could say that."

"A boyfriend?"

Ellen nodded sheepishly.

"Well, young lady." The doctor was in his late forties and had a fatherly way about him. "I'd say it's time you remove him from your life before the situation compromises your health."

Ellen nodded again.

After that she thought long and hard about her relationship with Jake.

They shared what seemed like a lifetime of happy memories and she loved him more than ever. They rode bikes along the shores of Mackinac Island, sailed on Little Traverse Bay, and cuddled together at Magnus Park under the shade of the leafy maple trees. They made fancy egg omelettes and laughed until Ellen thought her sides would burst. He was charming and romantic and the ultimate challenge. Jake Sadler was the only man she wanted in her life. But his unfaithfulness was affecting her health and something had to change.

The holidays passed and Ellen ushered in the New Year with a single resolution. She would give Jake an ultimatum. One more chance. If he couldn't be faithful, they were finished.

On a bright Saturday morning she drove to his house, prepared to share her decision. She was on break from the University of Michigan, but they hadn't talked much for the past week. They'd both been busy — she working at a steak house on the beach in Charlevoix and he working construction in the days.

Ellen pulled up in front of his house and saw that his parents' car was gone. She was slightly disappointed. She loved Jake's parents dearly and looked forward to seeing them. They had become like family to her.

Still, if they were gone that meant Jake was alone. Ellen smiled at the thought. She looked at her watch as she climbed out of her car. It was only eight-fifteen. If his parents were gone, Jake would still be sleeping. She walked up the front steps and knocked loudly. When no one answered, she knocked again.

"Come on, Jake, get out of bed," she whispered.

Suddenly the door opened and a leggy blond with tousled hair stood before her. She was wearing Jake's bathrobe.

Ellen was too stunned to speak.

"Yes?" The girl had sounded annoyed, her voice raspy from sleep. She was definitely suffering the effects of a hangover.

Ellen's heart began to race and she felt faint.

"Are you selling something or what?" the girl asked impatiently. She seemed anxious to be done with Ellen.

"No. Nothing." Ellen was in a fog of disbelief. She turned toward her car.

"Who are you?" the girl shouted after her.

Ellen ignored her and sped away. Angry tears streamed down her face as she drove aimlessly through the streets of Petoskey. She could not go home and face her parents' questions but her heart was racing so fast she thought she might have a heart attack. She wrestled with the idea of driving to the hospital, then convinced herself there was nothing physically wrong. She was having another panic attack.

She drove to Magnus Park and found a deserted plateau overlooking the freezing bay, a spot where she and Jake had parked a number of times over the years.

"I hate you, Jake!" Her heart responded by beating even faster.

She had trusted him, believed in him, given him everything she had to give. And he had betrayed her. No wonder her heart was racing. Her life was out of control and it was her own fault. She had stayed with Jake Sadler all these years, knowing that he wasn't faithful. Now she had no one but herself to blame for what was happening. She drew a shaky breath and decided that control was hers for the taking.

"It's over, Jake." She wiped her tears. It didn't matter that she had said the words a hundred times. She felt like blinders had been removed from her eyes. And there was too much at stake — primarily her health — to turn back. "I mean it this time."

With that declaration, Ellen's heart skipped a beat and then slowed considerably. The panic attack had left her tired and aching from the finality of her decision. Filled with a determination she had never known, she started her car and headed home. Her mother met her at the door.

"Jake called."

"Thanks." Ellen walked past her mother toward her bedroom. Her father intercepted her in the hallway.

"Ellen? You've been crying, honey."

"Yes, but I'm okay."

"Jake?"

Ellen rolled her eyes and released a sad, short laugh. "Who else?"

"Honey, you need to let that boy go. He's not ever going to change. Not even for you."

Ellen nodded and hugged her father. "I know, Daddy. Thanks."

When she didn't return his phone calls for two days Jake appeared at her house late one night. He tapped lightly on the door. Ellen saw who it was and she summoned her determination. The time had come to tell him good-bye. She slipped a parka over her turtleneck sweater and went outside.

"Hi." Their eyes met and she looked away. He was no longer welcome to see into her soul.

"Hi." He stuffed his gloved hands nervously in his pocket. Two feet of snow covered the ground even though the skies had been clear for a week. At that late hour the temperature hovered just above zero. "Ellen, what's wrong? You haven't called me in two days." Jake shivered and moved closer. "I've been calling you every few hours."

Ellen ignored him. She walked toward the porch swing and sat down. Jake followed. His eyes looked deeply troubled and Ellen guessed he probably knew what was coming. She thought about the years they'd been together, the memories they'd built, the love they'd shared. . . .

She looked at him now and was still struck by the sight of him. *Will there ever be anyone like you, Jake?* They had planned to spend their lives together, raise children and take them fishing on the bay, camping in the wooded pastures of the Upper Peninsula. But now it was over. It had to be. Her eyes filled with tears and she stared at the ground between her feet.

"Ellen, what is it?" Jake put an arm around her shoulders and she recoiled as if he'd slapped her.

"Don't touch me, Jake. Not now."

"Ellen, I —"

"Don't." She held up a single hand and stared into his eyes. "I came by the house Saturday morning."

Jake's body jerked as if he'd been slapped.

"Don't defend yourself." Her voice cracked. She was neither angry nor hateful, only sad at what they were both losing.

"I can't keep doing this, Jake." Her eyes were full of pain, and Jake looked away.

"Ellen, I can explain. I was drinking with the guys and I had a few too many. It wasn't —"

She shook her head. She was twenty-one years old and she had listened to Jake's excuses for six years. "I should hate you for what you've done to me, Jake, but I love you too much. Isn't that stupid?" Fresh tears welled in her eyes. She brushed them away and shivered as she stared intently at him.

"I have something to say so listen to me, please," she said softly. There was silence for a moment. "We're finished, Jake. For real this time."

"Ellen, don't do this." His eyes grew watery. There was a fear in his eyes that Ellen had never seen before. "I can't live without you, you know that."

"Yes, but I can't live *with* you. I've tried, Jake. Really." She pulled one hand from her lined pocket and touched his cheek gently with her freezing fingertips. "I love you. I'll probably never love anyone the way I loved you. But you'll never change, Jake. It's time for me to go my own way."

"Ellen, why can't you believe me? She was nothing —"

"Jake!" Ellen raised her voice for the first time that evening. "Please. Don't." Tears streamed down her freezing cheeks but her voice remained unaffected, determined. "There's nothing you could say to change my mind. It's too late."

She stood up, and Jake rose to her side.

"Can't you just hear me out? Can't we try — ?"

"Jake, go. Please."

He slumped in defeat. For a moment he stared at his feet, as though understanding for the first time the finality in her words. Then he came to her and circled his arms around her waist. For the last time she let him. "I love you, Ellen." He clung to her.

She could feel his heartbeat through their jackets, and suddenly she was terrified to let him go. She had to get inside before she changed her mind.

"I'm a jerk. I blew it and it's all my fault. But I'll never stop loving you."

Ellen felt his tears on her forehead and

she ached to tell him it was all right, they could try again. She closed her eyes tightly and held him a moment longer. Then slowly, for the last time, she pulled away.

"Ellen, give me time. I'll change and then at least let me call you."

"I need to go on with my life. I've spent six years waiting for your phone calls. So, please. Don't make me promises. Not now."

"But . . ."

"Jake, go. Please."

He met her gaze, and it struck her that he looked as if he'd lost his greatest treasure. She understood. She felt the same way. In the end they had both lost.

Without Jake in her life, Ellen's panic attacks stopped immediately. She busied herself with extracurricular school projects and housecleaning. In the evenings, when she was sorely tempted to call Jake, she forced herself to visit her girlfriends, especially Leslie Maple.

That year Leslie had become a Christian and there was something undeniably different about her — a joy, a light in her eyes that hadn't been there before. Two weeks after the breakup with Jake, Ellen spent a weekend with Leslie. The two prayed and read Scripture, and for the first time in Ellen's life she understood that Christ desired a relationship with her. She cried, picturing Jesus on a cross dying a painful death while she, Ellen Barrett, was on his mind. That was a kind of love so real it was intoxicating. She had believed in God. She had gone to church and catechism and confession. But she hadn't really known the Christ. That weekend, in those quiet, prayerful moments with Leslie, she understood that the physical relationship she had shared with Jake was wrong, not because of a list of dos and don'ts, but because God had different, better plans for his children. And now Ellen wanted nothing more than to follow those plans. That Sunday morning she went to church with Leslie and afterwards she accepted Jesus as her personal Savior in a way she had never done before.

She'd never known the kind of joy that decision brought her. It surpassed anything she'd ever felt before. "Does this last?" she asked Leslie with a grin.

Leslie smiled. "As long as you keep Christ your main focus, yes. But there are a lot of things in life that can come between you and your faith."

"There's only one person who could come between me and the Lord," Ellen admitted.

"Jake?"

"Jake."

"Well, girl, let's pray about it." Leslie grinned and took Ellen's hands in hers. "God alone can help you where Jake's concerned."

They did so. Ellen took the lead and asked God to protect her heart and to forgive her for the physical relationship she'd shared with Jake. She asked the Lord to teach her, to guide her, to show her how to keep anything from coming between her and him.

When the prayer was over, Ellen and Leslie smiled at each other.

"There's a wonderful, Christian man out there for you somewhere, Ellen." Leslie's eyes were shining. "I'm sure of it."

Ellen joined a campus fellowship when she got back to the university and her heart soared with a joy she hadn't known before. God loved her deeply and in that there was a freedom she hadn't realized existed. She was his alone. There was comfort knowing that if she listened to his voice, he would lead her along the right paths. Her quiet moments talking to the Lord satisfied a need deep in her soul, a need not even Jake had been able to meet. She began telling her parents and siblings how powerful a relationship with Christ could be.

"I only wish you could both join a Bible-believing church, Dad," Ellen told her father one day. "The Catholic church has so many traditions and things that aren't in Scripture."

John Barrett raised an eyebrow and pulled Ellen aside. "Let's get one thing clear. We have no choice but to accept your decision about leaving the Catholic church, but don't expect us to leave just because you did. Catholics love the Lord every bit as much as Protestants."

"I'm not talking about Protestants *or* Catholics, Daddy," Ellen insisted. "I'm talking about Christians. Bible-believing Christians."

John Barrett smiled patiently. "Believe it or not, I, too, read the Bible. Nearly every day. It doesn't matter what label you wear. What matters is that you know Jesus and have a relationship with him. There is one faith and one Lord, after all." His voice had grown softer then. "You and Jake broke up and now you've found comfort in God's Word. I'm glad for that. If you think you can be closer to God at a different church, then we accept your decision. Every day since you were born I've prayed that you children would grow close to God. But don't go thinking your mother and I don't love the Lord as much as you do just because we're Catholic."

Ellen never again tried to convince her family to leave their church. Instead she prayed that their faith would be strengthened, and over the years she saw those prayers answered.

Weeks after the discussion with her father, Ellen was back in Petoskey for his crash course in sports reporting. Six months later she met Mike.

She and Jake saw each other just once after that, when they met by chance at Glen's Market in Petoskey. Ellen remembered her prayer and managed to leave the store after barely exchanging greetings with Jake.

That was nine years ago.

Ellen picked at the damp grass around her. She wondered if he had changed, if he still had a string of girls or if he had finally gotten serious about life.

A truck turned and headed down the street. Ellen's pulse quickened as the vehicle came closer and finally stopped in front of her house.

The truck was new, a full-size Chevy with an extended cab. A man climbed out slowly. Jake. She would have known him anywhere. He studied her as she stood up and brushed the grass off her shorts.

"Hi ya." The soft greeting was one she'd

heard from him a thousand times before.

"Hi." She was thankful he couldn't see her red cheeks from across the yard.

He walked around and opened the passenger door, watching her carefully as she climbed in. He closed her door, walked around and climbed into the driver's seat. He drove several houses down the block, then pulled over.

"Ellen." He turned to her, searching her face. Gently, he took her hands in his, but he said nothing. There was no need. Ellen could read his piercing blue eyes as easily as she had the day they'd met. They were adults who had shared everything at a time when life was most impressionable and the memories were there for both of them.

"I know," she said quietly.

Then without a word they hugged each other, bridging the awkwardness between them and erasing the years in a single instant.

EIGHTEEN

Ellen pulled away first, smoothing her T-shirt and wrestling with her emotions. Jake stayed close. He stared into her eyes, watching her carefully.

"Are you okay?" he whispered. "About your dad, I mean?" There was concern in his voice, and Ellen caught the scent of his cologne. Mixed with the smell of the truck's new leather interior it was enough to make her flustered, unsure of herself — and her motives for calling him.

Lord, what am I doing here? What am I looking for?

As had happened so often lately, the only answer she received was silence. Drawing a deep breath, she steadied herself. Jake had spent so much time with her family that he would understand what she had lost. He had loved her father, too.

And that, Ellen realized, more than any other reason, was why she wanted to see

Jake after so many years.

She wiped at an errant tear. "I miss him, Jake."

"He was something, wasn't he?" Jake's eyes were distant and sad. He looked at Ellen again. "You okay?"

"I guess. It wasn't a surprise or anything. I just . . . I just needed to talk to someone who would understand."

"Well, I have all night." Jake started the engine and pulled back onto the street. "Why don't you relax a minute and you can tell me all about it when we get there."

"Where are we going?"

"You'll see."

She sank deep into the leather seat and studied him as he drove. He wore a blue tank top and athletic shorts, and it was easy to see that he was still lean, still remarkably fit. His hair was darker than before, cropped short at the neck and slightly longer on top. He was still tan, his eyes still as blue as the water in Little Traverse Bay. But there was something different. Something . . . more steady, more mature. He turned onto Mitchell, and Ellen saw he was heading toward the water. The silence between them was easy, and when she turned to watch him again he caught her gaze and smiled.

"I'm glad you called."

She shook her head, chuckling wryly. "I still can't believe I did it. I thought you'd think I was crazy, calling after all these years."

"Come on, Ellen. Did you think I'd forget you?"

She stared at her hands. "No."

"Well, that's good."

Ellen smiled to herself. Jake was trying to keep things on a surface level, and that *was* good.

"You have to admit it's a little strange, calling you out of the blue after nine years and asking you to come get me."

"You can always call me, Ellen. You know that." Jake's voice was kind, and Ellen felt it wrap around her, warming her wounded heart. Hot, unexpected tears pricked at her eyes at the compassion she heard in his voice, saw in his eyes. No doubt about it, Jake had been a head turner when they were younger. But this kinder, gentler manner . . . this sincerity and compassion that she felt from him . . .

That took him way beyond attractive — and right into dangerous.

They drove another ten minutes to the plateau along the beach at Magnus Park. A thicket of trees surrounded the secluded spot but opened just enough to offer a spectacular view of the bay. It was nearly nine-thirty and the sun was beginning its trek toward the water.

Ellen settled more deeply into her seat and sighed. She and Jake had parked here so often before. The plateau was where they had broken up and gotten back together a handful of times over the years. This was where she'd come after going to Jake's house that last time and finding another woman there.

How strange it was to be here again.

Jake turned off the engine and leaned back, facing her. He was silent, studying her.

She laughed nervously. "Kinda familiar, huh?"

Jake didn't laugh. "That's not why I brought you here."

"I know. It just brings back memories, that's all."

"We can go somewhere else."

"No," Ellen said quickly. "This is fine. I like it here."

"So," Jake said. He folded his hands behind his head and leaned against the window of his truck. "I'm listening."

"Well, it's a long story."

"About your dad?"

"No. I mean, I'm dealing with my dad's

death. At least I think I am. Actually I'm so busy fighting with Jane that I hardly have time to think about my dad."

Jake shifted so that he was slightly closer, and Ellen realized he could still make her feel safe and secure, still soothe away her pain without a single touch.

"I wondered how things would be between you two this week."

"They're terrible. Isn't that crazy? We come together for our dad's funeral, travel the country so we can be here in our hometown and bury this man we all loved, and we can't even get along with each other."

"Ah, just like old times."

Ellen stared at him. "Huh?"

"Come on, Ellen. You and Jane always fought. Don't tell me you don't remember."

Ellen was quiet a moment. She stared out the windshield at the waning sunlight. The bay had become a shimmering expanse of silver and gold. She drew a deep breath and turned to Jake.

"When I think about Jane I remember hanging around her at school and sharing secrets late into the night. Dancing on a flatbed truck one New Year's Eve. And a thousand happy memories growing up together."

"Those are all good, Ellen. But there were bad times, too. Remember the year you

331

shared the apartment?"

Ellen frowned. She remembered. "We disagreed once in a while back then, but it's different now. She snaps at everything I say. It seems like she hates me. I don't know how to get along with her, I don't know what to say around her, and I don't know what I've done to make her so mad. When I couldn't take it anymore I called you. And here I am."

Jake inclined his head but said nothing.

Ellen went on. "I was closer to my dad than she was."

"I remember. You think that's the problem?"

Ellen stared out the windshield again. "I don't know. It seems like she's taking it out on me, like she resents me or something." Tears made their way quietly down her face. "She tells me I shouldn't talk about her children, and then she ridicules me for not having any of my own." She closed her eyes. "She accused me of choosing my career over having children." She gave a short laugh. "I can't believe she thought that. I want kids; for a while I wanted them more than anything in the world. But Mike and I have tried and it just hasn't happened." She opened her eyes and met Jake's gentle gaze. "I've had two miscarriages."

His eyes filled with sympathy. "I'm sorry, Ellen. Really."

She nodded and sniffled loudly. Jake handed her a tissue from his glove compartment and Ellen was thankful she had called him. There was still a certain chemistry between them, but there was no spark, no hint of anything less than proper. She was a married woman talking heart-to-heart with an old friend, with the one person who understood everything she was going through. It was nothing more than that.

"I remember once when we were having pizza at the Cookery with Leslie and some of the others," Jake said. "One of the girls was Cindy, that girl Jane hung out with once in a while. Remember?"

"I think so."

"You said something about sharing a room with Jane but being too busy to talk to her for the past week. Something like that."

"Right, I remember."

"And that girl, Cindy, she said she was surprised you two shared a room because Jane had always talked like the two of you never got along. She told you Jane couldn't stand you. Remember?"

The memory came flooding back. Ellen sat up straighter and curled her legs beneath her on the seat.

"You were hurt for days afterward," Jake reminded her. He smiled gently, and again Ellen was glad she was with him. He did understand, even about her struggles with Jane.

Why can't Mike be more like that, Lord? The thought no sooner drifted into her mind than she pushed it away. She didn't want to think about Mike now.

"If I remember right, everything was fine in a week or so," he continued.

"I asked her to be honest, to tell me if she was upset and not talk about it with the kids at school."

"After that you were best friends again."

"You're right."

"And what about that John Bronson? That fireman guy you met at the health club one of those times when we were broken up? The two of you went on a date and you found out later that Jane had a crush on him. Remember?"

Ellen cringed. "That's right. She didn't speak to me for two weeks."

Jake nodded. "It hasn't always been rosy, babe."

The term of endearment caught Ellen off guard, and, from the look on Jake's face, it had surprised him as well. *Ignore it,* she told herself, hoping she was right. But still her

334

composure was shaken. She forced herself to sound unaffected. "So you think Jane and I were never close?"

Jake leaned nearer still, shifting to a more comfortable position and stretching his legs. "No, that's not what I'm saying. You were close enough to fight and still love each other at the end of the day."

"And you think that's all it is now?"

"Probably. I'm sure she's upset about your dad. Maybe there's something else bothering her. I don't know, why don't you ask her?"

Ellen hesitated. "I guess I could."

"Just remember she doesn't hate you, Ellen. Not anymore than she did when we were all kids at Petoskey High."

Ellen allowed a few moments of silence while she considered Jake's explanation. The sun was slipping beneath the horizon now and the sky across Lake Michigan was streaked with pink.

"Back then at least I knew why she was mad. Either I was too outgoing or too attracted to a guy she liked." Ellen kept her eyes on the sunset. "Now I don't know what's going on. If she has something against me, she sure hasn't told me about it."

"Yeah, but think about how unhappy she

is. I mean, you probably had a chance to tell your dad you loved him before he died. I'll bet she can't even remember when she talked to him last. That's how it was back when I was around, anyway. She lives in Arizona, right?"

"Right."

"And I'll bet she usually talks to your mom when she calls home, right?"

Ellen nodded and cocked her head, smiling warmly. "How come you know so much when I haven't seen you in nine years, Jake Sadler?"

"I was there a long time, remember?"

His voice was soothing, the same voice she had been in love with such a long time ago. Despite her good intentions, Ellen felt her stomach flip.

"I remember."

"Then trust me. It's just a phase. It'll pass and everything will be fine again before you know it."

"Okay, but what about the others? Aaron and Amy are fighting, and Megan's filled with all these unrealistic ideas about us being a family still because that's what Dad would have wanted. Meanwhile Jane and I are about to tear each other's hair out, and I just want to go back to Miami. I keep thinking there's supposed to be all this love between us because that's what I remember when I think of our childhood. Mom and Dad and us five kids moving from place to place. We had no one else back then, Jake. We needed each other." She bit her lip. "Now I find myself sitting around a room with those same people and it feels like we're strangers, like everything's changed and we don't even like each other."

"Your dad hasn't been gone a week yet, Ellen. You're all trying to find a way to let him go."

"And that's why everyone's being mean to each other?"

"That's why nothing feels right. Your dad was a great man. It's going to take a while for everything to be back to normal. In some ways it'll never be the same again."

The truth of those words stuck her deep. Jake was right. Life was never going to be the same again. Fresh tears rolled slowly down her cheeks. "What am I going to do without him, Jake?"

"Ahh, Ellen." Jake leaned over and wiped two tears from either side of her chin. "I'm sorry. Really, I am."

"I want to see him so badly, just once more. So I can talk to him and ask him what to do about Jane. Sometimes I don't think I'll survive without him."

Jake watched her intently. "I know how that feels."

"Yeah, but your dad's still alive."

He paused a moment. "I still know how it feels."

Ellen did not examine his statement but reached for another tissue instead. "So, you think things will work out for me and Jane? You think we'll have an understanding between us again?"

Jake smiled and brushed a lock of hair off Ellen's forehead. "If there's one thing your father left behind, it's love. He loved his family the way some people never love in their lifetime. I watched him all those years. He was a wonderful dad, a real maker of memories."

Ellen sniffled again. "He was, wasn't he?"

"Yes. And everyone in your family loves each other with an intensity that goes beyond words. I've seen that for myself, too. No matter what Jane says to you or how she's been acting lately, I know she loves you, Ellen."

Ellen looked doubtful. "I don't know, Jake. You haven't seen her in a while. Something's changed. I know I said it already, but I don't know any other way to describe it. It's like she hates me."

"She doesn't hate you. The two of you

have your differences, that's all. Maybe it's best that you live in Miami and she lives in Arizona. But that doesn't mean she doesn't love you."

Ellen sighed. "I don't know. These days it's hard to see any love in her at all."

"Give it time. Watch for a chance to reach out to her. Maybe she'll open up and tell you what's wrong. Maybe it's more than your dad's death, maybe she's dealing with something else."

Ellen nodded. "Okay. I'll try. At least I don't feel like jumping on a plane and heading back to Miami tomorrow morning." She looked at Jake and smiled, wiping her eyes with her fingertips. "Thanks. Somehow I knew you'd understand."

"No thanks needed, Ellen. I'm always here for you." His steady gaze held hers. "I hope you know that."

They talked a while longer, filling in simple details about the years that had passed. It was ten-thirty when they pulled up in front of Megan's apartment, and the lights were off inside. Jake cut the engine and turned to face Ellen. His voice was soft, gentle.

"Don't take this wrong, but it was good to see you again."

Ellen's eyes grew moist. "I know. After all

these years, who'd have thought we'd ever have a night like this?"

"Yeah, you weren't exactly speaking to me last time I saw you."

"I spoke to you." Ellen pushed him playfully in the chest. "Just not any longer than you deserved."

"Touché." His smile faded then, and Ellen could see his regret. After nearly a decade they could kid about what had happened between them, but it still wasn't funny. Not really. It never would be.

"Ellen, I've always wanted to tell you —"

"Jake, don't say anything. I didn't call you looking for a bunch of apologies. The past is behind us."

He let it go, but he looked pensive. "Are you happy, Ellen? In your life, I mean?"

She sighed and ran her fingers through her hair nervously. She caught Jake's eye, saw him watching the gesture, and quickly dropped her hand. It was something she'd always done, and he'd know it wasn't a good sign. She shrugged. "Most of the time, but . . . oh, I don't know. Mike and I are having a little trouble right now, I guess. There's a distance between us. He doesn't like to go out of his way for me, and sometimes that gets old. Like staying home while I attend my dad's funeral."

Jake listened, but again he maintained his silence. Ellen appreciated that he didn't try to fix things, to offer her solutions or explanations. It was becoming more and more evident Jake's physical appearance wasn't the only thing enhanced by the years. Jake Sadler had learned that sometimes it was better just to be silent and listen.

Ellen settled into her seat again, feeling safe and free to talk. "Mike's a wonderful man and a brilliant broadcaster. But I miss the romance we had at first. Most of the time it's like we don't even want to be together anymore." She shrugged. "Just something we have to work out, I guess."

"Ellen." Jake looked anxious, like he wasn't sure if he should say what was coming. "Do you ever wonder?"

Again tears stung her eyes and she released a shaky sigh. "Oh, Jake. Of course. How could I not?" She leaned back against the seat and stared straight ahead at invisible memories floating in the summer breeze. "You were my first love. You took my heart by the hand and led me on a wonderful ride. And when I think about the bad times now, they're not so terrible. Just sad."

"Time does that, doesn't it? Makes the bad times not so bad after all."

Ellen nodded. "I wouldn't have stayed

around if the good times didn't make up for it. I guess I always thought we'd stay together."

"Me too."

She hugged herself tightly and kept her gaze on the trees outside. "You know, Jake, there were times after we broke up when I could have killed you for not being faithful. You ruined all our plans." She glanced at him and saw that his eyes were wet, too. "I talked to your mom once after Mike and I were engaged and you know what she said? She said, 'Are you really sure, Ellen. I always hoped you would wait until Jake grew up.' "

She laughed self-consciously. "I had second thoughts about marrying Mike for more than a month after that. I kept wondering if she was right, if maybe it was only a matter of time before you really did grow up and everything could be like I always wanted it to be."

She fell silent, then nodded slowly. "Yeah, Jake. I wonder." She smiled sadly at him. "But I know what would have happened. In time we would have hated each other, because as charming as you were, as much as I was in love with you, you didn't have it in you to be faithful. And if we had gotten married, your cheating would have destroyed me." She drew a deep breath. "How are things for you? Megan says you're not married."

Jake shook his head.

"Seeing anyone?" She was ashamed of herself, but in some ways she didn't want to know, didn't want to feel the familiar pangs of jealousy where he was concerned.

"No. There's no one. I date once in a while, but nothing serious." His eyes narrowed as if he was trying to see into her soul, the way he had so easily when they were together. "I guess I'm still looking."

Ellen raised a wary eyebrow.

"I know what you're thinking, but it's not like before. Actually, I haven't been on a date in months. No time, really." He paused and seemed to struggle for a moment. "I'm not the same guy I was back then, Ellen."

She smiled. "We've both changed, Jake." For a moment she considered telling Jake about the biggest change in her life since they'd broken up, about becoming a Christian. In some ways she owed her conversion to him, since it had come in the wake of their breakup. She wanted to thank him for that . . . but if she told him about it, she'd also have to tell him she had prayed for God to keep him out of her life. And, somehow, it just didn't seem right to do that right now.

"Well, I know I'm different. I was a jerk,

and I learned my lesson."

"At my expense."

He spoke slowly, deliberately. "At *our* expense."

Ellen sat up straighter and reached for the door. They had crossed into dangerous territory and she knew better than to stay. "Well, on that note I should probably go in. The week's pretty much planned for me. I told my family to work things out without me tonight so they'll probably have a whole list for me to do tomorrow."

"When's the funeral?"

"Saturday morning." Ellen stretched and then reached down to tighten the laces on her tennis shoes.

"Would you mind if I go? I loved him, too, you know."

She sat up slowly and studied Jake's face, remembering the reasons she had fallen in love with him. "You did, didn't you?"

He nodded.

Ellen smiled sadly. "I'm glad you want to be there. I could use the support."

"You don't think it'll raise any questions?"

"Of course not. You're a friend of the family, a friend of my father. Everyone would understand."

Jake nodded again. "All right. Then I'll see you Saturday."

"Okay." Ellen watched as he got out of the truck. He ambled gracefully around to her door and opened it so she could climb out. When she stood before him she saw he had grown several inches over the years.

"You're taller."

"Yeah, runs in the family. My dad grew a few inches in his twenties, too."

"It looks good on you."

"Thanks." He stared at her, his gaze intense. "The years look good on you, too."

They studied each other, and Ellen was keenly aware of the narrow space between them. A gentle wind sifted through the trees above them, and Jake's eyes grew soft as he stared into hers.

The sudden image of Mike's eyes, Mike's face, drifted into Ellen's mind. She stepped back. "I'd better go." It was hardly wise to linger in the moonlight on a summer night in Petoskey with the breeze from Lake Michigan dancing in the trees above and Jake Sadler so close she only had to lean forward to kiss him.

"I hope things get better with Jane."

"Me, too. Thanks again, Jake." She smiled, sadness filling her, then turned and ran lightly up the walk toward the apartment.

"Call me again if you need a break," he yelled softly after her. "I'm taking tomorrow off to catch up on things at home."

She nodded and waved once more before going inside.

When her eyes adjusted to the darkness she saw that Jane and Megan were sitting on the couch watching television. They turned and stared at her, and she felt like a schoolgirl caught out past curfew.

"Where were you?" Jane stared at her hard.

"Out." Ellen did not feel obligated to share the truth with her sisters. They probably wouldn't understand, anyway.

"With whom?"

"A friend."

Jane cast a disgusted look at her older sister. "Fine. Don't tell us."

Megan seemed sad as she turned away from the program and looked at Ellen. "We missed you tonight. You should have stayed around."

"I needed a break."

Megan shrugged. "I know. Mom understood. It's just that the week is going fast, and I'd wanted us to spend as much time together as possible before we go our separate ways."

Jane snorted softly and Ellen forgot all the comforting words Jake had said. He was right. There had to be something else wrong with Jane. *Help me find out what it is that's destroying her, Lord. I can't do this on my own.*

"We made a decision about the eulogy." Jane turned to the television again.

"What?" Ellen remained by the door, her cheeks still flushed from the warm summer air and Jake's nearness.

"Everyone's writing something and reading it at the funeral. Just like Mom wanted."

Ellen felt her anger rise, but she stayed quiet. She could picture Jane gleefully orchestrating that decision to spite her.

"Did you hear me?" Jane stared at her impatiently.

"Yes. Who decided that?"

"All of us. You went out socializing for the night so you'll just have to go along with it."

Ellen thought of a dozen smart comebacks, but she refrained. Jane wasn't going to ruin what had become a nice evening. Not this time. "Fine," she said when she had a handle on her temper. "I'm going to sleep. Good night."

Megan spoke up. "By the way, we're not planning much for tomorrow. Mom has some things she wants to do on her own. We're invited for dinner and I thought we could all hang out there during the day. Maybe go for a walk or something. Then

Thursday we'll shop for funeral clothes and a casket. That's what Mom said, anyway."

"Okay. Fine." Ellen crossed the room in front of them and headed for the spare bedroom, which she and Jane and the children were sharing.

"Is there any other place you could sleep?" Jane called after her.

"You have a better suggestion? A hotel, maybe? A park bench?"

Jane swore under her breath. "You're so sarcastic, Ellen. I just wondered if you could please sleep on the sofa tonight so you don't wake the kids. Last night I didn't get any sleep with all of us crammed in there."

Now Megan rolled her eyes. "Oh, brother! The room's small. Deal with it."

"Whatever." Ellen sighed. "I'll sleep on the couch. But seeing as you guys are watching television, what am I supposed to do until you're ready to go to bed?"

Jane released a forced burst of air and stood up in a huff. "I'm going. Don't worry." She glared at Ellen. "Just like old times, huh, Ellen? When Ellen speaks, people move. Daddy's precious Ellen has to have whatever she wants as soon as she wants it." Jane picked up her pillow and stormed out of the room.

When she was out of earshot Ellen looked

wearily at Megan. "What's the deal with her?"

"I don't know. You two get in a fight before Dad died?"

"Not that I can remember. But there must be something going on. I've never seen her like this."

Megan nodded. "I know. I see it, too."

Ellen remembered Jake's words earlier that night. *Maybe there's something else bothering her . . . why don't you ask her?* "Oh, well. Tomorrow I'll talk to her and get to the bottom of it."

"I hope so. Maybe she's just upset about Dad."

"That doesn't give her the right to act like this."

"I know." Megan sighed and rubbed her neck absently. "Well, I'm turning in, too. I'll get some blankets for the couch."

"Okay. Thanks." Ellen began moving pillows to make room.

"Hey, Ellen . . ."

Ellen turned, distracted by memories of the evening with Jake. "Hmm?"

"Let's hope tomorrow's a better day. Daddy wouldn't have wanted everyone fighting with each other."

Ellen sighed and flopped onto the couch, clutching a pillow to her midsection. "I know it. But things are different now, Megan. Everything has changed so much." *Even Jake Sadler,* she thought sadly. *Just a few years too late.*

"You're right." Megan hugged her rib cage. "But it's so hard on Mom this way, with you and Jane at each other all the time."

"I'm trying my best." The insinuation that Ellen was partially to blame for the problems was frustrating. "What more can I do?"

"It's Jane's problem. Everyone can see that. But try to get along. For Mom's sake."

Ellen nodded. "I'll do my best. Tomorrow's another day. Maybe we can talk things out, and she'll be back to her old self."

"I hope so." Megan turned toward her room. "Good night, Ellen. Love you."

"Good night. Love you, too."

Ellen watched her sister disappear into her room. When she was alone, her shoulders sagged slightly forward and she crawled between a pile of blankets. She wondered absently what Jake was doing, what kind of house he lived in. Then she pictured Mike, alone in their house in Miami. The two images were still battling for position as she fell into a restless sleep.

NINETEEN

Mike was standing next to her, his eyes full of questions as he held a bouquet of red roses.

"Come on, Ellen, make up your mind," he said. Then he said it again.

Somewhere in the background Jake was laughing. He walked up, winked at Ellen, and took the flowers away from Mike. He kept his eyes on Ellen's as he ripped the flowers, one at a time, into a dozen pieces and dropped them onto the carpeted floor. But then the carpet changed and it was an endless field of lush green grass. She and Jake were sitting in wooden chairs, laughing about something.

Mike was there, too, crying softly as he leaned against a tree. He started to speak but no sound came out, and Jake asked him to leave. Before Ellen could protest, Mike's crying grew louder and louder.

Ellen opened her eyes, unsure where she

was. She blinked, disoriented. She'd been dreaming . . . dreaming that someone was crying —

No. She listened carefully. Someone was crying. A soft, sobbing sound was coming from Megan's room. Or was it? Ellen sat up, breathless, and the last wisps of her dream cleared.

She waited a moment and when she was sure the sobbing was real, she stood up and padded quietly into Megan's room.

For a moment she watched her sister, not willing to intrude on her privacy. Megan had four photo albums spread out before her and she looked as if her heart were breaking. The albums contained pictures of the Barrett family, from their parents' wedding through Aaron's high school graduation.

Megan turned a page and ran her fingers gently over a photograph as tears streamed down her face.

"Megan?" Ellen said quietly.

Her sister jumped. She obviously hadn't expected anyone to be up for another few hours.

"You scared me."

"Sorry." Ellen went to sit next to her on the bed. She looked at the picture albums and saw a photograph taken at the Detroit

Zoo. The five of them were lined up against a stone wall, oldest to youngest, with Mom at the end holding a squirming baby Aaron. As usual, Dad wasn't in the photo because he was behind the camera, making memories for another day.

"I miss them." Megan ran a finger over the faces of the small children.

"Me too." Ellen blinked back tears as she turned the page. There was a photo of her and Aaron with their brand-new bikes. Their birthdays were both in early July and their parties were usually on the same day. She flipped the page and saw her and Jane with their arms around each other. She and Amy holding hands. Megan and Aaron sitting in the same wagon, smiles on their faces.

One after another the pictures shouted the truth. Things had changed.

"Do you think Jane hates us?" Megan sniffed.

"I don't know. Nothing's the same with Dad gone, I guess."

"But Jane doesn't have to be so mean. I can't understand what's gotten into her."

"I don't have to what?" Jane leaned into the room and scowled. "What are you guys doing? Talking about me behind my back?"

"We thought you were asleep," Megan explained quickly. "Are the kids up, too?"

"No, don't worry. The kids won't bother you. They're asleep. So, why're you talking behind my back?" Jane stood in the doorway, her hands on her hips.

Ellen lost her temper. "You know, Jane, why don't you go back to Arizona if you can't be civil to the rest of us." Poor Megan had merely wanted a quiet morning to grieve the loss of their father and the family they used to be. Jane's selfishness wouldn't even allow that.

"Mind your own business," Jane sneered.

"Darn you, Jane!" Ellen stood up and yelled at her sister. "What happened to you? You're so full of hate you can't think of anyone but yourself."

"Maybe you just bring out the worst in me."

Ellen was silent, seething inside.

"Come on, you guys. You promised to get along today. Let it go." Megan was crying harder now, and Ellen caught the sound of a baby whimpering down the hallway.

"Way to go. Now the kids are awake!" Jane shouted at Ellen. "I hope you're happy."

"I'll be happy when you leave." Ellen muttered the words under her breath and Jane whirled around again.

"What?"

"I said —" Ellen raised her voice — "I'll

be glad when you leave. I can't stand the way you're treating Megan and me. And Amy, too."

"I suppose that's what you were talking about when I walked in?" Jane ignored her crying child.

"No, in fact it's not. If I want to say something about you, I'll say it to your face. Are you listening?"

Jane glared at Ellen.

"I think something must be terribly wrong, Jane, something you're not talking about and I think it's time to get it out in the open."

Shock ran over Jane's face, and for a moment Ellen thought her sister was going to burst into tears. She didn't give her the opportunity.

"This is your chance, Jane. Are you going to tell us what's wrong or should we take turns guessing?"

Jane's features hardened again. "Fine. Know what's wrong with me? Very simply, it's you. Ever since we were kids you've bothered me, Ellen. I'm sick of you. You think you're better than everyone else and that everyone should bow at your feet." Jane moved a step closer. "I guess I just don't like you, Ellen. I'm having a hard time pretending that I do."

She wheeled around and stormed out of the room.

"Forget pretending!" Ellen shouted after her. "I'm leaving anyway."

Megan watched the argument from her bed and shook her head in frustration, angry tears spilling onto her cheeks. "You two are the most selfish people I know. Dad's dead! And you guys can't stop picking on each other long enough to love each other through the hardest week of our lives." She was sobbing so hard she sounded hysterical.

"Megan —" Ellen began, but her sister jumped up and stormed into the bathroom, slamming the door behind her and turning on the shower.

Left alone in Megan's room, Ellen stared at the phone. Jake's words came back to her. *Call me again if you need a break. I'm taking tomorrow off . . . tomorrow off . . . tomorrow off.*

I need to talk to Mike. She sat down on the bed and picked up the telephone, dialing quickly. The phone in her Miami bedroom rang five times before the answering machine came on. Ellen hung up and looked at the clock. 7:05. Mike was gone to work.

She tapped the phone with her finger and wrestled with her conscience. Then beyond the bedroom door she heard Jane shout at Megan, her voice shrill and angry. Ellen closed her eyes and wondered if she could stand another day with Jane.

Call me if you need a break. I'm taking tomorrow off.

Ellen reached for the phone and dialed a number she had memorized only the night before.

Jake was up early that day and had already shaved and showered when the phone rang. His work crew would be handling the office calls and he was in a particularly light-hearted mood. Seeing Ellen had always had that effect on him.

"Yup?"

"Jake . . . it's me."

Ellen. He sat down slowly, surprised to hear her voice again so soon. "Uh-oh. What happened? You and Jane again?"

"I don't know what to do! She's driving me crazy. I can't stand it."

Jake sighed. "Listen, you need to get away for a while. Get your thoughts together and let her do the same."

"Any suggestions?"

"I'll be there in thirty minutes. We'll go to Mackinac Island, rent bikes, and lay in the sun. Or just sit and talk."

"But you had some personal stuff to take care of."

"It can wait. Come on, no protests. You're gonna lose it if you don't get away for a while."

A sniff sounded. "Okay. I'll be ready."

Half an hour later Ellen walked out of Megan's room wearing a navy one-piece swimsuit underneath shorts and a T-shirt. She held a towel under her arms.

"Where do you think you're going?" Jane asked. She was spoon-feeding the baby and overseeing breakfast for the other two children. Megan was reading a magazine nearby.

"To the beach." Ellen grabbed her purse and headed for the front door. "I'm spending the day with a friend."

"No cares, no worries, right, Ellen?" Jane scowled. "Did it ever occur to you that Mom might want you around the house today?"

"You aren't really leaving, are you?" Megan was shocked.

"Yes. I really am. I'll be back for dinner. Tell Mom I'll see her then."

Without waiting for a response she walked outside and propped herself against a tree where she watched for Jake's truck. Ellen knew her sisters did not for a minute think the friend she spoke of might be Jake Sadler. As he pulled up in front of the apartment she hoped they were not watching.

She settled into the dark brown leather seat. It was like entering another world. *Forget Jane. Forget Mike. Forget everything.* After all, it wasn't her fault Jane was acting vicious or that Mike had forgotten how to love her. Maybe if she disappeared for a day, her sister would have time to think about her behavior and everything would make sense again.

Jake opened the sunroof and slipped a Chicago CD into the car's player. He raised the volume on the stereo as they drove. A warm breeze circulated through the car, and Ellen's anger dissolved like April snow. She leaned back into the seat, saying nothing, enjoying the easy silence between them.

After a few miles, Ellen raised her eyes and searched the tops of the towering pine trees that lined the highway. She had missed them, living in Miami. Somehow the sights and smells of the Michigan pines and Jake's nearness carried her back in time, back to the days when her father was still healthy and strong and she and Jake believed in forever. She closed her eyes and savored the sensation.

In thirty minutes they began seeing signs that directed them toward Mackinaw City's main strip and the ferry boats that made regular runs to the island and back. She drew a deep, cleansing breath and grinned at Jake.

"Feels good, doesn't it?" He returned the smile.

Ellen took another deep breath and nodded. "I miss Mackinac Island. The way it looks and sounds and smells. It's been a long time."

They were quiet again, and Ellen absently twisted her wedding band. What would Mike think about her spending a day with Jake like this? What would her father think? *Help me not to do anything I'll regret, Lord.* But even as she prayed she knew she was being double minded — and wondered if it wasn't already too late.

Her thoughts poked pins at her conscience and she closed her eyes again. When she opened them, upper Lake Michigan lay spread out before her and thoughts of Mike and Jane and her father, even of her faith, were suddenly a million miles away.

Today there would be only Jake.

That same morning, a thousand miles away, Leslie Maple was studying Paul's words in the book of Romans, but she couldn't get Ellen out of her mind. She had wrestled with whether to call Ellen or not. Years had passed since they had talked last, and Ellen might not feel like talking so soon after her father's death. Especially to someone she hadn't heard from in so long. Leslie wasn't even sure she had Ellen's Miami phone number.

She tried reading the Scripture before her again but it was no use. *All right, all right, God, I'll do it. It's been a long time, but I need to call her. Maybe this afternoon.* She felt a sense of urgency at the thought. *Then again, maybe right now.*

Leslie shut her Bible, found her address book, and thumbed through it. She remembered that, because of her position as reporter, Ellen still used her maiden name. She found the *B* section and scanned the page. There it was. Ellen's number in Miami. She was probably already gone, back home in Petoskey for her dad's funeral. Leslie thought of how Ellen and Jane had sometimes fought. If she were already gone, then she would be dealing with more than her father's death.

Poor Ellen. Leslie's fingers flew over the buttons. *Please let me catch her, Lord. Let*

*me pray with her before she goes to face her
family.*

Mike was on his way out the door when the
phone rang. He lunged for the receiver.
"Hello?"

A woman's voice responded, "Oh, I'm so
glad I caught you in time."

Mike frowned. What on earth? "Who is
this?"

"Leslie Maple, Ellen's friend from high
school. I just heard about Ellen's dad the
other day and I'm so glad I caught you
before you left for Petoskey. Can I talk to
her? Is she there?"

Mike glanced at his watch and knew he
had to leave. He had only stopped home
between assignments to change clothes. "Ellen left a few days ago. You can reach her at
her parents' house. I can get the number
for you if you'd like."

Silence. Then, "She went by herself?"

Mike's gaze drifted to the kitchen table
and the unopened Bible lying there. Guilt
seemed to be coming at him from all direc-
tions. "Yeah. Hey, listen, I've got to get going. Did you need that number?"

"No. No, that's all right. I have it. I was
just hoping to pray with her before she left.
How was she? Before she left, I mean? Did

you guys get a chance to pray together?"

Mike sighed. The questions couldn't have been more probing if God himself had called. "No, not really. It all happened kind of fast, I guess."

There was a short silence. "When are you leaving, to join her?"

"The funeral's Saturday, if that's what you mean. I have to work this weekend so the plans are kind of up in the air."

Silence again. Apparently Leslie thought as much of that as Ellen had.

"Well, then. I guess I'll try to catch her at her parents' house. Thanks."

"Sure thing," Mike said. "Thanks for calling."

Leslie hung up the phone and took a moment to consider all she had just learned. Ellen's father's death had been sudden, no doubt leaving Ellen grief stricken. In the wake of the shock, she and her husband had neither prayed together nor taken the same plane to Michigan.

Which meant Ellen was back in Petoskey surrounded by her siblings, frustrated by her husband, and without a friend in the world.

Years may have passed since Leslie had last seen Ellen but some things did not change, and she knew that if things got too painful, too tense between Ellen and her family, too lonely without Mike, there was only one person she would turn to.

"No," she whispered aloud. "She wouldn't think of calling him. That was years ago."

Out of nowhere Ellen's heartfelt prayer that Sunday afternoon so long ago came back to her. *"Jake is my strongest weakness, Leslie. Pray for me. Pray that we stay away from each other."*

Suddenly she knew what she had to do. She picked up the telephone and dialed a local number. "Hello Martha, this is Leslie." She drew a calming breath. "I have an urgent request for the prayer chain."

TWENTY

Jake and Ellen parked in the lot at Shepler's Ferry and blended with a throng of tourists headed for the dock. People from all over the country came to Northern Michigan to see Mackinac Island's seventeen hundred acres and eight miles of shoreline. Ellen had always appreciated the island's historical background. She and Jake picked up a brochure as they boarded the boat.

"I didn't know Mackinac was founded in 1715," Jake said idly. There wasn't a cloud in the sky and the boat filled quickly with tourists headed toward the island.

They continued to read. Mackinac had at different times served as a fur-trading station, a military post, and a summer home for the East Coast elite. Cars were not permitted and travel was done one of three ways: on foot, by horse, or by bicycle. As they read, Jake strained to see over Ellen's shoulder. Occasionally, their elbows would touch and one of them would pull slightly away.

They sat on the boat's upper deck and laughed as the wind pulled at their hair and stung their eyes. The ride was exhilarating, and fifteen minutes later the boat docked along Mackinac Island's main thoroughfare.

Dozens of fudge shops and other specialty stores lined Main Street. At the end of the busy strip stood the famous Fort Mackinac, where an 1880s unit of American soldiers once guarded the straits of Mackinac from enemy forces. The buildings had been restored to look as they had a century earlier, and authentic shooting demonstrations took place throughout the day on the quad.

Most of the tourists stayed on the main stretch, browsing through shops, eating fudge, and touring the fort. The remaining seven miles of island shoreline was relatively free of people. Jake and Ellen rented two bicycles and set off toward the quiet side of the island.

"Remember that time we were riding this path and that kid walked out in front of you," Ellen turned sparkling eyes toward Jake. They were out of the city and, other than an occasional cyclist, there was no one else around.

"He didn't even look. Just crossed the path right in front of me."

Instead of running over the child, Jake had ridden off the path and tumbled down a rocky embankment toward the water. His knee was skinned raw in the resulting fall.

"Still have the scar?" Ellen locked her elbows, enjoying the wind in her face as she steered her bicycle around a pack of tourists.

"Yup. It's faded, but it's still there. My battle with a bicycle."

They laughed and rode on, side by side leaving the tourists behind them. The deep blue water spread out a few feet to their right and a forest of evergreens towered to their left. It was easy to feel at least a little of what the early settlers must have felt: like they were the only people in the world.

"Life must have been hard for the people who lived here a hundred years ago."

"They didn't have fudge shops, that's for sure." Jake raised a teasing eyebrow and Ellen's heart soared.

On the heels of that elation came a Scripture verse flashing across her mind. Proverbs 4: *"Above all else, guard your heart, for it is the wellspring of life. . . . Make level paths for your feet and take only ways that are firm. Do not swerve to the right or the left; keep your* foot from evil."

Ellen swallowed hard. She stared at her feet and the firm, level path before her. Somehow she didn't think that was what the Lord meant by those words. *I'm not doing anything wrong,* she protested silently. *After all I've been through I deserve at least this.*

They rode nearly three miles, then pulled into an alcove and parked their bikes. A stretch of sandy beach lay just in front of them, hidden from the bike path by a thicket. Jake cast a questioning look toward Ellen.

"Ready for some sun?"

"If you don't laugh." She brushed her fingers quickly over his tanned arm. "Some of us work too hard to have much of a tan."

"Ellen! I'm surprised at you," Jake teased. "Living in Miami and missing out on the beach life. Maybe you need a vacation."

It was not yet ten, still too early for anyone else to have discovered the private beach. They found a spot near the shore and lay their towels side by side.

"It's beautiful here." Jake walked back toward the bicycles. He wore red swim trunks and as he walked he stretched and slipped off his T-shirt. Next he grabbed a miniature ice chest from his bike basket and carried it down near their towels.

He smiled, tossing her a bottle of suntan lotion.

"Do my back?" He turned around and positioned himself in front of her.

Ellen snagged the lotion and stared down at it. *What am I doing here? Alone on an island beach with Jake Sadler, about to rub suntan lotion onto his back?*

She drew a deep breath and slowly released it. *Don't let your paranoia run wild,* she chided herself. *It's just a day with an old friend.* She squeezed a handful of cool, creamy lotion into her palms and rubbed them together. Then, like a hundred times before, she rubbed it across the width of Jake's shoulders.

"Mmmmm," he said. "That feels good."

Ellen blushed. She wrestled with her emotions and she was thankful they were on a public beach in broad daylight, even if there wasn't another soul in sight. She continued to rub in the lotion, moving her hands in tight circles down the center of his back and toward his waist. His muscles flexed beneath her touch and Ellen noticed chill-bumps along the base of his neck.

He turned around then and his gaze caught hers. For a moment their eyes spoke a hundred things that neither of them was ready to say. He cleared his throat and took the lotion from Ellen's hands.

"Your turn."

Ellen stared at him, then looked down at the lotion in his hand. An image of those hands rubbing the lotion into her skin swam before her mind's eye . . . and those warning bells that she'd managed to ignore for the last day or so were suddenly clanging so loud she thought she'd go deaf.

Okay, okay, Lord. I get it. She gave a quick shake of her head. "No, thanks. I'm . . . uh, I'm not ready to take my shirt off yet."

Something akin to disappointment sparked in his eyes, but he just nodded and put the lotion away.

They lay down on their individual towels, but Ellen couldn't help being keenly aware of Jake's nearness. Five minutes passed and Jake shifted. As he did so, his elbow ended up touching hers. Had he moved that way on purpose? And were his senses, like hers, completely focused on the spot where their skin touched?

She closed her eyes and tried to listen to the gentle surf, tried to find a voice of reason within her. But there was no getting around the one pervasive thought that filled her mind: the chemistry was back, as powerful as ever, working on her heart and mind and soul. She tried desperately to think about Mike, but he seemed part of another life. The sun was warm, the breeze soothing. In all the world there was only her and Jake, side by side on a sandy, secluded beach on the distant shores of Mackinac Island.

An hour passed and suddenly there was something freezing cold against her neck. She jumped and Jake grinned. In his hand he held a wet can of soda he had taken from the ice chest.

"Come on, sleepy head. Get up," he teased. "You'll get sunburned. Especially with that working-woman white skin of yours."

"Ooooh!" Ellen stood up and adjusted her T-shirt. She grabbed a handful of ice cubes from the chest and ran after him. "I'll get you, Jake Sadler!"

She chased him toward the water and caught him just as he reached the shore. Grabbing his arm she rubbed the ice on his back and laughed when he arched from the chill.

"Got you!" She grinned.

He pulled away easily and she chased him again. Then suddenly he turned on her, picked her up by the legs, and moved unceremoniously into the water.

"Jake! Don't! It's freezing."

He continued deeper into the lake, still holding her around her thighs, until the chilly water was up to her knees. She placed her hands on his shoulders to steady herself.

"Tell me I'm the nicest guy who ever walked the earth," he shouted into the breeze.

"Ha! Name, rank, and serial number. That's all you'll ever get from me!" She was laughing so hard her words barely made sense.

"What's that? Does the prisoner dare speak against her captor?" He swung her precariously near the waves, threatening to drop her.

"Jake, put me down!"

"You got it." He let go and she fell directly into the lake. When she came up her shorts and T-shirt were drenched and she was intent on revenge.

"That's it, you've had it!" She spit water and brushed her wet hair off her face. She reached down, cupped her hands in the waves, and splashed Jake as fiercely as she could until he, too, was soaked.

"Now you're gonna get it!" He retaliated, and the game was on. With an almost reckless abandon, they chased each other along the shoreline, teasing and splashing — and all the while Ellen kept desperately reminding herself that they were no longer young and in love.

When they were exhausted and breathless, they lumbered through the warm sand and headed for their towels.

"I'm freezing." Ellen picked her towel up off the ground and wrapped her body tightly. They sat down together, and she tried to catch her breath.

"Wimp."

Ellen kicked a bit of sand at him. "Not."

For several minutes they were silent, enjoying the sun as it soaked through their freezing bodies. A group of noisy cyclists passed by on the path above them and then disappeared into the distance. There were dozens of small private beaches lining the shores of Mackinac Island and the one they'd chosen remained empty otherwise.

"Makes me wish we had a blanket and a backgammon game." Jake pushed his bangs off his forehead, pulled his knees up to his chest, and turned to face Ellen. He dropped his head onto his arm and stared at her.

"We had fun, didn't we?" She turned and gazed at the horizon as she tousled her hair and pushed it off her face. She refused to look at him, afraid of what she might see in his eyes.

"More than fun."

She nodded absently, busying herself by searching for the suntan lotion and reapplying it to her pale arms and face. He watched her the entire time.

"Good idea. I could use some of that." He reached for the bottle and touched her hand instead.

She nearly gasped. "Jake, I —"

He gave her a bland look. "I just want you to rub some more lotion on my back."

She nodded, feeling foolish for making more of his actions than he intended. She did as he asked, this time as quickly as possible. When she finished she handed him the bottle.

"Okay, Barrett, get yourself up and let's play a little Frisbee." He reached into his backpack and pulled out a white plastic disc.

Ellen was thankful for the distraction, thankful they hadn't discussed the feelings she knew had come alive again between them. She stood up and ran down the shore until she was positioned just right.

Jake tossed the Frisbee in her direction and she snagged it expertly, returning it to him in a single motion.

"You haven't lost your touch," he shouted. "Try this one."

He flung it into the air so that it hung on

the breeze and floated gently toward her. She ran forward, concentrating on her timing. Then, just as she was about to pull it from the air, Jake picked her up around her thighs and threatened to dump her in the water again.

"Jake Sadler! Come on. I'm still cold from last time."

"Tell me I'm king of the beach!" He laughed and swung her precariously near the water.

"Not on your life!" She flailed at him, jabbing him beneath his upper ribs and trying to push herself free.

"Tell me I'm the handsomest man in the world!" He spun her around in the shallow surf, and she could feel the cold water on her feet.

"Get real!" She struggled harder, laughing at the same time.

Suddenly he stopped. With deliberate slowness, he lowered her in front of him. He placed his hands tenderly on either side of her face and his voice was soft when he spoke again. "Tell me you still have feelings for me, Ellen." His eyes searched hers and he wove his fingers into her hair.

"Jake . . ." She was having trouble breathing, and tears filled her eyes as she looked into his. Breaking the connection, she hung her head, wrapping her arms around herself protectively. "Jake, I can't."

There was silence for a moment, then Jake stepped back from her. "I know. I'm sorry." Ellen saw from the look in his eyes that the apology was sincere. "I shouldn't have said that."

"Sometimes I think you know me better than anyone," she said, tears spilling onto her cheeks. "What do you see when you look into my eyes?"

He spoke quietly, studying her face. "You still feel. For me."

She nodded. "A part of me will always love you. But that doesn't change the facts, Jake. I'm married. It's wrong for us . . . for me . . ."

"Don't say it, Ellen. I understand. I was wrong to push it." He reached out as though to touch her cheek, then let his hand fall to his side, a crooked smile on his face.

Ellen fought a sob. "I love my husband, Jake." At his steady look, she shook her head. "I know, I know. I called you. I agreed to come here with you. I . . . I don't know why. I wanted to find something, to feel something." She met his gaze again. "But I can't have some cheap affair on the beach while Mike thinks I'm here mourning my father's death." She moved away from him, angry with herself as she trudged toward her towel. He followed and they sat together in silence.

"Okay, then," Jake sighed and his sad smile nearly broke Ellen's heart. "Tell me about Mike."

Ellen drew a deep breath and stared at the endless deep, blue waters of Lake Michigan. It was colder and more intense looking than the Atlantic, and Ellen realized how much she had missed it. The breeze was stronger than before and clouds had formed in the west, blocking the sun.

"Mike is bright and funny and handsome. And a very good broadcaster. The execs at the network have their eyes on him for a national spot."

Jake's eyebrow arched slightly and he hesitated. "That's not what I mean, Ellen. . . . Tell me why you love him."

She sighed and hugged her knees close to her body. "Oh, Jake. Don't ask me that. Not now."

"I'm not trying to stump you. I just want to know what he has. What's so special about him? How come after you two met you were finally able to let go of us?"

Ellen pondered his question. What had been special about Mike? For one thing, he'd shared her faith and because of that she'd been certain God had brought Mike into her life. She was still certain. But after what had almost happened between her and Jake she was embarrassed to talk about her faith. She knew she wouldn't sound convincing. Not now when her faith was being tested and her feelings for Mike were so shaky.

After a while she turned her head and stared at Jake. "I trust him," she said simply.

Jake looked as if she'd taken a hammer to his gut. His face filled with regret and he turned away, gazing out at the water.

When he said nothing, she continued. "You let it happen, Jake. I was coming to your house that day to tell you I would be there forever. I only wanted to know I could trust you."

He lowered his head.

"Then that . . . that girl answered the door. Wearing nothing but your bathrobe."

He reached for her hand and squeezed it once before letting it go. "I'm sorry, Ellen. I've been sorry ever since. Really. You deserved better."

Ellen nodded. "You broke my heart, you jerk," she said softly. Her eyes were wet again. "All I ever wanted was to stay in love with you the rest of my life. But you weren't content with that. I wasn't enough for you, Jake."

He was silent, pensive as he watched her.

"That's what I love about Mike," she said finally. "I trust him. I'm enough for him." She paused. "And he won't ever break my heart."

Jake nodded. "Good. I'm happy for you, Ellen. Really, I am."

"I'm not saying it's perfect. But being with you these last two days I've really had to think about my life and what's important. There are reasons you and I broke up, and reasons Mike and I married. I can't forget that now that I'm here with you again." There was silence for a moment before she continued. "My marriage is important to me, Jake. I want it to work."

"I know. Forgive me?"

She studied him. "Forgiven."

"Let's forget about it, okay? I guess it's only natural for us to remember how we felt about each other."

"I guess."

Jake smiled at her. "Made you forget your family for a while, though, didn't I?"

She tossed a fist of sand at his feet. "Jake Sadler, I thought you'd grown up and quit your incessant teasing."

He grinned. "Some things never change."

She thought of the way he made her feel and she uttered a short laugh. "That's for sure."

For the rest of the day they kept their conversation on safer topics. Her job at the newspaper, his business. By midafternoon they'd caught up on nine years, all the while keeping a careful distance from each other. Finally, they climbed back on their rented bicycles and continued the rest of the way around the island. After they turned their bikes in, they walked along Main Street and sampled Island Almond Fudge and Northern Nutty White Chocolate.

At four o'clock they boarded a ferry headed back to the mainland. The air had cooled considerably and Ellen started when something came over her shoulders. It was Jake's shirt. He'd draped it around her without saying a word. She smiled her thanks, and he nodded. Though he didn't touch her, his nearness had an almost physical impact on her. The boat arrived at the dock and they walked across the parking lot to his truck. He led her to the passenger side, and before he opened her door, he wrapped his arms around her waist and pulled her close.

They had lost a great deal, and they both knew they could never have it again. The rules had been established. But for that moment they needed to say good-bye to what they'd found on a secluded island beach in the middle of Lake Michigan.

"Thank you," she said finally, tilting her head, looking up into Jake's face. "Thanks for today. Thanks for understanding."

Jake's hands tightened ever so slightly about her waist and their faces were inches from each other. If he lowered his head now, kissed her, Ellen didn't know if she could stop herself. *Don't let him do it, God. Please! I'm so weak and if he kisses me, I'll never go home again. Help me here, Lord.*

Seconds passed and finally she saw him clench his jaw and pull back. He took her hands in his.

"It was a day from the past." He smiled. "I won't ever forget it, Ellen."

Thirty minutes later he dropped her off a few houses away from her parents' home.

"Just in case our being together might cause trouble with the others," he said.

Ellen smiled tenderly. "Thanks again for today," she whispered.

He squeezed her hands gently. "Don't thank me, Ellen. I never thought I'd see you again and . . . well . . . I'll always remember today. I haven't had a day like that in years."

"Years?" she teased.

He didn't laugh. Didn't even smile. "Nine years, to be exact."

She looked down at her hands, unsure of what to say. Her eyes fell on her wedding band.

"You go on," he said finally. "Call me if you need me."

Ellen nodded and reached for the door handle. "Thanks for understanding . . . about me and Mike. It was good for me to talk about him."

Jake smiled sadly. "Me, too. He's a lucky man, Ellen." He paused. "Don't think I wouldn't give anything to be in his shoes, because I would."

"Jake . . ."

"I know. We had our time. But don't ever mistake how I feel about you. No amount of time can change that. Now go inside before I drive away with you and whisk you off to some undiscovered island to live with me forever."

"You're crazy."

Again, there was no humor in his level gaze. "I'm honest. Now go."

She smiled, thanked him again, and said good-bye. After a few steps, she turned to wave again, but her hand froze at her side. She'd caught sight of Jake's face just before he drove away . . . and there had been tears running down his face.

TWENTY-ONE

Jane's children were down for a nap in her parents' spare bedroom and she was wandering around the hallway looking at framed photographs. Megan, Amy, and Aaron were in the den finishing lunch, trying to figure out what to say at their father's funeral. For that moment at least, peace reigned in the Barrett household.

Jane came upon an old, gold-framed photo and studied the roughly colored print of Ellen and her at four and two years old. Even back then Ellen looked confident while Jane looked uncertain. Jane noted how, in the picture, she had leaned on her older sister for support.

That had certainly changed.

Now her support came from Troy. She wished he were there so he could calm her down, make her less angry around the others. They had all misunderstood her. It wasn't that she was mad at them. She simply couldn't relate to their sorrow and so had become increasingly frustrated. She could hardly wait for the week to be over so she could return to her calm, peaceful life in the Verde Valley.

She heard footsteps and she glanced out the window to see Ellen, looking tanned and relaxed. Jane's mouth twisted. How was it that while Jane was wrestling with the memory of being raped, struggling with indifference over her father's death, Ellen was off sunning herself with an old friend on the beach all day?

Ellen flung her things on an oversized chair and smiled tentatively at Jane. She was still savoring her day and the last thing she wanted was another fight. "Hi, how's everyone doing?"

Jane uttered a short laugh. "Like you care."

Fine, Ellen thought. *End of discussion.* She shrugged and without saying another word headed toward the den where the others had turned off the television so they could talk.

"I can't think of what to write," Aaron was saying as she walked in.

He was stretched out in their father's easy chair, his mannerisms almost identical to those of their dad. Ellen sat next to Megan on a comfortable old sofa that had been in the family for years.

"What's the discussion?"

"Where've you been?" Amy asked. There was no accusation in her voice, but Amy looked nervous and intimidated by her siblings.

"The beach."

"By yourself?"

"No, with an old friend."

"Who?" Megan asked curiously.

"No one you'd remember," she lied. "So, what're you guys talking about?"

"Trying to figure out what to write for Dad's funeral." Amy studied a page of notes in front of her and wrinkled her face. "Any ideas?"

"Well, it's supposed to be a private thing. I mean, you're supposed to write what *you* remember about Dad. Not what any of the rest of us remembers. Am I right?" She looked to Aaron and Megan.

Aaron snorted in frustration and slammed his notes onto the table next to the easy chair. For an instant Ellen remembered that her father had kept his medicine on that table after his bypass surgery. For three months he convalesced in that chair until both thirty-six-inch incisions, one down the center of his chest, the other along the inside of his left leg, had healed. How could a person smoke again after that?

She brought herself back to focus on her brother. "What's wrong, Aaron?"

"You."

"Me?"

"Not you. What you said," he barked. "You say it's supposed to be our own writing, but I'm not a writer. I can't put things down on paper like you and Megan and everyone else. I need a little help. Is that all right with you?"

"I wasn't trying to start a fight, Aaron. I only want you to understand the purpose of doing separate eulogies. It's what each of us individually remembers about Dad. Not what someone else remembers."

"Okay, but what am I supposed to say?"

"Exactly," Amy joined in. "How are we supposed to come up with the right words? I want to write something, say something that comes from my heart. But I can't think of anything."

"Okay, tell you what —" Ellen looked at Amy, her mind racing — "start with you, Amy. Tell me what you loved most about Dad. What you'll always remember."

Amy squirmed uncomfortably. "Well, he was bigger than life, kind of like my hero, I guess." Her eyes grew damp and Ellen tilted her head in empathy.

"He was, wasn't he."

Amy nodded, wiping a stray tear.

"Okay. What else?" Ellen coaxed tenderly, aware that Aaron watched them intently.

"I remember when we moved to Petoskey and I was a little girl. I fell in the backyard and cracked my chin on the patio."

"You were four, I think," Ellen said.

"Right." Amy's eyes grew distant at the memory. "Daddy picked me up in his arms and took me to the hospital. I don't remember how they fixed me up or what happened after that. Just that he took care of me."

"Okay, now you're getting somewhere. He was bigger than life, he took care of you. Jot those things down."

Amy did as she was told and Ellen turned to Aaron.

"Now, Aaron, you do the same. What do you remember?"

Aaron thought awhile, and Ellen could almost see the memories battling to take shape in his mind. But before he would give them a chance to materialize, he forced the chair's footrest down and stood up in a sudden burst of motion.

"Forget it!" He hitched up his jeans and turned to leave the room. "All I remember is how he paddled my butt while you girls got off easy."

Ellen stared at him, completely baffled. Not so much at what her brother had said as the fact that he seemed to believe it. "Aaron!" she called him back into the room. She did not expect him to return, and when he did, she pointed to the chair. "Sit down. We need to talk about something."

"What?" It was more of a grunt than a word but Aaron sat down and waited.

"Those things that happened to you when you were a child, they're in the past. They weren't Dad's fault, they were ours, mine and the other girls'. But I can tell you now, one adult to another, that everything we ever did to you was done in fun." She hesitated. "You might not have thought it was funny, you might have felt picked on. But you were our only brother, and we felt it was our duty to gang up against you. It was just a way of getting a few laughs."

"I didn't laugh then," he said, surprisingly articulate. "And I'm not laughing now. How would you have liked being the only boy with four girls picking on you all the time? And no matter what I said back then, Dad took your side."

"Is that the whole story, Aaron? Really?" She made sure she had his attention and she continued. "I remember things a little differently. Every Saturday you and Dad went out and had fun while Mom and us girls stayed home and cleaned the house. How do you think that felt? And what about your bedroom? Do you think any of us girls wouldn't have been thrilled with a room of our own?"

Aaron was quiet.

"Dad loved you, Aaron. You were his only son. Don't tell me about how bad you had it."

Ellen saw Amy and Megan stare at their brother. *Oh, please, Jesus. Don't let any of them jump in and say anything that will anger Aaron. Just this once, please, let things be peaceful.* Ellen knew they were all hurting now; it wasn't the time to fight about Aaron's leftover emotional baggage. The girls remained silent and Ellen breathed a sigh of relief.

When Aaron's anger seemed to subside, she continued. "Maybe you could write about something that happened in the last few years. Like when you and Dad spent all that time golfing."

Aaron put his elbows on his knees and covered his face with his hands. His shoulders sank but otherwise he was silent, unmoving. The others watched him carefully, and though he didn't make a sound, they could see huge tears dropping onto the floor. Ellen felt her throat constrict. The ice was melting.

Jane entered the room then and looked around at the faces of her siblings, unaware of the moment taking place. "What's going on?"

"We're trying to figure out what to write about Dad," Amy said quietly. "Thinking of memories."

"Hmph." Jane crossed her arms. "You have to have memories to think of them."

"You have memories." Ellen heard the weariness in her voice. "All of us have memories."

"Yeah, well some of us have better memories than others," Jane said pointedly. She sat down next to Amy and picked up a magazine from an end table. Thumbing through the contents she found an article and began to read, seemingly uninterested in the conversation around her.

"Aaron," Ellen tried again. "Pretend you're in a room all by yourself and an imaginary person wants to know what you remember about Dad."

Aaron grunted.

"Write down whatever you would tell that person. That's all you need to do."

Aaron nodded, sniffing loudly and discreetly wiping his eyes. "Okay. I'll try."

He stood up and lumbered from the room. It was just after six o'clock and he had a date that night with a girlfriend he'd seen the previous year. It was a date he'd clearly looked forward to. He picked up the phone and dialed.

"Jen, I have to cancel," Ellen overheard him say. "That's right. I need some time by myself. Right. Okay, talk to you later."

Aaron straightened himself up and there was an air of determination about him. He picked up some paper and a pen, grabbed his keys, and left the house without another word to his sisters.

When the door closed behind him, Ellen looked at the others. "I think he'll get the eulogy written."

Megan nodded. "His feelings are there, they're just buried so deep it's hard for anyone to find them."

"Yeah," Ellen agreed. "Even him."

Amy studied the notes she had written in the past few minutes and sighed. "Well, I guess I'll go home early tonight. I think I can work with these notes and put something together. At least I hope so."

"You'll do fine," Ellen said.

Jane looked up from her magazine. "Don't tell her how she'll do! She doesn't need your opinion to make her efforts worth something."

Ellen leveled an ominous glare at Jane as she stood and turned to Megan. "I'll be in Mom's room lying down. Wake me for dinner." She started to leave and then stopped again. "Oh, and another thing. Tell Mom I'm staying here tonight. It'll be easier on everyone."

Megan looked disappointed but she didn't argue. "You're probably right."

Jane watched Ellen go, angry that her older sister had given up so easily. If only Ellen cared enough to take her aside and ask what was wrong, Jane might consider telling her about the rape. Maybe then they could work through the barrier between them and find love again, even friendship. Tears stung at her eyes and though her vision was blurred, she stared down at the magazine and pretended to read so no one would see her cry.

TWENTY-TWO

Ellen was tired from the bike ride and her day at the beach with Jake. She lay down on her parents' bed and hugged one of the pillows to her stomach.

She thought back on the day, remembering how close she had come to giving in to Jake.

Then just as quickly another Scripture, this one from James, besieged her. *"Each one is tempted when, by his own evil desire, he is dragged away and enticed. Then, after desire has conceived, it gives birth to sin; and sin, when it is full-grown —"*

Stop! She shouted at herself. *Enough of that! I needed Jake today and besides, I didn't do anything wrong.* But the argument sounded unconvincing, even to her.

It was wrong. It was wrong to be with him, a voice within her said. *And dangerous.*

She pressed her lips together. If Mike had come with her this week, she would never have called Jake. And she certainly wouldn't be wrestling with old feelings that should have died a long time ago.

Mike. At the thought of him, Ellen had to fight off tears again. What had happened to them? Things had been so wonderful at the beginning. Their first date was a complete hit, and after that Mike had been full of surprises, like the time he took her to Canada for the day or out to dozens of wonderful restaurants. At their wedding Ellen remembered looking into his eyes and thinking she would love Mike Miller for the rest of her life.

The trouble had started a few years later. They lived in Detroit at first, and Ellen was used to making the trek back and forth to Petoskey. Especially during summer.

"Mike, my dad wants us to come up this weekend for a barbecue," she remembered telling him one summer.

"Sounds good."

The week passed, and when Friday arrived Ellen reminded him of their plans. "Are we leaving tonight or in the morning?"

"Leaving?" He sounded clueless.

"Yes. For Petoskey. Remember? My dad invited us up for a barbecue this weekend."

"Oh, that. Hey, hon, I don't think I'll go this time."

Ellen's mouth had dropped open. "What?"

"Sweetheart, I never really said I wanted to go." Mike looked suddenly pained. "I said it sounded good."

"When someone says something sounds good, it's typically safe to assume the answer is yes."

"Well, you go ahead and go. I have to research the games for next week."

"I won't do that to my father. He's expecting us and I want us there. You said you'd go."

"I did not. I said it sounded good."

"It's the same thing, Mike. Besides, you can do your research in the car. I'll drive."

Mike had exhaled dramatically. "All right, fine. I'll go. But it would be nice if one of these days you could see things from my point of view. It takes four hours to get to Petoskey and it wastes the whole weekend."

While Ellen talked with her parents and caught up on the latest, Mike grabbed a magazine and found a quiet corner. In the end, Mike made the trip miserable by distancing himself from the others and arguing with Ellen until they were back home again. There were a dozen such incidents like that in the early years of their marriage.

"Tell them I don't want to go," Mike would suggest.

"You don't understand, Mike. My dad really loves you. He thinks you *like* spending time with him. How do you think he'd feel if I called and told him you didn't want to come for a visit? That you had better things to do and wanted me to make the trip by myself?"

The worst part, Ellen thought now, was that whenever Mike did accompany her to Petoskey, he made sure she knew it was against his will. In doing so, he robbed her of the joy she might otherwise have felt about the trip. Mike had not pursued a relationship with her parents, and now that her father was dead Ellen was angry at him.

At least Jake knew and loved my dad.

She pushed the thought aside, feeling disloyal.

There were other problems that developed between her and Mike once they moved to Miami. Birthdays, for instance. Year after year she looked forward to Mike's birthday. She plotted and planned for a month until she had picked out the perfect gift. One year it was a surprise vacation to the Keys, another year it was tickets to Wisconsin so he could take in a Green Bay football game with his aging grandfather. She had created personalized wall hangings for his office and put his baby pictures together in a quilted scrapbook with his name embroidered on the front.

She loved Mike and she wanted her gifts to be a reflection of that love.

Mike's approach couldn't have been more different.

He generally did his shopping a day or two before her birthday and was usually gone not more than an hour. One year he gave her a bright orange nylon dress that she wore exactly once before giving it to Goodwill. Another year he bought her a bulky beige purse with double straps that looked more suitable for her grandmother.

But the worst birthday of all came four years ago. Ellen planned for them to spend the weekend at a hotel south of Miami. Friday night was wonderful with a walk along the beach and a shared bath later in their hotel room. Then, when her birthday dawned the next morning, Mike explained that he had not gotten her a gift.

"Honey, I've been so busy lately. You know how it is."

Ellen did *not* know how it was. She stared at Mike and tried to understand. "Did you get me a card?"

Ellen had always made it clear to Mike that in lieu of a present she would always be thankful for a handwritten card or letter.

She was not interested in expensive baubles or costly floral bouquets. But a gift should be a reflection of love and to that end Mike was a dismal failure.

That weekend, after the shock wore off, Mike tried to sound hopeful. "Hey, Ellen. I can go sit on the patio right now and write you a letter if you want."

"No. I don't want a letter now that my birthday is already here. It's too late."

"Don't be mad. I meant to get you something. It's just that the days got away from me."

"Mike, it's very simple. May is followed by June, which in turn is followed by July. There is nothing random about the way we arrive at a given date. I don't understand how the days can 'get away' from you if you really love me."

"Ellen, don't make this an issue, darling. Of course I love you. Gifts don't reflect how much a person loves another person. Think about last night."

"They matter to me, Mike." She picked up her towel and headed for the door. "You know they matter and still you don't make an effort. How am I supposed to feel about that?"

If there had ever been a summer when she was tempted to call Jake Sadler, it was the summer of 1994. After the birthday incident, one of her fellow writers at the paper in Miami invited her to his wedding.

"I can't wait," she told Mike that evening. "We haven't been on a date in months and this will be even better. We can dress up and dance. Can you make sure you're free that afternoon?"

"Ellen," Mike moaned. "I can tell you right now I don't have a game that day. But I don't even know the people getting married. Why don't you go and use the time to catch up with some of your coworkers?"

Ellen could feel her anger rising. "Mike, this is a simple thing I'm asking you. I haven't been feeling great about our marriage and it is very important that you accompany me to this wedding."

They discussed it for weeks but in the end she attended the wedding alone and afterward came home and parked in their driveway. She sobbed angry tears for two hours before going in. Thankfully, Jake lived in another state because if she'd had somewhere else to go that night she would have gone.

There were other occasions after that. Concerts, get-togethers with friends. Mike would only go when Ellen badgered him.

Even then he would let her know it was an effort.

She rolled over in her parents' bed and thought again about Jake. In some ways, he and Mike were complete opposites. Jake had brought her flowers and given her jewelry and surprised her with picnics on the beach and walks through Magnus Park. With Jake, Ellen never had to wonder if she was loved.

But she did have to wonder about other things.

Suddenly she pictured the blond in the bathrobe. Yes, Jake had been attentive, but he had also been dishonest and unfaithful. In the end she had been willing to let go of the romance in hopes of finding someone she could trust, someone with a love for God like she had known in those lonely days after leaving Jake.

Someone like Mike.

Mike did love her. He showed her in a dozen unique ways every day of their lives. He wrote songs for her and did the dishes when she was too tired to move after a day's work. He was loyal and fun loving and utterly faithful.

She rolled over once more and pulled the pillow more tightly to her body. *What is it, Lord? Why aren't things like they were between us?*

Again, no answer. Tears ran down Ellen's cheeks. Sure, Mike made mistakes, but his faithfulness had to mean something. He must love her, and more than Jake ever had.

She closed her eyes and tried to believe it was true.

Twenty-Three

For the first time that week, curled up in the king-size bed where her father had spent every night for the past twenty-one years, Ellen slept soundly. The room even smelled like him, and she fell asleep dreaming about being a small child, scurrying to her parents' bed for protection during one of the fierce Midwestern thunderstorms.

Sometime later, she grew vaguely aware of someone standing over her, touching her face gently, pulling the covers up over her. The sense she had was one of safety and care, and she burrowed deeper into the pillow with a sigh.

She awoke the next morning to find her mother lying beside her.

"Good morning, sleepy head." Her mother's smile was tender.

Ellen smiled in return. "Morning." Then she stretched. "Sorry to take over your bed."

Mom plumped her pillow and sat up

against the headboard. "You were sleeping so soundly when I came in last night, I knew you needed the sleep. I just pulled the covers over you and left you there."

Ellen glanced at the clock; it was still early. It would be some time before Aaron was up, before the family members and relatives started calling. For a while she and her mother said nothing, staring at the ceiling, comfortable in the silence between them.

"I still can't believe he's gone," her mother said finally. She kept her gaze on the ceiling, talking more to herself than to Ellen. "I wake up, ready to climb out of bed and make him coffee. Sometimes I even get halfway down the hall before I remember. Then it hits me. He's gone and he's not coming back."

Ellen felt her gut twist with her mother's words. She had been so busy that week, fighting with Jane, dealing with Aaron, angry at Mike . . . struggling with her feelings for Jake. It had almost been enough to make her forget why she was there. But the truth wouldn't go away. Not for long. She could ignore it, push it to the back of her mind, walk around it. But the fact remained. Her father was gone.

"I loved him, you know, Ellen. I wonder sometimes if I said that enough."

"Oh, Mom, don't be so hard on yourself." Ellen rolled onto her side and faced her mother. "Of course you said it enough."

"No, I don't mean to your father. I told him every day. But I wonder if you kids knew how I felt."

"We saw how you waited on him, if that's what you mean."

Mom shook her head. She turned onto her side and propped her head up on one hand. "That's not what I mean at all. I waited on your father because I loved him. Because he would have done anything for me through the years."

"We knew that. Otherwise you wouldn't have treated him the way you did. Still, I always thought he could have been a little more helpful, to tell you the truth." She paused. "It seemed like you had to do all the housework yourself. Especially after we girls were gone." She shrugged. "But that didn't change what was obvious about you and Dad. Everyone knew you loved each other."

Her mother sighed. "I didn't do that much, Ellen. Sure, I made him coffee and brought him a Diet Coke when he asked. I made dinner and did his laundry. But he did things that couldn't be counted or measured. He made a wonderful life for me.

He made me laugh and made our marriage an adventure. Everything we ever did with you children was his idea." She was quiet then and Ellen saw her lip quiver. "He made us a family, Ellen."

Ellen reached for her mother's hand. Suddenly she knew she would always remember this moment with her mother. The thought brought a fresh pang of regret. If only they had shared more times like this over the years.

"We're still a family." Compassion swept her. "I guess that's his legacy, huh?"

Her mom looked unsure. "You children aren't what you used to be, you're not as fun loving and close. There was a time when you got along beautifully together."

Ellen thought of Jake's words and pursed her lips pensively. "I don't know, Mom. I think we always fought. Even in the best of times."

"Sure, but nothing serious. Nothing like you and Jane now."

Ellen sighed. "I don't like it anymore than you do. But every time we're together she says something hateful. At least that's how I see it."

"I know. But couldn't you at least talk to her, ask her what's bothering her? She's always been moody, but Ellen, even you must admit this just isn't like her. It's obvious something is very wrong."

"I'll try, Mom. I've been trying since I got here. But she's been treating me different for a long time — long before Dad's death."

They were silent again. Finally Mom slipped out of bed, stood up, and stretched. She straightened her nightgown and checked her reflection in the mirror.

"I have more gray now, did you notice?"

"Not much. It's flattering."

"That's what your father said. Sophisticated, he called it." She took a deep breath and turned back to Ellen. "We're going shopping this morning at ten so we can find something to wear to the funeral. You're coming, aren't you?"

"Of course. I'll call Megan and make sure they're up and getting ready."

Mom looked pensive. "Ellen, have you talked to Mike?"

At Mike's name, Ellen felt the heat rise in her face. "Why do you ask?"

"I don't know. I just sense that things aren't great between you."

Ellen sat up slowly and hugged her knees to her chest, leaving the bed sheet tucked around her. "We had a fight before I left."

"Have you talked to him?" she asked gently.

"No. I've been too busy."

"You've had time to visit with friends."

"Mom," Ellen groaned. "I'm a grown woman. I can handle my marriage just fine, thank you."

"I know. But I think it's time you called him. You don't even know when his plane's coming in for the funeral."

"I don't even know *if* his plane's coming." Ellen instantly regretted making the statement.

Her mother raised an eyebrow. "Then it's worse than I thought." She waited a moment, appraising her oldest daughter carefully. "It's true, you're a grown woman, Ellen. You can make your own choices. But if you know what's best for you, you'll be on the phone sometime today patching things up."

Ellen was silent.

"The years go by too quickly to waste them in silent prisons of hate."

With that, she turned around and headed for the kitchen, leaving Ellen speechless and overwhelmed. All her life she had thought her father to be the poetic one, the parent who could best relate to her creative side. But once in a while her mother would surprise her by coming up with something meaningful enough to be remembered for a lifetime. *Silent prisons of hate.*

Ellen peeled back the sheets, stood, and stretched. If only Mike had come with her in the first place. She wandered absently toward her father's nightstand and opened the top drawer. Assorted pens and pencils, a calculator, and a couple of paperbacks. She shut it and pulled open the next drawer. Suddenly she caught her breath and stared. There was her father's old Bible.

Fresh tears stung her eyes. "Oh, Daddy," she whispered. "I knew you read the Word, but . . . I didn't know you kept it here . . . so close." She lifted it carefully from the drawer and ran her fingers over the worn leather cover. She traced his name, embossed in gold on the lower right corner. Holding his Bible made her feel nearer to her father than she had felt all week.

It also made her miss him more.

She opened it gingerly, wondering if he had written in the margins. Her eyes fell on the dedication page. "To my beloved John, on our first anniversary. Yours forever in love, Diane." Ellen felt a stab of regret for all the times she had questioned her parents' faith. She flipped gently through the text and saw that, indeed, he had written many notes alongside favorite verses. Her eyes fell on one that her father had highlighted and underlined: 1 Corinthians 10:12–13. *"So, if you think you are standing firm, be careful that you don't fall! No temptation has seized you except what is common to man. And God is faithful; he will not let you be tempted beyond what you can bear. But when you are tempted, he will also provide a way out so that you can stand up under it."*

Her father had drawn several asterisks near the verse and written his own comments. *"Hold fast to your faith. Temptation is a given; look for the way out! It is possible to fall!"* The words cut Ellen as deeply as if her father had been standing before her, saying them himself. She squeezed her eyes shut, and two tears fell onto the delicate paper. Dabbing at the page, she considered the message from her father — or her Father . . . ? She was supposed to be looking for a way out, a way to withstand her temptations. Instead she'd been entertaining thoughts of Jake Sadler from the moment she'd boarded the plane to Michigan.

Oh, Lord, help me stand up under it all. She read the verses and her dad's words again through blurry, tear-filled eyes. She glanced at the nearby alarm clock. It wasn't yet seven in Miami so Mike might still be home. She composed herself so that he wouldn't know she'd been crying, then she picked up the phone and punched in the number. He answered on the second ring.

"Hello?"

She paused a moment. "Mike, it's me."

"Ellen." There was something stiff and unyielding in his voice. He was probably angry with her for waiting so long to call. "I wondered whether you were going to call me this week."

"Of course. I've just been busy."

"Are you okay? Is everyone getting along?"

"I'm fine, we're all fine." There was no need to get into it now. She could tell him the details later. "How's work?"

"Busy, but great. They've got me working another couple games this weekend. They both have national attention."

The hair on the back of Ellen's neck bristled. "This weekend?"

"Yeah. Is that a problem?"

"The funeral's this weekend, Mike. Saturday morning."

He hesitated. "You told me you didn't want me there. Right? . . . Wasn't that you?"

Ellen released a loud huff. "That's not what I meant and you know it! I was mad because you wouldn't come for the whole week."

"Well, I took you at your word, Ellen, and

now I'm booked. It's too late to change my plans."

"I don't believe this. You couldn't possibly have thought I didn't want you here for the funeral. I need you."

"Look, Ellen. You told me you didn't want me there. Then you didn't call for almost a week. What was I supposed to think?"

Ellen was silent, furious with him. "I don't know. But I think it's pretty clear how much I mean to you if you can't even take time from your schedule to attend my father's funeral with me."

"You told me you didn't want me there," he insisted angrily.

"But if you loved me you'd have come — no matter what — I was angry. You know I didn't mean what I said."

"It's too late now, Ellen. Lighten up."

"Don't tell me to lighten up." Her voice was frigid. The sudden image of Jake sitting beside her on the shore of Mackinac Island flitted into her mind. "Forget it, Mike. I'll have plenty of support."

"Listen, Ellen, I'm sorry. Don't be so angry. I've missed you all week and I can't wait to see you. I even read my Bible last night. First time in a while."

"Good for you."

"Ellen, stop. I know this must be hard for

you, but it would have been almost impossible to get the weekend off. Especially at this time of the year with the pennant race heating up."

"What exactly do you think it means to be married, Mike?"

"What kind of a question is that?"

"A pertinent one. Marriage should be more than a convenience, more than a body to warm your bed." Ellen closed her eyes and her mind filled with the image of Jake. When she spoke again there was a catch in her voice.

"When you love someone you do whatever it takes to be by their side." She was talking to Mike, but she knew deep inside she was describing Jake, the way he was now. "You stand by them and make yourself available when they need you."

"Come on, Ellen —"

She cut him off. "No. I mean it, Mike. That's what love's all about. But that isn't you at all. The pennant race is worth more than me."

"Oh, Ellen, come on. Stop being so dramatic. You know I love you."

Ellen felt the sting of tears. Her husband had rejected her when she needed him most; she had no desire to fight him now.

"No. I don't. And that's the saddest part

of all. I need you, Mike." She uttered a short laugh. "And you're not here. How am I supposed to know you love me?"

Mike was quiet. "I don't know what to say."

She waited a moment and then reached into her purse beside the bed for her airline tickets.

"I'm coming home on Flight 252 at 5:30 Sunday evening." It was her professional voice, the one she used at work. Business-like, without a trace of the pain that was strangling her heart. "Will you be there or should I take a taxi?"

"Of course I'll be there. I'll come straight from the game. Hey, when we get home let's go out and talk."

"Fine. Listen, I'd better go. We have things to do this morning."

"Ellen, don't be mad."

"I'm not mad. I'm hurt —" She broke off. "You don't understand me at all, do you?"

Mike sighed. It was a totally dejected sound. "I'm sorry, Ellen. I guess we need to communicate better."

"Good-bye, Mike. Do me a favor and don't call these next few days. I need some time to think."

There was a painful silence. "Whatever you want, Ellen. I'll see you Sunday."

"Fine."

As she hung up Ellen struggled with her anger. How could he be so insensitive? He knew how close she and her father had been. The urge to call Jake was strong, but instead she closed her eyes. *Help me, Lord. Help me before I give in to my heart and completely destroy everything you've ever given me.* She took a deep breath and as she did the phone on the nightstand next to her rang. Her heart lurched and she reached for it, wondering if maybe it might be Jake.

"Hello?"

"Ellen?"

"Leslie?" An answer to prayer, but not the one she'd been wrongly hoping for. "Somehow I'm not surprised you found me. How did you know I was here?"

"Mike told me. Ellen, I'm so sorry about your dad."

Tears filled Ellen's eyes and spilled onto her cheeks . . . tears of loss. But Ellen wasn't sure if they were over her father — or her marriage.

She talked then, telling Leslie how badly she missed her dad and of the struggles with Jane and the others. As they talked, Ellen quickly remembered why she and Leslie had been friends for so long. Nothing ever changed with Leslie. The two might not talk for years and still they could pick up where they left off. They had that kind of friendship. Especially after that weekend when Leslie led her to Christ.

When it seemed like their conversation was winding down, Leslie's tone of voice suddenly changed. "Okay, come on, Ellen," she sounded gently suspicious, almost parental. "What else?"

"What do you mean?"

"Please, Ellen. I've known you longer than that. I know you're upset about your dad, but there's something else going on. I can see it in your eyes."

"You can't *see* my eyes."

"Okay, then I can see it in your voice. But I *can* see it. Clear as if you were standing in the same room with me. Mike isn't there, and that's bugging you big time."

Ellen sighed. "Is it always like that? The person who leads you to the Lord can see right through you when you're blowing it?"

"Talk to me, Ellen. What's happening out there?"

"Oh, Leslie, I don't know. Everything's so mixed up right now."

"Can I tell you something?"

"Go ahead."

"When I found out you went to Petoskey by yourself I had this crazy thought that I

416

should pray for you, that maybe, even though it'd been years, you might call Jake Sadler."

Ellen uttered a short laugh. "Well, that settles it."

"What?"

"God knows what he's doing. I mean, are you serious? You've been praying for me?"

"Mm-hmm. Hoping you wouldn't do anything you'd regret. Did you, Ellen? Did you call him?"

"Yes." The word came out hoarse. "But not because I wanted to get back at Mike. Nothing like that. Leslie, I keep thinking back to when my dad was healthy and everyone got along. I have a million happy memories, and Jake is right there in the middle of all of them. I had to call him. He's the only one who really knows how I feel."

"So you've seen him?"

"A few times. He's changed, Leslie. He's grown up and he's a wonderful man, honest and considerate. He's been there every time I've needed him."

"Is he married?"

"No."

Leslie hesitated, then went on, her tone cautious but firm. "Ellen, don't take this wrong. But you and Jake had something very special, beyond the usual high school

417

romance thing."

"So?"

"So don't you think, if you're really honest with yourself, that it's possible Jake's still in love with you?"

"Have you been following me, Leslie?"

"Am I close to home?"

"Very close. I never would have thought it was true, but now that I've seen him I'd be lying to say he doesn't still care for me. He does."

"And you?"

"Well, you know that special something we shared in high school and afterwards? It's still there. Whatever it is it hasn't gone away with time."

"Okay, this is totally off the subject." Leslie paused. "And it might be a long shot, but how are you doing spiritually?"

Ellen had no response.

"I thought so." Leslie sighed. "Oh, Ellen, I feel so bad. I haven't called or prayed for you or done any of the things I should have done over the years."

"It isn't your fault, Leslie. Life goes on and people go their own ways. You weren't responsible for my walk with the Lord. I was."

"You still believe, don't you?"

"Of course. It's not that we denounced

418

our faith or anything. We just sort of dropped out of the whole Christian circle." Ellen shifted to a more comfortable position, leaning back against the headboard as her mother had done earlier. "You wouldn't believe how easily it is to let that go when you're both working full-time during the week. It's like we convinced ourselves that the weekends were ours. We were too busy for church. Before long we were too busy to pray and too busy to talk about God. You think there's a connection, right?" She altered her voice so that she sounded like a newscaster. "Christian couple strays from God and winds up on the skids."

"Don't you?"

"I don't know. It seems more complicated than that. Mike doesn't love me like he used to. No one should have to stay in that kind of relationship forever."

"I don't care how far from God you are today, Ellen, God hasn't moved."

Ellen wanted to get angry, but there was so much compassion in Leslie's voice that she couldn't.

"God's there," Leslie went on, "and he expects you to honor your marriage vows. Satan would love to make you think you and Mike don't belong together anymore. He'd love to destroy the knot that God himself tied. I only wish I'd called sooner so we could have prayed about it before now."

"I don't know, Leslie. I don't think it would have helped. Mike isn't going to change. Not for me, not for anyone."

"So you've written off the Word, too. Remember Luke 1:37? Nothing is impossible with God." Leslie waited a moment. "I don't want to sound trite, like I'm giving you just another pat answer. But it's true. You loved Mike with all your heart, Ellen. You loved him for all the right reasons. Somewhere, buried deep within the man, those reasons still exist."

"And you think prayer will change him back to the man he was?"

"Or help you to see the man he still is, deep down. You should know how powerful prayer is, Ellen. You've seen God work in your life. You prayed about the job at the *Gazette* and got a position when no one else with your experience would have been considered. You prayed that God would help you forget about Jake and next thing you know you're dating the handsome *and* godly Mike Miller. Have you really stopped believing in prayer?"

Tears stung Ellen's eyes again and she blinked them away. She thought of her miscarriages and how things had changed with Mike. Her throat was thick when she could finally speak. "Maybe I have."

"What about Mike?"

"I don't know. He and I don't pray together, we don't read the Bible anymore." She bit her lip and the tears trickled down her cheek. "I guess neither of us should be surprised that we aren't doing well."

"So do something about it. Put Jake out of your mind and get busy."

Ellen's voice was barely a whisper. "What if I don't want to?"

"What do you mean?"

"I'm mad at Mike. I don't want to pray with him and work everything out. Right now I don't even care if I do something that'll hurt him."

"I can think of someone you could hurt more than Mike."

"Who?"

"God. Your Lord, your Savior. Remember him? Remember reading the Bible with me that day in my bedroom and realizing for the first time what Jesus suffered. Remember? When you finally understood that he took his place on the cross that day because one of the faces on his mind was yours? You couldn't stop crying. He loves you. And he's the one you will hurt the most, Ellen. He's the one you'll be unfaithful to." She paused, then asked softly, "Do you really want to treat God the way Jake treated you so many times?"

Ellen's shoulders sagged forward and the trickle of tears became a stream. She still wanted to call Jake, even now. Wanted to see him so badly, to spend time with him even though it would hurt Mike. Or maybe because it would hurt Mike. But picturing the Lord in pain because of her selfishness was almost more than she could bear.

Leslie's voice was thick when she went on, as though she, too, was crying. "Marriages take work, Ellen. Hours of communication, moments of honesty when needs are expressed and problems worked through. But most of all they take prayer, from both of you. If you and Mike aren't praying and worshiping together, then you don't stand a chance. None of us would. A cord of *three* strands is not easily broken."

Ellen sniffed and wiped her eyes. She hoped none of the others would look for her now that the morning was wearing on. She needed time to think.

"It-it kills me to think I might be making God sad." She sobbed softly. "Oh, Leslie, I've blown it so bad."

"No. That's where you're wrong. You haven't blown anything. Not yet. God is there with you. You can leave him but he'll never leave you, Ellen. Never. Remember that night when you asked Christ into your heart?"

"Mm-hmm."

"You prayed that God would keep you away from Jake. He was your strongest weakness then and he's your strongest weakness now. Pray it again, Ellen. Come on, right now."

Ellen was crying even harder. She couldn't bring herself to say the words. "I can't. You pray."

"Okay."

Ellen squeezed her eyes shut as her body shook with each silent sob. She listened intently to Leslie's gentle words.

"Lord, precious Savior and Father, we come before you and lift up Ellen. She's hurting now and she needs your touch. Give her peace and wisdom and comfort so that she will survive this week, the funeral of her father, the strained relationships with her family. The nearness of Jake Sadler. Lord, please keep her strong in the face of temptation. As she prayed so long ago, we pray again, Lord. Keep her away from Jake. And please restore her love for Mike. I pray that they will feel a desperate need to be back in your presence, in the shelter of your church, and the strength of your Word. Thank you, Lord. In Jesus' name, amen."

There was silence for a moment.

"Ellen, you okay?"

Her tears under control now, Ellen cleared her throat. "Thanks. Keep praying for me, will you, Leslie? I know what's right, but the only way I'll do it is if I keep my eyes on God."

"And off Jake Sadler."

Her heart constricted at the truth. "Right. Listen, I gotta go. I'll call you later and let you know how things went."

"Okay. Give my love to your family."

"Yeah. Thanks. And thanks for being there, Leslie. I needed you."

"Hey, I love you, Ellen. Mike loves you. I'll be praying for you guys. And you know what?"

"What?"

"Somewhere, I believe your dad is praying for you, too. When I think of people who lived their entire lives in faith, I think of him. Follow his example, Ellen. Please."

"Thanks. Talk to you later."

Slowly Leslie hung up the phone. Ellen's words, the pain in her voice, rang in Leslie's mind. Quickly she lifted the receiver again and dialed Imogene Spencer at the First

Baptist Church office.

"Imogene, it's me, Leslie. About my friend, the one on the prayer chain, I want to make that prayer request a bit more specific."

Ellen hung up the phone, wishing she felt better.

Leslie was right, of course; there was only one right thing to do. But still Ellen was confused. In fact, nothing about that week's events made sense. Ellen fingered her wedding ring and knew one thing for certain. Her entire future depended on the decisions she would make in the days to come.

She pulled the sheets off her bare legs and climbed out of bed. It was time to get ready. The others would be there soon and she didn't want to hold them up.

She twisted out of her nightshirt and climbed into the shower. As the hot water ran down her body she struggled to clear her mind. But no matter how hard she tried, one question remained.

If you love me, Mike, why aren't you here?

TWENTY-FOUR

Later that morning everyone but Aaron piled into the family van and headed for the mall. After two hours of shopping only Jane had not found a dress for the funeral.

Ellen was ready to scream.

"What exactly are you looking for, Jane?" Mom tried to sound patient.

"I don't care; whatever I can find."

"Honey, we have a lot to do today and I wanted to take you girls to lunch. We've been to three stores and you haven't liked anything yet. I'm just wondering what you're looking for."

"In other words, could you hurry and find something," Ellen added. She had been on edge since talking to Leslie, as if the battle for her heart was intensifying with each moment. It was taking every fiber of her control to keep from calling Jake and spending the afternoon with him.

"Lay off, Ellen," Jane snapped.

Their mother placed a soothing hand on Jane's arm.

"Girls," she said, her voice calm. "Let's not get angry with each other." She turned to Jane. "I was only trying to help you narrow your options so we could finish up and get to lunch."

Jane stared at Ellen and then their mother, her face twisted in frustration. "You know, I'm doing my best. You'd have a hard time, too, if you were trying to find a dress with three children pulling at you."

"Here, dear." Mom reached down to take Koley's and Kala's hands. "Let me watch the children while you look."

"Fine," Jane snapped again. She turned around and walked toward the women's clothing, pushing Kyle's baby stroller while Koley and Kala linked hands with their grandmother and walked along behind her. Ten minutes later Jane had picked out a dress and paid for it.

"Satisfied?" She looked at Ellen.

Megan sighed impatiently and Amy remained motionless. Their mother looked at the faces before her and forced a smile.

"Well. Now that we're all getting along so well, let's go to lunch." There was not a trace of sarcasm in her voice.

Ellen marveled at her mother. The woman

always had the ability to don a smile regardless of the circumstances. She and Jane used to accuse their mom of burying her head in the sand because she never wanted to discuss anything remotely controversial. Now she was starting to wonder if it wasn't just her mother's way of doing her best to hold her family together.

They moved silently through the mall, back to the car, and said nothing to each other as Mom drove to a nearby Italian restaurant. After the meal they headed home and rested until Aunt Mary arrived to watch the children. It was three o'clock and they had an appointment in thirty minutes. It was time to pick out a casket.

Three cars made the trip to Stone's Funeral Home. Ellen rode with Megan, Mom took Amy and Jane, and Aaron rode by himself. By that time their father's body had been embalmed, dressed in his best Sunday suit and tie, and made up to look "lifelike."

Ellen was thankful they wouldn't have to see him yet. That would come the following night, Friday, at the public viewing. Today was the final day of planning, of meeting with the director of the mortuary so they could choose a casket and coordinate the funeral plans.

The mortuary was conservatively set back

from the road. It had beige siding and a black, shingled roof. Each window had decorative shutters accented in white trim. Stone's Funeral Home had been in business since 1899 and had a reputation for being one of the most capable in Northern Michigan. The grounds were a carefully manicured carpet of deep green, and not far from the main entrance an American flag flickered in the afternoon breeze.

Ellen thought it was probably supposed to look like a very large family home. It did not. For all its careful upkeep, it still looked like death.

They filed quietly into the somber building and waited in a lobby for someone to help them. Ellen glanced down and noticed a standing ashtray near the foyer. *For future customers.*

"Smells weird," Megan whispered, and Ellen nodded.

"Hello there." A thin man reminiscent of Ichabod Crane appeared and ushered them into a spacious office. He spoke in hushed tones, exuding an appropriate aura of respect for his clients' loss. "You're the Barrett family, I presume."

"Yes." Mom clutched her purse tightly.

"Fine. Take a seat." He motioned to the padded chairs around the room. "I've been

429

expecting you. I'm Mr. Whitson."

Everyone in the Barrett family remained silent, waiting.

"Now —" the man said, reaching into his desk drawer and retrieving a leather-bound catalogue — "these are the coffins we can have available for the Saturday funeral. Whatever you choose, it can be here by morning. Of course . . . there's a wide price range."

He paused and looked at their mother. "Did you have some idea of your price range?"

Ellen squirmed and hugged herself tightly. Her stomach was beginning to hurt.

"Yes, we'd like to stay under three thousand dollars, if that's possible."

The man nodded quickly. "Definitely. Very possible." He flipped open the book and thumbed to the back section. "We have a wide variety of oak and walnut caskets in that range. Of course the price goes up depending on the definition and degree of difficulty in the engraving on the wood."

He flipped from one page to another, quietly allowing their mother to see for herself the many designs. Amy sighed softly and stared out a small window at the sunlit afternoon outside while Megan crossed her legs and nervously tapped her foot up and down. Each of them waited for their mother to say something.

Mom looked from one page to another and then directed Mr. Whitson to flip back to the first model he'd shown her.

"What's the difference, Mom?" Aaron's voice was loud and disagreeable as he broke the silence. He obviously did not care if he embarrassed her.

Ellen felt sorry for their mother. Mr. Whitson was too clinical, too businesslike. They weren't buying a new refrigerator after all, they were trying to bury their father and get on with their lives. A sales pitch on types of wood was unnecessary. Still, her brother's attitude was only making the task more difficult.

"No one's going to see it," Aaron continued. "What's the big deal?"

Mr. Whitson cleared his throat and discreetly excused himself for a drink of water. "I'll be back in ten minutes. Why don't you talk about it and we'll see what we can work out."

He disappeared and Mom looked wearily at Aaron.

"Your father was not a wealthy man, Aaron. He was not an important man by the world's standards and certainly not a famous man. But I'd like to see him buried as comfortably as possible."

"That's disgusting," Jane blurted. "He's dead, Mom. Good night! How can you talk about him being comfortable."

"That's not what I mean. I'm talking about his body. The coffin is his final resting place and I think it should be as nice as possible."

Ellen looked at her mother tenderly. "If that's what you want, Mom, and if you think that's what Dad would have wanted, I say get the best casket you can afford. It isn't time to be cheap."

"Oh, Ellen, that's ridiculous," Jane hissed. She turned to her mother, speaking like she would to one of her children. "I agree with Aaron. It's a waste of money. I say get the cheapest one there is and use the rest of the money to buy him a nice tombstone, something we could at least see. The coffin will be underground, for heaven's sake."

"With that logic, a tombstone's not worth wasting money on, either," Ellen mused aloud. "It's just an oversized rock. We don't need a larger one than normal to remember him. At least I don't."

Jane rolled her eyes. "Do you always have to have the last word, Ellen? Why don't you be quiet and let Mother decide for herself."

Ellen stared at Jane and stood up. Once

again, Jane had pushed her beyond her limit. She searched her purse for a few silver coins, and then stared at her mother. "I'll be back. I have to make a phone call."

Mom gave her a knowing look. "Good, dear," she whispered in Ellen's direction. "It's time."

Ellen ignored her mother's comment and despite Jane's angry glare she turned and headed for the pay phone in the lobby. She had spotted it on the way in and made a mental note that if things got too tense she would excuse herself and make the call, regardless of her battered conscience.

Her mother didn't know about the earlier conversation she'd had with Mike. Apparently she thought Ellen was about to call her husband and patch things up. A wave of guilt assaulted Ellen as she arrived at the pay phone, and for a moment she almost turned back to join the others. Then she thought of Jane, how their relationship was unraveling faster than a half-made sweater.

She thought of Mike, too. *It's too late to change my plans . . . too late . . . too late. . . .*

She picked up the phone.

Don't do it, a voice inside her head screamed. *You're married. You're a Christian. You're crazy. This isn't about Jane, it's about Mike. You've been looking for an excuse to*

433

call Jake ever since this morning. Come on, Ellen, remember what Leslie said.

Her conscience challenged her and threatened her, tempting her to hang up the phone. Leslie's words came back to her. *Don't do it, Ellen. Don't do it.*

She slipped the coins into the slot and dialed his number.

"Hello?" Jake sounded tired and Ellen almost hung up the phone.

"It's me."

"Ellen," he said her name slowly and it sounded like velvet on his tongue. His voice was filled with concern. "I've been thinking about you. I wanted to call but I was afraid you'd be uncomfortable."

"I know. I've thought about calling you all day."

"Things worse?"

"Yes." Her voice was choked with emotion and not very clear. "I'm at the mortuary, Stone's Funeral Home on Mitchell Road."

"I know it."

"Please come, Jake. I need to talk."

Jake was quiet and Ellen knew his struggle. In that instant she was certain he still loved her. He was afraid to see her again, terrified that he couldn't keep his distance. Jake didn't have to say a word. Ellen knew what he was thinking because she felt the same way about him.

"What time will you be done?" There was resignation in his voice.

Ellen looked at her watch. It was four o'clock. "Around five-thirty. I'll send the others home without me and I'll wait here for you."

"Where should we go?"

"How 'bout back to your house. Just for a few hours."

"Are you sure?"

Ellen understood the deeper meaning behind his question. Perhaps they were asking for trouble, allowing themselves to be alone together at his house. If so, Ellen didn't care. Mike didn't want to be there. She and Jane were no longer on speaking terms. Worse, the constant friction between them made it impossible for her to think about her father. His funeral was in two days and she hadn't even had time to mourn his death. What did it matter if she spent a few more hours with Jake? The week would be over soon enough and they would return to their separate lives, thinking of each other only on occasion as they had before.

"Ellen?" His voice was a caress.

"Yes," she said quickly. "I'm sure."

"Okay, five-thirty. See you then."

Ellen hung up and returned to the office where the others had reached an agreement on an oak casket. It was lined with white satin and engraved with tiny roses around the base. There were six brass handles stationed along the sides where the pallbearers would carry it from the hearse to the church and back.

"What do you think?" Mom pointed to the picture of the coffin in the catalogue. She had dark circles under her eyes and she seemed anxious to be done with the selection process.

"I don't know. It's a coffin." Ellen stared at the wooden box in the picture and thought of her father, full of life, sitting at a Michigan football game. She tried to imagine that same man lying in the carved oak casket and she shuddered. "It's hard to picture."

"I know, dear. I understand that. But I want us all to agree on the coffin and this is the one we've picked out. Could you please tell me what you think?"

"It's fine."

"Okay, then that's it." She turned to face Mr. Whitson, who was once again sitting patiently behind his desk while the family made their decision. "What's next?"

"We need to work out arrangements for tomorrow night's viewing and transportation to the church and cemetery. You do have a plot picked out?"

"Yes, that's taken care of."

Megan shut her eyes, and Ellen thought she was probably holding back tears. Amy stared at the floor, and Ellen clenched her fists, pressing them into her stomach to ease the knots that grew there. Aaron slipped on his dark glasses. Jane remained motionless.

The plot was located in St. Francis Cemetery, a small tree-lined park situated on a steep bluff overlooking Little Traverse Bay. The view was incredible from any spot in the cemetery, and there was a generous amount of space between plots. Earlier that week their mother had chosen a plot directly underneath a large oak tree. It was not far from the split-rail fence that bordered the edge of the cemetery and the embankment that led down to the water. Mom had not taken them all to see the plot. Ellen was just as glad. They would see it soon enough.

For an hour the five Barrett siblings sat quietly, together but very much apart, as their mother worked out the logistics of the viewing, funeral service, and burial. Ellen thought her mother was holding up remarkably well. She made notes and jotted down key details as they worked through the planning process.

Ellen watched and wondered if funerals were always like this. The planning took so much effort that there was no time to grieve. She had expected her mother to break down and cry, to be unable to get through this part of the week. Instead she was stoic and calm, well organized and efficient. Ellen wondered when the reality would hit.

"Well, that's all I have. I think we've worked everything out."

Mr. Whitson stood up and shook their mother's hand. He looked at the others and barely smiled. "We'll see all of you tomorrow night. You should get here at least an hour before the public viewing but you can come any time after two o'clock."

"Thank you," Mom told him as the group filed quietly out of the office. As soon as they were outside, she announced that they were all expected back at the house for dinner.

"Is that okay with everyone?" She held the keys to the van and looked at each of them expectantly.

"Uhh, I still have some work to do on that thing I'm writing for the funeral," Aaron mumbled. "I thought I might go to the beach and work on it."

Their mother's shoulders dropped in disappointment and she sighed heavily. "Aaron, I thought we'd all be together tonight."

"Mom, if you want me to get that thing done then don't complain about me missing dinner. Maaaaan, I mean it. Give me a break, will ya?"

Ellen cast a disgusted glance toward her brother and Amy rolled her eyes.

"Okay, okay," Mom smiled calmly, caving under Aaron's implied threat of a temper tantrum. "Go ahead, honey. Drive safely."

Aaron mumbled something, slid behind the wheel of his truck, and drove off. She looked at her daughters. "What about you girls?"

"I can come over for a little while but the children need to get to sleep earlier than last night." Jane crossed her arms impatiently. "Troy's coming in at 10:30 tomorrow morning so I don't want to stay up late."

"Amy?"

"Frank wants me to meet him for pizza with a few of his friends. We'll come back to the house later. Around nine or so."

"I'll be there," Megan said. She looked accusingly at her sisters. "This is a time

439

when we should be together."

"Ellen?" Mom raised her eyebrows hopefully.

"I have plans, too. Sorry, Mom. I won't be late."

Her mother sighed, and Ellen was glad she seemed too preoccupied to ask what her plans were. "All right. Let's get going, then."

Her mother, Amy, and Jane piled into the van and drove away leaving Megan and Ellen. They walked slowly, silently toward Megan's car.

"I don't need a ride, Megan." Ellen tried to sound casual.

Megan stopped and stared at her. "Why not?"

"My friend's picking me up here."

Megan narrowed her eyes and studied her sister. Ellen could see the suspicion in her face. "What gives, Ellen? Who's the mystery friend?"

Ellen nudged the tip of her shoe at a few loose rocks on the asphalt. She refused to look at Megan. "Just an old friend."

Megan lowered her face so that she could see directly into Ellen's eyes. "I'm your sister, remember, Ellen? I know most of your old friends. Who is she?"

Ellen hesitated. "He."

"He?"

"Yes." She drew a deep breath. "Jake Sadler. We're getting together to talk."

"What?" Megan's voice rose.

"Shhh. You heard what I said."

"Why on earth are you doing that?"

"I've seen him twice this week. I called him that night when Jane told me I was stupid for not having any children. Remember?"

"You saw him that night, too?" Megan was clearly astonished and Ellen felt a twinge of guilt. "Is that who you went to the beach with?"

Ellen nodded. "Mackinac Island."

"Ellen, are you having an affair?"

Megan sounded as if she was about to collapse from the shock and Ellen took her arm and led her gently to her car.

"No, Megan. It's no big deal. Don't worry. Just a couple of old friends remembering the way things used to be. He loved Dad, too, remember?"

Megan emitted a brief laugh that was completely void of humor. "Who are you trying to kid? I might have been younger than you, but I wasn't blind. Listen, Ellen, you and Jake Sadler were *anything* but friends."

"That was a long time ago."

"Not long enough." She thought a moment. "Does Mike know?"

Ellen shook her head.

"You guys are fighting, aren't you?"

Ellen set her jaw. "Mike and I are fine. This has nothing to do with him."

"Then why, Ellen? I can understand Jake's motives, but what about yours?"

Ellen was immediately defensive. "That's not fair. Jake's matured a lot since high school."

"I don't care what he's done since high school. You're a married woman and you have no right spending an evening with Jake Sadler."

Ellen was silent, her arms crossed stubbornly.

"You know I'm right."

"I know that whatever you say isn't going to change my mind." Ellen was matter-of-fact. "Please, Megan, go home and spend some time with Mom. I can take care of myself."

Megan frowned at Ellen and turned away. She opened the car door, slipped inside, and started the engine. Then she rolled down the window and stared hard at Ellen. "Do what you want, Ellen," she warned. "But Jake Sadler is trouble. He's been trouble since the first day you met him."

"If anyone knows that, I do," Ellen replied

442

quickly. "I said don't worry about it." She was beginning to feel nervous because it was almost five-thirty and she didn't want Jake to pull up and see them arguing about him.

"I think you're making a big mistake. Obviously I can't stop you."

"Good-bye, Megan," Ellen said simply.

Megan shook her head. "I have one more thing to say and then I'll go."

Ellen shifted her position impatiently.

"Please be careful." The accusation in Megan's voice was gone.

"Megan, don't worry. I told you there's nothing between us."

"Don't lie to me, Ellen. I know how you and Jake were. That isn't something that goes away with time."

"I know," Ellen finally conceded. "I'll be careful. I promise."

Megan nodded and then drove away. Ellen watched her go and then walked across the parking lot. She sat on the wooden bench in front of the mortuary and waited anxiously for Jake. She was restless, watching for his truck and feeling more nervous than she had all week. Not because of Megan's warning. She was not afraid of Jake Sadler's intentions.

She was afraid of her own.

TWENTY-FIVE

Ellen heard the low rumbling sound of Jake's truck seconds before it pulled into view. He climbed out and walked toward her, hesitating for a moment before pulling her into a hug. She buried her face in his pullover.

I can't go with him. It'll just hurt us both. "Thanks for coming," she whispered.

Jake's eyes filled with concern, and Ellen's doubts dissolved like summer days. He was her first love, but he was also her friend. In all the world he was the only one she wanted to be with at that moment.

Unbidden, another verse drifted into her mind: *"The way of a fool seems right to him, but a wise man listens to advice."* She felt her cheeks go red.

He slid into the truck and put his seat belt on. "Everyone gone home?"

"Finally." She closed the door and was surrounded by the scent of leather and cologne. She sank into the seat and released a heavy sigh.

"That bad, huh?"

"Worse. I don't know, Jake, maybe it's me. Jane's still on the warpath and my mom's wanting us all to be together every last minute leading up to the funeral. Aaron's a time bomb and Megan's playing peacemaker. Same old story."

Jake pulled out of the parking lot and headed west on Mitchell.

"Where do you live?"

"Harbor Pointe, out in Harbor Springs."

Ellen raised an eyebrow. "I know the area. Why didn't you tell me you lived in the estates?"

"They're not really estates. Just large subdivision homes."

"I can't believe you live in Harbor Pointe," she said absently. She stared out the windshield and ran her fingers through her hair. "Guards at the gate, tennis courts, the bay in your backyard. Who'd have thought it? I mean, weren't you the guy who was out to live life up and avoid commitment at all costs?"

Jake grinned sheepishly and his eyes twinkled with laughter.

"You couldn't be serious about anything back then, Jake. Now look at you."

He grew pensive and remained silent.

"You're happy about it, aren't you? The success I mean?"

"Sometimes. The house is nice, the cars and boat and hot tub. They're all fine. But sometimes I think my life was richer when I was twenty-one and lived paycheck to paycheck."

"Hmm." Ellen nodded slowly. "I think that way, too, sometimes. Between Mike and me we do pretty well. We live in a nice, gated community with a two-story house a few blocks from the ocean. Nice cars, nice clothes, good jobs."

"Doesn't really help you sleep at night, does it?" He glanced at her and she shook her head, shifting so she could watch him drive.

She studied him, remembering him as he was and wondering what would have happened if, like his mother once hoped, she had waited for him to grow up. She saw that his eyes were distant. He seemed a million miles away, lost in some long ago memory.

"What're you thinking about?"

"Choices. Passages. Moments that make a difference for a lifetime."

She considered his words and smiled. *Choices. Passages. Moments that make a difference for a lifetime.* This was the Jake she remembered, the one she had shared her heart with, the one she could talk to for hours without growing tired. For an instant she saw him as he used to be — a tan, fresh-faced boy who could see directly into her soul. She held the image and allowed herself to miss him as she hadn't in years.

She turned away then and tried to remember the flip side. The strange phone calls from other girls at odd hours, unfamiliar notes left on his doorstep or under his windshield wipers. The impatient blond in his bathrobe. Ellen sighed. As good as things had been when they were together, it hadn't been good enough.

She gazed out the side window, her back to Jake. Leslie hadn't been the only one to warn her about him. Her father had seen it coming, too.

"He's a fine boy, Ellen," he'd said once. "I love him like a son. But I see how he is, the way he looks at other girls. He has 'em dropping like flies." He touched her cheek gently, a gesture he'd done since she was a little girl. "You deserve better than that."

"Okay," Jake interrupted her thoughts. "Now it's my turn. What're you thinking?"

She turned toward him and answered quickly, "My dad."

Jake was sympathetic. "You miss him?"

447

"I haven't really had time. I keep thinking I'll go back to my parents' house and he'll be in his easy chair watching a golf tournament or a baseball game or something."

"Is there a viewing? At the mortuary?"

Ellen wrinkled her nose. "Yes. Tomorrow night. I'm dreading it."

Jake nodded. "I bet. But his death will be more real after that, Ellen. You'll be able to accept it better."

Ellen thought about seeing her father's body in the cold, satin-lined casket. "Yes," she conceded. "I suppose so."

They drove around the bay and continued along the water, through the town of Bay Harbor. In less than fifteen minutes they arrived at the gate. Jake waved to the man in the booth, turned left, and drove further out onto the peninsula. As the strip of land narrowed, he slowed the truck and turned left again into an impressive stone driveway.

"This is it? This is your house?" Ellen raised her eyebrows appreciatively.

Jake nodded and shrugged. Ellen studied Jake's house. Some of the places they had driven past had been pretentious. This house was very different. An inviting Victorian, Jake's home looked warm and filled with light. It seemed cared for and lived in, the type of house she might have picked for herself. Soft slate gray siding accented with white trim and an old-fashioned, white wraparound porch. It was a two-story home with dozens of white-rimmed French windows. The roof was the color of caramel. Heavily shingled, it peaked over a handful of smaller windows.

For all its homey warmth, Jake's house was stunning, surrounded by a lush landscape and delicate petunias that bordered the home. There were panoramic views of the bay on one side and Lake Michigan on the other. The porch wrapped around the front of the house and from where Jake was parked, Ellen could barely see a redwood deck stretched out across the back. The bay was literally in his backyard and Ellen felt like she was surrounded by sandy beach.

"Jake —" She clasped her hands in delight — "it's breathtaking."

"Thanks." He moved around the truck and opened her door. "I'm glad you like it."

She followed him to the front door.

"Hungry?" He turned the key.

"Starved." She hadn't realized it until he asked, but she hadn't eaten since late that morning and she was famished. They walked inside and she stopped to take in the beauty of the place. The numerous French windows allowed the room to bask in sunlight, bathing the white walls and walnut trim in warmth. The ceilings were vaulted, accented with skylights and plant shelves. His leather living room set looked warm and inviting.

"You did this?" She moved into the room and began wandering through the house.

"The doors and windows are mine." She could see the pride in his eyes. "I hired a decorator for the rest."

"Job well done. You could have *Home and Garden* here tomorrow and they'd do a centerfold on the place."

Jake grinned and headed for the kitchen. "Want me to order pizza or something?"

She followed him, sliding onto a bar stool and leaning across an expanse of granite countertop. "I have a better idea."

"Okay, what?" He opened the refrigerator door and twisted around to look at her.

"Omelettes. Filled with cheese and alfalfa sprouts, tomatoes and olives. Sour cream and salsa."

Jake laughed and his eyes danced at the idea. "I haven't made one of those in years."

"Remember? We'd get home from the beach and be starved and we'd raid your mother's fridge. You made the best omelettes, Jake. I mean it."

He bent over and riffled through the icebox looking for ingredients. "Let's see.

Lots of eggs. Sprouts. Cheese." He straightened, his arms filled with the ingredients. "You got it. Two omelettes coming up."

She stood up and moved into the kitchen, pulling open several drawers until she found a knife. "Hand me the tomatoes. I'll help chop."

He backed away in mock fear. "Be careful with that thing. You never were much good in the kitchen."

She wielded the small carving knife back and forth through the air, pretending to be dangerous.

"No, you don't." He grabbed her wrist with one hand and tickled her side with his other hand.

"Stop or you'll be sorry." She laughed, squirming to break free from his grasp. He let go and pretended to give up, but as she turned toward the cutting board he poked her once more in the ribs.

"Unless you want me to get the ice cubes and start an all-out war, you better stop, Jake Sadler." She was flushed from laughing, breathless from the feel of his hand on her wrist.

"All right, all right. Get busy chopping."

"Thank you!" she huffed. She caught three tomatoes as he tossed them her way.

They worked for twenty minutes preparing ingredients, and then Jake set to work. When he was finished he had two plate-sized omelettes, each oozing with vegetables, cheese, and sour cream.

"Mmmmm, smells like a restaurant."

"Remember, I was going to open my own omelette shop on the beach somewhere."

"That's right." She set two place mats side by side on the counter and filled two glasses with ice water. He joined her with the food and they sat down. "The way these things look you still could."

"Nah. You'd be my best customer and you live a million miles away."

"Eighteen hundred miles, to be exact."

"Like I said," his voice was suddenly serious, "a million miles away." He glanced at her and their eyes held for a moment too long.

He grinned, trying to break the tension. "So since you can't be around, the shop would probably go bust in a week. You're the only one who ever liked my omelettes."

She opened her mouth, teasingly astonished. "Jake! You mean you cooked omelettes for someone other than me? Shame on you!"

"I know." He grinned. "The ultimate betrayal."

"That's right. Don't forget it, either."

They laughed, and Ellen savored how comfortable they were together. He excused himself and slipped a Christopher Cross CD into the player. Music filled the house through an intricate sound system, and Ellen smiled. They had both enjoyed Christopher Cross years ago and she remembered listening to his songs between movies at the drive-in theater. The atmosphere was soothing and she felt herself relax.

Ellen ate her omelette slowly, remembering dozens of times when she and Jake had done this before. It was a simple thing, really. Eating omelettes in the waning afternoon sunlight, sitting side by side alone in his house, listening to Christopher Cross. But it took her back, made her keenly aware of him and the fact that they were alone.

What did you expect? she chastised herself. She didn't even try to answer that. She was afraid to do so. When they were finished they washed dishes together and put away food. Their conversation was light and when their elbows touched on occasion as they worked, they pretended not to notice.

"I'm stuffed." Jake stretched.

"Me too." She focused her attention on the pan she was drying. "You forget how filling an omelette can be. Especially if it's been created by the master omelette maker himself." She grinned at him.

When the kitchen was clean they went out back onto the partially covered wooden deck. The sun would set in a few hours and Ellen gazed thoughtfully across the bay toward Petoskey. A gentle breeze flowed across the water and the sky was free of clouds, a vast expanse of vivid blue.

Ellen walked to the edge of the deck and leaned against the railing, studying the sandy beach below. "You're right on the sand."

Jake moved up beside her and leaned against the railing. "Hmm. I guess I always did have a thing for the beach."

Ellen smiled, enjoying the easy sense of camaraderie they shared. It used to be like this with Mike. They used to share long, lovely days just being together, enjoying each other. She stared across the water and studied the distant shoreline. She could make out Petoskey State Park and Magnus Park. She could even see the pier at Bayfront with its dozens of sailboats and yachts, the flags that flew year round, and the beautifully kept softball fields. After a while she wandered toward a porch swing and sat down.

She looked at Jake and patted the empty spot beside her. He sauntered in her direction and sat down, careful not to brush his legs against hers. She was silently thankful. Her resolve was vanishing at an alarming rate and any contact with him was bound to make things worse. As if he could sense her feelings, he moved casually toward the outside of the swing, allowing a comfortable distance between them.

"Dad always wanted a house like this," Ellen said. She set the swing gently in motion. "On weekends we'd come look at these houses, and he'd talk about starting a business with his computer." She looked at Jake. "There was always a reason why that business never got started, always something in the way."

Jake sat there, watching her, listening.

"When I was little I thought my dad was the best man in the world, the most fun, the strongest. He could do anything he set his mind to. The whole nine yards."

Jake looked intently into her eyes. "And now?"

"I'm not sure."

He looked puzzled and she shook her head quickly.

"Don't get me wrong. No one could ever take his place. But when I grew up I saw a clearer picture of him. I don't know, maybe it's only gotten clearer since his death. I think about his dreams and intentions, the times he was going to stop smoking, start a diet."

Her eyes narrowed, seeing a thousand missed opportunities, and suddenly she felt the tears building. "You know what he said when he came out of heart surgery last year? He said he was through making excuses. Through procrastinating. He was going to be a new man, whatever it took."

Jake's face filled with compassion. "It didn't happen."

"No." She shook her head sadly, a single tear spilling from each eye onto her cheeks. "He wasn't strong enough."

"That bothers you?"

"Yes." She raised her voice. "I thought the world of him, Jake. But in reality he was just like anyone else. Just a man struggling to follow through with his intentions and failing in the end."

The swing had slowed and she set it in motion again.

"Are you mad at him?" Jake's voice was barely a whisper.

"That's hard." Ellen gazed thoughtfully at the sky. The sun was beginning to set, blazing a brilliant trail of pinks and oranges as it disappeared. She looked at Jake again. "I guess I am, in some ways. He could have had a house like this, a yard like this. He could have started the business and made it fly, and when he had to go through emergency bypass surgery it could have been a turning point in his life. He had the chances, Jake, but he didn't take them. He wasn't strong enough. That's what kills me."

She spread her fingers on her chest. "In here, where the little girl I used to be still lives, I know he could have done it. I guess a part of me thinks he didn't try. He gave up and sold us short." Her voice cracked and she stopped swinging. Then slowly, she dropped her elbows to her knees and buried her face in her hands.

"Why, Jake? Why didn't he at least try?"

Jake reached over and rested his hand on her shoulder. His fingers made soothing circles just beneath her neck. "I'm sure he tried. At least give him that."

"Not hard enough." She looked up, knowing she must look blotchy and tearstained and not caring. "What's a pack of cigarettes compared to us? What's a cheeseburger or a bag of fries compared to your family? I mean, how hard could it be to give up that stuff when the alternative meant dying young, leaving us alone?"

"Ellen, come on. You're not being fair. If it was that easy, heart disease wouldn't be the killer it is today. You know that."

She slumped over her knees, her face in her hands again. "I know."

Taking deep breaths, she worked to calm herself down. She wiped her eyes with her fingertips. Jake's arm was still on her shoulder, but when she sat up he removed it.

"Was he always like that?" Her voice was tired. "Weak, unable to follow through with things?"

"You tell me, Ellen."

She thought a moment. "He worked three jobs to keep food on the table when we were little. And every Christmas there were so many toys under our tree it looked like something out of a fairy tale."

Jake nodded. "He put you through college, didn't he?"

"I paid for my books with tips from the restaurant. But he paid for everything else." Ellen grew quiet. "And he sent me to Canada for a vacation after I graduated."

"He wasn't weak, Ellen. He just had some nasty habits, habits that were too hard to break."

"Habits that killed him." Ellen wiped at several fresh tears forging a new trail down her cheeks. "I loved him so much, Jake. Now that he's gone nothing makes sense. My whole world is falling apart."

She began to sob again, squeezing her eyes tight as if she could shut out the pain. She felt his arm go around her.

"I know." His voice was deep and filled with understanding.

Ellen opened her eyes and gazed at the sky, but her tears kept coming. The blurred pinks and oranges were fading to dark now and the moon appeared in the distance, a shiny sliver in the sky. Time passed and still they sat that way, Jake with his arm around her while she cried for her father. Gradually her tears slowed and then finally stopped. She lifted her head and remained silent, allowing the breeze to dry her face and clear her eyes.

"You okay?" Jake broke the silence first. He took his arm off her shoulder and turned to face her.

She gulped, searching for her voice and nodded. "I have to let him go. I guess this is just the beginning."

Jake smiled tenderly. "It wouldn't hurt so much if he hadn't been such a great man. Do you see that now?"

"I never doubted that." She stared at him thoughtfully. "I only wondered if the man I admired wasn't perhaps some wonderful figment of my imagination, someone who never really existed at all."

"He existed, Ellen. I can see him in your sorrow, in my own memories. Believe me. He existed."

Ellen smiled self-consciously and released a short laugh as she pushed her hair back from her face. "I must look awful."

Jake wiped his thumb just below her right eye where her mascara must have run. "No, Ellen. You've never looked more beautiful."

Ellen laughed again and sniffed. "Right."

Jake studied her a moment longer, then his face lit up. "Hey, you haven't seen the hot tub."

Ellen rose slowly from the swing, stretching her back and taking a deep breath. "Lead the way."

He moved easily down a circular redwood stairway off one end of the deck. At the bottom of the stairs, toward the left side of his house, there was a neatly manicured lawn that butted up against the sand. The hot tub was centered on a grassy knoll in the middle of the lawn. It had a spectacular view of the bay. Ellen saw that it was easily large enough for six people. Three sides were covered with redwood lattice that lent intimate privacy but did not block the view.

Jake lifted the edge of the tub's cover and steam released into the cool night air.

Ellen whistled appreciatively. "Looks good."

Jake raised an eyebrow. "Wanna go in?"

She shouldn't. She knew she shouldn't. Not alone with Jake, not as vulnerable as she was feeling right now. Instead she should ask Jake to take her home before she forgot why it was important to do so.

Jake was waiting. She shook her head. "I don't have a suit."

"Ah, come on, Ellen. I have a spare lying around somewhere."

Ellen tilted her head and gave Jake a sad, knowing look. She thought about her conversation with Leslie, her argument with Mike. And about her father's Bible. She saw his words in her mind again: *"Hold fast to your faith. Temptation is a given; look for the way out! It is possible to fall!"*

When she spoke, her words were little more than a choked whisper. "I can't, Jake."

Ellen watched him and knew he understood. He reached for her hand. "Okay. No hot tub. Let's go back up and watch the lights." He smiled softly at her. "There's one spot along the deck that has the most incredible view."

Ellen exhaled softly and allowed Jake to lead her back up the stairs. As they walked, she thought about sitting beside Jake, watch-

461

ing the dazzling lights of Petoskey across Little Traverse Bay while hot water swirled around them. She shivered. *That was close. Thank you, Lord.*

When they reached the top of the stairs, Jake directed her to an alcove with a cozy wooden bench. The railing dipped along that part of the deck so that the view of the bay was unobstructed. They sat down together, gazing out at the water.

"Beautiful." Ellen's eyes narrowed as she took in the distant lights and the bay as it shimmered under the glow of the moon. They sat there in comfortable silence, eventually leaning back and taking in the stars as well. Ellen closed her eyes and felt the tension melt away.

She grew vaguely aware of something . . . something that bothered her. A strange buzzing sound. Opening her eyes, she looked down to see a bumble bee making its way up her shoulder, toward her back. She screamed and batted at the insect, knocking it off her arm — but not before it stung her.

"Owww!" She jumped to her feet, glancing about, making sure the insect was gone.

Jake was up and at her side instantly. He took her arm gently and examined the red welt that had already appeared. He frowned, concerned. "Looks like he got you."

Ellen winced. "I know. I can feel it." She furrowed her brow and strained to see the sting. "Can you see a stinger?"

Jake moved closer and examined the raised area. They stood toe-to-toe, a breeze from the bay swaying about them, separated only by a thin veil of night air. "It's hard to see in this light." He ran a finger over the sting. "Wait. I think I feel it." His face was inches from hers. He gently pulled the tiny stinger loose and examined it. "There. I think I got it all."

"Ooo. It hurts." Ellen strained once more to see the welt.

"Sometimes if you rub it real good it doesn't hurt so bad." He still held her arm with one hand, and with the other he rubbed his fingers firmly over the sore area. "Is that better?" He looked up and their eyes locked.

The mood changed instantly and the air around them seemed suddenly charged with electricity. The familiarity of the moment, the impossibility of it, enveloped them. Almost of its own accord, Ellen's arm went up and around Jake's neck and he pulled her imperceptibly closer.

They were twenty years old again, crazy in love and aware of no one but each other.

Their gazes locked, their faces inches apart. Then even that distance disappeared until it seemed to Ellen that the only thing she'd ever wanted to do was give in to the desire that had grown between them that week.

Ellen's breath rasped in her throat; her pulse pounded so she was sure Jake could hear it. *Just once. I'll kiss him and then let him go. Just once.*

But even as she tried to justify her intentions she knew she was lying to herself. If she kissed him now, it wouldn't stop there. If she became involved with Jake Sadler after so many years, there would be no turning back. No marriage to go back to. No faith to restore.

Once again, a verse drifted into her thoughts: *"The wise woman builds her house, but with her own hands the foolish one tears hers down."*

Ellen felt as though she'd been hit in the chest. Hard. She struggled to breathe, to move, but she couldn't.

It was Jake who came to his senses first.

His cheek brushed hers as he drew close, pausing with his mouth near her lips, taking her breath away. Then, ever so tenderly, he kissed her forehead instead.

"I don't know why," he whispered. "But I can't."

Slowly, Ellen lowered her head and let it rest on his chest. She was trembling from both desire and shame. She knew why Jake couldn't kiss her. After Leslie's prayer, God simply wouldn't let him. And, as though a voice was speaking in her head, in her heart, she heard: *"He will not let you be tempted beyond what you can bear, but when tempted he will also provide a way out."* She closed her eyes, feeling desperate. *What if I don't want a way out, Lord? Please, please show me. I can't do this on my own. I can't walk away from this —*

Jake's voice interrupted her thoughts. "If you weren't married . . ." Each word was an effort and she could see he was fighting with himself. "I'd do everything I could to make you mine, Ellen."

He pulled her close, resting his chin on the top of her head. Then he pulled away, his eyes filled with regret. "But not like this."

Only when she exhaled did she realize she'd been holding her breath, waiting, afraid of what would — or wouldn't — happen. She remembered a hundred times when they had given in to these very feelings. But not now. Not when it could only bring them pain. All of them.

"I was thinking no one would know but us," she whispered, ashamed but needing to be honest with him.

His hold on her tightened. "No one else would need to know." He drew a shaky breath. "Because we would never, ever forget."

She nodded then, knowing what he meant. "A day wouldn't go by when I wouldn't remember. Wonder. Want you."

"Me, too." He took one hand away and tenderly brushed a lock of wispy hair off her face. "I couldn't live like that, Ellen. And neither could you."

He let her go and framed her face with his fingertips, studying her intently, as though memorizing her features. "I love you. I loved you before Mike, and I love you still. But you belong to him; he was better for you than I was. He treated you like I only wish I'd treated you when I had the right. But I lost that right. And you still love him. You told me so yourself."

She nodded, savoring the feel of his fingers against her face and remembering the first time he had done that on a park bench near his parents' home, the first time he had kissed her. She knew she should pull away, but there was one more thing she needed to ask him. She covered his hands with hers.

"What if I had waited for you? If Mike

and I had never met?"

Jake's eyes grew moist. "I've asked myself the same question dozens of times, and I always come up with the same answer." He shook his head. "I don't think it would have worked, Ellen." He looked as though his heart might break. "I think maybe it took losing you for me to see what kind of man I was becoming, for me to change."

She nodded and lowered her hands slowly, staring down so he wouldn't see her cry. He pulled her head to his chest again and stroked her hair as her tears spilled onto his canvas tennis shoes.

Jesus, I wish I was stronger. I wish I could just walk away. But it's so hard! It hurts so much. All I want is to be loved, Lord. Like Mike used to love me, like Jake loves me now. . . . Is that so wrong?

This time the answer was swift, and it pierced her to the depths of her heart: *"I have loved you with an everlasting love. I have drawn you with loving-kindness. I will build you up again and you will be rebuilt. . . . I will lead you beside streams of water, on a level path where you will not stumble, because I am your father."*

The tears started afresh then, and she felt as though her heart was breaking. She'd been looking to Mike to love her. And her father. And, yes, to Jake. But the only one who could fill the void inside her was the very one she'd been turning away from.

Forgive me . . . forgive me . . .

After a while Ellen's sobs lessened, and she sniffed, wiping her eyes and raising her gaze to Jake's. "So, Bucko, where do we go from here?" She already knew the answer to that, but she needed to hear it from him.

"We do the only thing we can," he said. Gently he pulled himself away, separating their bodies. He let his arms drop to his side and he took a step back.

"I'm listening."

"We see each other in a few days at your dad's funeral, and then we go our separate ways."

There was silence for a long moment.

"You mean we say good-bye." The idea of losing Jake now after finding him again and seeing how he had changed, cut deep. But she knew he was right. She wondered how much pain a person could take in a single week.

Jake moved further away and stared across the bay at the glittering carpet of lights in Petoskey. "Yes," he said, looking at her once more. "We say good-bye."

The tears came again and neither of them could talk. When she could trust her voice, she searched his eyes.

"I'm not sorry I called you."

Jake didn't say anything. He didn't have to. His eyes said it all.

She went on. "No one else understood what I was going through this week. Not even Mike."

"I'll never be sorry you called."

"When I remember the happy times, the years when my father was well and the rest of my family got along together, I see you, too, Jake. Being with you this week, talking with you, brought those memories back. Made them alive again. Made Dad alive again."

"For me, too."

She paused and stared out at the bay. Then slowly, she lowered herself back onto the bench. Jake watched and joined her, allowing a distance between them.

"Don't forget me, huh, Jake?" She tilted her head back toward him, took his hand in hers and allowed herself to be lost in his eyes once more.

"Ellen." Her name seemed like it was born on his lips and she could see he was still struggling to maintain his distance. "I never have," he whispered, his tears brimming, ready to spill. "I never could."

Ellen nodded and the impossibilities hung

in the air a moment longer. Then she sniffed and released his hand. "Take me home, okay?"

Without saying a word they stood and returned to the house. Twenty minutes later they pulled up in front of Ellen's parents' house.

"I guess this is it." She stared at her hands folded tightly in her lap.

"No, I'll be at the service. I promised you and I'll be there."

She nodded quickly and gulped back a sob. "But it'll be different."

He leaned over and pulled her to him, hugging her one final time before letting her go. "I do love you, Ellen. Now go home and make the best of things between you and Mike. Don't cheat yourself of that because of what happened between us this week."

She nodded and, summoning every ounce of resolve, pulled away from him. "Goodbye, Jake," she whispered. She touched his face once more and then slid out of his truck. She closed the door and without looking back she walked away.

In that instant she knew with all her heart that God was still there for her, still listening. That night he had answered a prayer she had whispered nine years earlier. Because now, after seeing Jake again and knowing how he felt about her, only an act of God could have kept her from giving up everything and staying here in Petoskey with Jake Sadler.

TWENTY-SIX

Family members began arriving at the Barrett home early Friday morning, and the long week leading up to the funeral came to a sudden end. There were Mom's three sisters and one brother and their families, and Dad's sister from California with her children and grandchildren. Dad's parents had died years earlier, but Mom's aging parents arrived with one of her sisters. After that there were other cousins, aunts, uncles, all arriving, all talking.

Family members flowed through the house, many of them with tearstained eyes. The house was full of living reminders, of testimonies to how much John Barrett was loved, how much he'd be missed.

As planned, Ellen and her siblings were dressed and gathered at their parents' house by ten that morning, prepared to greet out-of-town relatives and help their mother with last-minute details. There were casserole dishes to receive, flowers to arrange, and conversations to take part in.

Uncle Jess, Mom's only brother, arrived with his wife, Betsy, and their six children. They lived in Grand Rapids, four hours south, and would spend the night at a local motel. They planned to be at the viewing later that night but had stopped at the Barrett home as soon as they got into town.

Dressed in a straight gray dress and gray pumps, Ellen watched the relatives arrive, but it all seemed unreal. She still ached from the night before, feeling almost as bad as she had nine years earlier when she and Jake had broken up that last time. But now that Friday had finally come, Jake was no longer first on her mind. Somehow, with the arrival of relatives, her father's death was indeed more real. They were gathered for one reason alone. John Barrett had died and it was time to say good-bye.

Ellen looked around the room, thankful that Troy had arrived from his convention in time to distract Jane. The two sat together at the dining room table, and for the first time that week Ellen didn't feel under attack. The children were quiet, watching a Disney video in the den and enjoying the company of Uncle Jess's little ones.

Across the room, Aaron filled up the living room chair, assuming John Barrett's place in the family's unspoken seating schematic. He was dressed in slacks and a slick white shirt with a subdued silk tie. He wore the dark sunglasses again and sat motionless, his arms crossed in front of him. Well-meaning relatives stayed clear of him, and Ellen knew that was what Aaron intended. The glasses hid his eyes but not the fact that he, too, was hurting.

Megan looked stunning in a navy skirt and sleeveless jacket, her hair pulled back conservatively. She sat on the couch beside Ellen, with Amy and Frank on her other side. They were somber, lost in their private worlds of grief and the inevitability of the approaching funeral.

Mom remained standing, greeting her siblings. She wore a black wraparound with pearl accents. It was a dress she had worn for her and Dad's thirtieth wedding anniversary and Ellen wondered if anyone would remember.

"Diane, how are you? Really?" Uncle Jess hovered over her. He was a large man with lumberjack hands and he had always reminded Ellen of Aaron. Her uncle spoke in hushed tones. His eyes were damp as he took their mother in his arms.

"It all happened so fast," she said.

"I know, I know." He rubbed her shoulder. "What was it? Just last month we were up for that beach party at Petoskey State Park?" Mom nodded, too emotional to speak. All week she'd held up so well, but now, looking into the eyes of her relatives, the sorrow seemed about to consume her.

"Ellen, Megan." Uncle Jess turned and nodded his greeting to the girls. He looked at the others then, one at a time. "I'm sorry about your father. He was a great man, one of a kind." His voice rang with sincerity. "One thing I'll always remember about your family —" he looked from Jane to Aaron and around the room to the others — "you really loved each other. Not because you had to, but because you liked each other. That was really special. Somehow I think your dad had a lot to do with that."

For a brief instant Jane's eyes met Ellen's, but both turned away. Uncle Jess looked to Mom again and hooked arms with her. He led her out of the room as they continued talking.

The air was heavy as Uncle Jess's words rattled around the room.

"He doesn't know us very well, does he?" Megan muttered. She crossed her arms in front of her and stared at the floor.

Jane sighed and pretended to doodle invisible designs on the tablecloth. Ellen clucked her tongue softly and fiddled with her fingernails. Amy and Aaron stared into space, apparently intent on ignoring the uncomfortable currents in the room.

The doorbell rang, and it was Aunt Betsy and her family from California. Their plane had arrived the day before at Detroit Metropolitan Airport and they had rented a car. They planned to stay several nights after the funeral so that Mom would not be alone once the others left.

Aunt Betsy was crying as Megan welcomed them inside.

"I'm so sorry about your dad." She hugged Megan and turned to the others. "It's hard to believe he's gone. He was so . . ." She searched for the right word, struggling with her emotions. "I don't know, so full of life."

Aunt Betsy sat down, joining the circle of siblings. Amy asked her about her flight.

"It was fine, not that I noticed." She wiped her tears daintily with her fingers. "I thought about your family the whole time. The trips to the lake, the ice-skating and football games. You kids have always been so close, such a great family." She paused a minute. "Me and your uncle, we divorced years ago, you know. The two kids went their own way

476

and well, I guess we never were much of a family really. But you guys —" she looked at them — "you guys had something really special. Whenever I think of how a family is supposed to be, how the kids should be close and the parents should love each other, I think of you." She wiped her eyes again and pulled a tissue from her purse.

"My brother must have been awfully proud of the family he raised. I'm so sorry he's gone." She looked at them, her eyes making a circle around the room. "At least you still have each other. No one can take that away from you."

She stood up then, dabbing at her face as she went to search for their mother.

Ellen squirmed uncomfortably in her chair, as did Jane and Megan. Was that really how others saw them? A close-knit, loving family? Apparently so, for that same sentiment was expressed continually for the next two hours as people stopped to visit and then returned to their various motel rooms to prepare for the viewing.

How fortunate Ellen and the others were, they would say, raised in a family where love had no limits. How close their relationships with one another were compared with other families . . . how blessed they were to have each other.

Silently, Ellen was struck by the irony. She exchanged furtive glances with her siblings and saw by their faces they were feeling the same thing. *When did we change so much, Lord? Or were we ever really the family everyone else remembers?*

Finally it was two o'clock and the house cleared as relatives left to ready themselves for the evening viewing. Diane Barrett waited until only her children and their spouses remained before addressing them.

"I'm going to the mortuary now so that I'll have a few minutes alone," she said. She only hoped she had the strength to endure what was coming.

"Are you sure you should go by yourself?" Megan looked concerned.

"Yes. I'll be fine. I'd like you children to join me in a little while." She looked at Jane. "The kids are taken care of for the evening, right?"

Jane nodded. "A friend of mine is keeping them until late tonight."

"Good. Well, I'm sure I'll see you there within the hour. I'll take the small car. Ellen, why don't you drive the van."

Diane looked at the stiff way her children sat together and she was struck, again, by the fact that they were clearly not the family they had once been.

"I know you haven't gotten along this week and I think that's to be expected. We're all under a great deal of stress." She searched their faces, pleading with them. "But please, for your father's sake, try to be a family tonight and tomorrow. It would have made him so sad to see you like this."

Her request met with utter silence and finally, with tears welling up in her eyes, Diane picked up her purse and left.

TWENTY-SEVEN

"Well, that was nice. You guys are really something," Aaron sneered at his sisters. "All Mom wants is a little reassurance that everyone can get along these next few days and no one says a word."

Ellen raised an eyebrow. "Don't look at me, Aaron. I've done everything possible to get along this week."

"Oh, so I guess that makes me the bad guy," Jane piped in. Troy put his hand over hers and squeezed gently. They exchanged a knowing look and Jane seemed to lose interest in the argument.

"Why'd you have to start a fight, Aaron?" Amy's eyebrows creased in frustration. "Everything was fine until you opened your mouth."

"Look, you little witch . . ." Aaron rose from his chair and towered over Amy. Ellen watched as Frank pretended to read a magazine, but she saw how he sat a little straighter, moving closer to his wife and keeping an eye on her brother.

"You girls are the ones fighting this week," Aaron shouted. "I haven't said a word."

"Well, you also haven't done a thing to help Mom. So don't blame us for getting her upset." Obviously Amy was not in the mood to back down. "I guess you think the girls will do everything just like we always have, right?"

"You want me to do something, Amy?" Aaron's voice boomed as he took giant strides toward the kitchen. "Fine!" He picked up a dish and threw it into the sink, shattering it into a hundred pieces. "I'll do the dishes." Ellen cringed. "Here's another one." He smashed a second dish against the sink.

Then suddenly he stopped his tantrum and stormed out of the kitchen. He grabbed his truck keys and slammed the front door behind him.

"Same old Aaron," Ellen mumbled.

"You know, Ellen, why don't you lighten up?" Jane glared at her sister. "All week you've been feeling sorry for yourself, wishing you didn't have to be around the rest of us." She stood up, ignoring Troy's efforts to stop her.

"Things start to seem a little tense around

here and what do you do? Run off and spend time with your *friends*."

Megan raised an eyebrow and stared at Ellen accusingly.

"Did you ever stop and think that maybe there's a reason why the rest of us are so edgy? Maybe Aaron's life isn't as good and golden as yours. And maybe my memories of Dad aren't straight from a storybook like the ones you have. Did you ever think of that?"

Ellen crossed her arms tightly and stared back at Jane. "I don't need to listen to this." She started to get up but Jane blocked her way.

"No. Don't leave. Not this time." Jane put her hands on her hips, her face flushed with the intensity of her anger. "Did you ever think that maybe there's a reason why Amy's so quiet and Megan's so sentimental? Did it occur to you that maybe there's a reason why Dad's funeral has me so edgy? Or that there just might be an explanation for Aaron's anger?"

Ellen stood staring at her sister, waiting impatiently for her to finish her tirade.

"Let me say this, Ellen. If there was a reason, you sure wouldn't know it. Because all you care about is yourself. Is Ellen having a good time? Is everyone being nice to

Ellen? Is Mike doing what Ellen wants him to do?"

Ellen sucked in her breath at the mention of Mike. She hoped Megan didn't notice. "That's not true. I care about everyone here and you know it."

"You care about us if everything's going good and we're all happy-go-lucky. But when there's a problem, you split. That's what you've been doing all week."

Amy shifted uneasily and reached for Frank's hand. Jane's anger seemed to fade suddenly, and Ellen was surprised to see her eyes fill with tears.

"We're here for one week together, Ellen, and I'm sorry if I haven't been very nice. But you're so caught up in yourself you can't even see the way the rest of us are hurting."

Ellen's eyes stung with tears at the accusation. "That's not fair. I'm hurting, too, you know. I don't remember anyone asking me how I was doing."

"I asked you," Megan said quietly.

Jane's tears came harder now and she looked from Megan back to Ellen. "When we were younger we were like best friends. I still think of you that way. But what kind of friend are you when you don't even ask me what's wrong? I have things I'm dealing with this week that you know nothing about."

"Is it my fault you don't tell me what's wrong?" Ellen cried.

"Yes! I thought you were my friend, Ellen. I know I haven't been very nice to you, but did you even once think that something might be bothering me?"

Ellen released a burst of air, frustrated by Jane's summation of the week-long struggle between them. "If you want me to be interested in your feelings then think of mine for a change." Ellen maneuvered past Jane and found her bag. "You've been hateful toward me since we got here. Now you expect me to pretend that didn't happen, paste a sympathetic smile on my face, and ask you how you've been? Well, you can forget it, Jane." She looked at the others. "I'll be at the mortuary."

Then she stormed out the front door.

The room fell suddenly silent as Jane stared at the door Ellen had just slammed. She'd tried. She really had. And look where it had gotten her.

She swore under her breath. But instead of sounding angry, it just sounded desperate. She felt a hand on her arm and turned to see Troy standing there, his eyes filled with understanding.

She turned to him and buried her head in his chest, finally sobbing as she hadn't all week.

TWENTY-EIGHT

Ellen drove to the mortuary like a woman on a mission. She was determined not to let Jane's outburst affect her. She cared about Jane; the others had to see that. But it was impossible to be interested in the problems of a person who spent so much time on the attack. Ellen thought about Jane's statement and wondered vaguely what had been troubling her that week. But she refused to play games. If Jane wanted to talk then she would have to make the first move.

As she drove, images from the past week demanded her attention and suddenly she could no longer shut them out — she and Jake making omelettes . . . she and Jake at the beach, on the swing. She could feel his fingers entwined with hers.

She slammed her fist onto the steering wheel and the images disappeared. Five minutes later she was at the mortuary. The public parking lot was empty except for her mother's car and Ellen parked alongside it, cutting the engine.

The truth hit her then. In a moment she would come face-to-face with her dead father's body. How many times had she walked into her parents' home, rounded the corner toward the den, and seen him sitting in his easy chair? How many times had he looked up, noticed her, and burst into a smile, stretching his left hand toward her?

"Hi, honey," he'd say. "Come sit down."

She would walk toward him, tucking her hand in his warm one and bending to kiss him on his cheek. Somewhere through the passing of the days, he had greeted her that way for the last time. And she hadn't even known it.

She leaned back in the van, sitting in the seat that had been his alone, and closed her eyes. If only she could remember the last time he had done that so she could savor the moment forever. She wanted something real and alive to remember him by. Otherwise the lifeless body she was about to see would be her final memory of him. She drew in a deep breath and steadied herself. Then she climbed out of the van and headed for the mortuary.

It was quiet inside; the lights reverently dim. Ellen moved through the lobby and entered a narrow doorway leading to the front of a small chapel. Twelve wooden pews lined the room on either side of a center aisle. Ellen glanced to her right and saw the oak casket they had chosen the day before. It was propped open, and her mother knelt before it on a padded kneeler, her head bowed, lips moving in silent prayer.

Ellen headed soundlessly toward her mother. She refused to look at her father's body until the last possible minute.

"Hi, Mom." She put her arm around the older woman and knelt beside her. Then she turned toward the casket and felt her breath catch in her throat.

There he was. Hands folded peacefully over his considerable abdomen, graying blond hair neatly combed. His suit was pressed and starched, the shoes shined. She stared at him and felt herself about to collapse.

Her mother looked up then and studied him, too.

"He's at peace now," she said. Her voice was calm but tears spilled down her face and her eyes searched her husband's still face.

Ellen nodded, unsure what to say. She was horrified by the sight of her father like that and needed a moment to grasp what she was seeing.

Her mom struggled to her feet. "I'm going to go make a few phone calls," she whispered. "Will you be all right?"

Ellen nodded quickly, thankful for the chance to be alone. When her mother was gone she tentatively reached toward her father's hand and touched him.

He was cold and stiff, and she recoiled as if she'd pricked her finger on a needle. She narrowed her eyes, studying the face, the body that once housed her father.

His skin was pale, dusty from the makeup they'd used. It wasn't how she remembered him, and she thought how different a body looked when there was someone living inside.

She studied his eyes, closed for all time.

If only he could open them once more, smile at her the way he had all his life. She had the urge to nudge him, to wake him up and help him out of the satin-lined box so that everyone could see he was all right. Her eyes moved slowly up the lid of the casket and she shuddered thinking of the moment when they would close it, shutting him in darkness for eternity.

Get up, Dad.

But he remained motionless, nothing but a shell of the man he had been. She wanted to talk to him, to say something she might have said if he were alive and only sleeping.

"Dad," she whispered as tears sprang to her eyes. "I love you."

She had brought something for this moment. Reaching into her purse she wrapped her fingers around them, familiar with the way they felt. She opened her hands and tried to make out the items through eyes blurred with tears. There they were . . . she could see them clearly now. A worn white handkerchief and a plain black comb.

She had visited her parents a year earlier when her father was hospitalized with chest pain. Deeply concerned, she accompanied her mother to the operating room where doctors performed the final test to determine the cause of his discomfort. When they saw the gravity of his condition, they quickly decided to perform emergency triple-bypass surgery.

Ellen had been devastated, certain he wouldn't survive the surgery. But the urgency of the situation left them no time for lengthy good-byes. Instead, just before they wheeled him into surgery, he took his handkerchief and black comb from his hospital table and folded them into the palm of her hand.

"Hold these for me, Ellen." His lower lip

quivered slightly and his voice was choked with emotion. "I'll be back for them. I promise."

She had nodded and clutched them purposefully. For three hours, while doctors searched for the perfect vein in his leg with which to replace the arteries leading to his heart, she kept his handkerchief and comb in her hand, praying he would survive.

Three months later she was going through the nightstand next to her bed when she found the comb tucked inside the neatly folded handkerchief. After that she looked at them now and then, running her fingers over the threadbare cloth and remembering how thankful she had been when he had come out of the operation alive.

They were the first items she packed as she prepared to come to Petoskey to bury him.

Gradually, relentlessly, sorrow welled up in her chest as she held the handkerchief to her cheek and closed her eyes. Tears spilled onto her face and she surrendered as deep, gut-wrenching sobs exploded from the center of her being.

She cried for every single distant memory, moments she would have given anything to have again. Scenes from the past flashed through her mind and she grieved for each of them, crying for the little girl she had left behind and the father who would never again take her hand or swing her around the backyard.

She stared at him, thinking of the football games when he patiently taught her the difference between the quarterback and defensive back. And the times when he had listened to her read her game stories over the telephone so he could catch her mistakes before her editors did.

She sobbed harder and reached toward him once more. She knew what to expect this time and she didn't pull away. Instead, she ran her fingers gently over his hands, remembering the way those same hands had loved her and her sisters and brother through the years. The hugs and hand-holds, the ball-tossing and shoe-tying . . . hands that had been loving and warm, gentle and strong.

"Dad, I wish we had more time," she whispered. The sobbing finally slowed but the tears continued, as did the empty ache in the depth of her heart.

Suddenly she couldn't stand to see him that way a moment longer and she closed her eyes. Why was she doing this to herself, participating in a ritual that meant nothing? He wasn't there, resting in a casket. He had moved on to a better place, the place for people who have loved God and done his work on earth. She knew the Lord was watching over her that very moment, wishing he could comfort her, willing her to know that her father was all right.

She opened her eyes and looked into the coffin again. Dad's body would be buried there, but not his soul, his heart. No one could bury that.

She clutched the handkerchief and comb tightly, holding them to her face a final time. Then she gently tucked them under his hands.

"Dad," her voice was choked with tears. "I have to give them back now. I . . . I can't hold them anymore."

She hung her head and cried again, knowing that Jake had been right. For the first time, her dad's death seemed real. She looked at him once more, still, lifeless.

"Daddy," she cried softly. "You were the best. You believed in me . . . encouraged me, cheered me on. You were always there for me. Even when I was wrong you never let me down." She was quiet a moment, tears streaming down her face. "I love you so much."

She gazed toward the heavens then, her voice barely a whisper. "I love you, Daddy."

The sadness was like a lead weight as she stood up and moved to the back of the chapel. She had said good-bye. She found a seat near the back of the chapel and sat down to wait for the others.

The remaining adult Barrett children arrived within five minutes of each other and met in the parking lot. Aaron did not say where he had disappeared to earlier, but he was outspoken as they gathered near their parked cars and prepared to enter the mortuary.

"I don't know what problems you all have between you," he said waving his hand at Megan, Jane, and Amy. He stared at Jane, who stood quietly by Troy. "I know there's something going on between you and Ellen, but I don't want to hear the details or whose fault it is. Right now it's time to put our differences behind us. All of us. Dad would never have wanted us fighting right up until the moment of his funeral."

He looked at each of them slowly. "I want you to listen because I don't say a lot, and this is the way it's got to be. If you have a problem, hide it. In two days we'll all go our separate ways and you can think whatever bad things you want about this family. Right now, though, we're in this together."

Jane looked stunned. "Fine," she mumbled. "It's just two days. I can pretend with the best of them."

"Fine." Aaron was satisfied. "Now let's get in there. Mom's waiting."

Ellen watched in silence as her brother and sisters came into the room. She continued watching as, for the next two hours, they took turns kneeling by their father's casket, staring at his body, and reckoning with the fact that he no longer lived there. When Megan took her turn bidding their father good-bye, she cried much the way Ellen had. *Probably regretting the lost years with Mohammed,* Ellen reasoned.

Amy's grieving was quieter, more reserved. She seemed awestruck by her father in death, much as she had been when he was alive. She didn't fully give way to her grief until she had risen from the spot near the casket and returned to the pew where Frank sat. He stood, holding his hands out toward her, and she collapsed against him, sobbing.

Ellen remained at the back of the chapel where Megan and Amy approached her at different times to see if she was all right. For a time, her mother came and sat next to her, but then as the others seemed to take turns grieving she tried to make herself available for them, too.

Jane never even looked Ellen's way. She did spend a short time kneeling near Dad's casket before returning to sit with Troy for the remainder of the viewing. As the evening went on, Ellen couldn't help but notice that Jane appeared neither concerned for the others nor anxious for their comfort. She was the only one who did not cry.

Aaron was the last to approach the casket and he did so reluctantly. He wore his sunglasses and his tall frame looked uncomfortable as he knelt before his father's body.

Ellen watched from a distance, and although Aaron neither moved a muscle nor spoke a word, she knew his pain. Not because of anything obvious about the way he grieved for his father. But because of the angle at which she was sitting. He had his back to the others, but she could see his face, the dark glasses. And the steady stream of tears that ran from beneath them the entire time he remained on his knees.

At five-thirty the first of the relatives began to arrive and the Barrett siblings found their separate places in the chapel from which to watch and remember. It was a quiet time and within two hours everyone but Ellen, her siblings, and her mother had left for the night.

"Mrs. Barrett, it's time to seal the casket." It was the director, Mr. Whitson.

Mom had been talking quietly to Amy and Frank and she seemed startled by his statement. "Oh. Of course." She stood up and looked at the others.

"You can join me if you want," she said in a voice loud enough for them all to hear. She positioned herself close to the casket and stared a final time at her husband's face. Ellen watched Megan rise and move to their mother's side. She placed an arm around Mom's waist for support. Aaron joined her, too, bracing Mom on her opposite side, while Amy and Frank joined hands and stood nearby. Ellen and Jane remained in their seats on different sides of the chapel.

"Good-bye, John." Mom's smile was tender through her tears. "You made me so happy."

Ellen rested her arms on the back of the pew in front of her and let her head drop. She couldn't watch, couldn't bear to see him disappear behind the closing lid of a coffin.

She heard them unhook the coffin lid and lower it. Then there was the sound of someone moving around the casket as they tightened a series of latches so that it was sealed.

There was nothing left to do but go home. They did so, each in a separate car, returning to the house to discuss the logistics for the following day, who would drive which vehicle, when they needed to be where.

Ellen found a quiet spot in the den where she studied the eulogy she had written earlier in the week. The others milled about the living room where they finished plans and shared a late snack. There was little conversation, and even from the next room Ellen could feel the cool way in which her siblings regarded each other.

She read her eulogy again and sighed. It still wasn't exactly what she wanted to say. She'd been inserting words and crossing out others for what seemed like hours. Finally, she set her pen aside.

Closing her eyes, she leaned her head back. She just couldn't handle this right now. The image of her father's lifeless face came to mind, and she pushed it aside. *Think of something else. Anything . . .*

Jake's laughing face came to her, and she felt the familiar pang. What was it about him that captured her so? She couldn't let him go no matter how she tried.

Help me, Lord, she prayed desperately as

she considered the memories of her times with Jake over the last week. *Am I going to be haunted by him for the rest of my life?*

"This is a shadow of the things that are to come; the reality, however, is found in Christ."

Ellen frowned. Why had that verse come to her now of all times? What could it possibly mean? Jake? A shadow?

Dimly she heard the doorbell ring. Someone opened the front door and in the distance Ellen heard muffled conversation. She pushed the distraction away as she focused again on the images in her mind.

Jake on the beach . . . Jake holding her . . . Jake, Jake —

"Ellen." Megan poked her head around the corner and peered into the den.

"What?" Ellen looked up, startled. She felt completely drained.

"You have a visitor."

Ellen's throat constricted and sudden fear assailed her. Jake? Had he come to talk with her again? *Oh no, no, Lord. I won't be able to send him away again. Please —*

"Who?"

That's when she saw him. A man, standing there in the doorway to the room, looking rumpled and tired and still dressed in his work clothes.

For a moment she was sure it was Jake,

and then the image faded, and Ellen stared, her face going hot, and then cold. Quick tears flooded her eyes.

"Mike."

TWENTY-NINE

Ellen stared at her husband in disbelief. He had come. He had found a way to be with her, and her heart soared.

Their eyes met and spoke volumes. She studied the unrestrained love in his eyes, the hope and apprehension on his face, and suddenly the Scripture was utterly clear. "This is a shadow of the things that are to come. . . ." That was what Jake had been. A shadow. An image of something Ellen had convinced herself she wanted. Yes, he was real, but their relationship wasn't. Not the way she'd been thinking about it. All she and Jake had was a shadow.

She took in Mike's appearance, the dark circles under his eyes, the rumpled suit, the wedding band . . . he was the reality. The reality Ellen had found through Christ. For that's who had joined them. Forever. She remembered her anger of a week ago and felt ashamed. She had been wrong about

Mike. Yes, he had botched things up, he had left her alone too many times to count and he seemed to have grown cold to all that mattered. But she, too, had let her faith go by the wayside.

Now, if only they could cling to the Lord as they had in their early days, perhaps the love they once shared would return. Perhaps they could survive after all. Ellen felt a peace come over her as she considered her husband. At least their life together was real. Not an idea or a dream or a shadow. They would have to talk about the future, the expectations on both sides. As in the early days of their marriage, they would need to pray together, find a church family where they could grow. But looking at her husband now she believed they would find a way to work it out.

Tears filled her eyes as she smiled at him, and in his face she saw the young sports-caster with whom she'd fallen in love. Mike had always been faithful beyond anything she'd ever dreamed. But in those early days there had been so much more love. Mike had supported her decisions and encour-aged her writing career. He had taken time for walks on the beach and candlelit din-ners at little-known restaurants. Back then he had written poetry for her and rubbed her back when she ached with tension from a day of deadlines. He never let her go alone to anything.

She saw him now and remembered their early days as if they were only weeks ago. She had never doubted back then that Mike was the man she belonged with. Theirs had been a wonderful relationship — intimate, satisfying, deeply rooted. It was a life she knew they could have again. And one she never would have had with Jake. Now, at last, she understood that.

At the thought of Jake a wave of guilt washed over her and she hoped Mike couldn't see in her eyes how close she'd come only twenty-four hours earlier to breaking her wedding vows. She refused to think about that now. Leslie had prayed for her, and although the bond between Ellen and Mike had been tested that week, it had survived. Thank God it had survived. Even before Mike made the decision to be there for her.

Megan discreetly left the room, and Ellen moved toward Mike. His arms opened, and she went into them, sliding her hands along his back, pulling him to her, overwhelmed with gratitude.

"You came."

He pulled back slightly so he could look

503

into her eyes. "You needed me."

She sighed and hugged him tightly. "Oh, Mike. It's been such a long week."

"I know. For me, too. Do you still hate me?"

She shook her head against his chest. With him here now, solid and reassuring, things were so much clearer. What she and Mike had once shared — what she knew they would share again — was so different than what she'd shared with Jake all those years ago. With Mike, love was steady and real, without the uncertainty Jake had brought to her life. Mike was here and he was real. He was today and tomorrow — and that meant more than all her yesterdays combined.

She leaned up and kissed him tenderly on the lips. "Thank you . . . for coming."

He reached down and cupped her face in his hands, holding her gently but firmly. His eyes held hers. "I love you, Ellen. I'd go to the moon to prove it to you."

"Not always." She smiled sadly.

Mike's face fell. His hands moved down her shoulders, brushing her arms, until he took her hands in his. "I know. I've done a lot of thinking. Praying. I spent most of yesterday reading the Bible and begging God to make things right between us again. It was like the Spirit literally picked me up and set me at the Lord's feet."

Ellen thought about Leslie again and knew that since their phone call her dear friend had probably not stopped praying for them.

"How could we drift so far from everything we believe?" Ellen's voice cracked. *Jesus, forgive us.* Her heart felt as though it would break with regret.

"I know. I feel the same way. I've been selfish and faithless. You deserve better than that. Things are going to be different, Ellen." He met her gaze. "Forgive me. Please."

Ellen nodded and rested her cheek against his chest. She squeezed her eyes shut and felt tears fall onto her face once more. "I forgive you, Mike. Is everything okay between us then?"

He pulled back a few inches so he could study her eyes. "I don't know. Is it?"

She thought of Jake again and nodded. "A lot has happened this week. I was having my doubts about us, but God helped me work through a few things while I've been here. I do love you, Mike. I don't ever want to lose you. God gave you to me, and he wants us together."

"Then get your things." He smiled and patted her on the behind. "We've got a hotel room waiting for us."

The morning dawned chilly and overcast, unusually cool for July. The clouds would probably dissipate by noon but Ellen thought the weather seemed appropriate, as if the sky were mourning her father's death as well.

Still, the Baywinds Inn was perfectly tranquil that morning. The room she and Mike shared had a balcony with a distant view of the bay.

Ellen crept outside and sat down, letting the cool morning air wash over her as she stared across the water. In two days she would be gone and everything about the week would be behind her.

The night before, she had told Mike about the problems between her and Jane and the others, and he had kindly refrained from making cutting remarks about her siblings. Instead he assured her the week was nearly through. She would be going home the next day and could put the entire ordeal behind her. Then they talked for hours about their past mistakes. When Ellen finally told him how seriously she had considered leaving him, Mike cried.

He'd reached out for her, gathering her close and holding her tightly. He buried his face in her hair, and she stroked his back as he cried. When he could speak again, he pulled back and met her eyes. "I was a fool, Ellen. I took you for granted. I took everything I believe about the Lord for granted. In the process I let our marriage grow cold."

His words filled Ellen with joy — and gratitude to God, who had kept her faithful at her weakest moment. What she saw reflected in Mike's eyes moved her more deeply than anything she had ever experienced. They talked some more after that and then they did something they hadn't done in years. They prayed together. Finally, in the early morning hours, they fell asleep in each other's arms.

But still she said nothing about Jake. Not yet.

Mike had a game to cover Sunday morning, so he would leave later that evening on a flight back to Miami. Their hotel room was quiet as he dressed in a sleek Armani suit, and Ellen wondered how Jake would react when he saw them together that morning at the funeral. The two men had never met. She forced herself not to think about it as she slipped into the navy rayon dress she had worn from Miami a week earlier.

They arrived at the Barrett house by eight that morning. Everyone was there except

Megan and Jane's family.

"Good morning, dear." Ellen's mother smiled sadly, greeting Ellen at the door and kissing her on the cheek. "You look pretty."

"Thanks, Mom. You, too."

"Hello, Mike. We're glad you could make it."

Mike nodded in response and straightened his tie, clearly unsure what to say.

Ellen's mother wore an elegant black dress with dark hose, but her makeup wasn't done yet and she was slightly breathless with the rush to get ready on time.

"Your Aunt Betsy put together a breakfast tray for us, pastries and fruit, that kind of thing." She pointed them toward the dining room table. "I still have to do my face and hair. I'll be back out in a while."

Ellen watched her disappear down the hall and in the distance she heard Aaron's voice boom through the house.

"Mom, where's the blow dryer? I can't find it anywhere."

Amy and Frank were dressed, sitting at the dining room table eating. Ellen nodded to them as she fixed a plate of food.

"How's it going, Frank?" Mike asked. He took his plate and found a seat next to Ellen.

"Good. You?"

"Fine."

They heard Aaron's voice again.

"Mom, where's the hair spray? It's always in this cabinet."

"I've got it. Just a minute, Aaron," Mom yelled in response.

Ellen nibbled at a pastry and thought how familiar the scene felt. It had been this way a handful of times before, when the Barrett family had been up early in the morning preparing for a big event. They had done this from a motel room in Ann Arbor before her graduation from the university, and again before her wedding. Later the same scene played out in this very house before Jane's wedding and then Amy's.

There was that same anticipation, the readying for an event that would mark a milestone in a lifetime of everyday occurrences. It seemed strange — almost twisted somehow. Every other time the event had been a celebration. Ellen thought something should be different about preparing for a funeral.

She excused herself and went out back to read her eulogy once more. She'd worked on it late into the night, getting up again after Mike was asleep, and she felt satisfied with what she had written. Now she wanted to be familiar with it so she could read it despite her emotions.

Jane and Troy and the children piled into Troy's rented car at eight-thirty on the morning of the funeral. Jane was particularly quiet, and Troy allowed her enough space to deal with her feelings.

"Here we go," she muttered as they pulled out of the parking lot.

Troy looked over at her, and she caught his curious glance.

"You okay?" he asked.

"No, I'm not." She rubbed at a spot on her dress where Kala had spilled oatmeal. "How am I supposed to do this today, Troy? I mean, the whole week's been a disaster. Ellen and I aren't speaking to each other, and now I have to pretend to be broken up by my father's death."

Troy sighed loudly and slammed his foot on the brake. He pulled over and brought the car to a stop on the side of the road.

"Something isn't right here, Jane."

She looked at him, startled. He sounded as though his patience was waning. "What do you mean?"

"First of all, you've been snapping at everyone in your family since I got here yesterday. You act as if they should under-stand what happened to you the night your father left. Second, last night at the viewing you were working a little too hard to convince yourself that your dad's death doesn't matter to you."

He gripped the steering wheel with both hands and stared out the window for a moment. "I think you're kidding yourself, Jane." He turned back toward her. "I think you're hurting as much, maybe even more than the rest of your family. You wrote him off years ago, and now you have to live with that. Nothing you say or do can give you those years back."

Jane couldn't respond.

He paused a moment, and the children grew restless in the backseat. "Jane, it's time you let down your defenses and stop trying to fight the world because of what happened that night. The Bible says not to let the sun go down on your anger, but you've been doing that for more than a decade. No wonder you're miserable. Your bitterness has all but strangled you."

"I thought at least you'd understand," she cried. "You know why I feel this way."

"I do understand, Jane." He reached over and touched her face. "But you need to let it go, hon. Put it behind you. As long as you blame Ellen and your father, you're never going to be free of the past. You'll never be at peace with God or anyone in your family."

"It's not like I've been this way forever, Troy. It's just this funeral thing. I don't know how to deal with it."

He shook his head. "That's not true. You've been upset with Ellen for years. Sure, there are times when you two get along better than you have this week. But you blame her for what happened, just like you blame your father."

Jane hung her head, the fight gone.

"Ellen doesn't have any idea what's eating you, what's been eating you for the past decade. Neither did your father."

"I wanted her to ask," Jane said weakly.

"That's not fair, Jane. No one could guess something that terrible had happened to you. Not even Ellen."

Jane sniffed and raised her eyes meekly. "Have I been that bad?"

"Quite honestly, yes."

Jane sighed and stared at her hands, absorbing the truth in his words. "I'll talk to her."

"What about your dad? You have to deal with it, Jane. After today you might never have another chance."

"I know." She drew in a shaky breath. "I'll take care of it."

He reached out and pulled her close, hugging her. "Okay. Now we're getting somewhere."

Silent tears fell onto her lap, but she said nothing.

"Honey," his voice was gentle. "I'll be pulling for you."

Megan was pacing her apartment, frantic about what she had written for the funeral. She had not expected to have any trouble with the eulogy, but all week none of the words had fallen into place. She had memories of her father from when she was a little girl and memories from the past two years. But she had been gone so much of the time in between that she hadn't found a way to bridge the gap on paper. She had something else planned, something no one knew about. But she still hadn't pieced together the eulogy.

She stopped suddenly and remembered something she had forgotten until that instant. Years ago she had been in counseling after breaking up with Mohammed, and she had successfully survived a month without calling him or returning his phone calls. To celebrate the victory, her father had taken her to a fancy steak house for dinner. He told the waitress they were celebrating his daughter's special anniversary, but the woman misunderstood and thought it was Megan's birthday. When the meal was over a dozen food servers brought her a piece of cake with a candle. They sang her a birthday song and their waitress snapped a picture of her father with his arm around her.

For a long time she had kept that Polaroid snapshot on her dresser as a reminder of her father's unending support, an encouragement for the days when she felt like calling Mohammed. Later, when Mohammed was no longer a temptation and the picture began to collect dust, she tucked it away in a scrapbook. In the past week she had been too busy worrying about her sisters to remember the photo until now.

She disappeared into her closet, rummaging through a box of belongings until she came across the scrapbook. Flipping through the pages she searched frantically until she found it. There she was, side by side with her dad, silly expressions on their faces as they celebrated her independence.

That picture said more about her relationship with her father than anything she could have put on paper. She tucked it in her purse, grabbed her keys and an envelope that contained a single cassette tape. She was at her mother's house in five minutes.

Diane breathed a sigh of relief. All the kids were there now, and all but Aaron were ready to go. He was showered and dressed but he remained in his room, and Diane looked nervous. It was nine-fifteen and the service started at ten. They needed to leave in ten minutes according to her schedule.

"Aaron." She knocked gently on his bedroom door.

"What?" he barked.

"Are you almost ready? We need to leave in a few minutes."

"You go ahead. Go without me. I'll be there later."

Diane sighed softly. "Son, I want us all to arrive at the same time. Is there something I can help you with?"

Silence.

"Aaron?"

"I said go!"

"Can you open the door a minute so I can talk with you, please?"

There was a brief pause and then she heard the click of a lock turning as he opened the door.

"What?"

He had his dark glasses off, and she could see he'd been crying. "What's taking so long, son?" She kept her voice tender and calm. "I'd be happy to help you."

"Here —" He thrust a wrinkled piece of paper into her hand. "That's the problem."

Diane stared at the paper and read over the first few handwritten lines. "Is this what you're going to read at the funeral?"

"It's all I have, but I can't read it. It stinks. I've worked on it every day this week, and it just doesn't sound right."

She took a moment and read the opening lines of what he had written. It was jerky and not quite beautiful, but it came from his heart. She handed it slowly back to him.

"Son, this is what you remember, the way you remember him. It'll be perfect."

"You don't understand . . ." He began crying, and Diane watched him, deeply moved. This was the first time since he was a little boy that he had let her see his tears. "Dad deserved more than what I've written there. It's not enough."

Suddenly her tall, strong, strapping son was reduced to an oversized little boy crying for his daddy, and Diane's heart broke at the sight of him. She took his large, callused hand in hers and squeezed it tenderly. "You, all by yourself, are enough, Aaron."

He looked up at her, questioning, clearly

wanting to believe her. "What if I mess it up?"

She shook her head. "Your heart will speak for you, son. Believe me."

He sniffed loudly and wiped his face with the back of his hand. Then he reached for his dark glasses on his bedside table and put them firmly in place.

"All right, then," he said, his voice shaking. "I'll do this one last thing for Dad, even if it isn't perfect." He took his mother's arm in his. "Let's get going."

THIRTY

St. Francis Xavier Catholic Church stood tall and proud amidst the rows of gift shops and ice-cream parlors, novelty booths, and boutiques that filled Petoskey's Gaslight District. Jane's family drove in caravan toward the towering gray steeple that marked the church. The building was one of the oldest in Petoskey, and its brick-and-stone exterior made it appear stately and strong.

The hearse was there, across the street near the side doors. Jane and her siblings piled out of their cars and moved separately toward the black vehicle. They kept their distance from each other, aware of the tension that remained. The rear doors of the hearse were open, and two attendants prepared to place the casket on a rolling gurney.

An elderly woman appeared at the church's side entrance. "You're the family, is that right?" She wore a badge that identified her as the funeral coordinator. "And you must be Mrs. Barrett." She extended her hand. "I'd like you all to come in and have a seat about ten minutes before the guests begin to arrive."

"My son is a pallbearer," Mom said. "Can he sit with his sisters or does he need to sit with the other pallbearers?"

"Oh, no, dear," she said quickly. "He can sit wherever he'd like."

"Good. Thank you."

The woman nodded and disappeared back inside the church. The organist arrived and began practicing with the soloist, filling the air with dark, somber music.

Jane and Troy held hands and kept the children from running around. When Ellen and Mike approached and continued past them, Troy raised an eye at his wife.

"When, Jane?" he whispered.

"Later." She looked away. "I'll talk to her after the funeral."

Megan was standing next to their mother, and Jane saw her sister was shivering despite the fact that the sun was breaking through the clouds. Several feet away Aaron stood closest to the hearse, arms crossed, feet spread apart as he stared at the casket through his dark glasses.

Nearby, Frank put his arm around Amy as she leaned on him for support. She looked nervous and Jane wondered whether her youngest sister would hold up.

"Okay, everyone. Why don't you come in and take a seat," the coordinator said as she appeared momentarily at the door of the church and then vanished again.

Their mother motioned for the others to follow her. When they were huddled together inside the front of the church, she looked intently at their faces.

"I'd like you five to sit together in the front row with me." She pointed to a wooden pew that was easily long enough for ten people.

Jane started to roll her eyes, then caught herself. She stared at the ground instead.

"You mean I can't sit with Frank?" Amy sounded frightened.

"The men can sit in the row behind us with the children."

Amy looked at Frank, and he nodded slightly. She turned to her mother. "All right. That's fine."

"Is everyone okay with that?" Their mother glanced at each of them.

Jane and the others nodded and began moving stiffly into the front pew. Their mother sat on the far right with Aaron at the opposite side near the center aisle. Megan, Jane, Amy, and Ellen sat in the middle, spread out along the pew so that several feet separated them.

Let this day be over quickly, Jane prayed. *Please.*

Diane leaned slightly forward and studied her children, taking in the uncomfortable looks on their faces. They were sitting together, but they were still worlds apart. She bowed her head and whispered a silent prayer.

People were arriving and Ellen sat at an angle so she could watch for Jake. She had told Mike that she and Jake had spoken and that he might be at the funeral. Details beyond that could wait until they were back in Miami.

It was nearly ten and the church was more than half full when Ellen saw him. He was by himself and he entered the building through the back doors. Ellen watched him and saw him hesitate, searching the church for her. She stood up and moved toward the back of the church.

Jake had seen her stand up, and he remained in the back of the church, waiting for her. He was wearing a tie and Ellen thought it didn't quite look right on him. She would always see him in swim shorts and a tank top, the way he had been when they were dating . . . the way he had been that past week.

She motioned for him to follow her into the foyer.

"You okay?" he whispered when they could talk. He took her hand in his and squeezed it quickly.

"I'm nervous," she said. "I think my stomach's been in knots since last night."

"The viewing?"

She nodded. "Hardest thing I've ever done." She paused. "Thanks for coming, Jake."

"I cared about him, Ellen. And you."

"Jake, there's something you should know."

He waited, studying her silently.

"Mike's here. He came late last night."

Something subtle changed in Jake's expression, but he said nothing, only nodded.

"I had no idea he was coming, but I'm really glad he's here. I thought you'd want to know."

He straightened a bit and smiled at her tenderly. "It doesn't change anything. I still want to be here, if it's okay with you."

"Of course." She nodded. "Jake, I took

your advice. Mike and I stayed up late last night and talked about things. We even prayed together, which is something we hadn't done in years."

When he said nothing she continued. "I want you to meet him after the service. I —" she smiled gently — "I really think you'll like him."

Jake looked at his watch and Ellen stared at him closely, wondering what he was thinking.

"You better go, Ellen. The service will be starting any minute."

"Jake . . ."

He leaned toward her and hugged her, a friendly platonic hug that could never have been mistaken as anything more than a show of comfort for an old friend grieving the loss of her father. "Go," he whispered as he pulled away. "We'll talk later."

"Okay." She looked at him, trying to read his expression. "Bye."

"Bye."

She moved along the side aisle and found her seat in the front row once again.

Suddenly, the music began. People who had been rustling through their programs or looking for a seat settled in, and a heavy silence fell over the church. Ellen glanced once more over her shoulder and saw that

Jake had taken a seat in the back row. She looked at her siblings then and saw that they each were holding a folded piece of paper. She opened her purse and took out her memorial. Aaron was missing and Ellen figured he had gone to join the pallbearers on the side of the church. She closed her eyes and waited.

Suddenly the music changed, and Ellen opened her eyes. The wooden casket, covered with a brilliant spray of red roses, was rolled into the church. It sat atop an aluminum gurney and was flanked by Aaron and five other men. Aaron was stoic as he helped guide the coffin to the front of the church. When it was in its proper place, all the men except Aaron returned to their seats. The church was silent as everyone watched Aaron retrieve a large, framed photograph of his father and stand it gently on top of the casket. Aaron looked at it for a moment and then returned to his seat.

Father Joe, the priest who had never really known John, moved to the pulpit and welcomed those gathered there.

"We are here," he said, his voice hopeful, "to pay our respects to a man who touched the lives of many, a man who will certainly live on in the lives and love of his family." He paused and nodded toward the Barretts.

"It is at times like this that we must remember the way our dear Lord viewed death, not as an ending, but a beginning. A glorious beginning. We will certainly grieve, but we grieve for ourselves because in this life we are without John Barrett. We must not, however, grieve for the man who left our presence in the prime of his life. For he is in a better place now, a place with no pain, no tears."

The church echoed with the sound of rustling tissues and an occasional sniffle.

"And so, dear friends, this is not a time to mourn, but a time to celebrate. This morning you will hear songs John Barrett sang, Scripture he often quoted, and personal eulogies from each of his five children. This service is more than a mourning of his death. Rather, it is a celebration of his life."

The priest stepped down and Megan took the cue. She went to the pulpit. Glancing at the picture of her father on the casket, she stared at her notes. Then in a shaky voice she read the Twenty-third Psalm.

" 'The LORD is my shepherd, I shall not be in want. . . .' "

In the front row, Ellen squirmed. Glancing at her sisters and brother, she saw they were doing the same. She glanced toward the casket and the picture. When Megan finished she made her way gracefully back to her seat.

Ellen stood up then and approached the pulpit slowly. She spoke of how her father had loved the Serenity Prayer and then she proceeded to recite it. Afterward she returned to her seat and the church filled with music.

The mourners listened as the soloist sang the haunting strains of "The Old Rugged Cross." Ellen closed her eyes, silently mouthing the words to her father's favorite hymn. The music stopped and the crowd waited, aware that it was time for John Barrett's children to speak. The order had already been decided.

Amy stood, turned once to look at Frank, and then walked carefully to a microphone set up in front of the church, a few feet from the casket. She unfolded her notes and cleared her throat. For a moment she said nothing, only stared at the page before her. When she looked up there were tears in her eyes. She struggled to find her voice and then, staring at the paper in her hand, she began to speak.

"My father was a wonderful man and I'd like to share some things about him for those of you who didn't know him." She coughed, as though struggling to keep her throat from choking up.

"I will always remember the way my father took us on adventures each weekend. He was always laughing, he was bigger than life. Sometimes when the others would run off to play, I'd stay back with my parents and Dad would swing me around until I couldn't stop laughing."

She opened the paper a bit more and kept reading. "I also remember that whenever I needed help he was there."

In the front row Jane hung her head and closed her eyes. "I was the youngest of John Barrett's daughters. The quietest in the crowd." She smiled tenderly at her siblings. "I may not have as many memories as the others, but Dad made a difference in my life all the same. If it weren't for him, I would have been too serious about life. But he taught me how to laugh. I remember him playing water volleyball with us at Petoskey State Park and inviting our friends to stay for barbecues. He was generous and kind to others."

She looked up from the paper. "If you know me, you know that I don't say a lot. But I see a lot. I hear a lot. I hear his laughter even now." Her voice cracked, but she went on. "He was my hero and I'll miss him."

A sob caught in her throat and she turned to face her father's picture. "Good-bye, Daddy. I love you." She folded her paper and returned to her seat, dropping her head in her hands. There, she quietly gave way to her tears.

Megan wiped her eyes and slid close to Amy, circling an arm over her shoulder and hugging her tight. Aaron, too, moved next to her. He and Amy had not gotten along for years, and it moved Ellen to see him take her hand and squeeze it gently.

Mom saw, too, and smiled through her tears.

God was doing something. Ellen was sure of it. Not just for her, but for her whole family.

Aaron sat with his arm around Amy, talking to her quietly. His heart had broken listening to her, watching her up there. When he was sure she was all right, he clutched his letter and stood up. All eyes followed him as he lumbered toward the microphone and unfolded the paper. For a moment he stared silently at the notes he'd written, his eyes hidden behind the dark glasses.

"I was John Barrett's only son," he began. It was hard to talk through the emotions choking him, but he was determined to continue. "I want to talk about the way my father loved people." He paused. "Before I was born my father worked three jobs all at the same time so that we'd have enough food on the table. Later, when we moved to Petoskey, he bought a house with a big, porched . . . fenced yard because he . . . where he . . . he bought a house with a porch and a big yard so we could . . ."

He felt the frustration growing, building inside of him as he struggled to make sense of what he had written. He tried the sentence again. "Later, when we moved to Petoskey we bought a house . . . he bought a house with a large porch for people . . . a porch where everyone could meet and . . ."

He stared at the paper in his hands and then suddenly, swiftly he crumpled it and stuffed it deep into his pocket. Friends and family members throughout the church remained silent. Aaron glanced at the front pew and his eyes locked with Ellen's. She looked as though she wished desperately that she could somehow help him through the awkward moment.

"Forget it," he mumbled into the microphone. He took one step toward his seat, then his eyes locked onto his father's, staring at him from the photograph atop the casket. Aaron's shoulders slumped and he froze in place. *You can do it, son,* those eyes said.

Slowly, he returned to the microphone, took a deep breath, and leaned forward. Then he began to speak.

"I can't tell you about my dad's love by reading a handful of sentences from a piece of paper. His love lives here —" he put a hand over his heart and his voice cracked — "not on some written page."

He paused, shaking his head. "I have not always been an easy person to love. I know that. But my father loved me. I have no doubts. He cheered me on in Little League and took me fishing when I was a little boy. He took my scout troop camping on Mackinac Island and helped me build a Pinewood Derby car for my junior-high class project.

"But that is not where I learned how much my father loved me. I learned that on the golf course. People thought he and I went golfing because we loved the game." He looked at his siblings. "They were wrong. We went golfing because we loved each other. The golf course was our private world, a place of fairways and tall trees where we talked about things only a father and son can share."

Aaron paused, fighting the tears that threatened to choke him. "I always knew he loved me, but it was on the golf course that he told me so. I would tell him what was bothering me and he'd put his arm —"

He hung his head and drew a shaky breath. He stayed that way for a moment, then almost abruptly he straightened again. He had missed one opportunity. He wouldn't miss this one. He brought his hand to his face and pinched the bridge of his nose with his thumb and forefinger. He was fighting the tears with all his might. He let his hand fall back by his side, then he looked up and continued.

"He'd put his arm around me and tell me, 'Son, whatever it is we can work it out together.' Then he'd smile at me and tell me he loved me. He would always tell me he loved me."

Aaron crossed his arms in front of him and stared at his feet, silent for several seconds as the tears finally broke free and began sliding down his face. Around the church people dabbed at their eyes and in the front row he could hear his sisters crying.

"But there was a problem with that," he continued. "Even though he would always tell me he loved me, I never —" A sob escaped from deep in his throat. He swallowed hard and pushed on. "I never said

the words to him. Never said them to anyone."

He drew a breath, finding strength he
hadn't known he had. "But I do love. I love
my sisters." He removed the dark glasses
and looked at each of them slowly. "And
my mother. And I loved my Dad. He taught
me how to love."

Aaron wiped his face with the back of one
hand. "So today I promised myself I would
tell him how I feel. In front of you. For
everyone to hear." He took two steps and
faced his father's picture once more. The
eyes that smiled at him were alive, and
Aaron could see him preparing to tee off on
the ninth hole at the Bay View Country
Club.

"Dad," he sobbed, no longer ashamed of
his tears, the crowd forgotten. "I'm sorry I
never told you before . . . I love you, Dad.
Wherever you are, I hope you know that. I
love you."

He clenched his teeth and then returned
to his seat.

It was done. He'd said it. And for the first
time in his life, he felt free.

Ellen watched through her tears as her
brother slumped into the pew. He rested his
head in his hands and silently sobbed, his

back heaving. Amy motioned to Megan, and the girls moved next to him. Ever so gently, Amy took their brother's large callused hand in hers.

Ellen watched and felt the sorrow build in her chest. Her memories were filled with times when she and the other girls had gotten along with Aaron. She had always believed there were more good times than bad. And now Aaron had confirmed that. She moved toward her three youngest siblings and put her hand on Aaron's knee. He had allowed them to see him for who he was. Finally. They knew the truth now. Deep inside, he loved them after all.

Only Jane remained aloof, apart from the others, dabbing discreetly at her eyes. After a moment, she rose from her seat and released a heavy sigh as she made her way to the microphone. Her hands were unsteady as she opened a piece of paper.

"I'm not going to share a list of memories with you," she said. There was a tinge of defiance in her voice, and Ellen held her breath. She prayed Jane wouldn't do anything to spoil the service.

"Instead I want to use this time to read a letter I wrote to my father." She held up the piece of paper and cleared her throat.

Ellen frowned. A letter? What was this about?

Somewhat fearfully, she settled back against the pew and listened.

Jane stared at the paper in her hands. Then, with a quick glance at Troy, she began reading.

" 'Dear Dad' —" That was as far as she got. She was suddenly seized by an unexpected wave of emotion. Several moments passed before she took another breath and tried again. " 'Dear Dad, I know you can hear me, wherever you are, and you're probably wondering why I became a stranger to you. When I was a little girl I craved your attention, but for some reason I never thought I was good enough for you. You had other daughters with better talents and character traits than me' —" she glanced sadly at Ellen, then back to the letter — " 'and I thought you loved me less because of it.' "

People were silent, waiting.

" 'I was wrong and I want to explain myself. See, something happened twelve years ago that changed my life forever. It was something that I thought made me unlovable.' " Jane was seized by sudden fear, and she shifted nervously, unsure if she should continue. *I can't. I just can't.*

She looked at Troy and his eyes told her to go on.

Swallowing her fear, she started reading again. " 'Ever since then I have blamed you and told myself that you never cared for me. I blamed you and I blamed my sisters for not asking me what happened. I have become an angry, hateful person, and . . . I never thought they were interested in why.' " She caught Ellen's attention, and suddenly tears filled her eyes. " 'Especially Ellen. I have been so hard on her over the years.' "

Tears made their way down Ellen's face.

Jane's voice grew raspy. " 'But I have learned something this week. What happened to me was not your fault, Dad. I put myself in the situation and it was up to me to tell you about it. I could have allowed you to comfort me, but I kept the pain inside. I was wrong, Dad. And now it's too late. My stubborn heart refused to let you in and' —" A solitary sob escaped and the letter slipped from her hand onto the floor. Jane hung her head then, crying soundlessly, unable to speak, the pain so intense she wished she could die.

Watching her sister, Ellen finally understood. Jane wasn't angry at her, she was angry with herself. But there was something else, too. Something that Jane had said earlier in the week rang painfully true: Ellen had been too concerned about herself to worry about what was tearing her sister apart. She hadn't even tried to find out what was at the root of Jane's behavior. She'd been too busy taking the attacks personally and complaining about Jane to everyone who would listen.

Regret, piercing and heavy, seized Ellen, and she wondered for the first time what terrible thing her sister was referring to. What had happened twelve years ago?

Pulling a tissue from her purse, Ellen stood up. She moved across the front of the church, bent to pick up the letter, and then stood at Jane's side. She handed her sister the tissue and took her hand, squeezing it tightly, willing Jane to continue.

A small, sad smile came across Jane's face as she stared at Ellen for a moment. She blinked back her tears and then looked at the letter once more, struggling to find her voice.

" 'And so . . . you had to leave this life wondering why I had changed, why I didn't love you like I had before.' " She paused again and moved closer to Ellen, leaning on her. " 'I find comfort knowing, believing, that you are in heaven now and that somehow you can hear me. Dad, I never meant to hurt you . . . I love you, really I do. Please forgive me.' " She closed her eyes, then tilted her head heavenward.

"I'm sorry, Dad," she said so softly people had to lean forward in their seats to hear her. "I never stopped loving you. I always have."

Then she turned to Ellen and hugged her for a long moment, sobbing in her arms. Ellen's tear-filled eyes met her mother's tender gaze, then moved to Mike. His smile was proud and encouraging. Finally, Ellen sought out Jake, and she saw that he was crying too. She knew he was sharing her joy — that he was as thankful as she that the two sisters he had watched grow up together had once again found common ground.

Ellen took Jane's hand, and together they moved back to their seats, the distance between them finally dissolved.

Ellen closed her eyes for a moment, still holding Jane's hand in hers. *You are so good, God. Thank you . . . for Mike, for Jane. For all of this.*

Megan wiped her cheeks with a tissue and sniffled softly as she stood up and moved to the microphone.

She closed her eyes for a moment, steadying herself. Then she studied the Polaroid snapshot taken at the restaurant so long ago. She had no notes.

"My dad was not the kind of person who loved you based on what you did or how well you performed." She smiled sadly at Jane and then at each of her siblings. "I know there have been times when one or more of us thought that way about Dad, but it wasn't true. With so many children in one family we tended to think he loved those of us who excelled. Those of us who stayed out of trouble."

She stared at the floor, her shame apparent. When she looked up there were tears on her cheeks, but she continued, her voice strong. "For a long time I strayed away from my father, my family. I missed countless family outings and vacations and chances to be together. But during that time my dad never stopped loving me. Even after I had given up on myself, he believed in me." She looked at the photo again and smiled through her tears. "He knew I would find my way home . . . even when I was so lost I couldn't see the path."

She studied the individual faces in the crowd. "I could stand here and tell you that John Barrett was born in Battle Creek, Michigan. That he studied math and logis-

538

tics and became a brilliant computer analyst. That he made a difference at every company he worked for and left a legacy at computerized offices in a dozen major cities. That he went on to share that knowledge with hundreds of students.

"I could tell you that he was a family man who liked to take a drive to the beach and who, after leaving Detroit, never grew tired of Petoskey and the breathtaking views of Little Traverse Bay. I could tell you he liked classical music and Michigan football and a hot juicy hamburger straight off the grill."

She smiled, unashamed of the tears that streamed down her face. "But that is not what I will remember about my dad. It is not what I want you to remember." She held up the photograph now, showing it to the crowd. "When you think of John Barrett, think of the way he loved us. Even when we weren't very lovable. The way he celebrated our victories with us, no matter how small."

She lowered the photo and smiled at it once more. Then she turned and smiled at her siblings. "But most of all, when you think of him think of the love he left behind." Her smile faded then, her voice cracked. "Because now that he's gone, it's all we have left."

There was silence for a moment, and

Megan nodded to someone unseen in the choir loft. Suddenly music filled the church and she saw the surprised look on the faces of her family. The song was one sung by country-western singer Collin Raye, a ballad called "Love Remains." Despite her tears, Megan's voice rang clear and sweet. For three minutes she sang about the passing of time, of growing up and growing old, of living and dying. The last verse specifically dealt with relying on each other in times of sadness. The song's message was clear: people die, but there was still hope, still love. That love was her father's legacy.

When she finished singing, Megan clutched the snapshot to her chest and hesitated for a moment, thankful she had found the courage to sing for her father one last time. She returned to her seat then and took her mother's hand as her siblings surrounded her. Aaron took her other hand protectively in his.

There was brief rustling throughout the church as people reached for fresh tissues. They had witnessed something special and no one was left untouched. In the front row, Megan's mother squeezed her hand and leaned close to her.

"That was beautiful, dear," she whispered. "Thank you."

A hush fell over the crowd once more as people waited. It was Ellen's turn.

Ellen took a deep breath and stood up. She moved slowly to the microphone, lost in thought.

When she was in place, she considered her siblings, clustered at the end of the pew holding hands and crying. She stared at the eulogy she had written and knew that it was both eloquent and emotional. But somehow, in light of what was happening between them, it was not enough.

She folded it gently and wrapped her fingers around it. Her knees shook and she felt suddenly faint. She leaned forward and willed herself to speak.

"I have listened to my brother and sisters talk about our father and —" she crossed her arms in front of her, overwhelmed by the moment — "I have realized how little I knew him."

She looked into the crowd and for an instant her gaze met Mike's. Tears spilled onto his cheeks and his eyes silently encouraged her. She made herself turn away and look at the other faces in the church.

"I did not know until now that he was Amy's hero. Or that he and Aaron shared secrets on the golf course." She looked at

Amy and then Aaron, pain twisting her face, fresh tears blurring her vision. "I didn't know that he had given Megan hope when she felt worthless or that —" She began to cry in earnest and she paused.

"I'm sorry," she said. People waited for her to compose herself. She drew a shaky breath and continued. "I didn't know about Jane." She twisted her hands, unsure of what to say next. "My dad was exactly who he needed to be for each of us, and until today I only saw him the way I knew him. He was someone who believed in me and pushed me to succeed, someone who was excited about everything I did until his final week." She thought of Leslie's words then. "And his faith will be an example for me all my life." She sniffed. "That was the John Barrett I knew. And I loved him with all my heart."

She looked at her siblings. "But I know so much more about him now . . . and —" A sob welled in her throat as she directed her words toward her family. "I want to thank you for sharing him with me. Because I know him better now than I ever did when he was alive. I know all of you better, too."

She closed her eyes and when she opened them, she stared at her father's photograph. "You were the best. I'll always love you,

Daddy." She moved toward the casket and paused for a single moment, gripping the polished wood corner, not wanting to let him go. She lowered her head and sobbed once, too softly for anyone to hear. Then, with the determination that he had taught her, she returned to her seat.

For a long while no one said anything. The muted sound of people crying filled the church, and Ellen and her siblings and mother held hands in the front row, their heads bowed. Finally, Father Joe stood up and walked to the pulpit.

He cleared his throat and waited until he had the crowd's attention.

"I believe you understand now the reason we must view this service as a celebration. John Barrett was a man who truly made a difference in the lives of his family and friends. A man who lived life to the full. We would do well when we leave here today to follow John's example. And when you think of his passing, smile through your tears." He looked tenderly at Ellen and her family. "Because his life touched yours, and in that you have been truly blessed."

The priest looked once more at those gathered in the church and nodded his head. "You are dismissed. There will be a procession of vehicles to St. Francis Cemetery on Charlevoix Road just west of town. Maps are available near the doors." He paused a moment. "Let's pray."

Throughout the church people bowed their heads.

"Dear Lord, bless us today with the insight to understand death, to know that it is a necessary passage, a door to a better place. And let us, in our hearts, never forget John Barrett. Let us keep him alive in the love he left behind. And let us always smile when we remember him. In Jesus' name. Amen."

THIRTY-ONE

No words were needed as Ellen and her family formed an exclusive circle, exchanging hugs, unaware for the moment of the people milling about them.

"What was it, Jane?" Aaron asked. His glasses were in his suit pocket. "Can you tell us what happened?"

Jane glanced around, then pulled her mother and her siblings into a huddle, away from the milling crowd. She tried to speak and couldn't. She clasped her throat, as though willing her voice to work.

When the words finally came out, they stunned Ellen. "I . . . I was raped," Jane said simply. Her gaze fell to the floor and she allowed the tears once again.

Ellen's heart sank and Aaron's face filled with anger. For a moment they were silent as each of them absorbed the blow. Mom closed her eyes, and Ellen wondered if she was imagining her daughter being attacked and grieving that she hadn't been there to help her.

"Who was it?" Aaron demanded "Do you remember his name, Jane? He should be in jail."

She shook her head. "I didn't know him. It was the weekend Dad left. After he lost his job."

"You went to a party in Charlevoix," Ellen remembered. "When I asked you about it you wouldn't say anything."

Jane nodded. "I met some guy and took a walk with him. He . . ." She began sobbing and her family closed in tighter around her.

"It's okay, Jane, you don't have to tell us if you don't want to," Megan said softly. The others nodded.

"No. You don't need to know the details, but I have to tell you what happened. Otherwise I might never have another chance. Besides," she sniffed, "if I tell you what happened I won't have any reason to hold on to it anymore."

"Go ahead, dear," their mother encouraged.

"He — he raped me on a private beach at the end of the street." She paused, composing herself. "I screamed for Dad, but he was gone. He had left the day before."

"And you blamed him for not being there

when you needed him," Amy finished and Ellen understood now. As far back as she could remember, their father had always been there for her. But not for Jane. Not that night in Charlevoix.

Jane nodded, her eyes glistening with tears. "I blamed him. But it wasn't his fault. If I'd told him what happened he would have found the guy and dragged him to the police station himself. I know he would have. But I kept it inside. I didn't tell anyone until this week, right before I came here. Troy wanted to know why I seemed so . . ."

There was raw pain in her eyes and she cried unashamedly. "I was so indifferent. Like I didn't care. And finally I told him what had happened."

Ellen closed her eyes. She imagined how it would have hurt their father to know Jane was raped the weekend he disappeared.

Jane looked up through her tears at her family. "I'm sorry. I never meant to hurt any of you."

They surrounded her, hugging and holding her, murmuring words of forgiveness and comfort, proclamations of love. They cried because of life and its sometimes cruel hand and because they felt like a family again. Before they were ready to let go,

Aaron spoke up.

"I think Dad would have wanted us to pray," he said. Then, without waiting for a response, he did something none of the others had ever seen him do. He prayed.

"Dear God, thank you for bringing us back together today. Thank you for making us a family." He paused, his voice choked. "Be with our sister, Jane, and heal her from the scars of what happened . . . of that terrible night. Help us to follow our father's example, to love you and each other, even when it isn't easy. Amen."

When he finished, Ellen saw that people had gathered some distance away and were waiting for a chance to offer words of condolence. Her mother saw, too.

"Thank you." Mom looked into the eyes of her children, her face was tear stained but peaceful, as if a great burden had been lifted. "There is no greater gift you could have given your father or me today than to let the barriers between you fall. To finally love each other like you did when you were younger. I know things are different for us all. You're grown up and you have your own lives. It may be years before we are all together again like this. But after today I will always know that you still love each other. That your father's love really does live on."

She smiled then and motioned toward the people waiting for them. "Let's greet the others. We need to get over to the cemetery."

They pulled away from one another and turned to acknowledge the family and friends waiting to comfort them. Ellen glanced toward the back of the church and then scanned the rest of the building. Jake was gone.

She sought out Mike then and hugged him tightly.

"Everything okay?" He smoothed her hair away from her face and studied her eyes.

Ellen nodded and smiled; she was sure her face was red and swollen from crying. "Yes. It's going to be just fine." Later, when they were alone, she would tell him about Jane and together they could pray for her sister.

Mike looked around. "So where's Jake?"

Ellen shrugged as she searched the church once more. She was disappointed that he had left without saying good-bye. "I guess he's gone on to the cemetery. I'll introduce you later."

For ten minutes Ellen and the others mingled with the group of mourners, comforting and being comforted. Two attendants from the mortuary moved the casket back into the hearse and signaled the funeral coordinator. It was time to leave for the cemetery.

A procession of forty-seven cars made its way to St. Francis Cemetery, winding through town toward Spring Street and then turning right on Charlevoix Road. The park was a mile down the road just past the Knights of Columbus Hall where Ellen's parents had played bingo occasionally on Wednesday nights.

The cars proceeded into the park and pulled up near a yellow canopy. Clouds still covered the sky but they were breaking up and the sun was peeking through. A fresh breeze drifted off the bay and rustled the leaves of the sturdy maples that lined the cemetery.

The pallbearers gathered at the back of the hearse and carried the casket onto a device that would eventually lower it into the earth. There were six chairs set up before the flower-lined grave and the Barretts each took a seat.

The crowd grew quiet as the priest stepped forward.

"Dear God," he began, and around him people lowered their heads. "Help us to remember that our bodies are but dust and that to dust we must return. May the soul of John Barrett rest forever in your loving care. Amen."

Ellen looked across the bay and smiled through eyes damp with tears. She was glad her father's body would rest in a place overlooking the bay he loved so dearly. She could hear him even now. *"Behold, the beautiful bay."*

The priest was speaking tenderly to the crowd. "John Barrett, the John Barrett you know and remember, is not in that casket." He motioned gracefully with his hand. "Nor will he be buried in this piece of earth. We must remember that this is the resting place for his earthly body only."

He paused. "When you come here, when you bring flowers and remember him, do not look for him among the dead. Look out across the water and up to the heavens above. He lives in heaven as surely as our dear Lord lives there. And he will always live in the memories you cherish. You are dismissed."

Everyone except Ellen, her siblings, and their mother stepped away, quietly returning to their cars so they could drive back to the Barrett house. Ellen and the others remained in place, holding hands while their mother lay a single red rose atop the spray of flowers already covering the casket.

"Good-bye, John," Mom whispered. She touched the casket lightly and then stepped back, returning to her seat.

The priest took Mom's hand and squeezed it gently. "Call me if you need anything," he said.

"I will. Thank you." She smiled, and he turned and left them alone.

The mortuary attendants stood some distance away, discreetly waiting for the family to leave before lowering the casket into the earth.

No one moved for a moment. Ellen stared at the casket, knowing that in some ways, despite the priest's comforting words, it was her last opportunity to be with her father.

At least in this life.

Finally they stood and without saying a word returned to their cars where Mike and Frank and Troy and the children waited. Only then did Ellen look around and notice that Jake had not followed them to the cemetery.

She wanted to say good-bye to him one last time. But she understood his reason for leaving quietly without her knowledge and she thought again how much he had changed. She stepped over tree roots and onto the sidewalk, walking slowly, remembering. There had been a time when Jake would have gone to any lengths to keep her from loving another man. Now, though he knew she still had feelings for him, he had let her go. He had sent her back into the arms of the man she had married. The man she truly loved with all her heart. It was, in some ways, his final act of love for her. She glanced once more across the bay toward Harbor Pointe. Somewhere along the distant shore stood a gray-and-white Victorian house and a man she could never again go back to. A part of her heart grieved at the thought.

Mike took her hand then, and she smiled up at him, knowing she had made the right choice. As they left the cemetery she was struck by a comforting thought. That week she had visited the people of her past — Jane and the others. Her father. Jake. Leslie. Even God. She had made peace with them all.

Now it was time to go home.

THIRTY-TWO

Ellen drove Mike to Petoskey's Pellston Regional Airport where he would take a prop plane to Detroit and catch a jet home. The conversation between them was pleasant, and for the first time since her father's death, Ellen's mind was clear and focused on the future.

"I wonder how things are at the paper?" she said absently.

"I'm sure they're struggling without their ace reporter," Mike teased. "It's a wonder they could get by at all without the dirt you dig up for the front page."

"Stop!" She jabbed him playfully. "Hey, what's the deal with the rental car again?"

"You and Jane take it back to the airport tomorrow when you fly out. Makes things easier on everyone."

Ellen nodded. She was quiet for a moment, studying the light traffic and looking for the tiny airport on their right.

"I guess Jake must have left early," Mike ventured, glancing at her.

"Hmm. Guess so."

"You haven't said much about him, Ellen." Mike's voice was curious but without accusation. "Did you see him this week?"

Ellen remained focused on the road ahead of her. "Yes. A few times."

Mike waited.

She wanted to brush it off, to tell Mike it was no big deal. But she couldn't. She wasn't going to hide anything from him. Not now. *Okay, Lord. Help me say this right.* "I spent time with him, Mike. In some ways it helped me, because he was my sounding board, an old friend for me to lean on. But in other ways . . ." Her voice trailed off. She glanced at him, and the patience and trust she saw on his face encouraged her. "In other ways, I felt very confused. Jake listened to me. He showed me he cared in very tangible ways. And that felt good."

"What are you saying, Ellen?" Mike studied her but there was no accusation in his voice. "Are you in love with him?"

The question stunned her, but not nearly so much as the answer that resonated within her. "No." She smiled then and met his gaze. "No, Mike, not at all. There's only one man I'm in love with, and he's in this car."

She focused on the road again. "Jake knows that, too. I told him."

He reached out to take her hand. "That's all I need to know for now, Ellen," he said, and her love for him grew even deeper.

"There's more I need to tell you —"

He smiled. "Don't worry about it for now. You have other things to think about. When you get home, we'll talk." He squeezed her hand. "We'll pray then. And we'll be okay."

Ellen nodded and a peace that could only be described as divine filled her heart. They had been the most difficult seven days of her life, but in the end the past week had made her and Mike love each other again. More than that, it had restored their faith. Suddenly their future seemed alive with hope.

She spotted the airport then and pulled off the highway. In two minutes they were at the front entrance. She leaned over and gave him a lingering kiss good-bye.

"Tomorrow evening, five-thirty, right?" he asked.

"Right. I'm anxious to be home."

Mike caressed her face. "I know it's been a hard week for you, Ellen. I'll be glad when you're home."

She paused. "I really love you, Mike."

"I love you, too. See you tomorrow."

He kissed her again and then disappeared into the airport.

Casseroles and sliced meat, breads and salads, desserts and a dozen different dishes were spread out along the Barrett family dining room table when Ellen returned.

As she entered the house she realized that something had changed. The somber gloom that had hung over them at the funeral and later at the cemetery had disappeared. Instead there was laughter and conversation as people swapped fun-filled stories about John Barrett, remembering the good times.

Ellen realized then that there would always be sadness over her father's death, but there would also be times of celebration in remembering his life.

She smiled and joined in the conversation. This was one of those times.

Ellen and her family were about to share a final breakfast together before everyone went their separate ways. Conversation was pleasant among them and the tension that had plagued them all week had disappeared. Ellen guessed she had five minutes before it was time to eat and she disappeared to her parents' bedroom.

Thumbing through her purse she found

what she was looking for and dialed the long-distance number.

"Hello?"

"Leslie, it's me, Ellen."

"Ellen, how are you? I've been thinking about you constantly. How was the funeral?"

"Amazing. I'll call you when I get home and tell you all about it. Listen, I only have a minute, but I wanted to tell you about Jake. Everything worked out okay, Leslie." She paused as a lump formed in her throat at the thought of her long-lost friend praying for her on the phone earlier that week. "Thanks for praying."

"I'm not surprised," Leslie said, a smile in her tone. "God wasn't going to let you go, no matter how confused you felt. What about Mike?"

"He came. It was . . . amazing. We talked and prayed together and worked things out. Or we started to. We need the Lord in our marriage, Leslie, just like you said. We're going to start going to church again as soon as I get home."

"Oh, Ellen, I'm so glad. Hey, let's not let so much time pass before we talk again. Okay?"

"Okay. And thanks again. For praying, I mean. I think I know what would have happened otherwise. Remember that Scripture in 1 Corinthians, you know, the one about temptation?"

" 'God will not let you be tempted beyond what you can stand, but when tempted he will also provide a way out.' "

"That's the one. It was sure true this week. You prayed and God showed me a way out."

"It's a battle, Ellen. Prayer is our most powerful weapon. Don't forget that."

"Never again. Listen, I gotta go. I'll call you next week."

The conversation ended and Ellen returned to the table to join the others for breakfast.

"I'm stuffed," Ellen said thirty minutes later. She wiped her mouth with a napkin, glanced at her watch, and turned to Jane. "I think we'd better get going. Our planes leave in six hours and we'll need time to check in."

Their bags were already packed, lined up near the door, and Troy began loading them into the rental car. When he finished he buckled the children into the backseat and stood by the car waiting for Jane and Ellen.

Megan approached her sisters and smiled, her eyes brimming with tears. "I told myself I wasn't going to cry today and I'm not."

She hugged each of her sisters. "I love you guys. Write, okay?"

Ellen and Jane nodded, their eyes damp.

"And you come out and visit sometime," Jane told her. "The kids would love to spend a week with their Aunt Megan."

"Hey, Megan, it was too crazy yesterday to tell you, but thanks for that song," Ellen said. "Dad would have loved it."

Amy left Frank at the table and moved to join her sisters. "I feel like we should have another week together now that everyone's getting along." She smiled sadly, hugging Ellen and Jane.

"Now, let's not push our luck," Jane said. The others realized she was joking and they formed a circle then, laughing because it was easier than giving in to the flood of tears they each held back.

"Remember how we used to be when we'd leave some city and move across the country?" Ellen asked. They remained in a tight cluster, thinking back. "The four of us girls. I thought we'd be like that forever."

"Me, too," Megan added.

"Inside here —" Jane spread her fingers over her heart — "we're still those little girls." She looked at each of her sisters. "Let's stay in touch, huh?"

"We have to," Amy said. "It's too much

work to be strangers."

They all laughed again and gently pulled away. Aaron approached them and hugged Jane first, then Ellen. "I can say it now." His voice was gentle and warm and it seemed that the dense layer of ice that once covered his heart had finally melted. "I love you guys. Take care."

They hugged him and repeated his sentiment.

"I was proud of what you did at the funeral, Aaron," Ellen said.

He nodded. "I should have done it sooner."

"Well, take care of yourself."

His eyes grew watery. "I'll miss you. Really."

"Hey, none of that now. We'll be together again sometime," Ellen's voice was thick with emotion. She looked at the faces around her. "We'll have to have a reunion or something, right?"

Everyone nodded and moved about uncomfortably, not wanting the moment to end. Finally their mother cleared her throat and stepped forward.

"You girls have a safe flight. And call me tonight so I know you got in safely."

Ellen and Jane looked at each other and laughed.

"You thinking what I'm thinking?" Ellen asked.

"Some things never change, right?"

"Right."

"Now, girls, I'm only concerned for your safety," Mom defended herself, grinning at them.

"I know." Ellen smiled at their mother and hugged her. "I'll call."

They pulled Jane into the embrace then, and Jane's voice was raspy. "Me too."

"Love you," Mom said, holding on to them a bit longer.

"Love you, too," they replied.

Then waving once more at their brother and sisters, Ellen and Jane turned and walked toward the car. As they had done so many times when their father was alive, the remaining Barrett siblings filed onto the sidewalk and waved good-bye until the car bearing their older sisters had disappeared from sight.

THIRTY-THREE

The airport was busy and by the time they arrived inside the terminal, Ellen and Jane were running late. Ellen's gate was five minutes away from the one where Jane and her family were flying out, and the two sisters suddenly found themselves forced into a hurried good-bye. Troy and the children stood several feet away giving them a few moments of privacy as a constant stream of travelers flowed around them.

Jane looked at her sister, her face filled with regret. "Ellen, I wanted to say something to you yesterday but there were always so many people around that I —"

Ellen held up a finger. "Don't," she said gently. "You've already said it. Besides, you were right. I should have asked you what was wrong a long time ago."

"But I treated you so badly. How can you forgive me?"

"Jane, do you really think I could ever hate you?"

Jane looked down, staring at the bag in her hands. "I could understand if you did."

"I don't. I never have hated you."

"Well, now, there were a few times there . . ." Jane's voice trailed off and she grinned.

Ellen smiled, glad to see her sister's sense of humor again. She'd really missed it. "I don't know when we'll see each other again."

Jane nodded and tears glittered in her eyes. "You and Mike'll have to come spend some time with us."

"Or vice versa. There's always room for your family at our house if you need some time at the beach."

"You know, Ellen, despite all the mean things I said . . . you'd make a great mom." Jane took Ellen's hand in hers. "I'll pray for you . . . that next time there won't be a miscarriage."

Ellen nodded, too choked up to speak.

There was an awkward silence then, and Jane looked at her watch. "Well, I'd better get going. The plane leaves in twenty minutes."

Ellen nodded, blinking away her tears so she could see clearly.

"Jane, remember when we were little, what

we used to say to each other every night?"

"Sure," Jane smiled, her eyes distant. "I remember. Why?"

"I don't know. I just wondered if you remembered."

Jane's smile faded then and she rushed into her sister's arms. She held her for several moments, unaware of the people around her. Her voice cracked when she was finally able to speak.

"Good-bye, Ellen, I love you. See you around."

It wasn't exactly what they had said to each other all those years ago but it was as close as they would come. Ellen smiled, her tears falling onto Jane's shoulder.

"Good-bye, Jane," she mumbled. "I love you, too. See you around."

They pulled away then and studied each other one last time before turning, and without looking back, going their separate ways.

The plane took off smoothly over the Detroit area, circling gently around lower Lake Michigan and heading back across land toward the Atlantic coast. Ellen sat next to the window watching Detroit disappear behind them. She wore her sunglasses again, her back turned slightly to the passengers beside her. She wanted the next three hours to herself so she could remember all that had happened that week, to try to make sense of it.

She had made peace with everyone, it seemed. Her father, her sisters, her brother, Mike. Even her Savior. But she hadn't really made peace with Jake. There were things she would have told him if she'd had a chance at the funeral.

She stared at the tree-covered land below, thinking. Suddenly, she knew what she had to do.

She opened her bag and found the pad of lined paper and a black ink pen. Gazing into the endless blue sky, she pictured him sitting beside her in his truck, splashing in the waves with her at the beach, letting go of her on his redwood deck. Perhaps things would have been different if she'd met Jake later in life. Or if she had never married and run into him again. But that wasn't the way it had been . . . and everything about Jake Sadler was borrowed from a place where yesterday lived.

She began to write.

"Dear Jake . . ." The pen moved effortlessly across the page and Ellen paused, drifting back. With a sigh, she continued.

I wanted so badly to talk to you at the funeral but you left before I could say good-bye. I think I understand. Mike was there and you wanted the two of us to be alone together. Like we should be.

I'm in the air as I write this, suspended between your world and my world with Mike, and I feel compelled to talk to you one last time. I cannot put into words what seeing you this week meant to me. It was as if all the years between us disappeared in an instant. And yes, it made me wonder.

I think of your question on the beach, when you asked me if I still had feelings for you, and I can tell you honestly that I do. You were my first love and my heart has not forgotten. It never will. I needed you this week and I will always be glad I called.

But you were right to let me go, to send me back to Mike. Because what you and I shared has come and gone, and I believe you understand that even better than I. As you said, if we had stayed together it would never have worked. Right now we'd still be fighting over some different girl in a different bathrobe standing on your grand front porch. And I'd still have a broken heart.

I guess I'm trying to thank you for loving

me enough to leave what we shared in the past. You have grown into quite a kind man, Jake Sadler.

You should know I'm doing all right about my dad. The sadness has faded somewhat, and when I think of him now I see him where I will always see him: sitting with us five kids at a Michigan football game, his cheeks red from the cold, his fist raised in the air and that smile stretched across his face.

I keep finding myself thinking about what you said that night when we were on the way to your house. "Choices. Passages. Moments that make a difference for a lifetime." Seeing my dad that way is one of those moments.

So were you, Jake. You must know that a part of me will always love you, always remember what we shared. And every once in a while I will think of you, as I know you will think of me.

By the way, about that omelette shop, I really think it'd be a winner. And I'm never wrong, you know. Except once when I was a kid and I thought I'd grow up to marry my best friend. I was wrong about that.

You have changed so much since then. You've made a wonderful life for yourself, and I know one day you'll find the right person to share it with. When you do, I pray you'll place God at the center of your home. He alone can make the difference when troubled times come. That much I know from experience. I never told you, but I gave my life to Christ after we broke up. And even though I'm still growing, Jesus has never given up on me. His peace and love truly do surpass all understanding. It might sound like a cliché, but my life really would be nothing without the Lord.

Anyway, I wish only the best for you, Jake. I guess that's all. I don't expect you to write back or call me when you receive this. It wouldn't be right. Just know that I enjoyed this past week, being with you again, remembering a thousand memories of the way we were. The way everything was. It was a passage of sorts, another moment. But most of all this past week gave me a few precious days in the place where yesterday lives.

Thanks, Jake. I won't forget you.

Love always, Ellen

That same moment, in a small country kitchen in Maplewood, Pennsylvania, Imogene Spencer placed a telephone call to Erma Brockmeier.

"Erma, I've just got word from the church office. That young woman we were praying for? You know, Ellen Barrett?"

"Yes, how is she?"

"Everything worked out just fine, dear. You can take her off the prayer line."

"Oh, that's wonderful. Praise the Lord. I'll be sure to tell the other ladies."

"Yes. Now about that other couple, the one in Ohio whose son is in the hospital? Here's what I think we need to pray . . ."

Dear Reader,

Thank you for traveling with me through the hallways of Ellen Barrett's past. My guess is that the journey will have taken you back to your own yesterdays as well.

Scripture says, "Forget the former things; do not dwell on the past" (Isaiah 43:18). Certainly there can be no growth for today and tomorrow by remaining where yesterday lives. Still, the Lord gave us our ability to remember. He provided us with the ability to capture scenes and log them in a storehouse to be brought out and played again when the occasion allows. I hope *Where Yesterday Lives* provided such an occasion.

If so, it is my prayer that by remembering, by visiting once more that place where faith and family and love are born, you were convicted again of the truth that Jesus Christ is our only hope. Unless the foundation is built on him, it is merely shifting sand.

However, if Ellen's journey led you on one that was painful, filled with memories of a life devoid of Christ's love, then there is no time like the present to begin the greatest journey of all. By putting your faith in Christ today, you will start a trail of yesterdays that will one day conjure up beautiful memories.

Faithfully yours in Christ,
Karen Kingsbury

ABOUT THE AUTHOR

Karen Kingsbury is the bestselling author of eighteen books, with a total of more than 1.3 million copies in print. She is also a recognized author with the Women of Faith Fiction Club. One of her books was made into a CBS *Movie-of-the-Week*. Karen lives in Washington state with her husband and six children.